WILD SOULS

THE KINGSON PRIDE

KRISTEN BANET

Happy reading!

KBANET

To this wild journey called life,
And those who have taken it with me.

AUTHOR'S NOTE

Here we are, at the final book of the Kingson Pride series. What a journey it's been for me. Riley and her Pride have taken such a piece of my heart that I'm scared of letting them go, even for a moment. Which is why I'm writing this note to you, the reader.

The story isn't over. This just marks the end of the Kingson Pride series. More stories will come from Wild Junction, more shifters have tales that need to be written. Riley and the Pride won't be forgotten. Their world will continue to grow and change around them. You'll see them again, along with the rest of the cast.

I'm excited for the future, and I hope you are too.

Happy reading,

Kristen Banet

1

RILEY

*un. Go until your paws bleed. Don't stop. Don't look
back. Ignore the rocks. Ignore the pain. Ignore the
exhaustion.*
Just don't stop running. Don't get caught.
Don't forget what happens when you get caught.
The leather and metal. A rusty taste.
She stumbled and rolled to a stop.
Hounds bayed.

"FUCK!" Riley sat up in her bed, hair flying around, as her
heart beat a hundred miles an hour and the curse flew out
of her mouth. Star scurried off the end of the bed to her own
smaller one as Riley took a few deep breaths. Two nights in
a row. Fucking nightmares. She had too much to worry
about without them, and now they decided to make an
appearance?

She pushed herself from the bed, gasping for air as she
stumbled a little to get away from it. She couldn't have a
panic attack now. She couldn't. None of the guys were in her

room, and she didn't want to drag herself to one of them for this. Everyone was on edge, they didn't need this too. Not with her father prowling around, the guards, and the threats against them.

"Shit. Fuck," she mumbled, making it to her desk and sinking into her chair. She leaned back and sighed heavily as she laid a hand over her heart and took deep breaths. "Slow down, mother fucker. Please. I can't do this right now."

Her heart did eventually slow down, but the entire incident made Riley irrationally angry. There was nothing to fear anymore. She'd won. She'd freed her pride; she'd taken out that piece of shit, Abel. He was going to prison for a long time, and it was unlikely that he would cause anyone problems for the rest of his miserable life.

"Why are these nightmares so much worse than the ones after the first kidnapping?" she hissed, leaning her elbows onto her desk. "I just...want everything to be normal again." She blinked back tears.

Two days. In the two agonizing days since her father and the SSTF had shown up, nothing showed any signs of being normal again. The SSTF was breathing down their necks, getting into their shit, and causing general mayhem around the property. Her father...

Well, Riley snarled to herself, *that asshole is a whole different load of problems.*

She checked the time on her computer and groaned. It was only three in the morning. The only people who would be awake would be their protection detail. The night crew, anyway. Those guys were even weirder than the ones she dealt with during the day. Like fucking creepers, they didn't talk. They just wandered the grounds like a bunch of goddamn serial killers.

She stood up slowly. A shower might help her relax, so she made a beeline for her bathroom. She turned the water on as hot as she could get it and pulled off the very little she had worn to bed. Normally she slept nude because one of the guys stayed with her, but the last two nights she hadn't been in the mood.

And then the nightmares started back up and she was thankful they weren't there for it. They would have flipped out, and she definitely wasn't in the mood for *that*. They would have called the doe, Abigail, and forced her to sit down with the therapist again. Not that Abigail was bad, and nearly every shifter in Wild Junction was using her at this point. Riley just didn't have the patience for it.

She hadn't needed therapy for the first kidnapping, and she didn't want it for this one. After telling Abigail about what she'd done to Abel, Riley had made it clear that any more interaction between them would be personal, not professional. Riley wanted a friend, not a therapist.

The hot water nearly burned her, but Riley soaked in it for a long time, letting it pummel the stress from her. Her days since the protection showing up had been...too much. Her dad overstepped his role constantly with Brenton, the guards mumbled under their breath about them, and they were all constantly looking over their shoulders. So, after the first full day of dealing with the SSTF, she locked her bedroom door and painted instead.

She turned the water off slowly and dried off even more slowly. There was no hurry. She pushed aside thoughts on her nightmares and the drama to focus on the painting she knew was waiting for her on the easel. She'd started it today and wondered if she should finish it. She didn't want to, but something about it was calling her.

She didn't get dressed, noting the futility of it. One of

the guys would drop in before breakfast for a quickie, and whatever she had chosen to wear would just end up on the floor. Not that she minded, but sometimes just being naked when they popped in was a great way to surprise them. And it kept her from having to pick clothes up off the floor later.

She stopped in front of her easel and sighed, reaching to touch the painting but stopped just short. The edges were purposefully blurred. She couldn't remember those details, and so the viewer wouldn't be allowed to see them either.

It was an image from the hunt that was burned into her head; one that came back two nights in a row now. A nightmare, but something that needed to go on canvas. Maybe once the painting was done, the nightmares would stop.

She could hope. Right?

She grabbed her paints and brushes and slowly began to work on it, filling in the details she could remember. The forest in Texas where her sanity was on the line, and her pride hadn't been there to save her. She'd had to save herself that time, and she'd won.

Goddamn nightmares. She'd won, and yet it still haunted her. Winning should have fixed this.

"Winning should have fixed this," she whispered softly, an edge of desperation in her voice. It was a creeping feeling, the desperation. The feeling of being hunted, of being just barely out of their reach. The knowledge of what failure meant. Those were the things that haunted her. Not Abel's face. Not the cold hunter who had a cruel smile and a sick sense of humor.

She looked at her hands. They were still trying to finish the healing process. A few stragglers remained, small scars that would fade, one of the deeper cuts still slightly scabbed.

Thank god for fast shifter healing, she thought, or her hands would have been wrecked from the event.

She lost track of time while she worked, forgetting the drama around her. Her focus and her memories were locked on the painting and what it showed. She wondered if the emotions it evoked in her would be what a viewer felt when they saw it.

A knock on her door caught her attention, and she was momentarily startled. A quick check of the time showed six am, and she knew it must have been one of the guys.

She grabbed her robe from the back of her desk chair and swung it on as she walked to the door. She barely opened it and saw Zachary standing patiently outside her door.

"Good morning," she whispered, a small smile forming at the sight of her pale, inked, and massive white tiger in only his sweats.

"Good morning, baby," he whispered back. She saw his ice blue eyes drift down and knew he was taking in the sight of her in her robe. She could see the appreciative gleam that filled them. Yeah, staying undressed had definitely been the right decision. "Can I come in?"

"Of course." She pulled the door open and he stepped past her. Star ran out of the room as Zachary entered it, making him curse as he tried not to step on the tiny tripod. The moment she closed the door, he scooped her up and, with a gentleness only Zachary could surprise her with, laid her on the bed.

"Love," she chuckled softly, "I was painting. Can I go back to that?"

"I didn't see you yesterday," he growled softly, nuzzling into her neck, his large body over her own, making her feel tiny. She was tiny, but Zachary and Brenton both had a way of making her feel so terribly small underneath them: small in ways that Andrew, Troy, and Gabe couldn't. "Except at meals, and even then, you disappeared the moment they were over."

"I'm avoiding him," she sighed, a shiver running through her as he bit down on her neck with enough pressure to remind her who was in charge.

"We know," he murmured, licking the spot he'd just bitten. That made her wet, the primal urge to submit to the dominant tiger making her want to beg for his attention. "Brenton fucking hates him, by the way."

"I couldn't tell," she said with a dripping sarcasm that made Zachary laugh.

"I do, too," Zachary whispered, his hand reaching down to pull on the rope that held her robe closed. The knot she'd hastily tied came undone, and his deep growl at her nudity made her hotter than hell. "But let's not talk about your dad right now. There seems to be something much more important that needs attention."

"What's that?" she asked, a shake in her voice as his large hand traveled leisurely up and down her left thigh.

"You," he snarled, capturing her mouth. She moaned as his tongue dove in and played with hers, and she ran her hands up his arms to his shoulders.

When the kiss broke, Riley was momentarily dazed, forgetting all the things that had been weighing on her mind before he'd come in. These men could do terrible things to her and her attention span, that much was certain.

Zachary was kissing his way down her body when a second knock interrupted them. He growled into her breasts before turning to glare at her door. She laughed and slapped his shoulder.

"You're dressed, go answer it," she chuckled. "I'll cover up, so they don't see anything."

"Fine," he groaned, lifting off her, and she watched him stomp to the door. She ignored his growling, knowing he was just being a cranky-butt at the interruption.

The scent hit her when the door opened. A lion. A male one at that. She stiffened only for a moment before she recognized it was Brenton.

"Well, I was beaten to the punch it seems," their Alpha chuckled, looking from Zachary to Riley. She smiled at him, and teasingly pulled the robe over herself, making him narrow his eyes. Never had she denied him the sight of her, and she relished the near predatory way he disapproved of it.

They hadn't had sex since before the hunters captured them, and they both knew why. It was time to change that. She wasn't going to let Abel take her love and pleasure away from her.

She was also horny as hell thanks to Zachary, and the thought of both of them in that moment was something that made her very excited.

"Going to come in?" Zachary pressed, leaning against the door frame. Brenton shook his head slowly, and she felt wanton at the look he was giving her.

"No. I'll be back for you later, beautiful," Brenton growled softly at her. She raised an eyebrow and bit her bottom lip as Zachary laughed, looking between them.

"Alright, brother," Zachary said, closing the door as Brenton strolled away. By the time he looked at back her, she was frowning a little.

Something about Brenton not wanting to join them made her a little upset. Zachary must have noticed because when he got back to the bed, he kissed her slowly.

"He wants some alone time with you, and so do I," he murmured, ending with a growl.

"Oh," she gasped as he latched onto one of her nipples and stroked it with his tongue. "I thought he..."

"Was avoiding you?" Zachary growled after releasing her poor nipple. "Never."

"No, just..." She sighed and shook her head. "Nothing."

"You two need some time alone, and things will work themselves out," he whispered, kissing her collarbone. "Let him order you around a little and feel powerful. He's feeling a little out of control right now. And you need to remember that he loves you more than anything. We all do."

"And I love you," she whispered, and his responding growl told her things were about to get a bit rough. He moved over her body, a grin spreading over his face.

"Roll over," he growled, "and I'll make you say that again. Let's stop with the heavy shit for the morning."

"Good idea." She smiled and rolled over, pushing her ass up at him. He rolled his hips against her ass, and she could feel his hard on, ready and willing to send her to heaven.

He grabbed both her wrists and pulled them over her head, forcing her chest to the bed. The robe slid and bunched up on her back, leaving her bare to him. He must have freed himself with one hand while he held her with the other, because she moaned at the feeling of his bare cock rubbing against her.

"Zachary," she whimpered. But he didn't give her what she wanted. Instead, that free hand slid between her legs and began to rub her clit, making her buck into him.

"Riley," he growled back.

"Don't tease me!" she begged, trying to look at him. He was a presence looming over her, massive and in control. He slid a finger into her and she moaned, trying to move her hips for more. She was more than ready for him, and they both knew it.

"I'll tease you as much as I please, baby," he growled, shoving a second finger into her. She gasped as he slowly fucked her with his fingers. She grew hot, her cheek pressed into the sheets. He released her wrists and sat up while he toyed with her. She grabbed the sheets and moaned into the bed.

"Z-Zachary," she whimpered, and he only chuckled at her in response.

She felt him hit her g-spot and bit back a scream as he worked his fingers inside her. She felt the orgasm build and build, taking her thoughts far, far away from her worries.

Then he stopped, and, before she could complain about it, she felt his cock slide into her with a single, forceful thrust.

"Oh, fuck," he growled down at her. She hissed in pleasure at the full feeling of him seated completely inside her.

She felt him pull out slowly and ram into her. This time the scream couldn't be stopped, and he snarled as he picked a back-breaking pace. She felt like he would rend her in half as she shoved her face into a pillow. Zachary was able to hold the headboard as he thrust into her.

Her first orgasm, already primed thanks to him, came quickly. Her eyes rolled back a little as he sent her over the edge. The ripple running through her lower abdomen and the release of it only made her greedier, though. She pushed her ass back toward him, letting him know to continue the rough pace he'd set.

"Damn it, Riley," he snarled, slowing for a moment. He let go of the headboard and grabbed her hips, and she knew he was looking to control her. "You are going to kill me."

"Mm, good," she taunted. She tried to move her ass back onto him again, but this time he just held her and stopped thrusting.

"No, no," he growled, "bad girls don't get to pick the pace, you little arsonist."

"Zachary!" She gasped, indignant. This prick was serious! He'd never stop halfway like this, there was no way.

Then he pulled out of her slowly, and that made her whimper. He flipped her over and she blushed at the slow, hungry look he ran over her body. She squeaked when he grabbed her thighs and gasped as he slid back into her.

"Scream for me, baby," he snarled, and she obliged as he did things with his hips that she didn't think were possible. He rolled them like a stripper, and that blew her mind. She was pushed up into the headboard, that he was once again using as leverage. Her legs wrapped around him, and she felt her toes curl. The second orgasm didn't just happen. It crashed into her like a semi.

"Zachary!" she screamed, scoring his sides with her nails, as she rode out the explosive finish. He only kept pumping until a roar tore from the back of his throat, one that made Riley even more turned on and a little scared at the same time. She heard something crack above her as Zachary stopped moving, filling her.

"Oh, baby," he panted. "Fuck, I broke your headboard. Cracked it, anyways."

"I love you," she told him softly. She didn't care about the headboard. One of them would order a new one for her. Or she would. Someone would get to it eventually.

"There it is," he growled, pulling out of her slowly and moving to kiss her. After a gentle and deep kiss, he smiled. "I love you, too."

"Nap?" she asked with a small smile. "Breakfast won't be until sometime around nine."

"Are you asking me to cuddle?" he teased, and she nodded. "I can do with some cuddles. Hold on."

She let him rearrange them and after a moment, she found herself splayed out over his chest and under the blankets. She traced his tattoos lazily with a finger as he began to snore softly. She wasn't particularly tired, but these moments were everything to her.

"Stop," he growled softly. She looked up to his face and saw one of his eyes open, those icy blues that penetrated her no matter his mood. She could have sworn he was asleep already.

"Why?" She smiled to him, tracing one of his tattoos lower down his abdomen.

"I thought you wanted to nap," he said, grabbing her hand. "That is not napping."

"Aw, Zachary," she teased, kissing his chest. "Are you cranky?"

"No," he sounded petulant. She narrowed her eyes a little.

"You aren't sleeping, are you?" she asked gently, lifting herself to look down at him.

"Nap." He pulled her back down, and she huffed.

"Cranky cat," she mumbled, and he growled softly. "Fine, you nap, and I'll lie here."

"You aren't sleeping either, or you would have been dead to the world when I knocked," he huffed back at her. "Don't deny it."

"I'm not," she sighed, tracing his tattoos again. "Sleeping or denying it."

"Nightmares," he whispered. Not a question, but rather a statement of fact. "You should talk-"

"To Abigail. Yes, I know, it's why I was trying not to mention it," Riley groaned. "I don't want to talk to Abigail. Not about that. I don't think anything she'll say can change it. Plus, you don't talk to Abigail."

"I have no reason to," Zachary growled softly, almost defensive. Riley filed that away for later. She knew that Brenton, Zachary, and oddly, Andrew were the last holdouts in Wild Junction who hadn't talked to the doe yet. Troy and Gabe were more than willing to talk to her, for their own reasons and for what happened with the hunters, which made Riley proud of them. But the more dominant pride members, while willing to admit they all needed to talk, were still hesitant at doing so.

"Don't be a grumpy butt about it." Riley poked one of his pecs and made him grunt. "If you're going to convince me to talk with her, then you get to as well."

"I would rather hang with the wolves." Zachary curled a lip. Riley scoffed. Zachary liked the wolves, so his act to make it sound like such a bad thing completely failed on her.

"I'll make you a deal," Riley teased, scooting up to kiss her tiger's neck. The purr that began made her pleased. Zachary enjoyed being waited on, a little. Not in the same ways as Brenton, but if Zachary could kick back and just enjoy things for a moment, he was going to.

"Please," he murmured, rolling his head so she had more access to the sweet spot she'd hit.

"I'll talk to Abigail about...stuff if she and I can join you to hang out with the wolves." She threw in more kisses to his neck and his jawline. "And we can all hang out, like regular fucking people."

"Fine," he groaned. "We'll go in a couple of days. Brenton and I are still helping them set up. The Colorado wolf pack is a bit weird about Thomas and his boys being here, but we're working on allowing the guys to stay here in Wild Junction, on their own piece of property."

"So, why in a couple of days?" Riley inquired.

"We have to schedule it with our protection detail."

"Oh, for fuck's sake," Riley hissed. "I fucking hate those goddamn-"

"We agreed to it and with good reason," Zachary cut her off. "I take it a nap is now out of the question, since you seem to be very chatty this morning."

"Probably," Riley sighed, sitting up, causing the covers to once again fall from them. She took a moment to soak in the sight of Zachary stretched out on the black sheets. He was a glorious thing to see, her tiger. "And I know we need them for a little while. It wouldn't be a big deal but..."

"You should talk to him," Zachary whispered. "I know you despise the idea, and I can't blame you, but it might bring some resolution—or at least an armistice in the War of the Sterns."

"The War of the Sterns?" Riley chuckled. "What?"

"Just a little...nickname floating around..." Zachary shifted uncomfortably.

"Who started it?" Riley pressed. "Come on. Who's making bets?" She knew someone had to be.

"Uh..." Zachary began to sit up, so she jumped to straddle him.

"It was you, wasn't it?" She laughed. "You have nicknamed my drama!"

It should have upset her, but this...this was normal. She relished in the fact that some fun could be pulled out of the situation. Not for her, but for someone at least. She could admit it was all ridiculous. Her dad, a retired Navy Seal, was now a member of the Shifter Special Task Force when she'd had no idea she was even a shifter. Her dad, the once-husband to Lily Stern, also known as the infamous thief, Isabella Gordon. Wasn't that some shit?

"I did," Zachary choked out, and she grinned.

"You awful man," she teased.

"This is where I'm supposed to say, 'Yes, and please punish me for being so awful,' but I'm not one of the leopard brothers," Zachary growled with a grin before flipping them over. "I don't grovel, baby."

"Don't I know it," Riley whispered, pulling him down for a kiss. "Stop taking bets, though. It's not nice."

"Fine," he mumbled, returning her kiss.

"Want to hit the gym before breakfast?" She laughed. "A good workout might do us both some good."

"Well...we don't need the gym for a workout," he growled playfully.

She didn't miss the fact that he was ready for another round. No, they didn't need a gym for a workout.

2

BRENTON

The walls of the mansion are too thin, Brenton thought with a small frown. On any other day, when they didn't have company that roamed the halls or the property, the thin walls didn't bother him. He actually enjoyed them, since they let him know exactly what was going on. Specifically in terms of where Riley was enjoying herself.

However, standing in his office with Keith Stern while Riley and Zachary brought the house down was one of the rare moments where Brenton was increasingly uncomfortable with the thin walls.

"Brenton." Keith started tensely. Brenton could smell how uncomfortable and upset the man was with the... obviously healthy sex life his daughter had.

"Keith," he bit out. Brenton wished it was him up there in her room. It almost was, but Zachary had beaten him to the punch. Normally, that would have been fine, but he needed her alone for a moment; and he hadn't gotten that since...before.

"Is this funny to you?" Keith asked suddenly, pulling

Brenton from a momentary imagining of what time alone with Riley would be like.

"No," Brenton growled. "I think this is my life, and I enjoy it. I also think it is none of your business."

"Not my business?" Keith spat out with indignation. "My daughter-"

"Is the love of my life," Brenton snarled, "and you had better be ready to handle me pissed off, if you say whatever you might be thinking."

Brenton narrowed his eyes at Keith in the moment of silence that followed. Relative silence. Brenton could tell Riley and Zachary were just about to finish up. He should have stayed, should have crawled into that bed with them instead of coming down to the office to find Keith waiting. Why was Keith there? That was a question that Brenton needed an answer for.

"Brenton, I don't think I've seen you *not* pissed off yet." Keith frowned. "Are you this mad all the time? Or is this something new?"

"You have not really seen me upset." Brenton grinned. "But I am sure it can be arranged."

"What I was trying to say originally, was that my daughter-" Keith started again but Brenton only snarled to cut him off. He watched the human, with the same steel backbone as his daughter, go pale but not back down. No, Keith had the same steel spine as Riley, but none of the feline instinct to back down to the superior feline. It meant Keith was probably going to get himself killed one day.

"You are not fucking here to give opinions on Riley, old man," Brenton roared. "You are here because the SSTF tasked you and this fucking crew to keep my Pride safe and alive. Got that? In two days, you have successfully brought up Riley in nearly every conversation. Tell me why the fuck you are in my office this morning or get the fuck out."

"I..." Keith took a deep breath and Brenton watched his shoulders rise and fall with the action. Brenton watched the man carefully every time they spoke. He wanted to know everything, even how this asshole twitched when he had to fucking sneeze. "I was coming in to let you know that the night team reported a female lioness scent in the area but were unable to track it."

Brenton gave a silent prayer to the heavens. Finally. He'd been worried she had been hunted down just for being even remotely associated with them. She'd hidden fairly well, even from the Pride, sometime over the summer, but now she was out there.

Jessie Eriksson was out there on the prowl. It was only a matter of time before she gathered the courage to come up to the door and accept some level of sanctuary with the Pride. On top of that, he had a desperate need for her skills. While Zachary's training was good, it wasn't professional, and Brenton wanted to avoid asking for the SSTF's help on self-defense.

"She will reveal herself when she is ready," Brenton told Keith quietly. "Jessie Eriksson. We have had some business with her in the past. There should be no reason to think of her as a threat."

"What kind of business?" Keith pried, but Brenton shut his mouth before he let it slip.

Well, she once helped kidnap your daughter, but, a couple of betrayals later, she helped us by selling out the ones she worked with.

No, he wouldn't be telling Keith that. If the SSTF didn't know about the first round of troubles the Pride had, Brenton wasn't keen on letting them in on it. On top of that, the SSTF tended to ignore Pride versus Pride situations, since it could leave them seeming less neutral in the shifter world not to.

"Feline business," Brenton offered carefully, eyeing Keith's reaction.

"I hate those two words, Brenton." Keith crossed his arms, and Brenton sighed. He knew that. He didn't need Keith reminding him. "For some unknown reason, Riley is allowed to burn down a house and part of a forest, and my shifter teammates all just write it off as 'feline business'."

"If you are going to remain hung up on that, we are going to have problems," Brenton hissed. "More than we already do. This is our world, get over it."

"Maybe if you were competent, I would," Keith scoffed. "Such a reputation among shifters, but all I see is a young man with a temper. No professional training, no real-life experience, nothing. Most of my feline coworkers won't even tell me how you achieved your reputation, just that you have it. 'Feline business', they all say."

Brenton was very still for a moment. Keith was right on some accounts. Brenton had no professional training—no Alpha truly did. But every Alpha either learned quickly or they fell, forgotten to their world.

Brenton had learned faster than most, but that was a thought for a different time. First, he needed to get Keith out of his fucking hair.

"It does not matter," Brenton sighed, suddenly weary of the conversation. Not like he and Keith ever had a real conversation. They spent a lot of time growling and posturing before one of them walked away pissed off. "If that is all, please get out."

"Fine." Keith shrugged. With that, the human was out of his office and out of his hair. Brenton began the countdown.

It would be lunch when he saw Keith again, since the man was always finding reasons to come sink a knife in Brenton's gut over something. He wouldn't send any of the shifters to talk to Brenton. No, Keith felt the perverse need to bother Brenton directly, and Brenton had a strong feeling it had to do with more than just his relationship with Riley.

"Save me," Brenton groaned, looking at the clock. Breakfast wasn't for hours, but Andrew was probably already awake preparing it or doing something. He had no hope Troy and Gabe were awake. Those two would sleep in until the last possible moment, and Zachary was wrapped up in black sheets with Riley, most likely sleeping again.

He locked his office as he left and headed for the kitchen. Sure enough, Andrew was counting eggs and prepping for the massive breakfast he made nearly every morning.

"Help me?" Andrew asked, before Brenton could even announce himself. "It'll take your mind off things."

"Yeah, if you can tolerate me in the kitchen," Brenton sighed.

"Make those muffins," Andrew chuckled with a smile. "I've got the stuff for them."

"Really?" Brenton laughed. "It has been a long time...I am not sure I remember the recipe well enough."

"Right," Andrew huffed, disbelieving. "Just make the damn muffins." Brenton continued to laugh as he grabbed everything he needed and moved around Andrew, who was still prepping on his own section of the counter.

"Another Alpha would kick your ass for a comment like that."

Brenton bit back a snarl as Andrew tensed, uncomfortable with the implication.

The whisper had come from a guard watching them

from his station. Brenton eyed the wolf who stood on guard and bared his teeth, making the wolf break eye contact.

"Do not ever make comments like that in this house, dog," Brenton snarled. "I do not give a damn how other Alphas treat their prides and packs. No one questions how I treat mine."

"I didn't mean any offense," the wolf quickly continued. "Truly."

"You better not have," Brenton growled.

This was why Brenton didn't like people in his home. This was why he and the Pride had worked so hard to close themselves off from the world.

"You know, you don't need to stand guard here near the kitchen," Andrew cut in before Brenton could rail on the wolf like his instincts and temper demanded. "You can go and let Keith know. He'll put you somewhere else."

"Are you sure?" The wolf was edgy now, and Brenton was fighting hard to let Andrew's calmer, patient nature handle it.

"Yeah, go on." Andrew waved him off, and once the wolf was gone, he turned to Brenton. "Going to talk to me, Brenton?"

"About?" Brenton growled softly.

"About why this has you so on edge," Andrew finished, touching Brenton's shoulder with a light hand.

"I am not on edge," Brenton hissed. It was a lie, and they both knew it. Brenton wasn't sure why all of this had him so pissed off, which meant he wasn't going to talk about it, yet.

"Alright," Andrew sighed. "Make the muffins."

"Sure." Brenton went back to work. They would take time. It was a recipe the old butler had taught him and Andrew. Andrew had forgotten it, but it was the only thing Brenton remembered how to make by heart.

Brenton mixed the muffins from scratch. Chocolate chip with a dash of cinnamon to add something special to it. They weren't the greatest muffins ever, but they took him back to one of the few childhood memories he liked.

"I do not like any of this," Brenton finally whispered.

"I don't either," Andrew said just as quietly back to him. "But, Brenton?"

"Yeah?" Brenton looked over to Andrew while he grabbed the pan he needed.

"Anything you need, let me know." Andrew met his gaze as he spoke. "Anything."

Wasn't that a blast from the past? Brenton, for the third time that morning, found himself thinking about his childhood. Wasn't that some shit? The first time Andrew had said that to Brenton, they were probably seven or eight.

"Don't say that," Brenton finally coughed back, looking back to the batter that needed to go in the pan.

"It's the truth," Andrew reminded him. "I made you a promise, Brenton."

"Don't remind me," Brenton mumbled, pushing the pan into the oven. He just watched the timer as he thought about what Andrew was talking about.

Anything.

BRENTON

Age 9

"**B**renton, boy! My office! Now!" A roar tore through the mansion, causing the walls to shake. The thin walls that allowed the ruling Alpha to make his message clear, no matter where he was in the expansive building.

Brenton's head snapped up from the book he was reading. What did he do this time? He closed the book and sighed, standing up slowly from his desk. If he ran to his father, it would be considered weak. If he walked too slowly, he would be considered petulant and disrespectful.

As he left his bedroom, he ignored the maids wandering around, looking at him and barely able to contain their whispers. Some couldn't at all.

"I hope this isn't another...discipline thing. He's going to kill his heir, if he isn't careful," one murmured to another. Brenton didn't look at them. "He's only a child, what does our Alpha expect?"

"He obviously expects his son to be as strong as him," the other scoffed. "The Kingson Pride has always been ruthless, even to its only progeny. If he doesn't show the strength to take over, he won't."

Brenton moved silently down the stairs at a brisk pace but still only a walk. A speed he'd practiced, a speed that would keep him from getting beaten. He turned down the hall to his father's office and knocked once on the door, then waited.

"Come in," the growl shook the door. Brenton turned the handle and looked at his father.

They were mirror images of each other, except Geoffrey Kingson was aged. He was falling past his prime, while Brenton hadn't yet come into his own. Brenton ignored the others in the room, realizing they weren't Alphas themselves. If he gave them the time of day, even a glance, his father would see it as a weakness.

"I have some people I would like you to meet," Geoffrey began, "a few members of my inner circle and their children. You will take the kids and go do whatever it is you children do."

Brenton knew that was his cue to look at the visitors. A male, older, a little sleazy, an African leopard by scent. Two females, another African leopard and a snow leopard. The adults didn't bother Brenton so much, and his eyes fell to the other kids. Just a hair younger than him, they looked exactly the same except for their coloration. One was a snow leopard. Brenton could tell without needing to catch his scent. The boy shared the woman's strange silver and gray hair. Rare, snow leopards. The other boy was an African leopard, but by his coloration, it was easy to guess he was a black leopard.

"Of course, Father." Brenton inclined his head to his Alpha once he was done taking in the new faces. This was the first time Brenton had met one of his father's inner circle. He held out a hand to the male and shook his hand. "Brenton Kingson, sir."

"Michael Walker," the leopard responded politely, looking Brenton up and down then turning to his father. "Strong young man, Geoffrey."

"Isn't he?" Geoffrey chuckled. "I've been told the Woods will be here soon, as well?"

"Of course." Michael nodded as he took his boys' shoulders and pushed them toward Brenton. Brenton didn't help the two stumbling young ones. He knew better. It would have infuriated his father to help others like that.

"What's holding them up?" Geoffrey growled softly. "I told them to get their boy here to meet my son. That shouldn't be so hard."

"He's a white tiger," the female snow leopard sighed, "and you know tigers, Geoffrey."

"I don't particularly care," Geoffrey snapped. "You boys, go wait in the hall." He directed that last part at Brenton and the two leopards, so Brenton turned on his heel and left, letting the two young boys follow him.

Once they were in the hall, he eyed the kids.

"How old are you?" Brenton asked carefully as one grinned wildly. The snow leopard.

"Eight!" He answered brightly. "I'm Troy! This my brother, Gabriel!"

"Gabe," mumbled the other one. "Just, Gabe."

"You know Dad won't like if you don't go by your name," Troy whispered, as if the adults couldn't hear them in the office on the other side of the door.

"Troy and Gabe," Brenton confirmed softly. He'd use

Gabe. If that's what the leopard wanted to be called, then he would use it. "I am Brenton."

"It's nice to meet you, Brenton!" Troy laughed, reaching a small hand out to shake. Brenton shook it quickly and then Gabe's. "So, do you know why we're here?"

"I am assuming my father has some meeting with your parents," Brenton sighed, looking toward the door. "Let's step a little farther away so they aren't bothered by us."

"Of course!" Troy jumped up and down a little, and Brenton frowned at him. He was definitely an eight-year-old.

They moved farther down the hall, but Brenton was careful to keep them within sight of the office door. If he wandered off too far, and his father had to call him again, he would be in trouble.

The brothers whispered to each other as Brenton just waited. He would rather be reading or hanging out with Andrew, the cougar who lived in the servant's quarters. His father didn't know about that friendship, and Brenton was careful to keep it a secret. Andrew was calmer than these rambunctious brothers.

"Are you twins?" Brenton asked finally, looking between them.

"No, we're half-brothers," Gabe sighed. "Same dad, different moms."

"Ah," Brenton huffed, remembering the two women, the leopard and the snow leopard.

"We might as well be twins though!" Troy laughed, throwing an arm around Gabe. "Right?"

"Yup," Gabe confirmed with a smile.

Brenton shifted on his feet, a little uncomfortable as more shifters walked up to the office door. Two tigers, the Woods, Brenton realized. They were both so tall, and the male probably weighed more than his father. Behind them, with their golden bronze looks with dark brown and reddish hair, was a pale boy. Tall and lanky with hair as black as midnight, he looked terrified. And angry. Brenton could smell the anger from down the hall.

"Zachary," the male growled, "you'll be well-behaved for our Alpha, is that clear?"

"Yes, sir," the boy growled back.

Brenton felt a shiver go up his spine as the scrawny boy proved to be dominant enough to make his father snarl down at him. *Foolish boy*, Brenton thought as they all watched a hand crack across Zachary's cheek. *He didn't know how to play the game.*

"Watch your tone," the male snarled. Then they all disappeared into the office.

Only a moment later, the young tiger was back in the hall, Geoffrey behind him.

"Brenton, come meet Zachary Woods," his father said with a tense smile. Brenton walked back toward his father, leaving Troy and Gabe to their own devices for a moment. "You will become friends with these boys. Their parents are in my inner circle, and I expect they will all be in yours one day...if you make it that far."

"It's nice to meet you, Zachary." Brenton extended a hand, but Zachary only nodded quietly. The bruise on his cheek was stark and awful. "I'll take it from here, Father."

"Good lad." Geoffrey said nothing more as he shut and locked his office door, but Brenton heard the yelling anyway. "Are you two mad? You have the potential for greatness in that boy and look at what you do to him."

"You wouldn't understand," a female hissed. "We're trying for a second, who will be our heir. We can't have... that flawed child as our heir. If you want, you can keep him."

"I will, thank you," Geoffrey growled. "Are your two boys staying long term, as well, Michael?"

"Of course," Michael laughed. "A chance for them to foster in the home of my Alpha with his son? Such an honor can't be passed up."

Brenton grabbed Zachary's arm after that and dragged the growly, young white tiger with him. Politics. Brenton was only allowed friends because of politics. Brenton filed that away. He couldn't let these kids become too close to him. They could get him in trouble for their parents' own political gains. Maybe not Zachary, since it was clear his parents thought nothing of him, but that could also make Zachary the most dangerous. A throw away who would try to earn their affection by doing anything.

"So, what are we going to do?" Troy asked happily, looking between them as Brenton dragged Zachary over.

"We have a huge piece of property," Brenton sighed. "We can go for a run..."

"Any cool places to play out there?" Gabe asked softly.

"Uh." Brenton thought about that for a minute as Zachary tugged his arm free from Brenton's grip. There was, but it was his and Andrew's place: far enough away from the house where they wouldn't get caught playing. If he showed them...

"Master Brenton!" a voice called out, and Brenton turned with a smile.

"Jameson!" Brenton felt lighter at the sight of the butler, Andrew's caretaker.

"Who are your guests, Master Brenton?" Jameson stopped near them and smiled. Jameson was a cougar, like Andrew, with the same brown hair and brown eyes. Some cougars had sandy coloration, but they were generally more normal-looking compared to other shifters. Brenton could have passed for normal, but he shared his father's golden lion eyes. His mother, a lioness, had the same eyes.

"Ah!" Brenton turned to give introductions. Once that was concluded, including handshakes for all but the tiger, Jameson nodded.

"Good, good! You need more boys your age to play with. Speaking of, Andrew is free this afternoon as well. I'll send him out, and he can help you show your new friends around."

Brenton swallowed the hard lump in his throat and eyed the distant door of his father's office. Jameson's eyes followed.

"I'll take the blame, young Master, if he finds out," Jameson whispered carefully. "Go on."

Brenton said nothing else, just led the other kids out. They must have realized something was up, because even the leopard brothers were quiet as they exited out the back of the house and into the clearing before the woods.

"Who's Andrew?" Troy finally asked in a whisper.

"He's a cougar who lives in the servant's quarters," Brenton told him. "He's ten. Jameson takes care of him."

"Oh, snap," Troy laughed. "So, Alpha Kingson doesn't know you hang out with the help."

Brenton snarled and grabbed the snow leopard by his shirt and pulled him close, making the pale boy even more so.

"Do not call him that," Brenton growled the order. "He is Andrew and he is my friend. If you want to be that, you will need to deal with that. And you will keep it to yourself."

"I'm sorry," Troy gasped as Brenton released him. "I just-"

"Never again," Brenton growled. "Now, let's wait for Andrew, quietly please."

"You used that Alpha shit on him," Zachary snarled. "Fucking little prick."

Brenton turned toward the white tiger and growled back.

"Yeah, I did," Brenton snarled. "Got a problem with it?"

"Damn right, I do!" Zachary went to shove him. "I hate shits like you. Think you're better than everyone!"

Brenton was going to shove Zachary back, but Andrew was suddenly between them with a snarl, shoving the tiger instead.

"You don't talk about Brenton that way," Andrew hissed. Brenton looked at his best friend and tried to pull him back from the angry tiger.

"Andrew, it's fine, he's just angry." Brenton tried to pull Andrew away, but the fight had started. Brenton was pushed back as Zachary jumped on Andrew, and they both threw punches at each other.

"Uh," Troy and Gabe were both just gaping at the scene. Brenton knew this was trouble. If the fight caught the adults' eyes, they were all done for.

"You two, grab Zachary," Brenton told them. "I'll get Andrew."

They tried their best, but it still took way too long to separate the two.

"You don't touch Brenton," Andrew snarled. "You hear me?"

"You grovel at his feet if you want, but I never fucking will," Zachary snarled back.

"Andrew," Brenton gasped, pulling him further away, "leave it before we all get into trouble."

"He doesn't have the right," Andrew hissed.

"I'm not his Alpha, Andrew," Brenton growled, "and if

my father hears about you fighting a guest, then he'll throw you out."

"But you're my Alpha," Andrew growled back, "and I was raised with the belief that a pride member should do *anything* for his Alpha, no matter the cost."

4

ANDREW

The oven started beeping as Andrew was making scrambled eggs.

"Brenton. The muffins are done." Andrew took a quick glance to his zoned out Alpha. "Brenton."

"Oh, yeah," Brenton mumbled, finally grabbing an oven mitt. Andrew watched as Brenton pulled the muffins out.

"Where were you?" Andrew asked, going back to the eggs.

"The day we met Zachary, Troy, and Gabe," Brenton chuckled. "The fight you had with him."

"I still think I won that," Andrew muttered. "I couldn't today, haven't been able to since he hit puberty, but that day, I had him."

"We will never know," Brenton continued to chuckle, "but you are right about the second part. You can't beat him now."

"He still up with Riley?" Andrew asked, wondering why they hadn't heard anything from the upper floors since before the muffins went in.

"Give it a moment." Brenton pointed up. Sure enough,

Andrew heard the tell-tale sound of someone making Riley's morning.

"How?" Andrew sputtered with a grin, looking at Brenton incredulously.

"Zachary's recovery time," was all Brenton said on the matter. Andrew laughed, shaking his head at it.

"You two spend too much time together," Andrew finally said. "And to think, the day we met him, he and I threw down."

It was twenty years ago, now, that day in the backyard. Troy and Gabe looking a little lost and confused, but game for whatever they were told. Zachary would remain a pain for years to come, but Andrew was always there for Brenton, like he said he would be. Zachary might have become Brenton's right hand, but Andrew was the consistent one. That mattered to Andrew, since Brenton had taken such a risk with accepting Andrew as a friend to begin with.

"Have we ever told Riley that story?" Brenton asked, carefully removing the muffins from the pan.

"No, I don't think we have." Andrew thought about it long and hard. "We don't really...talk about the time before everyone...died."

"No, we really don't," Brenton sighed. "That's why all of this bugs me."

"Huh?" Andrew frowned. What was Brenton talking about?

"You asked earlier why this has me on edge." Brenton met Andrew's eyes again. "It reminds me of when my father ruled the estate and the Pride. Always watched, always needing to be careful. It reminds me of when we were kids before we were on our own."

"Brenton," Andrew sighed. "No one here is stupid

enough to tell you what to do, or who you can be friends with-"

"Keith is stupid enough," Brenton growled. Andrew finished the eggs and dumped them on a plate for the table. "Stupid enough to hear her with Zachary and try to say something."

"Keith is human," Andrew said carefully. "And if he thinks he can tell you that, he's going to find himself up against not just you, but six very angry and possessive shifters."

"Six?" Brenton frowned at him this time.

"You think Riley wouldn't be right there with us?" Andrew gave Brenton a smile and watched his Alpha's face light up just a bit.

"You are right," Brenton chuckled. "She is too feisty for anything less. God, I love that woman."

"Damn right." Andrew grinned. "Now bring those muffins to the table. I'll go wake up the brothers, they've been sleeping in on us."

"I was going to let them," Brenton said as he dropped the plate on the table. "This has been hard on them."

"It's all been hard on everyone." Andrew groaned. "And it's not over yet. We've caught a sweet little break over the last few days. Sure, the SSTF sucks, and we all fucking hate them, but it could be worse." Andrew knew it was going to get worse before it got better. No Pride dealt with problems on this scale without someone else trying to take advantage of the situation. And if there was a Pride with a target painted on it, it was this one.

"You do not need to remind me," Brenton whispered. "This is out of control."

"And you can't tolerate that," Andrew finished for him. "I

know. Let me get the guys, you can drag Zachary and Riley down. I just need to cook the bacon."

"You've gone into full house-husband mode, Andrew," Brenton chuckled quietly. "Please stop."

"My bad," Andrew said as he walked out. Sometimes it was needed, so Andrew didn't feel too bad about it. Not really. Jameson had raised him to always look out for Pride and family, and Andrew would do that in any way he needed to. It's why he started cooking.

He trotted quickly up the stairs to the brothers' room and didn't bother knocking on the metal door, letting himself in without a sound. Sure enough, both were still out.

"Guys?" Andrew called softly, closing the door before he moved closer. "Troy, Gabe. It's time for breakfast."

He reached to the one on the right side of the bed, but he couldn't tell who it was. The entire room smelled like both of them, and they slept with the blanket pulled all the way over their heads. He shook the shoulder he found and jumped back as Troy sat up quickly, looking confused.

"What?" Troy's speech was slurred from sleep, and Andrew chuckled.

"It's time for breakfast," Andrew told him again. "Get Gabe up."

"I don't want to," Troy groaned, lying back down and grabbing the blanket.

"You both need to get out of bed," Andrew laughed, pulling the blanket away from them. It left Gabe on the other side of the bed, groaning even louder than Troy. "Why are you both sleeping in like this?"

"We've been screwing with the night detail," Troy grumbled. "Those pricks said some shit when they got here, and we've been making them pay for it."

"What did they say?" Andrew asked softly. If it was bad enough for Troy and Gabe to start getting revenge, then Andrew would need to know and maybe tell Brenton.

"They called us freaks," Gabe growled. "It's not like we do more than sleep in the same bed. We don't fuck or anything. We only like messing with people, and they called us freaks and perverts. Plus, what's wrong with a good cuddle every now and then?"

"Screw their opinions," Andrew sighed. "Your antics make Riley laugh and..."

"Say it," Troy said, trying to slap Andrew's abs.

"I think they turn her on," Andrew choked out a little. "Which says more about her than you, really. And really, I've heard of worse things..."

"She's got them hot sibling fantasies," Gabe chuckled. "Who knew?"

"I don't think she did, but whatever," Andrew groaned, waving a hand. This was going toward a conversation he didn't want to have without her in the room. "Get up and stop messing with the protection detail, they do have jobs to do. If they give you guys a hard time, let me know. If I can't handle it, I'll take it up with Zachary or Brenton."

"Fine," Troy said, swinging his legs off the bed. "Give us a few minutes to put clothes on."

"Will do," Andrew chuckled, backing away to leave the room. Before he opened the door to leave, he looked back. "And please, start waking up on time."

"Sure thing, Dad-Andrew." Gabe gave a fake salute as he walked to his dresser. "I'm not sure what has you in a mood, but we'll listen."

Andrew wasn't sure either. Something about the entire morning, maybe even the last couple of days, had him in the 'house-husband mode' as Brenton had aptly called it.

Maybe it had started before the SSTF showed up though... Maybe it was getting back from the compound, being free from the hunters. Immediately, he had dived back into running the house. They'd also had a lot of company.

He passed Brenton sneaking into Riley's room and heard a growl from Zachary. Andrew grinned and continued the walk down the stairs. Hopefully those three wouldn't wait until the food got cold before they made it down.

Back in the kitchen, Andrew grabbed Star off the counter as she hissed at him and put her on the floor.

"You know better," he growled back. It was a real growl, since the cat only responded to the guys if they went a bit feral on her. She hissed again and darted away to terrorize some other fool. He tossed the piece of bacon he had caught her licking into the trash and washed the rest carefully, hoping she hadn't contaminated all of it. Not like her germs would kill any of them, but Andrew wasn't in the mood to deal with it.

"Andrew, right?"

"Yeah," Andrew growled softly, turning to see Keith standing in the kitchen. Andrew hadn't yet had the pleasure of Keith's attention. He didn't want it, either. "Why?"

"I wanted to ask you something." Keith shrugged. "I haven't had a chance to talk to all you guys yet."

"Ask away," Andrew grumbled softly, going back to the bacon.

"Why don't you hire any staff?" Keith began as he grabbed a seat at the bar.

"Why should we?" Andrew asked with a frown. "The Pride can manage a quick clean when it's needed, I can cook, and they all help me with laundry. We don't need someone to change the sheets for us. We're adults."

"Strikes me as strange." Keith shrugged. "Strikes my

entire team as strange, really. Don't get me wrong, makes this babysitting detail easy but it's odd."

"What you're trying to say is that you think there's a different reason for why we don't have staff," Andrew said hesitantly. Keith was fishing. Looking for something, but Andrew didn't know what. "And you would be wrong...Why are you asking me?"

Andrew had to be careful about lying to Keith. If he questioned another Pride member, they needed to have the same answer.

"Because you seem to be the one everyone-"

"Because he's nosy," Brenton growled as he walked in. Andrew checked the time. He hadn't stayed with Zachary and Riley for as long as Andrew would have guessed. Both of them followed Brenton in seconds later, looking thoroughly not ready to be in public. Zachary was only wearing sweats and Riley's hair was going in every direction, a complete mess.

"Well, good morning you two," Andrew chuckled as Riley ignored her father and walked to him. She was at least more dressed than Zachary, in her own yoga pants and a tank. With a bra. Andrew couldn't leave out that important detail since normally, she would go without.

"Good morning, love." She smiled, pulling him down to kiss his cheek. He smiled at her and kissed her back.

"Good morning," Zachary grumbled, looking around for food. Brenton grabbed him and pulled him away from the finished items Andrew had left on the counter.

"You'll wait for the brothers," Brenton said, leading Zachary out of the kitchen.

"But I'm hungry now," Zachary groaned from the dining room.

"We're coming," Troy called, trotting into the kitchen.

Andrew nearly laughed as he met Keith's angry gaze when Troy swept Riley into a kiss. Andrew threw him a wink to watch his face turn red. "Pretty girl, how did you sleep?"

"Well enough," she laughed, patting his arm. "I hope I didn't wake you."

"No, we're used to that. Aren't we, Gabe?"

"Yup." Gabe walked in, and kissed her forehead. Both completely ignored Andrew. He should have known they would, since he was the terrible person who woke them up. Pricks.

Eventually, it was just Andrew, Riley, and Keith. Andrew watched her carefully eye her father and wondered where this was going to go.

"It's too early to deal with you," she mumbled, dismissing him and turning back toward Andrew. "Need any more help in here?"

"No, just need to finish up the bacon," Andrew chuckled. He leaned down and kissed her again and purred softly as she ran a hand through his hair. A masculine throat being cleared called their attention away from each other, and Andrew looked over her head at Keith and bared his teeth. Riley hissed softly.

"If you don't like it," she snapped, "then leave."

"I was hoping you and I could talk sometime today," Keith said, trying to be diplomatic. Riley scoffed, and Andrew winced at the complete disregard she held for her father.

"We'll talk when I'm damn well ready to," she informed him. "Until then, you can wait. Patiently and, preferably, silently."

"I'm your father and never have I allowed you to talk to me like that," Keith growled. The idiot didn't realize that it would cause five big, dangerous shifters to growl back. Louder.

"You lost the right to pull that card years ago," she snapped, "and no one in this house will be on your side if you try to press the issue."

A simple brush of her hand as she strolled out of the kitchen quieted Andrew. He bit back the rest of his growl and went back to the bacon. If this was going to be every interaction between them, Riley and Keith were going to start a fucking war between the SSTF and the Pride within a week. The Pride wasn't going to tolerate this for more than a couple of days, and Keith seemed too bullheaded and stubborn to know when to keep his mouth shut.

"She's too strong for you to just expect her to fall in line, Keith," Andrew told the irate human. "You screwed her, and now you have to deal with the consequences. Or you can just leave. That would work well for everyone, too."

"I don't owe you an explanation," Keith responded tensely. "Don't act like I do."

"I don't need you to explain," Andrew snapped, pulling the finished bacon out of the pan. He dropped it on a plate, turned the stove off and shrugged. "I know her. And I know how hard her life was after it."

"And I've heard what she's gone through since meeting you," Keith growled, leaving his seat and stomping away.

Andrew grabbed the plate and walked into the dining room. He didn't need to say anything; the Pride would have heard the interaction. Riley looked furious, and Andrew quietly took his seat next to her.

"That ass," she hissed as she dished her own breakfast.

"Yeah," Andrew sighed. "He was bugging me about why we don't keep a staff. I told him we don't need one."

"We do not," Brenton responded blandly. And that was

that. Everyone knew that the story couldn't change. The truth was, they didn't keep staff because staff tended to try to kill the Alphas and Prides they worked for. It was another thing they had decided to not have involved in their lives. Creature comforts versus survival. Survival won out.

"Oh, Zachary and I were talking about visiting Thomas and the other wolves." Riley took a bite of eggs as she finished. "Can we get that done?"

"Zachary," Brenton sighed.

"I'll get it scheduled," Zachary chuckled.

"What else do we have going on?" Andrew asked, piling eggs onto his plate. "I've got meetings with contractors over the diner. We have a board meeting in three days. Troy and Gabe have..." He looked to the brothers and Troy shrugged.

"We were able to push our schedule back a few weeks, so we don't have deliveries for a little while," Gabe told them. "Figured it would be best with everything that's been going on, even though we're a bit behind. We'll be in the garage a lot."

"Good to know," Brenton grunted, distracted by something, and Riley turned a fake glare at him. Andrew looked down for just a second and saw Brenton's hand sliding up and down the inside of her thigh. Andrew held back a chuckle.

"I don't have shit going on," Zachary groaned.

"Yes, you do," Brenton sighed. "You have to coordinate with SSTF about getting bullet-proof glass in our vehicles and upgrading the more conventional security measures for the property. Remember?"

"Yeah, but I can do that here, at home," Zachary grumbled. "What about you, babe? Got anything you want to get handled?"

"I'd like to just keep working on my studio," Riley

laughed softly. "Which means I'll be hiding up in my room a lot, painting. I think I'm only about a fifth done with what I want to open with."

"This feels so normal." Troy frowned around the table. "Anyone else getting a weird normal vibe from this?"

"No," Riley scoffed. "I don't think it's weird. I'm happy it's fucking normal."

"Amen," Brenton purred, leaning back in his chair a bit more. Riley gave a small chuckle, and Andrew rolled his eyes. Every shifter in the room could smell where those two's thoughts had gone.

"Here, here," Andrew laughed, looking to a smiling Zachary. "A few more mornings like this, and we might actually start to calm down a bit."

"Once we get all of them out of the house." Zachary jerked his head, his smile turning a bit aggressive. Andrew looked to what he mentioned and sure enough, a guard was wandering the hall outside the dining room. "I'm not sure why they insisted on wandering the house."

"Beats me," Brenton growled. A phone started going off, and a curse came from Brenton. "Fuck."

"You can come see me later," Riley laughed as Brenton checked the screen. She rose and kissed his forehead. Andrew watched her gaze turn to him, and at a crook of her finger, he rose to follow, sticking a tongue out at their Alpha. Brenton bared his teeth but made no other move to stop him.

"What do you need?" Andrew asked quietly as he followed Riley up the stairs to her room.

"Not what you're thinking," Riley laughed, looking back at him. "We need to talk."

"Of course, darling." He smiled as he opened her door for her.

Once the door was closed, Andrew began to feel a little uncomfortable. Riley was silent as she locked it and turned to him.

"I was thinking about something this morning and decided to corner you first." She ran a hand down his chest and he swallowed a lump in his throat. "Why haven't you spoken to Abigail?"

"I don't feel much of a need to," he whispered, "and nothing you say can force me to."

"Are you sure?" She raised an eyebrow. He gave a soft growl.

"Positive." He grabbed her hand and turned her around. He held her tight to his chest and leaned down to her ear. "I still outrank you, darling. If anyone is going to make me sit down for that chat, it'll be Brenton or Zachary, both of whom also haven't gone for a chat with her."

"It was Brenton's idea to begin with," she muttered, a little petulantly. "Why won't you three talk to her? And I figured it would be like that for Brenton and Zachary but not you. At least give me your real reason."

He didn't have much of a reason to give her. He'd lived through worse? Because, while Troy and Gabe were knocked out on substances, he, Brenton, and Zachary dealt with problems and did things that would make the hunters look like chumps? The hunters terrified him, certainly. They had done something to her that was unimaginable, and that was why the hunters had bothered them. Andrew hadn't cared if he had died, Brenton and Zachary as well. It had been all about her.

"I don't have one. Let's leave this topic for another time," Andrew whispered, close to her ear. He felt a shiver run through her and let her go. There was no scent of fear to her, but they all tried to tread carefully around anything they identified as something that could frighten her. "I'm sorry."

"I'm fine," Riley sighed, turning back to him. "I wasn't scared. Thank you for caring, though."

"Anything for you, darling," Andrew purred, kissing her forehead. "You know, Brenton brought up something earlier, a story from our younger years. It's pretty funny. Want to hear it?"

"What?" Riley gasped, faking shock. "A story about young Brenton and Andrew? I must hear this."

"About the day we met Zachary, Troy, and Gabe," Andrew chuckled. Riley hadn't even been in their life for a year, and listening to Brenton earlier, realizing she'd never heard the story made Andrew realize they didn't tell her much. They had all been too wrapped up in the little life they'd made to ever think about stories of their childhoods and the time before their return to Wild Junction.

"Oh!" Riley laughed, clapping her hands together. "Come on, don't leave me hanging!"

"Zachary and I got into a fight," Andrew told her, making her eyes go wide. "To this day, I still think I won."

He told her about the fight. About Zachary shoving Brenton, and Andrew intervening. About taking them all to the rocks and jumping around for the afternoon while Zachary sat around, grumpy, even at nine years old. Brenton trying to reason with the tiger, and then finally telling Andrew that they would do whatever was necessary to get Zachary in. Troy and Gabe had fallen into Brenton and Andrew's friendship easily, but Brenton liked the challenge of Zachary and he wasn't going to stop until he claimed the white tiger as a future pride member.

"They were all going to foster with Brenton's dad for a year," Andrew finished. "It was considered a great honor to give custody of your children to the Alpha and allow them to be raised with his own. Zachary was a throw away for his family, but even Geoffrey Kingson saw his potential."

"When did...all their parents die?" Riley asked softly. "I know you wanted to tell me a happy story but...you guys don't talk about it. I can't blame you. I don't like talking about my dad and he's alive. And my mom...well, you know."

"It started slow," Andrew sighed. "One day we got word that Zachary's parents were gone, and he was officially a ward of the Kingson Pride and its Alpha, Geoffrey Kingson, Brenton's father. A few weeks later, it was Troy's mother, and, just two days after that, Gabe's. Their father was a bit harder to kill for whomever went after them, surviving another week. At that point, Geoffrey knew something was up. He was a cruel old bastard, but he was a smart one."

"How so?" Riley was now sitting on her bed, her legs pulled up as she listened to Andrew.

"It wasn't just their parents," Andrew shrugged. "Remember, I'm an outsider looking in on this. Geoffrey's entire inner circle was being picked off, one by one. He was worried Brenton would be next, and, at this point, he had full legal custody over Troy, Gabe, and Zachary. Not me. No, he didn't approve of me, but at this point, he also wasn't going to fight Brenton over it."

"You said people tried to throw you out," Riley added, and he saw a small bit of confusion on her face.

"Others, after Geoffrey was gone. I'll get to that," Andrew told her, collapsing onto the bed next to her. It smelled of sex, Zachary, and her. Brenton had never made it to the bed, it seemed. "So, cruel, intelligent Geoffrey wrote up an expansive amount of legal shit to protect his fortune and his son. It was all about Brenton, in the end. Zachary, Troy, and

Gabe were, legally, his brothers, thanks to the scheming. They couldn't be legally separated."

"What was his endgame?" Riley asked, and he looked back at her face. She looked genuinely curious about it, and that almost amused him.

"If he was going to go down, he was first going to raise the next brutal king of the Kingson Pride," Andrew answered, watching her eyes go wide. "He didn't get the chance. With his inner circle completely decimated, a glass of whiskey and a drive to clear his head became his down fall. Written off as drunk driving, he was poisoned and died before he hit the trees."

"Poisoned by who?" Riley gasped.

"Jameson, our butler," Andrew groaned. "The man who raised me. But we didn't find that out until later. Much later."

That had been a kick while they were down, Andrew remembered. Brenton and he had grown up with Jameson, and the other guys had fallen half in love with him. He'd been the caring father, the older brother, the lookout while they got into trouble.

"And then, the people Geoffrey had set up to look over us came in. They deviated from the plans Geoffrey set up. You know the short version of that story. They were pricks. We dealt with a lot of shit in those early years on our own."

"Why would someone go after the Pride so hard?" Riley continued to be curious. Andrew figured that it was because it was just a story to her. People she didn't know and children she had only met long after it happened.

"Geoffrey and the Kingson Pride Alphas before him, they were all ruthless. Half-running their own Pride, half-ruling over literally everyone else. They took the 'king' in their last name seriously." Andrew rolled his eyes at the memory. "Brenton has purposefully tried to avoid it but, in some ways, not having a Kingson on top has left the feline community with a power vacuum. No one has stepped up and enforced the unspoken rules of our kind in decades... which is probably why Abel thought he could get away with what he did to you. It's also probably why some shifter is out there selling our own kind out to hunters."

"For someone who didn't 'grow up' in the upper class, Andrew, you seem to know a lot about it," Riley murmured, playing with his hair.

"I had to learn, and, being an outsider, I could learn things that those in the game didn't realize." Andrew turned and buried his face in her stomach, rubbing his facial hair over her sensitive skin and eliciting a giggle from her.

"Stop that," she laughed quietly. "And thank you for telling me all this."

"It's...it's about time you know, really," Andrew sighed before kissing her side. "We let it fall to the wayside while we've been having a good time, and you're too deep in it now. You have to know."

"Could it be that none of you thought I was ready to know?" She tugged a lock of his hair, and he chuckled.

"Probably." Andrew rolled over and looked up at her, keeping his head on her stomach. "Would you have run screaming for the hills?"

"Maybe?" Riley shrugged. "If you told me I would get kidnapped twice, kill a bunch of humans who wanted to kill me, lose my best friend, and meet my father again, maybe. But, I like to think even with all that, I would stick around."

"Why's that?" Andrew smiled at her.

"Because I have you guys," she whispered, running a hand down his cheek. "What time is your meeting with the contractors?"

"Ten-thirty," Andrew groaned. "Shit."

"Shit is right. It's ten-fifteen," Riley laughed. "Go on, love."

"I love you," he whispered, sitting up to kiss her.

"I love you too," she whispered back, and Andrew stole the smile from her face with a slow, drawn out kiss goodbye.

5

RILEY

Riley sighed as Andrew left her room to deal with getting Starry Night Diner rebuilt.

"I couldn't imagine that happening," she whispered to herself, thinking about the losses her guys suffered as kids. "And I thought my family drama was bad."

She continued to think on it as she made it back to the painting that awaited her. It wasn't like she knew *nothing*. She knew about Troy and Gabe's younger childhood, the games their parents had played. She knew Zachary's parents were just a bit fucked in the head about him being a white tiger, a sign of inbreeding to tiger shifters. She knew Andrew had lost his mother to cancer at only five, and Brenton's mother was killed by Riley's own.

But to hear the full tale of the destruction that had left them completely alone was something else. It felt like it set the pace of their lives in a way that nothing else had. She'd been told they had reputations, and now, in the back of her mind, she truly wanted to know how the young boys, alone in the world, became the men she fell in love with.

"I should have asked these questions earlier," she

groaned, looking at the blurry painting. "I really should have."

She hadn't because they weren't her secrets. She'd wanted to continue the little peaceful life they'd lived, but the hunters had proven that ignoring things wasn't an acceptable way to live. She also hadn't known or realized the depths of her feelings, and those feelings drove her to need to know every inch of her men's lives. All of it, every little piece.

She also had her own problems, she remembered a bit sourly as she kept her eyes on the painting.

"Fuck this painting," she hissed softly, but she resisted the urge to destroy the canvas. "I'm going to finish it today and put it away. That will be the end of it."

She got to work, letting it take her away from the questions swirling in her mind. Back to the hunt and the feelings. The taste of leather.

She hated it, but the painting begged to be finished, and she couldn't stop herself once it was started.

The only thing that brought her out of it was her phone ringing loud enough to make her wince. She grabbed it and didn't bother to check the number when she answered.

"Riley Stern," she said sharply, with more than a little annoyance.

"Having a bad day?" Abigail's docile tone came through. "I was wondering if you wanted to get your nails done with me."

"Really?" Riley snorted. She looked down at her paint-covered fingers. She'd actually never gotten her nails done before. "Did someone ask you to call?"

"I may have gotten an angry text message from one of them..." Abigail trailed off into silence and Riley gave a heavy sigh. Probably Zachary, thanks to the talk they had earlier in the morning. "Really, though, I think you need to get out of the mansion for an afternoon, and there's no other female shifters around to get my nails done with."

"I'll need to get my guard, and make sure Brenton knows, and..." Riley rolled her eyes. "You know, all of that."

"Of course," Abigail laughed. "I was thinking sometime around one. That should give you enough time to get everything worked out. There's a place in the next town over where we can go."

"I know the place," Riley confirmed. There wasn't a nail place in Wild Junction, the closest being in another small town about twenty minutes away. "Make an appointment, and I'll tell everyone the time and get it worked out...I do want to talk to you about something, so this works out." Riley figured Abigail should know about the nightmares, and while it irked her to be having them, she also wondered if Abigail may have extra advice.

"I'll text you when I get the time!" Abigail sounded pleased, and they both quickly said goodbyes and ended the call. Riley shoved the phone into her bra, grabbed the painting, and shoved it onto her canvas rack.

"You're done, so please, stop haunting me," she hissed at it. "Now I need to find Brenton or Zachary, hurt one of them, and go get my damn nails done."

She went to the bathroom to clean the paint off, and then went on the hunt. She trusted her nose, and found herself heading into the gym, finding both of the dominant, beefy men she called lovers.

"Brenton. Zachary." She said plainly as Brenton spotted Zachary on the bench press. Brenton looked up at her with a confused look while Zachary grunted as he lost his partner.

"Yes, beautiful? Are we in trouble?" he asked carefully,

helping Zachary up for one last rep.

"You aren't," Zachary growled with a smile. "But I think I am."

"Abigail just called asking if I wanted to get my nails done," she began, crossing her arms and tapping a foot. Brenton choked back a laugh as Zachary sat up, actually laughing at her. "She said she may have gotten an angry text from one of you. My guess was Zachary, and it seems I'm correct."

"You would be," Zachary teased her. "Though, I meant the nail thing as just a thing for her to use as an excuse…"

"Very cute," Riley growled back, rolling her eyes. Brenton finally let loose on a loud laugh, bending to hold his stomach. Riley's phone dinged, and she pulled it out to see what Abigail had to say.

ABIGAIL: I've gotten us an appointment at 2pm. It might be easier if you have your protection pick me up as well.

"TWO THIS AFTERNOON," Riley told them. Zachary was standing up now, and she couldn't resist looking over them both, shirtless and sweaty. "You're lucky you're hot."

"Is that the only reason we're lucky?" Zachary growled with a grin. She swallowed and nodded.

"Yes." She raised her chin a little. "I'll remind you that while you outrank me in the pride, I control your sex life." That stopped their snickering quickly enough.

"You wouldn't," Brenton said with a wary glance her way.

"Try me." She stuck her tongue out and was thankful to be across the room from the teeth that Brenton and Zachary bared at her.

"Put that away," Brenton growled softly, beginning to close the distance between them. She kept the tongue out, making a childish noise, and turned to leave the room. She didn't walk out, though, she ran.

She didn't make it far down the hallway before a strong arm wrapped around her abdomen and she found her back pressed to a large chest. But something was off.

Like every time she got Brenton's scent, now, she could only smell the lion for a moment. With the playful adrenaline in her system from running away, she was suddenly in a different place. Fear lanced through her, and she gasped for air. The arm left her waist as she pulled away and spun around.

There he was, her glorious golden eyed lion. She reminded herself of it over and over. The lion in her home was Brenton, and he was her Alpha and one of the loves of her life.

"Riley..." he groaned softly, looking defeated. "I would never..."

"I know," she whispered, placing a hand over her accelerated heartbeat. "I...I just...I can't control it. I thought..."

"Tell me," he whispered, dropping to his knees in front of her, making himself smaller. Less of a threat. "Please tell me. What did I do this time?"

"I thought after...after I took down Abel that everything would be okay..." She took a deep breath, which helped her calm down more. "I was stupid to get playful and run like that. I think I just got worked up from the adrenaline. Then your scent hit me, and it reminded me of the compound and..." The hunt. And Abel.

"Okay," Brenton whispered. "No more of that from me, then."

She nodded slowly, swallowing a hard lump in her throat.

"I'll talk to Abigail about it..." she whispered. It would be the same thing anyone else told her. She leaned forward and kissed him gently. "Brenton, I love you. I've said it before, everything will be okay."

"I know...and I love you too," he sighed, kissing her back from his spot on his knees. It was the only way she was taller than him. He stood back up and looked down at her. "Go on. I'll deal with everything so you can go out with Abigail today."

"Oh...Zachary told me it would take a couple of days to go see Thomas and the wolves. If I can go with Abigail today..." She frowned at Brenton, who gave her a small smile.

"He took into account how much he doesn't want to deal with these new rules about our security, so it'll take him longer to get it done." Brenton leaned down and planted one more kiss on her cheek.

"Of course," Riley chuckled softly. She began to walk away and heard a grunt. She turned and saw a worried Zachary standing at the door of the gym. "We're okay, Zachary."

"Okay," he said, looking between them. "Come on Brenton, let's get her playdate scheduled."

"I hope it's not a playdate," Brenton said with his familiar, mild tone. Riley felt her face heat up.

"Brenton!" She laughed, swatting at him, and he only winked at her.

"We'll go get this worked out for you," he said, removing himself from her reach.

"Thank you." She blew a kiss to them. "I'm going to go bother Troy and Gabe for a minute."

"Have fun," Zachary called after her as she walked away.

She left them in the hall outside the gym and moved towards the garage, ignoring the SSTF agents wandering around. It was a hard thing to do, since they all gave her looks as she passed. She had a feeling what they were thinking but didn't dare ask. She'd barely interacted with any of them since they had arrived, and she had realized her father was a fucking member of the damn organization.

She slipped into the garage quietly and looked around. There they were, her other pair. They were frowning at the "bike" they were working on. Riley wasn't sure she could truly consider it a motorcycle, yet, since it was in several hundred pieces, scattered all over their work space, and they were basically looking only at the frame. They were so absorbed in it that they had no idea she was even in the garage yet.

"What's going on?" she asked loudly, making them both jump. As they turned towards her, she wandered closer.

"We think we need to rebuild it," Troy sighed, waving a hand at the frame.

"I wouldn't know anything about that," Riley chuckled, "but I'm sorry for your troubles."

"Why are you in here?" Gabe asked, pulling her close for a cuddle. She pressed her forehead to his chest.

"I just wanted to come bother you," she mumbled into him.

"Our gorgeous distraction," Troy chuckled, coming up behind her and leaning down. "Feeling playful?"

"Naughty man," she whispered, wrapping her arms around Gabe. "And no, Zachary has me thoroughly sore from the morning. I'm going out with Abigail later, and I just wanted to stop in and say hello."

"Ooooh. What are you two girls going out to do?" Gabe

asked, now rubbing her back, both hands drifting lower to her ass.

"She wants us to get our nails done, though I firmly believe Zachary has threatened her into it." Riley chuckled. "I've never gotten my nails done."

"Really?" Troy coughed with a laugh. "Never?"

"No." Riley smiled. "I like how that surprises you, but not Zachary threatening her."

"You've been in this house and with us long enough to know that Zachary threatening anyone really isn't much news, just an inevitability," Gabe laughed, giving her ass a firm squeeze. She did know that. "Are you going to let us get back to work, or do you need something?"

"I'll let you get back to work," she sighed, giving him a quick kiss and pulling out of his embrace. She turned to Troy and raised an eyebrow. "You want one, too?"

"Always," he growled softly, swooping down for one. "We've got to work, though. We're so behind it's stupid."

"Yeah, yeah," Riley sighed. After a few more attempts at leaving and a few more goodbyes, she left them to their work. She needed to get cleaned up and ready to go out, anyway.

RILEY WAITED in the Range Rover in silence as one of the agents went into Abigail's hotel. Brenton was paying for the room for Abigail's entire stay in Wild Junction because he was the one who dragged her out into the middle of nowhere.

She ended up having not just Cortez, the jaguar who said he was her personal guard on days, but also two others: Liam and Logan, a pair of huge bears that Brenton thought would scare off any real threats. Over-protective, her Brenton. She had to convince him that a bullet-proof vest just wasn't a good idea to wear out into public, especially not for a trip to the nail salon a town over.

"So, have you two met Sheriff, yet?" Riley asked the burly bears in the front. Logan turned to her slowly with a serious look.

"No, but there's not an SSTF agent that doesn't know of him," Logan replied in a rumbling, deep voice. It was like an earthquake of a voice and made her chest vibrate.

"Really?" Riley smiled tentatively. "He told me he was an agent a long time ago." Along with being a Green Beret, which Riley thought was cool as shit. Though, now that she thought on it, it mirrored her dad. A Navy Seal, then an agent with the SSTF.

"The fact that you know him at all, astounds me," Liam growled softly. It wasn't an aggressive growl but rather a grumpy sounding one. She heard it a lot from Zachary.

"Why? He's our Sheriff, not just in name, but literally," Riley chuckled and shrugged. "I just wanted to know if any of you agents bothered to go say hello to him or not."

"He won't let us on his property," Logan sounded a bit put-off and childish about it. "Or rather, his wife won't let us on the property, and he hasn't left his property since we've been in town."

Riley nearly laughed, but she didn't know what was so funny about it. It was just hilarious, though. She looked out the dark tinted window and finally saw Cortez coming out the door with Abigail. As Abigail climbed in, Riley gave her a smile and it was returned by the put-together doe.

"Are you ready to have a girl's day?" Abigail asked in that gentle tone. Riley had figured out one thing about Abigail— she had two settings: professional and kind of motherly. She had her long brown hair pulled back in a ponytail, and her dark eyes were warm.

"Sure, why not?" Riley gave her a thumbs-up. "I've heard of this place before. Apparently, they do a good job, but I wouldn't know from personal experience."

"This doesn't seem like your thing," Abigail chuckled softly. "How did you hear about it?"

"My friend Ha-" Riley stopped and leaned back in her seat. "A human named Haley used to talk about it."

Riley hadn't forgotten Haley, but it was still an adjustment to think Haley was just not her friend anymore, but an active enemy. Riley frowned down at her hands as Abigail put on her seatbelt and the Range Rover got moving.

"Haley?" Abigail asked quietly. Riley looked back over to the doe and shrugged.

"She was a friend until I met the guys." Riley sighed. "And she ended up not being a very good one."

"I've been given some information about what happened," Abigail said, now in professional mode. "Haley and her husband were recruited by the hunters after the Pride returned to Wild Junction, along with a couple others?"

"Yeah," Riley whispered. "She told me about this place, but she could never convince me to go."

"Where's Haley now?" Abigail continued, giving Riley a look she couldn't describe. It was expectant, as if she knew Riley knew and that was somehow...a thing.

"Around Denver?" Riley said with another shrug.

"All the humans associated with the attacks on the Kingson Pride are being monitored," Cortez said from the other side of Abigail. "Haley is currently living in Denver and has been issued a restraining order from Riley and any other members of the Kingson Pride. She's not allowed back in Wild Junction, and she's been convinced to give up any association with the hunters. Jeff was also given the same treatment, once he was released from the hospital."

"Thanks," Riley groaned, rolling her eyes. "I didn't really need to know all that."

"Change of topic in order?" Abigail asked, elbowing Riley a little.

"Please," Riley begged with a groan. "I just want a couple hours without...all of this." She waved around, hoping Abigail got her meaning.

"I can't blame you, though you said you had something to talk about?" Abigail turned a little more serious, if it was possible.

"I've had nightmares the last couple of nights," Riley mumbled. "Being chased and not getting away."

"Oh, Riley," Abigail sighed, looking over at her sadly. "I'm sorry to hear that. I could have warned you that what you did...it wasn't truly going to help."

"I felt like it did for those first couple of days. And today, after you texted, Brenton accidentally freaked me out. I had run from him and-"

"You don't need to explain," Abigail whispered, cutting her off. "You don't. It's easy to forget with everything going on how fresh this all is. Nothing is going to be perfect and better overnight. It could take weeks or months for everything to even remotely feel normal again on a consistent basis. And nothing is wrong with you. This is natural, and it sucks." Abigail took a moment to think and Riley just watched her. "I'll talk to Brenton, if that's okay, about things he can do to help not accidentally freak you out. That way you and he don't both end up just constantly feeling guilty over something you can't control."

"Thank you." Riley gave Abigail a weak smile, and

Abigail just took one of Riley's hands and squeezed.

"I already told Brenton that I can stay in town for as long as you need me, or any of the others I'm seeing," Abigail told her with that soft smile.

"Let's go get our nails done," Riley chuckled, trying to shift the topic.

"Alright." Abigail nodded. Riley was thankful for the doe letting the heavy topics slide away for the moment.

It was more therapeutic than Riley had thought it would be. She was ushered into a big chair, and her feet were then placed in warm water. Abigail told her last-minute that she got them appointments for pedicures as well. Riley wasn't sure what to think about that, but, as the women did their thing, Riley was able to close her eyes and enjoy it. She let Abigail choose what was done to her nails, and she ended up with red nails with little white skulls on them.

"I thought they suited you," Abigail said with a small blush, looking at Riley's finished nails.

"They really do, and now my toenails are black, which is just hot," Riley chuckled, looking down at them as well.

"You might want to be careful with those," Abigail laughed. It was like a wind chime, her laugh. Riley couldn't help but enjoy the sound when it was completely unhindered by serious topics. "I hear men are fascinated by painted toenails."

"I'll have to test that," Riley joked. "Who do you think I should test them on?"

She watched Abigail tap her chin with a long finger and finally make an "aha" noise.

"Brenton." Abigail grinned. "I think you should test them out on Brenton. Hide them and let him discover them on his own. I bet you'll both have a good time."

"You can be devious," Riley said with a note of

appreciation in her voice. "I like it."

"I know how the mind works." Abigail winked at her, which made Riley lose her shit. She was still laughing as they climbed back into the Range Rover. Their guards had been silent the entire time, trying to remain out of the way for the entire girly affair. Abigail had paid for it all, and Riley appreciated the gift. Riley didn't need her to, but it was nice.

"We'll have to do this again," Riley said as they were heading back to Wild Junction. "I never had these moments with other friends. Haley, Phoebe, and I would just meet up to go out, but not this small stuff. Not getting our nails done or anything."

"We do need to do this again," Abigail agreed with a smile. "Do you still hang out with Phoebe?"

"No, not really," Riley said with a shrug. "After my falling out with Haley, Phoebe and I just drifted apart, I guess."

"It happens. You entered a new place in your life, and some things in your old place get left behind." Abigail nudged her. "Give her a text, ask how's she doing. You never know, it might lead back into the friendship or you'll know it's over."

"That's a good idea." Riley nodded. "Maybe if things are good, the three of us can go out to Rocker's. I haven't been in ages."

"Is that the bar the wolves are thinking of getting involved with?"

"Yeah, though who knows?" Riley chuckled. "I don't think they know what to do with themselves."

"They don't," Abigail said emphatically. Riley howled in laughter at the expression on Abigail's face. She didn't know what had Abigail looking that way, but it had to be something hilarious.

6

ZACHARY

"What's up with you, man?" Zachary groaned as Brenton once again zoned out at his desk. Brenton snapped back to attention and shrugged.

"I don't know," Brenton mumbled.

"Don't lie to me, ass," Zachary growled, throwing a convenient pencil at his Alpha. Brenton caught it and snapped it in half.

"I have not had sex with Riley since before we were grabbed," Brenton growled. Ah, his Alpha just wasn't getting laid. That would make Brenton a little cranky. "And I am not sure I will ever get to again." That was much worse.

"Ah, that," Zachary sighed, leaning back in his spot on the couch. He looked down at the massive stacks of paperwork they were supposed to be going through. Shit they had missed while everything was going on.

"Yeah, that," Brenton growled more. Normally, Zachary was the one growling this much, but Zachary knew this was really eating away at Brenton.

"It's only been...shit, a little over a week?" Zachary

reminded him, shaking his head. "You're expecting too much too fast."

"I am not expecting anything," Brenton bit out, "but I would like to not terrify our girl every time I go near her."

"I don't know what to tell you." Zachary threw his hands up. "I'm not really good at this kind of shit. Talk to fucking Andrew, he's better at it. Or the doe, Abigail. She's a fucking professional."

"I will talk to Abigail when you do," Brenton crooned dangerously, and Zachary stiffened. He didn't want to talk to Abigail. He didn't want to admit he was having dreams of cages again. "I thought so," Brenton muttered after a long moment of silence.

"Not fair," Zachary growled.

"I am your Alpha. I do not need to be fair. I choose to be." Brenton smiled, and Zachary remembered that Brenton could easily end this by just forcing Zachary to sit down with her. Brenton was being nice by giving him the choice.

"I have a question," Zachary finally said, going for a change of topic.

"Let's hear it," Brenton huffed. "You know your words, Zachary."

Haha. Zachary bared his teeth at Brenton before continuing.

"Who's your best guess on the shifter who sold us out to the hunters?" Zachary kicked his feet up onto the coffee table, which was new. The last one had been destroyed when Zachary was stuck in the office while the hunters tried to raid their home.

"No ide-" A knock cut Brenton off and Zachary inhaled deeply before standing up from the couch to answer. Zachary pulled the door open and grinned at Andrew.

"What's up?" Zachary asked as Andrew walked in and fell onto the couch.

"One of the contractors quit," Andrew growled. "The one that has to remake the diner's kitchen. Caleb."

"Why?" Brenton asked, narrowing his eyes. Zachary was also curious.

"He didn't give me a reason," Andrew sighed. "Just said he would refund the deposit and that the project wasn't for him."

"That is...concerning," Brenton said with care. It was, Zachary thought, since they had hired shifter-owned companies to rebuild the diner. It was very concerning. The contractor for the kitchen was a golden eagle and popular to use in the restaurant business. He had a sixth sense about what chefs needed and how to create an optimal work space for them.

"Isn't it?" Andrew huffed. "And the cougar I was using for the displays and counters out front? He was lying to me today, but I'm not really sure why. I can't call him out until I figure out what his game is."

"What was the lie?" Zachary growled.

"He upped his estimate by about half a million dollars," Andrew groaned, "saying something about having to work around so many other people. It was utter nonsense."

"He is just looking for a fatter paycheck." Brenton gave them both a disgusted look. "We will pay him what he wants. If the work is shoddy, he will pay for it with something other than the zeros in his bank account."

"I'll let him know." Andrew nodded, pulling out his phone. "Where's Riley? I figured she would be in here under your feet at this point in the day."

"She went to get her nails done with Abigail," Zachary told him as he found his seat on the couch.

"I'll have to see it to believe it," Andrew chuckled.

"I do not like this," Brenton whispered, looking down at his papers. "No one has ever broken a contract with us before..."

"You still thinking about Caleb?" Zachary frowned at Brenton, who gave a slow nod. "Shit happens. There's been a lot going on. We'll hire someone else."

Zachary didn't like the look Brenton and Andrew shared after that.

"No one has *ever* broken a contract with us before," Andrew repeated, and Zachary huffed.

"I heard Brenton," Zachary growled, and, when he went to say more, Brenton continued.

"They are not scared of us right now," Brenton whispered. "This is only the beginning. We are about to find it very hard to find someone who is willing to work with us without a substantial amount of money being on the table."

"Oh fuck." Zachary looked between Andrew and Brenton, realizing where they were going with this. Andrew's phone went off and he sighed as Zachary kept talking. "I can beat him in court over it. It's really not a big deal, guys."

"I have a feeling you'll be in court a lot, if that's your plan," Andrew chuckled, holding up his phone. "Brenton is right, Zachary. This is only going to get worse before it gets better. That was the lynx working on the plumbing. He's backing out of the project."

"Goddamn it," Brenton groaned, rolling his eyes up to stare at the ceiling. Zachary grunted, grabbing Andrew's phone from him and turning it off.

"We'll deal with it," Zachary snarled. "I can't believe this shit. Half the people we hired for the diner also worked on this house. They know we pay well and stay out of their hair. They know we don't force them to grovel like other prides."

"It makes me wonder why they are all stepping back from us," Andrew added, grabbing his phone back. Zachary watched him shove it back in his pocket without turning it back on. Good.

"Andrew, I hate to say it, but the diner just really is not the highest thing on the priority list right now," Brenton sighed, leaning back in his own chair and kicking his feet onto the old desk.

"Oh, I know," Andrew laughed but it ended quickly. "No, what I'm wondering is why the contractors feel the need to step back from it."

"That is an important question." Zachary pondered it for a minute before looking at the papers. He really needed to get through those, and pondering some obscure question was only going to distract him. "You can file it with the other thousand questions we need answers to."

"Amen to that," Brenton grumbled. "Let's just get through this day by day and handle things as we can. We will not get anywhere trying to fix everything at once. And I would ask Gabe to look into the contractors, but that would only be a nightmare for him. We hired the best, so he would be seeing hundreds, if not thousands of people who contact them for work. We will hire humans if we have to for the diner."

"With that," Andrew sighed, "I'm going to lay here and take a nap."

"Alright." Brenton went back to his own work, and Zachary followed suit.

Zachary looked at Andrew and gave a small smile. It'd been a long time since the cougar had willingly hung out in the office. Watching him fall asleep, it was easy to forget that

Andrew was third, and, even though the pride only had six members, that meant something. He was calm and peaceful by nature, but underneath that was a strong mind and a dominance that could be a force to be reckoned with. Zachary knew that Riley could easily match that dominance, though, if she continued down the road she was on.

"He and Riley going to fight over third?" Zachary asked softly, once Andrew was too deep in the nap to wake up. "Well, not fight...you know what I mean."

"I do, and no," Brenton chuckled. "I thought they might, but I'm certain Andrew is never going to let her step higher than him. He's too stubborn to go lower on the totem pole than he already is. Not like third is very low but he had a hard-enough time letting go of second as it was."

"Good to know," Zachary huffed and with that, they both were back to work. At least Andrew and the diner conversation took Brenton's mind off Riley and what was going on there. Zachary hoped, at least.

7

RILEY

A fter dinner, which had been almost too normal, Riley wandered slowly down the hall towards the den. She'd shown all the guys her nails and was surprised by how completely fascinated by them they all were. The growl that had come from Brenton had made her break out in goosebumps. They were all growly when they thought something was hot, and she wondered what their reaction would be to the toes.

"Riley," Troy called to her from the door to the den. "It's your movie choice tonight."

"Let Brenton choose," she told him as she stopped to look at one of her favorite paintings, the deer. Captivated by the viewer, as if it knew the predators were always watching it. She had a hard time catching and eating animals in her feline form, but the guys had told her that it helped soothe the feline in her. They'd been right. Even now, she felt the cat prowl in the back of her mind, though it had gotten plenty of exercise recently. It remembered the hunt and the kill and craved it. It still remembered killing the hunter as she and Thomas made it back into the compound where her pride and his pack were held. "And I want to sit with him tonight. Is that okay?"

"I'll let him know," Troy chuckled at her with a smile.

She stood for another moment in silence, glancing towards yet another SSTF guard wandering around. She had yet to understand why they felt the need to be in the house.

"Good evening," she called to him, and watched the guard turn towards her with a frown.

"Good evening," he replied with a thick layer of confusion. She took a whiff and paid attention. He was a serval like her mother.

"How are you?" she asked, not yet ready to sit down in the den for a movie. She was also trying to be polite.

"Good," he answered, eyeing her with apprehension. "Do you need something?"

"No." She shrugged. This was the most stilted conversation she'd ever had. She wasn't sure what she'd been expecting by saying hi to him, but it wasn't this awkward exchange. "Just trying to be polite."

"No need," he huffed and continued on his rounds. She watched him walk away and sighed.

"Let's watch a movie," she whispered to herself, heading into the den.

Troy and Gabe were closest to the door, always on their right-side couch while Zachary and Andrew shared the left. Brenton waited, seeming tense, on her favorite middle one. He looked over to her as she walked up, and she noted he was all the way on one side, leaving her a lot of couch to give her space.

"What are we watching?" she asked him with a smile.

"A comedy. Something we can get a laugh at." Brenton kicked off his shoes and she wondered why he was still in his suit. He normally put on sweats like everyone else for movies. "Get comfortable."

"Alright," she chuckled, falling down onto the couch. Then, she decided to enact her plan. Abigail told her to let Brenton discover the toes on his own, and she was going to let him. "Think you can tolerate giving my poor feet a rub down, love?"

"I can do that," he grunted, patting his leg. She swung her feet onto his lap. She was wearing socks since it was November in Colorado, meaning it was freezing outside and a little chilly in the massive mansion. As the movie started, he got to work on her feet. He didn't pull the socks off, though, and Riley wondered how long it would take him.

She closed her eyes and leaned back, ignoring the movie in favor of Brenton's skilled hands on her feet.

"How thick are these socks?" he grunted after nearly ten minutes.

"I bought them for her," Andrew yawned from his spot, "so, they might be her winter socks, to keep her tiny ass little feet warm."

"They've got to go," Brenton growled, looking up at her from her feet.

"Go ahead. They were getting a little too warm anyways," she said nonchalantly.

She watched him pull off the first sock and listened to the growl that made her a little wet. He ran a finger over her big toenail and quickly revealed the second foot.

"Well, aren't these lovely?" he snarled, grinning at her. She felt some heat rise in her face at the hungry expression on his face.

"What?" Troy asked from his spot. Riley realized all the guys were watching her and Brenton now.

"She even got her toenails done," Brenton growled. "I like this..."

She gave him a saucy grin. She hoped he would catch the meaning behind it. He did.

"Fuck the movie," he snarled, pulling her up and into his lap. She laughed as he stood up with her. "You all can look at them tomorrow."

"Well, hot damn," Zachary laughed as Brenton carried her from the room.

"Trying to tell me something?" he growled playfully into her ear.

"Yes," she whispered back as he took the stairs two at a time.

They passed the serval guard, who looked at them like they were mad. Riley stuck her tongue out at him, which Brenton noticed, claiming her mouth to stop the offense. She found her back against the wall as he devoured her mouth.

"Stop that," he groaned at her, before continuing the kiss. He hooked a canine on one of her lip rings and tugged gently with a growl. A bit of throat clearing had him letting go of her and looking behind him. Riley peeked around him and sighed. The guard was still giving a wide-eyed look at them.

"Let's get into my room." She chuckled at Brenton, who nodded silently, pulling the door open and locking it once it was closed behind him.

"You know, just earlier today, I was getting fucking cranky about not being with you," Brenton growled against her neck before he dropped her on her bed. "It's been a fucking long day."

"It's been a long week," she gasped as he leaned down to kiss her neck.

"It has," Brenton murmured, running his hands up her sides under her tank top. "And I'm just fucking terrified of scaring you..."

"I've thought about that," Riley whispered as Brenton slowly rubbed her sides down to her hips and back up. "I think it's just when I can't see you, or you catch me unexpectedly."

"So, no more spooking you on accident," Brenton purred, and she realized he was becoming distracted.

"I'm not scared of you when you walk in the room, or when I see you in the halls," Riley continued, hoping he was listening at this point since he was doing a fairly good job making her lose her train of thought as he peppered kisses on her stomach. "I think I'm just...getting over it. It could be worse..."

"It could be," he agreed as he pulled her yoga pants down slowly. He left her thong in place, tracing it with a finger as she felt her heart beginning to do weird things. It wasn't sure whether it wanted to race or stop completely. "I think we need this."

"We do." Riley propped herself up on her elbows, but Brenton tsk'ed at her quietly.

"Stay on your back and just let me..." He took a ragged breath. She didn't know what he was looking at, but something had bothered him. "Let me make this good for you. Let me have some control, or I might take this too fast."

She nodded slowly and went flat on her back again. She kept her eyes locked on his; those molten gold pools were heated and filled with apprehension. He didn't want to go rough and scare her, which meant she couldn't taunt and tease him like she normally did. And Zachary was also right. He needed to feel in control for a moment.

He tore her tank top open down the middle and freed

her breasts, leaning down to trap a nipple in his mouth. She kept her eyes wide open and watched, even as a moan left her lips. She couldn't take her eyes off him being gentler than she had ever seen.

"You don't need to do this," she murmured as he slowly pulled the ruined tank off her.

"Yes, I do," Brenton told her as he slowly went over her body with kisses. It took her a long time to figure out what he was trying to do.

Every place the faint yellow of a bruise was still there or small scar, every place a bruise or cut had already healed, he kissed. Every place she'd ever gotten hurt since they met, he touched gently, as if he was trying to replace the memory with this moment.

He even got her hands and feet, once covered in cuts. He pulled her thong off with care as he went down to her feet.

"Yes, I do," he said more softly as he continued. He made it to her lips, and the kiss he gave her was scorching. She was sensitive and putty in his hands. Riley couldn't think straight. She couldn't think of anything except him, in that quiet moment, as he laid over her and kissed her.

"Brenton," she said airily as he pulled up over her.

"I love you," he growled softly. "And I am sorry."

"There's nothing to be sorry for," she whispered as he put his forehead to hers.

"Riley..." he growled softly. "My *family* did this to you. I brought you into this. I did this to you."

Riley wanted to weep. There it was, the real guilt, the real pain Brenton was dragging around. The cherry on top of the violent world she'd joined at his invitation. It wasn't just politics and vengeance, though those were bad enough. It wasn't just hunters and violations to their security and privacy. It was that he blamed himself for all of it, and she knew he didn't know how to fix it.

Wasn't this something she had just dealt with? Gabe had felt the same way—the underlying guilt and belief that it was all his fault. And she refused to believe that. She refused to allow the men she loved to believe it.

"Brenton," she said once more, stronger, taking his face in her hands and pulling him in for another kiss. "Don't do this to us. Don't let them get in between us. Don't let them win. I love you too much to allow it." She didn't have the power to back that statement up, but she hoped he could feel what she did in that moment. The overwhelming amount of love she had for him. For all of them.

"Okay," he sighed to her lips. "Okay, beautiful."

"Love me," she whispered, and he obliged, giving her a deep kiss as he laid out next to her. One of his hands ran down her side and over her stomach. She moaned into his mouth when he used a finger to rub her clit gently, and then he sank it inside of her.

Her back arched as he slowly slid it in and out of her, and she held his shoulders as his thumb leisurely rolled over her clit. She felt his erection pressed against her thigh, straining to get out of his navy-blue suit, but he made no attempt to undress himself. She pulled the buttons of his shirt open, making him growl as they flew.

"You just don't know how to slow down, do you?" he asked, pushing a second finger deep in her. He pressed both to that glorious spot and rubbed, making her cry out.

"No," she gasped as he continued his slow pace now with both fingers. She ran her hands over his pecs. She nibbled on his neck. She moaned into him and listened to the satisfied growls he answered her with.

"I'm trying to be normal, beautiful," Brenton snarled,

73

pushing her closer to an orgasm she refused to have until he told her she could.

"This isn't normal for *you*," she panted, holding on to him. "And I want you. *All* of you. Alpha. Dominant. Arrogant. Mine."

"Fuck," he grunted, rolling over her. He put his mouth next to her ear and growled one word. "Now."

She exploded. Stars danced in her vision, and she wasn't sure if they were the ones on her ceiling or just balls of light she couldn't focus on.

She felt a small breeze as he backed off of her. She tried to focus her eyes on him and watched him strip faster than she'd ever seen.

Then, he crawled up from the end of the bed, and she found herself underneath the massive man she called hers. But she didn't stay there.

"Let's do something else," Brenton growled softly. Then, he rolled over onto his back and pulled her on top of him. She smiled down at him as she bit her bottom lip. Well, she could make this work. "This way you can go however fast or rough you want."

"How thoughtful of you," she chuckled, grinding herself on his cock, making him growl. She was just going to have to drive him mad to get the dominant male she wanted. She kept up with that, wet and primed but refusing to take him in.

"Never mind," Brenton snarled, scooting up so he was propped against the cracked headboard. She laughed as he grabbed her hips and pulled her closer. He directed her over him and held her as she sank down on him. "Oh, fuck, Riley..."

She wrapped her arms around his neck as he began to thrust upwards into her. Her cries echoed through her bedroom, every thrust feeling deeper than the last. His hands moved to her ass and held on tight.

"Brenton!" she moaned before biting down on his shoulder. One of his hands left her ass and moved up to wrap in her hair and pull her head back. She met his eyes, and his lips crashed into hers.

The kiss felt like a prayer. It tasted like salvation and peace. Riley blinked back tears, and Brenton pulled back from the kiss. They only had eyes for each other in that moment. Nothing was coming between them now. This was just another piece of home to Riley, and she found a small piece of power in knowing Brenton was still hers, no matter what.

"Cum for me, beautiful," he growled, their eyes still locked together.

She did, his name falling from her lips as he rolled them over and he held her. He continued to thrust as she rode out the orgasm, growling in victory.

"Do not stop now," he snarled down at her. She felt him angle his hips, causing him to grind across her clit. The muscles in her lower abdomen continued to try to hold him as he gave one last, powerful thrust. They were both panting as he came in her. "Beautiful," he whispered, kissing her as his dick twitched in her. She moaned with a smile, satisfied.

"There's my Alpha," she whispered back. "Welcome back."

"I did not go anywhere." He frowned down at her, and Riley shook her head. She poked his forehead.

"Yeah, you did," she chuckled. "Somewhere up there, thinking I wouldn't want you here, in my bed and in my body." He grinned and lowered to kiss her.

"My apologies," he teased, kissing her slowly afterwards. "It is good to be back."

"Stay the night?" She asked, wrapping her arms around his neck again.

"If you want."

"I've had nightmares for a couple of nights," she admitted softly to him.

"Zachary told me," he murmured. "I will stay for you."

"Thank you," she told him as he finally slid out of her body. She noted he seemed to stand a bit straighter as he walked towards her bathroom for the customary hand towel he used to clean them up.

Only ten minutes later, she snuggled her face into his chest and absorbed his scent, reveling in it. He purred, and she wondered if he was even tired as his hands made trails of goosebumps over her.

"You know what I haven't done in a long time?" he asked with a small smile.

"What?" She frowned, wondering where he was going with this.

"This," he growled playfully, rubbing his head to hers. She laughed as he rubbed his hair and head across her cheeks.

"What are you doing?" She laughed until she cried. He rubbed his chest on hers and she nearly moaned. Her nipples were hard, and she felt a wave of heat between her legs.

"Marking you," he growled playfully. "So that fools know you belong to the Kingson Pride. Always. No matter what."

It made her heart skip a beat to hear. He hadn't done it since the day she had shifted for the first time.

"And it might help you remember my scent again," he whispered in her ear, pressed up to her. She bit her bottom lip at the feeling of him hard again.

"Thank you," she mumbled back, getting a little warm from the idea of a round two with Brenton.

"Anything for you," he growled, kissing her.

The second round was better than the first.

But it was accented with a single question.

"What happened to your headboard?"

"Zachary broke it. I thought you would have noticed this morning."

8

RILEY

She woke up to his scent and only thought of him. Her Alpha slept peacefully next to her, and she smiled at him from her spot. They weren't all wrapped up together, so she could open her eyes and see his face, void of any troubles.

She didn't say anything as she pushed herself up and then out of the bed. She checked the time as she passed her desk on her way to the bathroom. It was nearly seven in the morning, so she'd gotten a full night's rest...after she and Brenton had finished relearning every inch of each other since before the hunters.

She did everything she needed to do in the bathroom with a lighter step, knowing she and Brenton would be fine. She'd felt this way after knowing Gabe would be okay as well.

She left the sleeping lion in her bed as she got dressed. In her mind, there was no reason to wake him. Breakfast would be later today, and she could come get him up before it was on the table.

She considered what to do with her morning. She was

just too awake to cuddle with Brenton until his eyes opened. She considered a run, but then she would need to shower again before breakfast. That wasn't something she was in the mood for. Neither was painting. She would be doing enough of that later in the day and with *that* painting finished, she was almost a little scared to see what her mind would want to paint next. She wandered out of her room and began to head downstairs, wondering if anyone else was awake. Maybe she could read something in Brenton's office.

"Can we talk about how she's fucking not just one of them, but all of them?"

Riley stopped in her tracks on a landing on the stairs. She sort of recognized the voice, which told her that it was one of the SSTF agents. She just couldn't remember which one.

"I can only imagine how Keith feels about it," another voice replied, sounding bemused. She took a deep breath and held back a hiss. That fucking serval she'd tried to be polite to and a human.

"He's embarrassed as hell," the serval chuckled. "She's pretty blatant about it. Tiger for breakfast, Alpha for before-bed snack. I wonder where the leopards and cougar fall in on her daily schedule. And she's cute enough, I find myself wondering if she'll add a serval to the meal plan."

"Well, Isabella was well-known for opening her legs to get what she wanted, too. Maybe if your scrawny ass had something to offer her, she'd take you up on an offer," the human said, sounding sure of himself. As if it was a case of 'like mother, like daughter.' "Shit, Keith got wrapped up with all the wrong women."

"He didn't know who Isabella was until he joined the force," the serval said with a large dollop of pity. "He had no idea his daughter would turn out the same way. I was there the day we showed him open cases and he freaked the fuck out. He'd thought his *human* wife was killed by shifters. It was why he joined the SSTF. After learning that he'd practically been tricked by her..."

"He's been trying to catch her for what...seven or eight years? He was utterly convinced she wasn't dead. And he was finally proven right earlier this year."

Riley bared her teeth silently. He'd learned about her mom and then abandoned Riley to go catch her. He never told her. He never told her anything. He hunted a woman they had all thought was dead. One that should have stayed dead, but instead got back into the game just to have a fucking good time. Fuck her parents. Riley couldn't hold back a snarl.

Tears welled in her eyes as rage flooded her system. Fuck them both. They fucking deserved each other.

"Shit," the serval whispered. Riley heard footsteps coming toward her, but she couldn't bring herself to move. She was fucking furious. The serval came into her line of sight and looked up at her, paling.

"Go to hell," Riley snarled. "And to think, I tried to be fucking nice to you yesterday, you low-life piece of shit."

"Ms. Stern," the serval stammered a little. "Please, let-"

"No, I don't think I need your explanations," she hissed. "Not about what you said about my sex life, nor what you were just kind enough to share about my father. And before you go thinking he's the injured party in this mess, he fucking abandoned me." She took a step down and began stalking closer to the serval, who was smart enough to take a few steps back as she descended. "He didn't tell me what I was. He made some shoddy plans for me to go with his brother, who never fucking showed up, and I was dumped into fucking foster care. He doesn't get to play fucking victim, and don't *ever* try to pretend he is one in this house."

She took the last step and turned to see the human. She snarled at him as the serval moved to block her line of sight.

"Ma'am," he began but she wasn't fucking having it.

"Go tell Keith and the rest of your fucking crew that the next time I hear this shit, I'll fucking make your lives miserable," she growled, "and get the fuck out of the main house from now on. You aren't welcome."

"Uh." The serval looked unsure, but Riley only snarled louder. He made the correct decision of backing farther away from her, grabbing the human, and leaving. It wasn't because she was a real threat to them, but the Pride had been promised discretion and that the protection detail would be "unnoticeable". Talking shit about the Pride was not discretion, nor was it unnoticeable. Those two must have been fucking stupid to think no one would hear them gossiping about her like fucking children.

Now, she definitely needed a run, second shower be damned. She stalked towards the back door, white-hot rage still simmering inside her. She stripped quickly, ignoring the sounds and smells of other guards outside. She heard someone moving toward her as she entered the quick shift to her cheetah, and the cat snarled immediately, making whoever was coming close stop instantly.

She turned towards the approaching figure and took a sniff. She met her father's eyes, and he looked shocked. She growled viciously at him, making him step back. Behind him was the serval, who had the balls to snarl back while in human form. In her current form, she had him, and she was peeved he didn't recognize it. His feline form didn't match up to hers, either. Considering it was his shit-talking that pissed her off, she was irritated at him.

Fuck them.

She took off as Keith tried to call her back. She felt the earth pound beneath her feet as she tore past a wolf coming out of the tree line with a human beside it.

This was her home. These were her woods. And if she didn't want to be followed in them, she couldn't be. She knew every safe foot fall, every trail, and every errant branch, ducking them as she ran.

She hadn't truly run since the hunt, and it was exhilarating. Wind on her face, ears tucked back. The controlled posture of her cheetah form as she ran, a burn of energy she desperately needed.

She slowed to a walk when the house was completely out of sight. It would take any of them a good amount of time to gain the distance on her if they tried to follow.

She remembered the shocked look on her father's face and huffed. Did he forget she was a shifter? She knew he'd never seen her in her cheetah form, but she didn't expect him to be shocked over it. Maybe it was something they both needed. That recognition that they weren't the same species anymore. They never had been.

The November morning air had a bite to it, and Riley was cooling down from the run. She couldn't stay out too long, or she'd develop a chill. She trotted along, near the stream before cutting toward the field. The night before at dinner, Brenton had mentioned a lioness' scent on the property, and he firmly believed it was Jessie. Riley didn't pick up the scent, but it was something she knew to watch out for.

Not that any of them considered Jessie a threat right now. They had actually been a little concerned for her.

Ms. Stern. A male voice entered her mind and she let

the breeze bring a scent towards her. The wolf she'd screamed past.

Yes? She turned towards him and watched the black wolf tread carefully towards her.

We would appreciate if you didn't come out on runs alone. And if you don't want me following you, you should head back.

Party poopers. She huffed, adding in a real sigh to accent her point.

It's for your safety.

Yeah, I bet. He's wants to talk when I go back, doesn't he?

I'm not touching that topic with a ten-foot pole, Ms. Stern.

Really? She sat down and watched the wolf move around, looking uncomfortable.

I like having my body parts attached to the rest of me. I'm not willing to test whatever line I shouldn't cross that keeps them there.

I would never, she replied with a silent laugh. *I just burn houses down when the mood strikes me, it seems.*

Your males would.

Well, he had a point there.

Fine, I'll head back in, but I want him gone. I'm not dealing with him or that rank ass serval.

That can be arranged.

She followed his lead back, slowly but steadily. Sure enough, when she walked out of the trees, her father and the serval were both gone.

Thank you, she told him as they made it to the back porch. She shifted back into her human form before he could respond, and he trotted away, probably to report that he'd gotten her back to the house. She grabbed her clothing out of the chest and threw it on.

She didn't stop for anything as she made her way back to her room. She wasn't sweaty enough for a shower, but she was feeling the need to curl into the bed next to the lion she'd left there.

"Brenton?" she called as she entered her room. She smiled when she saw him.

"You went for a run?" he asked, putting his phone aside as she walked closer. He was still beautifully nude, propped up on the headboard and the pillows.

"You haven't decided to get out of bed yet?" she asked. He knew well enough by her scent that she went for a run.

"Hmm," Brenton sighed. "I can check emails from right here, and I figured staying here meant you would come back eventually. Plus, no one bothers me while I am in your bed. I have heard them knock on mine for the last ten minutes." She chuckled and laid out over her blankets next to him. "Why did you go out for a run?"

"I got angry about something and needed it," she answered, wondering how much she should tell him. If any of the guys heard about the incident, they'd go on a warpath, and Brenton would be the worst. Or Zachary. They might even kill someone.

"That does not sound good." Brenton frowned at her and pulled her to lean on his chest. "Are there any fires out there I need to call someone about?"

"Very funny," Riley snorted. "No, I heard a couple of the agents talking a bit of shit and chewed them out for it."

"What did they say?" Brenton growled softly.

"I handled it," she assured him, "and I'm going to continue handling it. There's no reason for you to get involved."

Then someone was knocking on *her* door.

"Why are we being looked for, Riley?" Brenton began pulling the covers back to leave the bed. "What did they say?" She was thankful he wasn't putting that Alpha oomph behind the question.

"Let me just...tell you what they said after I send a quick text..." Riley needed a plan right now, before she had to stop her Alpha from decapitating a certain serval and a couple of humans. "But I'm handling it. It's not your problem."

"Riley," Brenton growled louder.

"Hold on," Riley said quickly, grabbing her phone. She sent a text she never thought she would send before.

RILEY: Hey, can you get to the estate as fast as possible? I might need your help with something.

SHE HIT send and waited impatiently. Brenton was growling louder, and the knocking on her door had not stopped.

"Tell me, Riley," Brenton snarled.

"They talked some shit about us," she hissed, impatient about not getting a text back yet. "As in me, you, the guys. My sex life. Our sex lives. They also said some stuff about my parents. I'm *handling* it!"

The growl that came from Brenton was something feral, and she wondered if her Alpha was about to shift. The sound definitely wasn't human.

"Brenton, you can't go out there and kill any of them," Riley said quickly. "You absolutely cannot do that. These aren't people you just bury in the woods and no one will notice or care."

"Watch me," he hissed.

Her phone vibrated, and she read the response quickly.

"Who did you text?" Brenton asked sounding like violence and fury. A monster ready to attack helpless victims. He was, in that moment, the man-eating beast that people feared wild lions could be.

"Sheriff," she answered as calmly as possible.

SHERIFF: I'll use my sirens.

BRENTON JUMPED OUT OF BED, and Riley couldn't beat him to the door. Without a lick of clothing on, Brenton swung it open and revealed her father.

"I am going to fucking kill some of your agents, Keith. I recommend you start fucking packing all your shit and getting the hell out of my goddamn house before I decide it is your turn." The mild tone he said it in was probably more terrifying than the snarls and growls she had just heard. Then he roared, loud enough to shake the walls, and Riley took several steps away from the enraged lion filling her door frame. She'd asked for her ultra-dominant Alpha back. She'd gotten him.

To his credit, Riley thought, her father only staggered back a couple feet instead of completely falling to the floor.

Either response was acceptable.

RILEY COULDN'T STOP the madness that ensued after that. She could only watch the clock and hope someone bigger and badder than Brenton and Zachary would show up. She only knew one person who fit the bill and he was already on his way.

Brenton had woken up everyone in the Pride with the roar, and in minutes, she was in the hall outside his office, between him and her father. The serval was back, wide-eyed and deathly pale. Other agents were ready to throw down, and she could only keep her hand on Brenton's chest, hoping he didn't decide to tear past her and go for throats. He at least had clothes on, though.

Once he made the decision to start exacting punishment, there would be no stopping Zachary from following suit. Or Andrew, who looked genuinely furious. That was a rare sight. Troy and Gabe were more expectant, as if they knew something like this would happen eventually. That didn't mean they weren't pissed, too, and Riley had to remember they were just as dangerous as the big boys.

"Three fucking days," Brenton snarled. "You are here three fucking days, and you have not been able to keep your goddamn mouths shut about shit that is not your business."

"It's just a misunderstanding," Keith pressed, probably for the dozenth time. Riley rolled her eyes.

"There was no misunderstanding about it," Riley hissed back at him. "They talked some shit and deserve to be reprimanded."

"And they will be, but I'm not going to let Brenton kill them," Keith told her, frustrated, "and I definitely don't believe this reaction is necessary."

Brenton reached around her and grabbed Keith's shirt, yanking him forward. Riley found herself squished between them as Brenton growled into her father's face.

"All I am hearing is that you are a terrible father," Brenton viciously told him. "That you would dare say that those mother fuckers do not deserve exactly what I am about to give them only tells me that you really do not give a damn about your daughter."

"Brenton," a roar entered the hallway. She hadn't heard him come in, or anything else. She peeked around Brenton and sighed a little happily at the sight of Sheriff stomping closer. "They can send you to prison for assaulting an SSTF agent. For a very long time. Let him go."

Brenton just snarled, turning to the big bear. Sheriff growled back, and Riley was still trapped between her Alpha and her father.

"Please, Brenton," Riley whispered. "We'll get this figured out, but you can't kill any of them. I already chewed them out, and I was going to chew them out again after I cooled down."

"Go take a run, Brenton." Sheriff came closer and clapped Brenton on the shoulder. "You trust me to take care of Riley for a moment? I'll handle all of this. Kitten doesn't want you killing people, so I'm not going to let you."

"Yeah," Brenton growled, releasing Keith with a shove. "I'll go for a run..." He glanced down at Riley and huffed. "They don't get another chance after this, Riley. They open their mouths one more time, and I'll end them, fuck the consequences."

She nodded and watched him turn and leave. Zachary looked her over for a moment then towards Brenton's retreating back.

"Go with him?" she asked, and Zachary nodded, swooping down to kiss her cheek.

"You guys go get some food made," Zachary told the rest of them as he followed Brenton out the back. Andrew, Troy, and Gabe didn't say anything at all, leaving quietly. She watched them all go before sighing at Sheriff.

"I'm not going to ask them." Sheriff jerked his head to the agents still filling the hall. "What happened. So..."

"I caught a couple of them gossiping," Riley said with disgust. "Let's hear it, serval." She turned to the most offensive party. The human who'd been in that conversation was also there, staying close to his buddy. "You still want to join the meal plan? Think you got something to offer that I don't already have?"

"Ah hell," Sheriff groaned, grabbing Riley and pulling her away from the agents as the serval hissed at her.

"And what about you, Dad?" Riley growled. "Still embarrassed? Still letting all them think you just have a slutty daughter, and, oh no, it couldn't possibly have anything to do with you."

"Fuck," Sheriff growled, wrapping an arm around her and lifting her. She didn't fight it. Now that Brenton and her pride were out of the way, she could go off on the assholes like she'd originally planned. "Office. Only one of you, whoever wants to fucking explain." He pulled her into the office and waited, holding the door.

Keith was brave enough to step inside. She wondered if Sheriff realized who he was yet. He'd been getting his wife home, and Mrs. Johnson was Sheriff's top priority. Always.

"The rest of you go back to whatever the hell it is you're supposed to be doing," Sheriff commanded, shutting the door. He released Riley, and she huffed, straightening out her tank top as she walked to Brenton's desk. She sat in his chair and leaned back.

"This has been an eventful morning," Keith sighed. "Sheriff Johnson, it's a pleasure to finally meet you." He held out a hand to the bear, but Sheriff didn't take it.

"Don't," Sheriff growled. "I knew who you were the moment I saw you, and it's really not a pleasure."

She watched Keith get a little pissed at that, but he didn't say anything.

"So," Sheriff started, sinking into the couch. "Who wants to start?"

"I'm sorry my team said something inappropriate," Keith ground out. "It won't happen again."

"Yeah, because you won't be having them roam the halls of my fucking home," Riley hissed.

"That's not your decision," Keith snapped at her.

"My Alpha leaving me here to deal with you makes it my decision," Riley growled.

"I don't know what you see in him," he said with frustration. "You avoid the hell out of me, and, instead, hang out with a bunch of dangerous, out of control-"

"Don't go there," Sheriff warned quietly. "If you want any sort of relationship with your daughter, do not go there."

"Relationship?" Riley laughed, throwing her head back. "He doesn't want a relationship, Sheriff! The first thing he did when I realized he was even fucking here was compare me to my mother! He doesn't get to stand there and wonder why I won't talk to him."

"You set a man's house on fire!" Keith roared. "With people inside it, for fuck's sake!"

"I believe this has little to do with what Brenton was angry about..." Sheriff groaned. Riley heard it but ignored it.

"Abel Cartona is a monster! He's damn lucky I only burned his goddamn house down!" Riley screamed, standing back up. She slammed her hands down on the table. "You have no idea! You stand there and look at me like I'm some terrorist, and how I couldn't *possibly* be your daughter." She pointed at him. "And then one of your fucking friends out there practically called me a whore, wondering if he could stick his hand in the goddamn cookie jar, and you defended him! You won't even pretend to be upset that someone said that about me!"

"Hell," Sheriff sighed. "That would make the boys angry..."

"Maybe you shouldn't be sleeping with five men then!" Keith glared at her and she bared her teeth. "It's not normal!"

"Go to hell!" she yelled. "You don't get to judge me, you patronizing piece of shit! You walked out! You don't get to walk back in and say a goddamn thing! You damn sure don't get to let any of those mother fuckers do it, either!"

"Both of you stop yelling," Sheriff grumbled. "It's getting us nowhere."

Riley bit back the next thing she was going to say as Keith turned red.

"And what would you have us do?" Keith asked angrily.

"You'll keep your agents out of the main house. There's acres of land for them to patrol, and the security in the house doesn't need the extra hands, anyway. It'll preserve the Pride's privacy, and, if they want to gossip...well at least they won't get caught. You should put a stop to it though, it's unprofessional and a disgrace upon the SSTF," Sheriff told him sternly. Then he looked at her. Riley swallowed as Sheriff softened for a moment. "Kitten, he's your father. You two need to work out some of this other stuff in private." Riley could hear a small level of despair.

"No, he's not," she whispered. "My father is in the room, but he would never judge me for who I love."

She heard a choked sound and looked back to Keith. He looked stricken. He glanced wildly between her and Sheriff, and Riley almost believed he was hurt by what she'd said. Almost. But she was more worried about Sheriff than her father. The bear meant a lot to her, and he'd given her a real father-daughter relationship when she believed she'd never have one again.

Now, she felt like she had too many.

"Go tell your boys that we've worked out the situation with the agents?" Sheriff's question was thick with emotion, and she nodded. "I'd like to talk to Keith for a moment. Agent to agent. About the sticky situation you all seem to be in."

Liar. Riley could smell the lie. This had nothing to do with them both being SSTF agents. Former, in Sheriff's case.

She left the office, ignoring the scent of pain and anger coming from Keith. She refused to feel guilty.

But she didn't go far, once she was out of the office. She quieted and hung out near the door, alone in the hallway, and waited.

"I retired long before you joined," Sheriff growled, "but I don't think the protocols have changed all that much."

"Excuse me?" Keith said with shock.

"Agents are seen and not heard during protection assignments." Sheriff. "On top of that, you are her damn father. When I heard through the grapevine that you were here, I expected better. Oh, I figured it out, when I finally got her to open up about you. And I don't care about your excuses for leaving her alone in the world, no idea who or what she is. I don't think you can truly justify yourself either."

"I wanted justice for my wife," Keith strained. "And when I realized I couldn't get that, I decided I was going to catch her and bring her to justice. That's justification enough."

"You are a selfish man," Sheriff sighed. "And you wonder why she's so mad at you. You walk into this house, and all you think is about how her behavior embarrasses you. You think about what you went through, dead wife, losing your career to take care of a child. How you feel. You forgot the most important thing. You've already failed the most important mission you ever had."

"What's that?"

"Being a father," Sheriff whispered softly. "Trying to make the next generation better than the previous. And I pity you for not realizing how utterly sad that is."

"You don't understand," Keith growled. "You had your all-star career and then got to step away to have children and devote your time to it."

"I'm not the one who doesn't understand, Keith," Sheriff sounded like he was disappointed. "But fine. You don't want her? I'll take her. I heard you were in town, and my wife asked me to visit the Pride and I kept saying no. I didn't want to step on your toes. You're her real father. And on day three, I can see that I had made the wrong decision. So, my wife and I are going to be here every day. She doesn't get out of the house enough, in my opinion, and I think this entire lot of felines needs a couple of parents for a minute, so why not? I'll take all of them."

"They're all adults," Keith scoffed. "What makes you think they're going to want you underfoot any more than me?"

"I'm bigger than all of you," Sheriff said it nonchalantly. "Now, you go on and deal with your agents. I'll deal with Kitten."

"Wait. Why do you call her that?" Keith asked, sounding curious and cautious.

"Because she is one," Sheriff huffed. "She's the smallest cat I've ever seen. And she's feisty like a little feral one. This conversation is over, though."

Riley began to walk away in a hurry as she heard them

moving around. She hadn't meant to stick around so long. She made it to the kitchen, hoping Sheriff and Keith didn't see her.

She found Andrew, Troy, and Gabe all moping around the bar and sighed.

"We won't have agents in the house anymore," she told them, walking over to give each a kiss.

"Thank, fuck," Troy grumbled. "Now let's get the other two and eat something."

"Well, I'm not done," Riley began.

"She's going to tell you that I'll be over here every fucking day, now, with my wife," Sheriff chuckled, walking over to her. "Eavesdropper."

She winced a little with guilt and shrugged at the guys.

"Oh, great," Gabe mumbled. "Get rid of the agents, gain the bear."

"Why?" Andrew asked, frowning at Sheriff.

"Because if Keith doesn't want her and you all, I do," he huffed. "You all need allies right now, at that. But, let's keep this from getting too political."

"You follow feline politics?" Riley asked him, and he shrugged.

"I was already here as the sheriff when the last generation of the Pride started dropping like flies," Sheriff told her. "I was here for nearly fifteen years already. I had to pay attention."

"Why?" Riley tilted her head to the side, and Sheriff sighed.

"I needed to know which bodies to ignore," he groaned. "Brenton's father, Geoffrey, and I weren't allies by any means, but we had an agreement. He wouldn't mess with the town, and I wouldn't mess with him."

"Jesus," Riley exclaimed under her breath. How deep did

the ties between the shifters around her go? How many bodies were buried around Wild Junction?

"I'll go get Brenton and Zachary," Andrew said as he began to walk away.

"Thank you," Riley called after him. She gave a weak smile to the leopard brothers, who looked a bit worn out. "This has been an eventful morning."

"You're the one who thought Brenton would let you handle it," Troy chuckled, shaking his head. "What did you think the morning was going to be?"

"Yeah, that's why I called in the big guns," Riley sighed, pointing at Sheriff.

"Good call," Gabe groaned, leaning his head down onto the counter. "And fuck those guys. I'm so tired of them being in our fucking house."

"They just got here, all of you." Sheriff looked around, confused at the lot of them. "Good Lord have mercy."

9

GABE

"They've been assholes the entire time too," Gabe huffed at the bear. He checked his watch and groaned again. He only had an hour until a completely different meeting called his attention. The morning was totally wasted at this point.

"Really?" Sheriff frowned, taking a seat next to him.

"Yeah," Gabe mumbled, looking away from the bear. Gabe didn't know how to deal with him. They all let Brenton handle things, but their Alpha was running a temper out. "The night crew talks shit about Troy and me.

"Why didn't you bring that up?" Riley said with a huff, giving him a look. Gabe winced, and Troy took over.

"We took it up with Andrew. He was going to take it to Keith but then today happened, and, well..." Troy shrugged. "It's fine, pretty girl. We were getting them back for it until Andrew told us to quit."

"Felines," Sheriff grunted.

They quieted down after that for nearly twenty minutes.

"Are they out of my fucking house?" Brenton asked immediately upon entering the kitchen.

"They are no longer allowed to patrol the house," Riley told him quickly. Gabe looked up to the ceiling, thanking God for Riley being able to handle this. Gabe wasn't a violent person, but even he and Troy had been riled up thanks to Brenton's anger. If Brenton had decided to go to town on the SSTF agents, the entire Pride was going to back him up on principle. Not that Gabe wouldn't have beaten someone down for talking about Riley that way, but it was different when the offenders were federal agents.

"I want them off my property," Brenton growled, leaning over the bar to Riley, who just kissed him.

"We need them right now," she whispered.

"Three fucking days, Sheriff," Zachary snarled. "In three days, that lot have proven themselves completely incompetent."

"Yes, I gave Keith a dressing down for the unprofessionalism of his team," Sheriff told them. Gabe snorted. A dressing down, as if Keith Stern were a child. Troy was giggling, hysterical from it. Gabe looked over to Riley, who nodded.

"So, how long are you staying over today, Sheriff?" Brenton directed the conversation over to the bear with a wave of his hand.

"I'm going to go home, pick up Mrs. Johnson and we're going to come help y'all out," Sheriff chuckled. Gabe saw Brenton give a small smile.

"You are going to sic your wife on us?" He asked, a little bemused.

"Yeah," Sheriff said with a nod. "Give you kids a bit of parental help and a buffer between you and them." Sheriff gave a nod towards somewhere, but Gabe knew his meaning. A buffer between the Pride and the SSTF. "I'm going to come over as often as possible to make sure y'all aren't out here killing each other."

"We might actually need that," Zachary groaned. "And it's a strong show of having a bear with a reputation of his own on our side."

"I'm trying not to turn this political but yes."

Gabe frowned. Again with the politics. Gabe didn't like the references to them, didn't like that he didn't understand what they were trying to say. He looked at Troy, who shrugged, also confused. A glance at Riley but she gave away nothing. She was missing something, just like Troy and him.

"Gabe?" Riley asked him softly as Andrew and Zachary started giving out plates of food to everyone.

"Yeah, gorgeous?"

"You have a meeting today, don't you?" She moved a seat over and was right next to him. He leaned down and kissed her, maybe a little longer than he should have by the grunt Sheriff gave.

"I do," he answered. "With Abigail."

"Want to hang out afterwards?" she whispered against his lips. He smiled and nodded.

"I'd love that," he purred back, adding a suggestive note that made Sheriff start clearing his throat. Sheriff might be okay with the relationship Riley had with them, but the old bear didn't want to see it.

"Maybe we should ask Troy, too." She smiled back at him.

"Troy." Gabe looked past her, all the way down the bar, to his brother.

"Yes," Troy chuckled. "Obviously."

"I'm trying to eat," Sheriff groaned. "Brenton."

"Oh, no," Brenton laughed. "You want to hang around our house, deal with it. By the way, how's your leg?"

"Could be better. Healing slower than normal in my old age," Sheriff chuckled. "It works, and there's no reason to worry about permanent damage. Not the first time I've been shot, and it seems like it won't be the last. Though, first time since my boys got out of my hair."

"Well," Brenton sighed. "Feel free to relax in our hot tub if you need to, and we will get you anything you need. You have been a big help to us."

"You're already paying the medical bills. I don't need much else. Hell, I didn't need you to do that."

Gabe chuckled. The Pride was already paying for the bear's medical bills. And Sheriff didn't need it. Gabe knew the bear had a couple million in off-shore accounts as a nest egg for rainy days and when he finally decided to actually retire from public service. It wasn't that Sheriff was rich but Gabe's personal investigation into the bear proved the old guy was smart with money. How long ago was that now? Gabe must have done that when he was a teenager, being nosy about the bear that ignored them for the most part.

"I wanted to," Brenton said gruffly, taking a seat with the plate Zachary gave him. He picked the other side of Riley and elbowed her softly. Which meant she bumped into Gabe and Gabe grunted. "I'm sorry I lost my temper. I should have let you handle it. I just made it a bigger headache."

"It's okay," Riley said, a smile still on her face. "I knew you were going to be upset, but I wanted to be the one to tell you and not one of them, like Keith."

"Thanks for calling Sheriff in," he murmured, leaning down to kiss her. "I needed someone bigger than me to get me to back off. I do not want to hurt your father, he just makes it difficult not to."

Riley laughed. "I'm already over it. A couple of guys said

some shitty stuff. We expected this when we decided to...be public. I just hadn't been expecting it in our home."

"Chris' nonsense had already irked me," Brenton sighed, "so I could throw him out without a concern." Brenton gave a disgusted look. "What exactly did they say?"

"I'm not telling you the specifics," Riley said. "Nope. Not happening."

"Good call, Kitten," Sheriff chuckled. "Do you all have any idea how long these guys will be here?"

"No," Brenton said with annoyance. "Well, I know what needs to happen for the SSTF to feel comfortable leaving. They want to verify any hunter threats against us are not serious. Just a lot of angry, empty yelling."

"Only hunter?" Sheriff groaned. "That's right, the SSTF took on a position of neutrality. They used to help more often, but they were being used against Prides and packs in political maneuvers. It made them biased. You can't help one Pride against another, and then need to protect the other Pride the next day."

"Yeah, now they hate us all equally," Gabe jeered. "Dicks."

"They hate the hunters too," Sheriff reprimanded him. Gabe curled a lip, but he couldn't say Sheriff was wrong. The SSTF was working fucking hard on getting the hunters as disbanded as possible. They couldn't do too much, since making a law would out shifters to the general public, but the entire situation was much bigger than it normally was. A Pride like them was normally very safe from hunters. Which brought up a question on Gabe's mind.

"Why didn't the wolves getting grabbed before us raise any alarms like we did?" he asked Sheriff.

"Wolves don't hold public profiles the way you cats do.

You should know that." Sheriff gave him a look saying he thought Gabe's question was a little stupid. Gabe shrugged.

"They were an Alpha and his inner circle though," Gabe reminded him.

"That's a good point," Riley added, raising an eyebrow at Sheriff. It was Zachary who cut in with an answer.

"Wolves are territory-based, not family-based," he grunted. "So, the territory would just choose a new Alpha and move on. The idea is that only a weak Alpha and inner circle would be captured. We cats base our entire Pride around the tone set by our Alpha, not by territory or the resources it provides. A new Alpha for us would be a complete game-changer."

"Weird," Riley mumbled. "Do any other species have units like packs and prides?"

"Not really?" Brenton remarked. "Finn and Huck were standard foxes. A small family unit, maybe not even the entire family. Or a close friend. Even then, most foxes go it alone. Sheriff, standard bear. Settle in one area for as long as possible, and other bears will avoid him. You guys hook up with humans more often than not, right?"

"Female bears are incredibly reclusive, and I can't blame them. I never really cared to look for one. My Patty is perfect for me. But yeah, most bears are half-breeds or have several humans in their genealogy."

Gabe looked back at Riley. She was eating all this up. Until this hunter situation, she'd never encountered other shifters, except Sheriff, who was still a bit human in her eyes.

"Hyenas make some sort of unit, but those guys are rare as hell," Zachary threw in. "Anyone else?"

"Preys, all of them," Troy threw out. "They will make small communities in urban areas, hidden in the humans, just so they have other shifter company. But good luck finding one of those."

"This is all so cool," Riley sighed happily. Gabe grinned at her.

"You think so?" He laughed. "You're a cheetah, that's pretty fucking cool."

"That's lost its mystique," Riley said with a grin.

"Well if that's the case." Gabe heaved an exaggerated sigh. "I can only imagine how long it will be before having five boyfriends might lose its mystique too. Guys." He looked around her. "We're going to lose her. One day, we'll be boring."

Everyone laughed as Riley pulled his face back to hers and kissed him. He grinned against her lips.

"I would never," she told him. "Never, ever."

"You say that now," Gabe teased, kissing her nose. "Love you."

"Love you, too," she chuckled. "How long until your meeting with Abigail?"

Gabe sighed and checked his watch. Damn, out of time.

"She'll be here any minute," he told her.

"Go on." She patted his arm. "We'll send her to the office."

"Thank you." He kissed her cheek as he stood up. "Troy, get that design done while I'm doing this?"

"Can do," Troy confirmed with a mouth full of food.

GABE KICKED out his legs once he was on the couch. He leaned back and closed his eyes. He liked talking to the doe, he did. He needed it. Troy's meeting with her was tomorrow.

They both agreed to see her at least once a week, just to chat.

When she stepped in, he opened his eyes and watched her move behind Brenton's desk.

"I can smell it's been an eventful morning," she started, giving him a look.

"We had some drama with the SSTF guys," Gabe groaned. "They decided to have opinions about our...Pride dynamics."

"Oh." Abigail stopped for a moment and shuffled papers around on Brenton's desk. She looked uncomfortable. "People are still breathing, I hope?"

"Yeah, we got it worked out," Gabe chuckled. "The bear."

"Of course. So...What do you want to start with today or would you like me to pick the topic?"

"You can pick the topic," Gabe sighed.

"Let's talk about the pills," she decided softly. "Have you been feeling the need for any, recently?"

"No." Gabe smiled at her. "I'm actually feeling pretty good."

10

RILEY

Three days with the SSTF turned into nearly two weeks, and Riley was finally beginning to feel almost normal again. With Sheriff around constantly, she and Keith gave each other a wide berth.

"Troy!" She laughed as he jumped onto her bed way too early in the morning. "What are you doing?"

"I want your help with designs today," he laughed pulling the blankets off her. She tried to grab them back, but Gabe was there to help his brother.

"Come on, gorgeous," Gabe chuckled as Troy purred, looking her over. She hadn't worn anything to bed, and she looked at the guy next to her.

Andrew was glaring at the leopard brothers, looking like he might soon start making recipes out of leopard. He wrapped an arm around her and pulled her into his side.

"Mine this morning, you fuckers," he growled, grabbing the blankets back.

"Oh, come on," Troy groaned. "You had her all of yesterday with Sheriff and Patty. Let us have some time with pretty girl!"

Riley just snickered, her face buried into Andrew's chest as they all growled at each other. It happened on occasion, these small territory battles.

"Since it's so early in the morning," she started, trying to keep a straight face. "Why don't we all just lay in bed for a little while longer?"

"Now that sounds lovely," Gabe purred, crawling over to her other side and nuzzling his head to her neck. Andrew sighed, defeated.

Troy crawled up Riley's body and she smiled at him as he kissed her stomach.

"Did you get...that thing handled?" he asked, his voice thick.

"Yeah," Riley chuckled. "I was a couple weeks behind schedule on getting my birth control shot, but they think everything should be fine. I'm safe. No babies."

"Thank fuck," Andrew groaned, pulling her chin towards him and kissing her. "Though, maybe I should have asked last night."

"There's no reason you needed to worry about that last night," Riley mumbled, thinking about it. "Plus, you'd all be wonderful fathers. I'm just not ready to be a mom."

"Let's shelve the kid conversation," Gabe growled, taking a gentle bite on her ear. "For a decade from now. Maybe two."

Riley gasped into Andrew's kiss as Troy took one of her nipples between his teeth and Gabe kissed down to her neck.

"So, I was thinking." Riley's door opened, and someone started to laugh. "Well...never mind." Her door closed but she heard them walk over.

Brenton and Zachary gave each other looks before meeting her eyes. Troy didn't bother acknowledging them, and Gabe only gave a small growl. Andrew cursed under his breath. Riley almost felt bad for him. He'd really wanted an easy-going morning with just her.

"We need to get her a bigger bed," Zachary chuckled, low and dangerous, as he pulled off his shirt. "Because I'm getting in on this, space be-damned."

"We really do," Brenton laughed. "Instead of just replacing the headboard, I will get a new, custom-made bed."

"Sounds lovely," Riley purred as Zachary pulled Troy off her, "and why do I have all of you in here this morning?"

It wasn't the first time it happened, but it was still a rare occurrence. All five of them trying to crawl in her bed was a recipe for disaster they tried to avoid. There was only one of her and five of them. Take Zachary moving Troy. The dominant males would demand they go first, and Troy and Gabe would need to wait. The problem was that Brenton and Zachary tended to exhaust her, so no one else would get a chance. It's not like she didn't have a choice in it, but she didn't want her bed to become a war zone for the pecking order.

Luckily, Zachary just laid his head on her lap instead of getting frisky. Troy fell on the other side of Gabe and accepted his fate of losing the space between her covered legs.

"Well, we came in to bother you and Andrew," Brenton teased, sitting down and then lying out at the end of her bed. Her bed seemed to groan under the weight of all of them. None of the guys were under two hundred pounds, and the bed frame just wasn't made for that amount of weight. "But we were beaten to the punch."

"Why do I not get a peaceful morning?" Andrew

groaned, sinking downward and placing his head into Riley's neck. "Why me?"

"Because we're hungry," Zachary grumbled, "and you always cook breakfast."

"Save me," Andrew mumbled.

"Other than accidental poisoning and you being a good chef, why do you always cook?" Riley chuckled, looking down at him. "There's got to be a reason because I'm pretty sure Brenton knows how to pour a bowl of cereal."

"That is a story," Brenton sighed. "Remember guys?" They all gave grunts of confirmation while Zachary rolled over to his stomach and began nuzzling her thigh.

"Tell me," Riley chuckled, looking around at them and running a hand through Zachary's hair. "Come on. This has got to be good." She didn't hear enough about the little things. She'd always wanted to, but before she told them she loved them, it had always felt too personal to ask. And they knew her life, on paper, at least, but didn't weasel in on her old stories either. Now, the l-word had been said, and it felt like their lives were blending together in more than just physical ways. She knew them, but now she wanted all of it. Every little story, every laugh, every memory.

"I'll tell her," Andrew whispered. "You guys meet us downstairs."

Riley frowned at the sudden serious tone from him.

"I will stay," Brenton told him, as the other guys got off the bed.

"Thanks, my brother," Andrew chuckled darkly.

What kind of story was she getting?

11

ANDREW

Age 15

"Hey, everyone, sit down for dinner," Andrew sighed, looking between the other guys rough-housing around the dining room table.

"Yo," Zachary growled, "you aren't our fucking father, man."

"Fine." Andrew threw his hands up. "Let the food get cold in the kitchen. I'm not bringing it out while you all might knock me over."

"Sorry, Andrew," Brenton laughed at him. "We will calm down. You can let Jameson know we're ready."

"Man, did you see that play?" Troy laughed. "I wish we could join some of the local teams."

"You know we cannot," Brenton groaned. Andrew began walking off as Brenton reminded them again that they needed to stay under the radar. They weren't adults, and the people in their lives were shit enough.

Except Jameson. He was their only ally on the estate now. He and Andrew covered everything the old staff used to and kept the new adults on the property away from the guys.

Andrew walked into the kitchen and grinned.

"Jameson, is everything done?" Andrew walked over to the young-looking cougar. He was nearly fifty, but no human would have guessed that. Andrew elbowed Jameson once he was there, startling him.

"Ah! Andrew!" Jameson coughed, mustering up a smile. Andrew frowned.

"You okay?" Andrew asked quietly. "Something going on?"

"No, no," Jameson chuckled uncomfortably. "You can take all this out. I think I'm going to go lay down, though. A bit tired tonight."

"Sure, thank you for cooking tonight without me," Andrew said, but he couldn't hide his concern for Jameson. For ten years, Jameson had been his only family. The guys were cool but wild. Jameson was basically his father.

"It's nothing my boy," Jameson said gently. "You need to stay close with your Pride. That's more important than helping me out all the time."

"Thank you," Andrew whispered again as Jameson walked out. His Pride. They were just a bunch of teenagers. He and Zachary had nothing to their names. Brenton was locked down by education requirements, something he was powering through. Troy and Gabe had to be eighteen before they had their own resources. Not much of a Pride...

Andrew began picking up a few dishes and walking them to the dining room.

"Hey, can I get a hand?" Andrew asked as the guys chatted about the football game they had just gone to see. "Jameson needed the rest of the night off."

"Yeah," Troy said with a grin, jumping up. "Come on, Gabe."

The brothers followed him back and helped grab the rest of the plates. They had a rule about eating before everyone was served, so Andrew wasn't worried about leaving the voracious monsters, Brenton and Zachary, alone with the rest of it. They were all pretty close to being black holes, but those two were going to be huge. Already, Zachary was taller than Andrew, and Brenton was the same height.

"Alright," Andrew began but he looked down at the potatoes. They were not the right color to him. He wondered if the lighting was making them seem weird. "Wait."

"Why?" Brenton asked with a frown.

Andrew just held a hand up, even though that would piss Brenton off. He pulled the bowl of mashed potatoes closer and took a sniff.

They didn't smell right.

"Give me a few minutes," Andrew mumbled. "Don't fucking eat anything."

"Andrew?" Zachary growled. "What's wrong?"

"I need to make sure," Andrew whispered and rushed out of the room.

The moment he was out of sight, his heart began to race. No. He just had to make sure. Andrew picked up his pace and took off at a run. He shoved out of the main house, ignoring some bitch calling him rude. Probably one of the brothers' babysitters.

He ran all the way to Jameson's door. It was locked, but Andrew ignored that, forcing it open and breaking the handle.

"Jameson," he said, panting. "New recipe?"

"Yeah," Jameson whispered, a suitcase in front of him. "I'll teach it to you one day."

"Why?" Andrew asked, desperate.

"I killed his father," Jameson chuckled, not turning back to him. "Thinking it would mean that I finally got to be with the woman I love. But she asked me to stay here, stay with all of you. I love you, Andrew, I do, but you aren't her."

"Holy shit," Andrew gasped. "You..."

"We're felines, Andrew," Jameson said with a bitter laugh, finally looking at him. "You and me? We might be the help, but we're just as deep in it as anyone else. We aren't Geoffrey, who gives the dirty orders, we're the men who make them happen. And this is the last thing I need to do so I can finally be with her."

"Jameson..." Andrew stepped closer, but Jameson growled at him.

"Did you tell them?" Jameson snarled.

"I told them not to eat," Andrew said in a whisper. "And I'm not going to let them."

"Damn it." Jameson sounded...disappointed? Andrew couldn't place it. "You can come with me, Andrew. We can be a part of a bigger pride, a better one than the shit show the Kingson's have always been. Brenton is going to grow up to be his father, even if you can't see it. One day, you'll find yourself back in this building, wondering what happened. Go back, tell them you aren't hungry, and pack a bag while they eat."

"No," Andrew snarled. "I'm not doing that to them."

"Andrew-"

"Anything!" Andrew roared. "You taught me that."

"I can't leave to be with her until Brenton is dead, boy," Jameson growled. "Don't stand in my way."

"Who is she?" Andrew growled. "Who is more important than our Alpha?"

"Our Alpha? No, Andrew, *your* Alpha," Jameson sneered. "Geoffrey is the last Kingson I will ever serve. I was just waiting for the right time. And I'm not letting you stop me from ending that despicable family."

Andrew didn't have the size or reaction time to stop Jameson from jumping him. He was still shell-shocked by Jameson's betrayal. Jameson raised him. How could he do this?

Hands locked on Andrew's throat, and he couldn't breathe. Black spots started dancing in his eyes as Jameson's face became blurry.

No. He'd do anything for Brenton. Including this.

As he was running out of oxygen, Andrew threw punches towards Jameson's face. He was lucky enough to connect one with the cougar's nose, making him fall away, blood going everywhere. Andrew took a moment to breathe and began to scramble away as Jameson tried to grab him again. He needed a weapon. He couldn't die. He was the only thing between the guys and the grave.

Andrew dragged himself up as Jameson did the same, cursing and looking at the blood covering him.

"You fucking prick," Jameson growled. "They will never respect you. You will also be second-class to them. I thought it might be different, since you grew up with Brenton, but he lets you do his housework. He doesn't respect you."

Andrew growled but didn't respond. That was his biggest fear, his deepest insecurity. But he wouldn't let his own fear ruin the honor he had. Jameson was between him and the door. He was only getting out if Jameson was dead.

He looked around the room, desperate. A glass lamp. How fucking cliché.

He dove for it as Jameson went for him. He was able to grab it as Jameson collided into him. He closed his eyes as he slammed the lamp into Jameson's head. Jameson roared and backed away. Andrew still held a jagged and sharp section, and he shoved it into Jameson's gut, making the cougar grunt.

"He'll never care about you, you stupid boy," Jameson coughed, falling back. Andrew didn't say anything as he shoved Jameson and winced when he heard the cougar's head crack against the dresser.

Andrew didn't move for a long time. He needed to get back to the guys. They had to know something was wrong, now.

He closed Jameson's door and slowly walked back to the house, covered in blood. It was all over his hands, all over his clothes. He ignored a gasp as he walked through the mansion and back into the dining room, where all the guys were exactly where he left him.

"Did any of you eat any of this?" he asked softly, devoid of emotion.

"No," Brenton whispered, standing up slowly. "Andrew?"

"I'm cooking from now on. No one else. *Ever*," Andrew growled softly. "And I need help with something."

"What, my brother?" Brenton walked over to him slowly, and the others began to stand up.

"We need to bury a body," he whispered, finally cracking. He began to cry as Brenton wrapped his arms around him. Andrew fell to his knees, and Brenton went to the floor with him.

"Why?" Brenton asked, sounding terrified.

"Jameson," he sobbed. "Jameson poisoned the food."

"Andrew," Brenton choked out. It sounded like he would cry too. "Oh, fuck."

"We'll handle it," Zachary growled, kneeling next to them. "Me and the boys."

"Thank you," Brenton whispered, and Andrew just clung to him.

They had no allies. None at all.

12

RILEY

R iley was with Troy and Gabe, still thinking about Andrew's story hours later. Good Lord, Andrew killed someone at fifteen. Only fifteen. His near father, at that.

"You've been quiet all morning, gorgeous," Gabe whispered to her, leaning over her shoulder as she sat at Troy's computer, mocking up a design for a gas tank.

"Where did you bury him?" she asked softly. Was it near Cameron?

"Jameson?" Gabe sounded confused. "Shit, um, near the field." He sounded a little disturbed by her question.

"How many are out there?" She continued to question him.

"We put three out there," Gabe whispered in her ear, keeping his voice down, "including Cameron. How many are actually out there? We have no idea."

"How can you not?" she sputtered, turning around to look at him.

"Because every Kingson Alpha has buried bodies out

there," Gabe told her, his voice firm, "and we aren't about to go digging them all up."

"How is this okay?" she hissed. "How is any of this okay?"

"It's not," he growled. "None of it is. Jameson tried to poison five teenage boys who trusted him. He tried to kill the one he raised to finish what he intended. Cameron tried to shoot you in our kitchen. The last one is a young female who tried to stab Brenton in his fucking sleep after they fucked. Riley, none of it's okay, but it's what we are."

"I...I." She swallowed, trying to find the words to describe how this all made her feel.

"Abel fucked with you, and you burned his house down and sent him running for his life and freedom," Troy said from where he was hand-painting a tank. "It's second nature to us to be power-hungry and conniving. To live by the belief of survival of the fittest."

"How did I not notice this?" she whispered to herself, looking away from Gabe.

"Because we never wanted you to," he mumbled. "We were really happy after everything with Cameron, and...it just never came up."

"Of course," she murmured, standing up. She felt uncomfortable. She wasn't a killer like this. She didn't bury bodies in the woods and move on.

Except she was, and she did. She had to swallow that hard truth. Her father was right. Dangerous and out-of-control. She had killed hunters to defend herself and let Sheriff bury them on his property. She'd shot more in this very house. She'd stabbed Cameron in the kitchen.

She'd gunned down hunters in the compound without a second thought.

She'd burned Abel's house down and terrified him...and she had liked it.

"I can't believe..." She crossed her arms and frowned. Did she really regret any of it?

"Gorgeous," Gabe whimpered to her, "gorgeous, we never wanted any of this for you."

"Do you regret any of it?" she asked, meeting his glowing green eyes.

"No," he whispered. "Not any of it. Do you?"

"No," Riley sighed, "and I think that's what's bothering me the most."

"You can always tell us that you want out," Troy told her, full of sadness. "You can do that."

"And then I wouldn't have any of you." She shook her head. "Why don't I regret it?"

"Because we aren't murderers," Gabe said with a rueful smile. "We retaliate, and we do so without reservation. We crush our enemies without a blink, but we don't go out and start fights. You aren't a bad person, Riley. You've just stayed alive, and, sometimes, survival means bodies need to be buried in places no one will ever find them. Sometimes, people will never stop until you're dead, so you need to kill them first."

"You sound experienced in this," she huffed.

"We are," Troy growled softly. She looked over at him and realized he needed a haircut. *Such a mundane thing to notice*, she thought. His gray and silver hair was getting too long. He flicked her a glance, and she saw pain in those mercury eyes.

"I love you," she whispered. "I'm sorry. I don't know why...I don't know why Andrew's story got to me so much."

"We were kids," Gabe sighed, "and Jameson was...our only adult friend."

"Who was the woman he loved?" Riley asked with a frown.

"Brenton's aunt, Geoffrey's younger sister...Abel's mother," Gabe told her, going back to his tinkering. "He never could have had her. Geoffrey basically married her off for political reasons, even though she and Jameson had grown up together and were definitely in love. They both grew bitter over the years apart, and she finally decided to take the Kingson fortune from her brother as revenge. Geoffrey was already dead, and we've never figured out who got Jameson to do that, but we know that it left Brenton as the only person between her and billions."

"No shit," she hissed, shocked and a bit disgusted by that. "Why have y'all never gone after her?"

"It wouldn't do us any good, really," Gabe said with a bit of anger. Not at Riley though, she knew that. "We've considered it, a thousand times, but by the time we knew it was her, she hadn't been a threat in years. It would be an act of war over old insults, and we don't play that game. We don't hold the long game. We win, and we move on. We won with her. She failed in killing us, in her attempt to take the Kingson fortune, and now, killing Brenton wouldn't do her any good."

"Is that all this is for shifters? A game?" Riley asked, wrapping an arm around Gabe's waist and leaning on his back.

"To all of them? Yes," he whispered. "To us? It was survival, pure and simple. If we didn't go fast and go hard, without mercy, they would have never stopped trying to kill us. We wouldn't have lasted more than a few years on our own."

"I'm sorry," she whispered. "I'm in. I want you to know that. Anything the Pride needs, and I'm in."

"I never had any doubts," Gabe chuckled, grabbing her hand and pulling it up to his lips. "If Cameron and hunters didn't chase you off, I'm not sure anything will."

"You're right," she told him with a bit of levity. She was disheartened but not scared. She was sad because her men had such sad lives. She was angry at the injustice the feline world was ruled by.

But she would never leave them. She would never regret her actions. This was her family, and she was standing by for when she needed to walk in the fire with them.

"They used to call us wild animals, renegades, and fools," Troy laughed. "We broke the rules, those unspoken do's and don'ts of our world. We proved them right, every time. We were renegades. We were wild, and not just in the way people think they see Gabe and me."

"Damn right," Gabe growled with a grin, turning back to Riley. "We're dangerous men, gorgeous."

"Am I your dangerous woman?" She smiled at him.

"Yes." He leaned down as he spoke. "You definitely are," he growled against her lips. He kissed her deeply, and she moaned into his mouth as his hands moved to squeeze her ass and pull her harder against him. When the kiss broke off, Gabe was grinning. Troy was behind her, his hands wrapping around her front.

"You'll have to tell me more about how much of a renegade you were," Riley murmured against Gabe's lips, "later."

Work with us today, they had said. Work. Riley could laugh. They were never able to work for longer than a couple of hours.

"We can do that," Troy growled as his hands roamed up her stomach and then her ribs. He cupped her breasts, and even through her bra, her nipples got hard at the idea of his hands there.

"I shouldn't get hot at the idea of you being dangerous," she purred.

"You're a shifter, pretty girl," Troy chuckled.

"Yeah," Gabe continued, wearing his Cheshire Cat grin, "your cheetah knows that we're males who can handle her. Just like our leopards need a woman who can handle us. You've got to be wild to do that."

Gabe kissed her again as Troy nibbled on a sensitive spot where her neck and shoulder met. She could feel and smell they were both as excited as she was. She moaned as Troy dropped a hand and started sliding it into her pants.

"Excuse me," a rough voice interrupted them. It sounded uncomfortable and unsure. Riley looked over as Gabe turned around. Troy quickly removed his hand. It was Liam, one of their protection detail—one of the bears.

"Can we help you?" Gabe asked, polite and professional. The guards had been well-behaved, so the Pride would be.

"We were told to ask everyone to meet in Alpha Kingson's office," Liam said gruffly, before turning around and walking out.

Riley looked between the guys and shrugged.

"Let's go," she muttered with a hint of worry. She didn't like the sound of that.

SHE AND THE leopard brothers walked into the office, leaving Liam to do whatever he was supposed to be doing. She frowned at the crowd crammed into the room already. Brenton stood behind his desk with Zachary next to him on the right and Andrew on the left. Sheriff was sitting on one end of the couch. Her dad and Special Agent Corban were standing to the side, both holding several pieces of paper.

"Well," she mumbled, "I can imagine this is important."

"There's been some changes to the situation," Brenton told her and the guys as she walked over to him. She wrapped an arm around his waist as the brothers dropped onto the couch with Sheriff.

"We don't feel like we're needed here anymore," Keith began, holding up a file. "We've established that threats from those associated with the hunters appear to be empty, a nonissue. From there, any legitimate threats against you are from other feline shifters."

"Oh great," Riley snorted. "So, how long are you staying?"

"We aren't," Keith told her, meeting her eyes for the first time in over a week.

"We don't offer protection services in Pride to Pride situations," Corban cut in, giving Keith a look. "We'll give you whatever information we have, and we'll continue to monitor for hunter threats. But...situations you have with other shifters are your problem. We can't become biased between different factions."

"So much for upholding the law," she muttered, a bit angry.

"It's their policy," Brenton sighed down to her. "It's been like this for a long time."

"That's right," Keith confirmed, nodding. "So, we're going to spend a day packing up, and we should be out of here by dinner tomorrow."

"Really?" Troy sounded excited, but Sheriff grumbled.

"About fucking time you all made some headway on anything," he growled. "Back in my day, it only would have taken a week, and we didn't have the tech you do now."

"I'm sorry." Corban looked down at Sheriff. "We have a lot going on, and we've been working with both Mexico's and Canada's governments on finally busting up much of the systematic hunter situation."

"Give me the notes," Gabe said, holding out his hand. Once Keith handed them over, Gabe looked to Brenton, "I'll start running these after this little meeting."

"Of course. Thank you, Gabe," Brenton said with a smile. "But I don't see any reason for you to over-work yourself, so you can keep Riley for the day...or the next several, just in case."

Riley snickered as Gabe grinned her way. With a wiggle of his eyebrows, she stuck her tongue out at him, making all her men growl a little.

"Please, do not," Brenton groaned. "Please, not with other people here."

Normally, she would have stuck her tongue out at him for that, but while she was willing to test Sheriff's patience, she wasn't comfortable with Keith there. Keith, who disagreed with her relationship. Keith, the father who didn't even begin to understand the woman she'd become.

She had to reconcile that. If he was leaving tomorrow, she needed to talk to him. She didn't want to, but it felt somewhat necessary. She had no idea when, or if, she would ever see him again, and that felt...scarier than she thought it would.

He was her father, and he was looking completely okay with walking out of her life again.

"Is that everything?" Zachary growled.

"It is," Corban sighed. "I'm sorry we can't be more helpful to you. We have to follow the rules on this."

"Of course," Brenton said mildly. "Give me a few minutes with my pride, please."

With nods, Special Agent Corban and her father left the room. They all sat in silence until Sheriff grumbled incoherently, stood up and left as well.

"That bear," Andrew chuckled. "So, what now?"

"We get back to our lives," Troy laughed. "Fucking finally."

"Not so fast," Zachary cut Troy's excitement off at the pass. "Security is still a top priority. We don't know who sold us out to the hunters, since Abel didn't know. Anything in the notes about that?"

"Yeah, a bank account number," Gabe mumbled, flipping through pages. "I'll see where it leads us. They didn't go much further, since it ruined their neutrality in pride affairs."

"We need to get that mother fucker," Zachary growled at Brenton. "We can't let it slide."

"I agree," Brenton growled back. Riley didn't want to be in the middle of them when they started growling at each other, so she slipped past Brenton and cuddled into Andrew. "But we also need to live our lives. We can't get wrapped up in some crazy revenge quest. No offense, Riley." He looked over to her as he said it, and she shrugged.

"None taken," she chuckled. Andrew rubbed her back, purring in her arms.

"Fine, but once we get a name, we go after that furball and end it," Zachary pressed Brenton.

"I know," Brenton said mildly. "Zachary, when are you going to learn that I very rarely disagree with you?"

"I..." Zachary trailed off and concentrated for a moment. "Good point."

"I know," Brenton said disdainfully with a roll of his eyes. "Sometimes, Zachary, sometimes I worry about you."

"Fuck you," Zachary snarled. Riley watched them and

saw their eyes meet. Then both were laughing like teenage girls with a secret.

"Weirdos," she mumbled.

"Aren't they?" Andrew chuckled. "Everyone gets on the Walkers, but they don't see Brenton and Zachary like this."

"Right?" Riley laughed.

"You two talking smack?" Zachary growled their way, and she shook her head.

"Not smack when it's true," she told him with a smug smile.

"I'll remember that," Brenton told her with a heated look. "Now, all of you get back to what you were doing. Time for us to move on from all of this."

"Thank goodness," Gabe groaned. "Well, not really. I still have some work."

"Later," Riley whispered as she walked out. She slapped his ass and got him to give her a look similar to the one Brenton had just given her.

"Naughty cheetah," he murmured seductively in her ear. "Do it again."

"Later," she whispered even lower. A crook of her finger had both the brothers following her back to the garage, where she intended to finish what they had started.

"That's impressive," she heard Andrew laugh.

"Right? They never fall in line like that for me," Brenton said with some humorous disbelief. "I might be a little jealous."

"I'm just happy they listen to someone," Zachary grunted, louder than the others.

13

ZACHARY

"There's only a few problems we need to discuss," Brenton whispered, closing the door. Zachary fell onto the couch and sighed.

"Yeah," he mumbled, "I've heard the chatter."

"I think everyone has," Andrew sighed. "Though, those three don't realize what a big deal it is."

"Other Prides view us as politically weak right now," Brenton said without preamble. "Using SSTF protection against hunters, having a bear as a public ally. Then there is letting wolves stay in our home, in our town."

"Do we count Thomas and them as allies?" Andrew asked, leaning on Brenton's desk.

"Not officially," Zachary answered, giving a shrug. "But I think we would be fools not to consider them friends. They know we did them a huge favor by letting them stay here until they figured out where to go and what to do."

"They can stay here permanently for all I care," Brenton said with without a care. "Thomas is a strong Alpha. James is intelligent, good with numbers, and a likable guy. Antonio is a hard worker and easy to talk to. They aren't trouble-makers. If they were, they would already be gone."

"I'm visiting them tonight for a couple of beers," Zachary reminded Brenton. "You can come."

"No," Brenton laughed. "Take Riley, she likes them."

"She and Thomas have some connection," Andrew chuckled. "You notice that?"

"They did the impossible together," Brenton sighed. "Coming back for us? I'm not going to question that friendship, even if he's another Alpha and that..."

"Little jealous, brother?" Zachary teased. "Won't happen. Riley wouldn't. Plus, he's a wolf."

"I know, which is why I am not questioning it. It is why I don't tell her she needs to stay away from them, and it is why I don't go hang out with them. I do not think being there, watching them be friends, is good for me, so I don't. One of you can, one of you not threatened by another Alpha."

"Thomas is an easy-going guy. He doesn't flex the Alpha in him enough, in my opinion," Zachary laughed.

"So, what's our play?" Andrew shifted them back to the correct topic. "We have allies, none are feline. We burned all our bridges years ago on that front. A bear who has a human wife, and he's law enforcement. He's really only in this for Riley, as it stands. Finn is our employee, not an ally. He's also just a fox."

"Foxes are cunning when they get the bug for it," Brenton said, pointing at Andrew, who just shrugged.

"Do you see Finn being helpful for the next year? Hell, the next decade?" Andrew groaned.

"No," Zachary muttered. A fox was a great asset, but Finn was fucking useless. Zachary dealt with him on upgrading their vehicles. He was happy when it was over because that fox could bring anyone down from the best of moods. Not that Zachary could blame him. If Zachary had lost any of the guys or Riley in that hellhole, he'd be a fucking mess.

The Pride had gotten lucky. So had the wolves. Only the twin, Huck, didn't make it, and that left Finn young and alone, with only some new friends to keep him walking in the world of the living. And none of them were particularly close with Finn because he was, by nature, elusive and reclusive.

"Thomas, James, and Antonio," Andrew continued, leaving Finn to be a thought for another time. "We need a show of force. Something that says we don't think this is a big deal. It might not work, but it'll be a start."

"We need to get back into Denver," Brenton added. "Also, I hate when you are in politics-mode."

"You hate when I'm in any mode except calm," Andrew laughed. "Come on. We can start really getting back into Kingson Inc. We'll hit every meeting. I'll hire humans to work on the diner, fuck shifters. They are all gone now, and I need contractors ASAP if I want to stay on schedule."

"I hate it when Andrew gets like this, too," Zachary groaned. "We bought him the diner to keep him occupied."

"You bought me the diner because we were coming back home so none of us would have to deal with this anymore. This was my role before we came back," Andrew chuckled. "We didn't want me to wander the house with nothing to do."

"House-husband mode," Brenton said with an exaggerated raise of his eyebrows. "We didn't want him permanently in house-husband mode."

"The fact that the boy once called the help is our political strategist honestly terrifies me sometimes,"

Zachary mumbled, giving Brenton a pleading look. "Please stop him."

"He is good at it, and he is right," Brenton said without meeting Zachary's eyes. He went and sat down. "So, we start moving back out into the world. Go back to our schedule while Gabe slowly picks apart what we got from the SSTF. You hire human contractors, a middle-finger to the shifter community. We keep our friends, and we keep this shit out of Wild Junction."

"That's right," Andrew said with a nod. "It might not stop more aggressive action from any enemies we have, but it's a show of force."

Zachary remembered why Andrew in this mode bothered him. Andrew was a dangerous man when he started thinking. He was calm, peaceful, and the kindest man someone could have the pleasure knowing. Until someone threatened him.

Until someone threatened Brenton. Brenton and Zachary were ruthless in their physical strength, but it was Andrew's idea to blackmail Cameron to hell and back. It was Andrew's idea for them to be the rule breakers and make names for themselves before they could get squashed under larger prides.

They needed to get Andrew back in his fucking diner, or the man was going to start master-minding a rise to power for Brenton that no one could stop. With Gabe's intelligence, Troy's jack-of-all-trades ability to get shit done, and now Riley's own cunning aggression, Zachary could see the wheels turning behind Andrew's eyes. Their Pride could be unstoppable, if they let Andrew off his leash. And Zachary felt like Andrew was itching for it. For over a year, he'd held back, kept his head down.

But there was a reason Andrew was Brenton's second

until they were in their early-twenties.

"Andrew," Zachary growled. "Please. You've done really well for the last couple of years. Don't slip back into it all."

"Slip back into what?" Andrew scoffed. "My job? Maybe if I had been doing it better, none of this would have happened. I would have been able to head shit off, like the hunters, before they became a real threat to us."

"None of us could have known about the hunters, Andrew," Brenton said quietly. "And Riley hates when we start playing the blame game with ourselves."

"Yeah," Andrew sighed. "Yeah. That was out of left field."

"It was," Brenton said with finality. "Zachary, talk to the wolves. See if they would mind going public as our allies."

"I can do that." Zachary nodded. "Meetings later this week in Denver?"

"I'll get them all scheduled. We'll all go, full Pride," Brenton said, looking through the large calendar on his desk. "Take Riley with you...and pick up Abigail. Those two have been hanging out a lot, and I think the doe might need something I have heard called a life."

"You mean a love life, don't you?" Zachary chuckled. Andrew was holding back a smile.

"I do." Brenton grinned. "She only spends time with Riley. For a mental health professional, that's not very healthy."

"I DO NOT KNOW why I am coming with you both," Abigail sighed as they turned down the dirt road to the farm house the wolves had claimed.

Zachary drove in silence as the women gossiped. He enjoyed seeing Riley have a friend again. She'd drifted from the humans in her life, and the Pride had never intended to sequester her away from the rest of the world.

"You need to get out!" Riley laughed, sitting in the back with the doe. "You can't just keep dragging me to the girly things and not seeing anyone else."

"But the wolves?" Abigail said with disdain.

"What's wrong with Thomas and the boys?" Zachary asked, curious from the driver's seat. The farm house came into view, and Zachary grinned. Time to drink some beers and kick up his feet.

And deal with some politics, but that would be easy.

"They're wolves," Abigail sighed.

"We're all predators," Zachary reminded her as they pulled into the driveway. Riley made an agreeable noise.

"They're wolves," Abigail pressed. "And I'm a doe."

"I'm missing something," Riley said, sounding confused.

"So am I," Zachary chuckled.

"It's nothing. Thomas and his little pack aren't a problem," Abigail said, trying to dismiss the topic.

"Do you not feel safe?" Riley asked, and Zachary could smell her concern. But what interested him wasn't that, rather it was Abigail's nervousness. There wasn't any fear in it at all. It was the same type of nervous Riley felt with...the Pride.

He needed to tell Thomas about that...and Brenton, since Brenton was a nosy son-of-a-bitch when it came to people in Wild Junction. It had gotten them Riley.

"Oh, I feel safe," Abigail muttered, and Riley began to laugh harder than before.

"Safe, she says," Zachary chuckled. She was probably hoping for that big bad wolf fantasy. Zachary was definitely telling the guys this one.

"Very funny," Abigail groaned.

"Okay," Riley snickered.

"We're here," Zachary snorted, "Let's go bother some wolves. Riley, I've got some shit to talk to Thomas about, so he and I are going to disappear for a moment."

"Yup," Riley said and hopped out of his Range Rover before he turned it off. Abigail sighed.

"So, what's really going on, Abigail?" Zachary asked, looking into the backseat.

"Nothing," she mumbled, getting out and leaving him alone in the vehicle.

Women were odd, he thought to himself. Just strange. At least Riley had been open and honest about everything in the beginning.

He got out and saw the wolves walking out. He grinned as Thomas gave Riley a hug, only to get smacked.

"You haven't visited the estate like you promised!" She growled as Zachary and Abigail got closer.

"I've been really busy," Thomas laughed. "I'm sorry, little cheetah. Next time, I'll be sure to come annoy you at your order."

"Good," she huffed and then turned to give the others a smile. "Where are my hugs, guys?"

"Ah, yes, our little savior wants hugs," James chuckled, wrapping his arms around her. Antonio went next.

Zachary shook Thomas' hand with a smile.

"Got enough beer?" Zachary asked as he watched the wolf Alpha look toward Abigail hanging out behind Riley.

"I should," he mumbled absentmindedly.

Well, wasn't this interesting? Yeah, he was going to be gossiping to Brenton like a teenage girl the moment they made it home.

"Let's get inside," Antonio said with a rumbled laugh. "Come on, we've got barbecue going."

"Yes!" Riley laughed, and Zachary watched her go inside behind Antonio and James, holding Thomas with him. Abigail took one look at them and decided to follow her friend inside as well, without a word to Thomas. Rude.

"What's going on?" Zachary asked Thomas quietly. It snapped Thomas out of watching Abigail walk away.

"About?" Thomas frowned at him.

"Any of it," Zachary said with a shrug. "Finances, future, politics, your brother...or maybe you can tell me why you're watching that doe like you want to eat her."

"The new Alpha in South Dakota agreed to give us something to use to restart, compensation for our previous positions in the Pack," Thomas sighed. "In return, I had to agree to never go after her, either by myself or helping Chris. She gave me the money and told me to stay here in Wild Junction, far from her. She doesn't want a fight, and we're not allowed back in the state."

"Have you touched base with the Colorado Pack?" It wasn't really Zachary's business, but he also knew that the Colorado Pack could run Thomas out of Wild Junction if they wanted to. And he wanted the wolves to stay.

"I was told that as long as I was here," Thomas said with a wave around the property, "that I would be fine. But I can't try to expand. I'm okay with that. I never wanted any of this, so I'm just looking to give me and the boys a place to relax and live out our lives."

"That's good," Zachary sighed. "I wish we could help more-"

"It's no big deal," Thomas laughed. "You and the Pride have helped enough. Speaking of, what does Brenton need?"

Zachary admired the fact that Thomas knew exactly why this wasn't a social call.

"He wants to know if we have you as an ally, publicly, in

case things get hot."

They were both silent for a moment. Thomas was weighing his options, and Zachary knew what that meant. The Kingson Pride tended to have trouble. Lots of it. If Thomas said yes, he not only got a huge boon from being associated with the Pride, but he also got the side-eyes and the Pride's enemies.

It was a dangerous place for him to be. Sheriff was almost a protected citizen in the shifter world due to his job and just being a bear. He would never leave Wild Junction and hunt down their enemies. Purely defense and a strong deterrent. Thomas would be seen as an active threat to the Pride's enemies.

"Yeah," Thomas whispered. "It's not really a question. I'm never going to leave you out in the cold, for the sheer fact that your girl didn't leave me out in the cold. If you guys need anything, call me. I'm not sure what me and the boys can really do, but you just ask, and we'll make it happen."

"Thank you." Zachary inclined his head in respect for the Alpha. "So, the doe. Abigail."

"Oh, man," Thomas laughed. "She wouldn't appreciate me telling you."

"So, something *has* happened!" Zachary roared in laughter. "Please, my man."

"You know, does are quite fast in their shifted form," Thomas chuckled, looking a bit sly.

"No shit," Zachary said with a roll of his eyes.

"We were out on a run, and she must have wandered onto our property. We hadn't marked the scent boundary yet. She freaked out. We chased."

"I can imagine," Zachary chuckled. "Let's get in before James and Antonio try to eat her. Riley wouldn't appreciate it. They're friends now."

"God have mercy on us," Thomas continued to chuckle. "And Zachary, if those two were planning on eating Abigail, she wouldn't be telling them no."

"Pervert," Zachary snorted.

"Says the big white tiger with a girlfriend and four brother-boyfriends," Thomas laughed, dodging Zachary's shove. "Seriously! You know, I expect a relationship like yours from a wolf pack, but felines? You guys are possessive as hell, and you somehow all share a gorgeous girl like Riley. It astounds me."

"Yeah," Zachary huffed. "We make it work, and it's been the best thing to ever happen to us."

"Oh, wait a minute," Thomas said, seeming to remember something. They both stopped walking toward the door and Zachary frowned. "I've been hearing the chatter."

"So have we," Zachary growled, "and let me tell you, right here, right now, the Kingson Pride is not, nor will it ever be, weak."

"Perception is important, Zachary," Thomas sighed. "Brenton knows that."

"Everyone in the Pride knows it, and we're working on it. The SSTF leaves tomorrow. They've decided the hunters aren't a threat anymore."

"The SSTF leaves tomorrow?" Thomas said, a bit shocked. "Really?"

"Yeah? Why?" Zachary frowned at him.

"I've been avoiding the estate because they were there," Thomas mumbled. "I didn't want Riley to know her dad and I have history..."

"No fucking way," Zachary growled. "No."

"He tried to recruit me to the SSTF. He and a few members of his team showed up at my house. I didn't put it together until the plane, hearing about him a bit more, and I damn sure didn't think he was going to show up here," Thomas sighed. "I would have warned her, but now I just feel like an ass."

"I can tell her for you," Zachary offered. "When were you supposed to tell her? The plane? After what we'd all just been through? The very few days between getting here and her burning a fucking house down? She had some other shit she needed to work through without him being on her mind. And how were you supposed to know that he would oversee our protection detail? She won't be mad. I think. I hope. I want your house to remain standing, so let's just not tell her right now. I'll tell her later."

"Oh, it's fine," Thomas chuckled. "We'll tell her tonight and that way, if she tries to burn down my house, we have Abigail on standby to talk her down."

"We're never going to let go of the fact that," Zachary snorted with a smirk, "she burned down that mother fucker's house."

"She did," Thomas said, covering his mouth to hold back the grin. "She is terrifying, you know that, right?"

"Yeah but joking about it makes it feel like she didn't go completely off the rails on us," Zachary told him. It was the truth. The Pride had wondered if she would ever really hit that point of no return in their world. They had avoided it, given themselves a life where it wasn't necessary.

"You guys used to be like that." Thomas was whispering, as if he were trying to keep it a secret. "I might be a wolf, but everyone knew that this new generation of the Kingson Pride wasn't afraid to break the rules and get dirty. People used to be scared of you. You used to be terrifying."

"Used to be," Zachary whispered as well. "A long time ago, it feels like."

"A couple of years isn't a long time in our world,"

Thomas said, looking off into the distance. "You might have to be terrifying again. The world thinks you've been brought to your knees by the hunters. By getting this female who went out and handled a problem for you."

"I know," Zachary growled. "Brenton, Andrew, and I have been talking about it."

"Good, and I take it you have a strategy." Thomas didn't phrase it as a question.

"We do," Zachary murmured, a bit dangerously, "and we need you as an ally."

"You got me, like I said. We need allies too, so it better be reciprocated." Thomas smiled when Zachary just nodded. They wouldn't leave the wolves out in the cold if they helped the Pride when the Pride called. This partnership had to be equal. "Let's get inside. I'll talk to Riley, and let's keep our fingers crossed I still have a house after it."

"Let's." Zachary gave a dark chuckle.

"What kind of trouble have you seen already?" Thomas asked as they made their way to the front door.

"Small shit," Zachary growled. "Shifters are cutting out of business contracts with us. Like the diner? We've lost everyone working on it. Troy and Gabe lost a couple of clients, but it's harder for them to attack those two. Brenton has had a few challengers on military contracts, real estate deals going a bit sour. Money things."

"Trying to take advantage of the distractions with your safety being the priority," Thomas groaned. "*Felines*. Wolves, we would try to kill each other."

"Oh," Zachary snorted, "it'll get there if we don't get this shit under control. Eventually, someone is going to look at us and decide it's time to play the game to its finale. And then things will get messy."

They let the conversation trail off at that. Once inside,

they watched James dish up ribs for the women, and Zachary went to push Riley around to steal off her plate.

"Zachary!" She laughed at him, swatting him away. "Get your own!"

"I don't want to," he growled playfully, licking a bit of sauce off his finger from when he nearly snagged one. "Please, give me one."

"Fine!" She huffed with a grin and held out a rib for him. He grabbed it in his teeth and growled. She let go of it, and he ate it quickly. She didn't start eating, though, and he raised an eyebrow.

"I don't think the wolves are going to poison us, babe," he whispered. She sighed and waved him away.

"I know," she chuckled. "I'm waiting on you."

He blinked and began to nod.

"My bad," he mumbled, wandering off to get a plate of food from James. "Thanks, man."

"Here," James laughed, handing him a beer as well. "Thanks for coming and hanging out."

"Yup," Zachary grunted, went to the couch, and dropped down next to Riley. A bit of sauce was on her cheek, and he grinned. He leaned over and licked it off her, and he watched the blush creep up her neck and cheeks.

"We're with company, in someone else's house," she hissed, and he could barely hold back the laugh. "Zachary!" She smacked his leg.

"They don't care," he chuckled, kissing the blush. In front of the other guys at home, it wouldn't have been a big deal, but this wasn't home, and these weren't her men. He still didn't regret it, though. "I'll stop embarrassing you, promise."

"Sure," she said with an eye roll. He started eating and

made sure she was too. His eyes fell to Abigail dodging a question from Antonio before she sat on Riley's other side.

"So, have you texted Phoebe yet?"

"Not yet," Riley sighed. "I'm going to wait for things to settle down. And I'm not sure I want to be in the position to keep secrets from her..."

"About being a shifter," Abigail finished. "You'll find a balance. We all do."

"Yeah," Riley mumbled, continuing to eat her food.

"Now might be a bad time to bring this up." Thomas came over and fell into a recliner. "But, no time like the present."

"Here we go," Zachary groaned softly.

"I knew your dad was in the SSTF," Thomas said quickly. "But I never had a chance to tell you before he showed up."

"Oh." Riley gaped for a moment, and Zachary watched her blink a bit.

"I'm sorry, and I feel like a total dirtbag for not saying anything sooner-"

"It's fine," Riley cut him off, waving a hand. "He and I don't deal with each other, and it's been a hectic time. You have your own thing to worry about, and...yeah, it's just a crazy time."

"We cool?" Thomas asked, looking concerned. Zachary had to give it to the wolf, he respected the hell out of Riley.

Who wouldn't when she'd been so ready to storm a building with nothing but her own fury? And her love. Zachary could never forget that her big, amazing heart led her back into that place for them.

"We're cool," Riley told him with a smile. "It's fine, Thomas, really."

"I didn't like him, by the way," Thomas explained to her.

"He was a prick back then, too. He had a general distaste for shifters. Honestly, I think his sense of justice is the only reason he didn't become a hunter himself."

Zachary nearly choked at that comment. Well, that was some impression Keith left on Thomas.

"Well, fuck me sideways," Zachary coughed.

"No, thank you," Antonio joked from the other side of the room, and Zachary glared at him, making the wolf bare his teeth in a grin.

"He's an ass," Riley muttered, full of spite. "A total fucking prick."

"Zachary said they leave tomorrow?" Thomas asked her. "You going to try and keep in contact with him?"

"No," Riley snapped. "I won't. Though, I'm going to talk to him before he leaves. See if there's any way to get some... resolution to it all."

The conversation continued, and Zachary just listened to Abigail, Thomas, and Riley talk about the difficulties of her family situation.

All in all, they had a good time. Zachary threw an arm around Riley's shoulders and watched Abigail nervously avoid the wolves for the entire evening.

"That's so silly," Riley chuckled as Abigail accidentally bumped into James and nearly dropped her plate. "It's adorable."

"You ran from us a little bit," Zachary teased her, remembering the first few awkward moments they had with each other.

"You all looked like trouble," Riley laughed. "And I was right."

"Too bad you're just as much trouble," he purred, kissing her softly.

14

RILEY

Riley wrung her hands together for a minute as she watched the SSTF pack away everything. And there he was, her father, directing them around, about to leave.

Again.

It shouldn't have bothered her, really. He had barely re-entered her life. Two weeks in her home hadn't brought them any closer, only marked the distance between them; a distance he had created by walking away.

"Dad?" She called out, making the chatter and conversation around her go quiet. He turned to her and frowned. "Can we talk for a moment? Before you go?"

He had walked out without a goodbye last time. She needed to know if he was okay doing it again. If she mattered so little to him. He was her fucking father—she couldn't mean so little to him.

Hanging out with the wolves, Zachary, and Abigail had done her a lot of good the evening before. Refilled her batteries and recharged her heart as she watched Abigail dance away from the wolves, who only wanted a friend. She and Zachary had a bit too much to drink and got home howling, James needing to drive them back.

He didn't answer, but he did walk over to her. She took a deep breath. This was it. Time to see if they could find some agreement. If she wanted one. She hadn't decided on what, yet, but she would at least give him the opportunity.

"Would you like to talk somewhere privately?" he asked gruffly, folding his arms behind his back. It seemed like he was reporting to her like he would a superior, and that pissed her off a little bit. She bit back the anger and nodded.

"Yeah, we can go for a walk," she mumbled, walking off the front porch and leading him around the house, away from the noise.

Neither of them said anything for a long time as she walked them closer to the woods. She raised her chin and sniffed at the wind. She didn't think there were any other shifters or humans around.

"I'm on a tight schedule, Riley," he reminded her, checking his watch. She reined the anger back a little more.

"Look," she said with a bite. She wasn't controlling her anger as well as she had hoped. "I'm trying to...I don't know, talk about shit, okay? Don't fucking rush me."

"What's there to say?" Keith huffed. "You are mad at me because I needed to go do something and screwed up on making sure you were taken care of. I'm mad at you because you have broken laws to get what you want. And that's ignoring the...*relationship*...you have, which is a whole topic that has been made clear to be off-limits."

She ground her teeth and glared at him.

"We can start at the beginning, then," she hissed. "You can explain what this thing you needed to do was and why it was so much more important than me."

"Where do I even start?" He sighed. "What all did you hear from Darcy?"

"The serval?" she snapped. "Oh, just that you've been obsessive about catching Mom."

"I thought shifters killed her," Keith mumbled. Riley winced.

"I did hear something about that," she whispered.

"Yeah," Keith grumbled. "After leaving the Navy to take care of you, I did some research. I was never comfortable with how Lily died...And I stumbled on shifters and what they are, how they are. What I didn't think is that your mother or you were actually shifters."

"Well," Riley huffed, "I'm a half-breed. A couple of different rules on that."

"I learned those later, too late," Keith said with a shake of his head. "I met hunters, but that all seemed too..."

"Awful? Despicable? Repulsive? Evil?" Riley threw out her favorite terms to describe hunters, wondering which would stick.

"All of the above."

At least they could agree on that.

"Continue," she mumbled. "Please."

"So, I dug deeper and found out about the SSTF," Keith shrugged. "And I contacted them. I had all the work experience and the knowledge for them to offer me a job. Suddenly, I had a mission again, a purpose."

"You already had a purpose," Riley growled, bitterly.

"I didn't know anything about raising a child, especially not a girl with an attitude and a wild streak," Keith scoffed. "Moving on, in my first week with the SSTF, I was shown the Most Wanted list. And there was your mother with a list of her known crimes."

"Really?" she hissed. "How long did you know who mom was when I didn't?"

"Two years," he sighed, looking at the ground. "For two years, I resented having been a fool for falling in love with a criminal. Oh, and the SSTF didn't hold it against me. They now had an asset, someone who knew where Lily...Isabella had been for years after her break from the Kingson Pride, while that Pride collapsed, slowly but surely. Your guys might not know this but the SSTF saw the Kingson Pride collapsing for nearly a decade before Geoffrey was finally killed. Growing weaker, being picked apart by their enemies."

"What do they think about the Pride now?" she asked, cautiously.

"They give you all about six more months before the Kingson Pride is forever disbanded," Keith told her, a deadly whisper, a prediction of the end. She almost didn't hear him, even with her shifter senses. She felt her heart rate pick up but ignored it. She wasn't going to let her pride fall, that was for sure, so the SSTF could go eat a dick.

"Why did you leave?" she asked, going hard and straightening her spine.

"There was an undercover mission that needed someone who wasn't on the system, our digital records. I'm not because of my ties with Isabella. The mission was to go into South America and bring down a Pride with major drug connections," Keith sighed. "I couldn't tell them no. Isabella had once done work with that Pride and it was opportunity for more information on her. And catching her is my life's goal."

"Why is everyone so obsessed with her?" Riley snarled. "You, Cameron Slater, fucking half the shifter community, and nearly all the felines. What the actual fuck?"

"I loved her," Keith growled at her. "That's why I'm bringing her in. So she can stand trial for her crimes."

"And you can say that you didn't love her more than your duty to home and country," Riley hissed with disgust. "Is that right?"

"Yes."

It was the only answer she needed. There it was, the truth laid out in front of her. Her father loved his family, sure...but he was ashamed of them.

"You love home and country more than me," she said, tears finally welling in her eyes. "Thank you for finally confirming that."

"I do not-"

"You made that decision, Dad, about eight years ago," Riley whispered. "Don't try to lie to me now."

"You look like her," Keith growled. "You know that? You are her, about five inches shorter, but I won't lie to you and say you look anything like me. If it weren't for the shifters around, confirming the familial scent...Riley..."

"You didn't think I was actually your daughter," she muttered with pure rage. "Are you fucking *kidding me*? Is that why, even when your plans for a new home for me failed, you didn't come back?"

"I had a very small window to make that work. Very small. I had one number and an address." Keith shook his head. "By the time I learned that he'd been unreachable, I was already on the mission, two weeks in and unable to back out. And, a few people thought it was safer for everyone if I kept on the mission and you just made do. Part of me..."

"Part of you what?" Riley yelled at him, making him jump.

"Part of me wonders if my superiors were trying to screw

you for being Isabella's daughter," he admitted, looking upset. "But they gave me a purpose, and they kept me a bit aware of your life. I knew you were having a hard time. I knew you graduated, though, and I was proud of you."

She took a couple of steps back and began to laugh until she cried. She covered her face and couldn't stop herself.

"Even they judge me for being her daughter," Riley laughed. "I didn't know they existed, and they hate her so much. I barely fucking know her, and I can't escape her."

"I never proved anything, and by the time I was done in South America, you had moved on with life. I saw you with that boyfriend...whatever his name was and thought it was okay. And I...I felt guilty for it all and stayed away."

"And you proceeded to ignore my existence for years," she said, finally calmed back down. The injustice of it all. Oh, she was still pissed, but she could at least control herself again.

"I thought it was easier on both of us," he mumbled, full of guilt.

"And when you showed up here?" She waved a hand around. "What the fuck was that?"

"I heard about what you did and realized you had gotten in too deep. Now, you are going to live in her world and behave like her. I was pissed off." Keith shook his head. "I still am. I'm *disappointed* in you, Riley. I thought maybe my influence on you as a kid would have made you different from her. You had options, and yet, you chose to go out and get revenge instead of trusting the authorities. And everyone in the SSTF knows you're also *my* daughter. All I heard for two days before I got here was how I fathered the new Isabella, off burning down houses and hanging out with the young, newer generation of the Kingson Pride."

He did not just go there again. He did not just say she was another Isabella. She was not her mother.

"You should go," she hissed. "Like right now. If you think you can compare me to her, then you should just go and stay gone. If you think what I did was in any way like her schemes, then just leave."

"I really should, since it looks like you aren't willing to admit there's anything wrong with what you did," Keith snapped. Then he added, just a bit gentler, "Have a nice life, Riley. I love you."

"Sure, you do," she mumbled as he walked away. "Sure, you do..."

She waited until she heard their vehicles leave before walking back towards the house. He had seemed to feel somewhat guilty for it all, but he also didn't seem to regret it. The fact that some underhanded asshole in the SSTF had convinced him that abandoning her was okay made her look down on the organization. She'd been sixteen...what had she done that deserved that? And he'd let them, never tried to prove they had done it to her on purpose.

"Riley?" a feminine, older voice called out. Riley looked up as she got closer to the back door. Patty was an older woman, though Sheriff said that she was still as beautiful as the day he met her. They had been married for nearly forty years and had several sons. She had claimed the bear's heart and held on to it with a patient, loving kindness that could break down even the angriest person. She had the kindest brown eyes and simple, long brown hair that she held back in a braid. Riley thought she was beautiful, not just in body, but also in spirit.

Patty Johnson gave her a sad once over and walked over. Riley didn't say anything as the human woman, nearly in her sixties, hugged her tightly. Riley wrapped her arms around Patty and held back another wave of tears.

"Why didn't they care about me?" Riley whispered, trying so hard to hold it all back. "Why did neither of them love me enough to stay?"

"I don't know, Riley," Patty told her, clinging to her and rubbing her back. "But my Sheriff loves you. And I do too, even if he tries to keep me from interacting with other shifters. The boys love you. We all love you, and hopefully, one day, it will hurt less."

"I hope so," Riley cried softly.

"I'll be your mom, because yours didn't realize how wonderful her daughter is," Patty continued. "I'll help you with boy problems, teach you how to bake, all of it. Sheriff will knock the boys around when they break your heart, sometimes. We might not be your real parents, but we've always wanted a daughter."

"I told Sheriff I considered him my father." Riley choked out a laugh through the tears.

"Oh, I know," Patty laughed softly. "He came home like he'd just saved the world. "'Riley loves me more than Keith!' It was the silliest thing I had ever seen. We'd never been blessed with a daughter, and you give him that. We've never been close, but...maybe in time you'll see how much I care for you, even if it was just through him."

"Thank you, Patty." Riley smiled, pulling back from the embrace. "Thank you for being around with Sheriff. I know the guys have been a bit on edge, but you've really brightened this place up for us."

"Come inside," Patty said, ignoring Riley's thanks. Riley chuckled as Patty pulled her along. Once they were at the door, Patty leaned in close. "Never say thank you for being loved. It's what you deserve."

Riley blinked back a new wave of tears.

"Come on, let's go eat something," Patty chuckled, wiping Riley's cheek. Patty was nearly six feet tall, and Riley felt like a child again with the older woman doting on her. She pulled her face away from Patty's hand, who only laughed. They were both smiling as they walked into the kitchen together.

Riley could rebuild. Hell, she already had rebuilt. This was just a stumble. She didn't need him. She hadn't needed him for years. He'd just reopened the old hurts and the old pain.

Now, looking at Brenton and Sheriff arguing over something or another, Zachary teasing the leopard brothers, and Andrew hauling food into the dining room, Riley realized who her family was. Not the mother who was off her rocker. Not the father driven by a sense of duty she couldn't fathom.

This was her family.

And that was all that mattered.

She would fight for them until her last breath because they were the first people to do it for her.

15

TROY

"Damn, I hate when I need to come to Denver with you," Troy groaned as Brenton chuckled.

"I know but it's been too long, and I need your help."

"Yeah, yeah," Troy said petulantly. He was being childish over it, but he really did hate it. He had an eye for business, could see the papers and the numbers like Gabe, which had made them successful, but Brenton used him as a damn assistant sometimes. He'd much rather be in the garage building another bike and making another gorgeous design into reality. Gabe looked at a motorcycle like a miraculous feat of engineering, but Troy thought it was art. Beautiful, dangerous, and completely freeing.

And yet, here he was in Denver, playing assistant because the Pride had to move on with their normal lives again. A year ago, hell, even two months ago, it wouldn't have made Troy so moody, but after the hunters, everything seemed different. Some things were less important while others were more important than they had been. This part was less important.

"So, what are we doing?" Troy asked as Brenton held his office door open.

"Going over some troubling numbers," Brenton sighed. "Had some deals go south and some other strange occurrences. I only trust your eyes on this."

Troy nodded absentmindedly and took a seat on one side of Brenton's desk. Brenton took his own and handed him a stack of papers.

"Look through those and tell me if anything seems off to you," Brenton whispered, low enough that nobody else could hear. "And if it does, mark it and I'll look over it. We'll talk about what makes it weird after you're done."

Secrecy. Troy knew why Brenton was being quiet. He didn't want this to get picked up on security. Weird numbers happened all the time, but something had Brenton bothered. If he only wanted Troy, then it meant he didn't know anyone outside the Pride who could be trusted.

Troy began flipping through the mismatched mess of papers Brenton gave him. By page three, the pattern was clear.

Other businesses were trying to attack Kingson Inc. through money. Partnerships ended. Contracts broken or backed out of. Deals stopped right before they were signed. It wasted the company's money. Millions of dollars were evaporating into lawyers' fees, and a thousand different other things. They were attacking the Pride through its finances.

"Brenton," Troy gasped. "Why didn't I know sooner?"

Shit. Fuck. The SSTF had been gone for a week already. Some of this was dated back to when the Pride was held by the hunters. Most of it was dated when the SSTF were around the estate.

"We have a perception problem, and Andrew does not know how to fix it," Brenton whispered. "We had plans, and we have been doing them. Coming out, living, moving on. Pretending to be strong, but we are all off, and other prides are noticing. You, Gabe, and Riley are not as keen on the politics. So, until I had more, I did not know what to tell you."

"Who are our allies?" Troy whispered, feeling a bit freaked. The Pride had never been attacked like this. Never so subtly or widespread. "This is going to escalate, Brenton. We'll be right back where we were as kids."

"I know," Brenton sighed. "I know. We have very few allies. Sheriff. Thomas and his guys. No felines. None of them particularly like us, which is our own fault."

Damn right it was their fault. Before coming back to Wild Junction, they had cut a path of danger and disobedience. They burned bridges, bit the hands that tried to feed them, and generally just caused mayhem to keep other shifters from fucking with them.

"What changed?" Troy whispered to himself. "When did we lose rep?"

"I do not know," Brenton said with a thoughtful and worried look. "Realizing a shifter sold us out to the hunters should have been the first sign, but the hunters kept us too busy to notice, and we didn't think about long term problems."

"We were too busy staying alive," Troy groaned, loudly and pissed off. "Fuck us. What's Andrew's play?"

"We keep moving. We do not let this shit phase us. They are minor annoyances, and we treat them as if they are nothing." Brenton was firm with it. This meant Troy could only do so much, though. "You can consider these things quietly. Find out who is making these calls. Is anyone pulling their strings? We need to find out if it is one enemy or several."

"Alright, Brenton," Troy mumbled. He pulled out Gabe's laptop and opened it. As Brenton went about his normal business, Troy got to work.

This scared him. This completely terrified him.

"Troy," Brenton whispered. "Look at me." Troy met his gold eyes. "We will make it through this, just like everything else we have been through. We have Riley, now. We have a life. We are not going to lose it, but we need to be careful. If the hunters could not bring us down, this will not, either."

Troy didn't smell a lie in Brenton's statement. But that didn't mean Brenton wasn't completely talking out of his ass, either. Troy would never admit to doubting his Alpha but after so much, after everything, he shamefully did. Brenton might be worried, but he was also a bit over-confident in his surety they would just pull through.

It had been a long time since Troy doubted Brenton. Last time, Brenton should have listened to him.

Troy hoped this time he was just feeling off.

16

TROY

Age 16

"I can't believe we're at a real fucking party," Troy laughed, holding up a beer he shouldn't have. Gabe howled, like a fucking animal at the bonfire they were at.

"Cheers to being free, my brother!" Gabe grinned, and they were suddenly laughing like fools.

Earlier in the day, Brenton had qualified for emancipation and taken control of the Kingson Pride. Troy no longer had to answer to the sniveling bitch lynx shifter that'd had control over them before. Brenton was now their 'guardian,' and there wasn't shit anyone could do about it.

"Freedom!" Troy roared, then took a swig of his beer. He looked around the party, all shifters from his age to a bit older than Andrew, like the twenty-three-year-old hotties who had brought the beer and liquor.

It wasn't that the guys never got to go to parties, but this was the first time they didn't have someone at home to berate them and tell them they were all failures. There was nobody to tell them they would never amount to anything.

He took another large swallow and grinned at a female that walked over. Her hand ran down his chest as she stood in front of him.

"I'm Sasha," she whispered with a smile.

"Troy," he chuckled. "Troy Walker, and this is my brother Gabe." He pointed his bottle at Gabe, who gave a sly smile. "And before you get started, do you have a friend for him?"

"I believe I do," she laughed, looking away and Troy watched her wave someone over. When Troy saw the dark-haired beauty move towards Gabe, he went back to the hot blonde in front of him.

"So, can I help you with something?" Troy whispered to her, touching her waist.

"I was hoping we could flirt, and then you could take me home," she whispered back.

"Well, babe," Troy sighed. They always asked, and he always had to tell them no. "We don't bring company home. I'm more than willing to play here."

"A pity," she pouted. "I heard the Kingson Estate was a pretty swanky place."

"It is, but we don't do company." Troy blew her a kiss, and she backed away from him. They never wanted to fool around, unless it was on their terms. Which told the Pride exactly what these women were looking for. A way in to their home. They never offered their own pads or places to crash. They just took the rejection and moved on.

The rule was only humans. Humans weren't as dangerous as shifters, weren't out to kill them. And after several brutal years, no amount of alcohol could convince Troy to trust any woman at this party to be in the estate while he and his brothers slept.

"Yours fuck off, too?" Gabe groaned, adjusting his pants. "Mine fucking nearly gave me a handy, until I told her she couldn't come home with me. Then she fucked right off."

"Yeah," Troy said, a bit perturbed by it.

They hung out for hours, chatting with different shifters, talking about the future. Troy had no plans. He didn't fucking care. He and Gabe were rich as shit, trust-fund babies to the extreme. He just wanted to have a good fucking time and fuck the rest of the world. Once they turned eighteen, the only person they would answer to, willingly, would be Brenton.

And Troy debated on that as he drank his fourth beer. He was feeling it now, and it felt fucking good. Gabe was next to him, smoking a joint, laughing at something Zachary said.

"Fuck," Gabe moaned with a grin. "I think it's time to head home."

"For you two?" Zachary growled with a smile. "Yeah, it is."

"Where's Brenton?" Troy mumbled, bumping into Gabe as he turned around to look for their Alpha.

"Hooking up," Andrew answered with a smile. "Zachary, help me drag these fucks into a truck."

"Can do," Zachary replied with a solid nod. Troy groaned as Andrew took his arm.

"What do you mean he's hooking up?" Troy asked with a slur.

"He's taking his own ride home, since he's sober. We'll have company tonight, but it's cool. He needs a break for once," Andrew answered. Troy frowned. He didn't like that. Even fucking wasted, he knew ladies didn't come home. But Andrew was the second, and that was that. He was the end-all unless Brenton stepped in.

"He shouldn't do that," Troy mumbled.

"I'll be fine," Brenton said, walking over to them. "You just get some sleep, my man."

"Brenton, that's a bad idea," Troy pleaded.

"She's eighteen, she's hot, and she has no ties to a major Pride," Brenton whispered. "It'll be okay."

Troy didn't believe him.

IT WAS NEARLY five in the morning when he rolled out of bed. Literally. He had rolled too far and hit the floor. He groaned and pushed himself up. After he stood, he wobbled a little bit. Gabe was passed out on who knew what. *Gabe knew how to fucking party*, Troy thought with a chuckle.

"I need some fucking water," Troy groaned, realizing how bad his head hurt.

He didn't bother putting clothes on, since they threw everyone out of the house, the staff and the damn legal adults. It was only the Pride now and if he wanted to walk around naked, he was going to. He stumbled down all the damn stairs and into the kitchen. That's when he caught a scent he didn't recognize. A lioness shifter. He growled.

"Oh, shit," she gasped, turning towards him.

"Who the fuck are you?" he growled, stepping closer.

"I...I'm Nicki. I, uh, came back with Brenton last night," she told him, quickly. "I'm just looking for a snack for us."

Troy bared his teeth but ignored her after that. He wished Brenton tied his women to the bed like Zachary did. Not that Troy wanted to think about what either did in their bedrooms, but if Brenton was going to start bringing women home, he'd like if they didn't wander around.

"Um, do you know where I can get a knife to-"

Troy growled and opened a drawer, shutting her up. He grabbed one at random and handed it to her. Then he grabbed a glass and went to the sink. He filled it up and began swallowing. Once it was empty, he did it again.

He continued to ignore her as he walked out of the kitchen. Wasn't his business. She wanted to make Brenton a cute little breakfast in bed to see if that bought her a morning of play time, then that was her business.

He made it all the way to his room before feeling that uncomfortable itch. He didn't like that she was in the house. He put his glass on his desk and sat down with another pained groan. Beer. Beer always did this to him.

He hit play on some anime and watched it quietly until he heard it.

A roar. A clatter.

He didn't waste time. He jumped up and began running. He ran all the way to Brenton's room, only to find the door locked.

"Brenton!" he roared. "Brenton!"

Were the other guys going to wake up? Gabe wasn't going to, that was for sure, but where were Andrew and Zachary? Why hadn't they gotten here yet?

He heard more banging from Brenton's room and pounded harder on the door. His fucking Alpha was in there, damn it. He knew what this was. He knew none of those women at the party could be trusted. He fucking *knew* it.

Zachary pushed him aside, finally, and began shouldering the door open. Andrew was there only a second later to help. Troy watched the two bigger shifters destroy the door and the three of them flooded into Brenton's room.

He stood over the girl, whose head was twisted

unnaturally to the side. He was pale, and there was a knife in his shoulder. One of the kitchen's knives.

Troy had given that to her.

"I was asleep," Brenton whispered in shock, "and she tried to fucking stab me. I woke up to this." He pointed at the knife in his shoulder, and Troy wondered if he could even feel it.

"Why?" Zachary growled. "Fuck."

"Doesn't matter now," Andrew murmured and cautiously began to approach Brenton. "Zachary and I will take care of that." He pointed at her body. "Troy, get the knife out of him and collect her things. Maybe Gabe can do some magic and find out who she is."

"I don't know shit about removing a knife," Troy hissed. "What if it kills him?"

"We will take that risk," Brenton growled. "I cannot go to a hospital. They'll wonder who fucking stabbed me."

Brenton winced as he walked to his bed and sat down. Troy walked to him slowly. He bit back the 'I told you so' and just stood in front of him. Brenton would need to say something first.

"You were right," Brenton growled, long after Andrew and Zachary were gone with the body. "And after tonight, we're fucking leaving this town. Could take months to plan, but we're doing it. And only humans from here on out. Well...you already follow that rule..."

"Really?" Troy asked, frowning. "Why do you want to leave? This is our home."

"Because I'm fucking done with it. We're going to go somewhere else and make a name for ourselves. Convince people to stop trying to fucking kill us. Then, we'll come home again and just fucking hide out. I'm tired of being attacked here. I'm tired of having nowhere safe, nothing safe."

"Okay," Troy whispered. "Let's get you to the kitchen, and I'll try and pull this out of you."

"Where's Gabe?" Brenton asked, wincing as he stood up.

"Dead to the world," Troy mumbled.

"Of-fucking-course he is," Brenton growled. "Why aren't you?"

"I accidentally rolled out of the bed and decided not to go back to sleep..."

"Thank you for getting here so fast," Brenton sighed as they walked from the room. Troy shrugged.

"I didn't do anything."

"You got here first. That's something," Brenton reminded him.

Brenton leaned on the counter as Troy used his phone to look up how to treat a knife wound. He had no idea what he was doing, and if there was a time to learn, this was not it.

"I'm going to train to be a medic before we leave town," Troy told Brenton as he put the phone down. His head hurt like a mother fucker and everything sucked. "And hopefully, if this happens again, what I'm about to do won't hurt so fucking bad."

"Good idea," Brenton huffed.

Troy pulled the knife out.

17

GABE

G abe frowned at his computer in the security room, a little angry at it. He had been going through the files Keith had left with them, and it pissed him off.

The SSTF had figured it out, but their dumb policy of neutrality had meant they hadn't done anything about it.

"Gabe?" Troy called out, opening the door. "You okay in here? You're upset."

"How was Denver with Brenton?" Gabe asked quickly, deflecting for a moment.

"No good," Troy groaned. "You know a lot of people are fucking with us right now?"

"I'm getting the picture," Gabe growled. "That bank account I was given? Along with all the other crap?"

"Yeah?" Troy closed them in and sat down in an extra chair.

"It's paying different shifters all over the world—ones we know. I've already found all of the contractors that broke rank on the diner," Gabe groaned. "And Jonathan Slater,

Cameron's boy. You know the one, he's our age, maybe a little older."

"Look for anyone connected to these companies," Troy sighed, dropping the files in front of him.

Gabe flipped through the papers and sighed. Yeah. He knew these names. He knew these companies and shell companies and accounts. He'd been staring at them for a week, wondering what piece he was missing.

"This account is being used to bribe people to break from us," Gabe whispered. "I fucking hate the SSTF."

"You think they put it all together, then walked away," Troy said quietly, under his breath.

"I know they did," Gabe hissed. "And Riley told us what Keith said. Six months. They are giving it six months before we..."

"He said disbanded, but what he meant was dead," Troy said, his expression dark. "He straight up told her that he and all the people he works with think we'll be dead in six months."

"How did this fucking happen?" Gabe growled, shoving papers off his desk. "When did we lose it? When did we lose our reputation? Are we going to start meeting people who want to have a drink only to drop from poison an hour later? How did we come back to this?"

"I don't know. I don't know Gabe." Troy shrugged. "But Andrew has ideas. Tell me, who doesn't connect with the business files? Let's start putting this together. And start tracing that bank account back to its owner."

"I've been digging for the owner since I got it. It's easier to see where the money is going, but it's getting to be a pain in my ass to find out where it's coming from," Gabe sighed, rubbing a hand over his face. "The first payout was in May. To the hospital that kept our records."

"Fuck," Troy mumbled. "Serious? That's how far back this goes?"

"Yeah," Gabe groaned. "After that? A ton of different people, human and shifter alike." Gabe pointed at a list. He'd already been working on a timeline. "All the way up until the hunters began attacking us. Then it stops. Takes a long break, until recently. They don't know we have it yet, but I don't think that will last long."

"Gabe, someone orchestrated...all of this. Is that what you're trying to tell me?" Troy sounded a bit sick.

"Yes," Gabe bit out, "and those files from Brenton prove that the same person from before the hunters, the person who outed us, is still fucking with it. And there was a substantial payment to Jonathan Slater in August. I'm still not sure what that one means or what it leads to."

"They tried to kill us," Troy whispered. "Gabe, this can't be about the annoying shit. This person or group tried to kill us. Now, they are just playing with us. Why?"

"Because they can," Gabe mumbled. "Because to them, this is a game."

They sat in silence for a minute, and Troy just rubbed his face. Gabe glared at his computer and bared his teeth.

Years of drugs, death, bodies, and *games*. And here they were, back in it, on defense. Again.

"I'm losing patience for this," Gabe growled. "I am out of patience for this. I'm tired of spending my days looking out for who may kill us, who wants to fuck with us. Dissecting lives, looking for secrets and blackmail."

"I know," Troy said, standing up. "Riley promised I could bother the shit out of her after I got back from Denver, before Brenton gets a chance to. Want to come?"

"I'll leave this on Brenton's desk for him then head up," Gabe sighed. He began printing several items out. Brenton,

Andrew, and Zachary could use all of this to make a more concrete game plan. While they did that, he was going to curl up with his love and enjoy some time with her.

"Alright," Troy chuckled, patting Gabe's shoulder. "Take your time."

With a wink, Troy was gone, and Gabe waited for things to finish. The paper wasn't cool, and he was out of the room with it.

He didn't knock, pushing his way into Brenton's office. Brenton just looked up and took his feet off his desk with a frown.

"Yeah?"

"This is all a game," Gabe told him quickly. "The SSTF gives us six months? They might be right."

"Excuse me?" Brenton growled. "Explain."

Gabe ran through it, pointing out the bank account, the connections in the businesses. The hunters, the timeline, where the money was going. And how he hadn't found where it was coming from yet.

"It'll take time for me to drag out the mastermind," Gabe sighed. "It's running, all set up. It could lead me to one person, or it could lead me to a dozen; I don't know."

"You did well," Brenton whispered. "Thank you."

"No problem. This is my job," Gabe mumbled with a shrug.

"It wasn't supposed to be," Brenton sighed, sad for a moment. "Coming back here...it wasn't supposed to be."

"We've changed," Gabe said quietly. "You, Zachary, Andrew, Troy and me. We're different. Remember Cameron?"

"Who doesn't?" Brenton growled, furrowing his brow and giving Gabe a dangerous look.

"Three years ago, we wouldn't have blackmailed him,"

Gabe hissed. "We would have walked into his home and fucking killed him for hurting a Pride member. We came back here, and we thought he was a one-off. A random mad man bent on revenge against a woman, and Riley was just his way of getting to her." Gabe gave a frustrated sound. "I can't be the only person who thinks that maybe....Maybe the chatter is right. Maybe the perception problem isn't just perception."

"We are not weak," Brenton snarled.

"No," Gabe sighed. "We aren't weak. But we are getting soft."

"Get out, and go play with your brother," Brenton growled. Gabe turned and began to walk out, knowing he'd just pushed Brenton too far. They were close, but Brenton was still a Kingson Alpha. "Wait."

Gabe stopped and looked over his shoulder.

"I will think on what you said," Brenton whispered. "You are not the only one...you are not the only one who has said it."

"That's all I hoped for," Gabe said with a weak smile. "I only said it because-"

"I know. Go, brother, have a good time. You have until dinner, then she is mine." Brenton was able to crack a smile at that last part. Gabe's smile got a little stronger as he left.

He hauled ass up the stairs and grinned fully when he realized Riley's door wasn't locked. Entering, he locked it behind him and watched the scene in front of him.

Troy was on his knees to the right of Riley, waiting patiently as she painted. She wasn't wearing anything except some thigh high, sheer, stockings. Wasn't that a fucking sight?

Gabe even noticed, just for a second, that Troy was already nude.

"Troy tried to interrupt me, and I need to finish this painting," Riley said with a trace of humor. "You can join him, and once I'm done, we'll hang out."

Was that the hottest thing Gabe had heard in his entire life? Yeah, it sure as fuck was. He chuckled and began pulling off his clothes. Once he was in just his boxer briefs, he walked closer to her, and she watched him.

"What if I didn't want to wait?" he growled softly, and she growled back. She didn't just growl, she looked over at him and bared her teeth.

"Don't interrupt me, Gabe," she rasped with a bite. "I am really behind."

"Tell me," he purred, "is that paint non-toxic?"

"Of course," Riley scoffed. He waited and watched the wheels turn. He knew the paint was non-toxic because Star lived in here, for the most part. And they could afford it, so why not shell out for the best? "Go wait, Gabe."

"Of course, gorgeous," he chuckled, hooking his thumbs into the waistband and pulling down his boxer briefs while she watched. She licked her lips with a small smile.

"I'm almost done," she whispered. Gabe heard Troy growl softly.

"How long have you been here?" Gabe asked with a chuckle, kneeling next to his brother. He noted the long swipe of blue paint down his brother's chest.

"Only about a minute," Troy moaned. "But look at her. She did that after I got here."

"That's just mean, gorgeous," Gabe laughed, letting his eyes slide up and down their girl. Those stockings were something else.

"Hmmm." Riley just smiled as she continued painting.

"I think she's been listening to Brenton too much," Troy whispered.

"I like it," Gabe mumbled with a smile.

"Me too," Troy chuckled. Gabe could tell.

"Now," Riley began with a devious smile, "this is done and can dry. But I seem to have two extra canvases sitting around." Gabe watched her put the painting away on her canvas rack and look back at them. "Some of my work is already there," she purred, walking closer. Her hand touched Troy's chest but not the paint stroke. They had matching tattoos now that she had designed. "Should I add more?"

Gabe purred as she touched his back and he leaned back into her legs. She was circling them.

"I think I should," she purred back.

"Can we paint with you?" Troy asked, his voice a little rough.

"Sure," she whispered. Troy was up first, and Gabe followed him. She laughed as Troy took some paint off his own chest to smear it on the underside of one of her breasts. Gabe grabbed a lovely green color he thought looked like his eyes and squirted some into his hand. Screw a brush.

He grabbed her hips and pulled her back into his chest as Troy kissed her. He liked the look of the green paint where he touched her. Blue was being left by wherever Troy touched, as well.

"What color do you want us to wear?" Gabe growled in her ear.

"Red," she gasped as Troy traveled downwards, kissing her breasts then her stomach. "Give me red."

He grabbed a candy apple looking color and she held out her hands for him to squirt some. He tossed the bottle back onto her table and began kissing her neck as she moaned. Troy was now between her legs, and Gabe saw her red hands leaving streaks on his shoulders and through his hair.

"More," she hissed, and Gabe just growled, biting down on her shoulder as Troy sent her to an orgasm.

"Pretty girl," Troy growled. "I've found a problem with this idea."

"What?" Gabe groaned, massaging her chest, mixing the green and blue together. Her nipples were so perky that he was betting they were incredibly sensitive. He flicked a finger over one of them and relished the sound Riley made. He rolled it between his index finger and thumb, purring.

"We can't use our hands on the good parts," Troy groaned.

Gabe thought about that for a moment and looked down at his dick. Sure enough, he'd somehow gotten paint on it already. He'd almost been hoping it was still clean, and he just wouldn't use his hands.

"Looks like we need to go shower then," Gabe chuckled, nibbling on Riley's earlobe.

"Showering with you two never ends up being just cleaning ourselves," Riley laughed.

"Does it with any of us?" Troy teased, standing back up. They had Riley standing between them, and that was exactly where they always wanted her.

"As a matter of fact, yes, sometimes I do get to take a regular shower with one of you. Just never you two," Riley snorted as she said it. Gabe just grunted with a shrug, picked her up, and carried her toward the bathroom.

"Take my stockings off!" Riley yelled, kicking her legs. Gabe dumped her on the counter and grinned. Troy was right behind him and together, they each rolled a stocking off her, kissing the skin they revealed. Troy claimed her mouth as Gabe threw the stockings out of the bathroom.

He got the water running next, and when it was the temperature he knew she liked, he waved Troy to bring her in.

"You both spoil me," she whispered as Troy carried her into the hot water. She leaned into Gabe once on her feet, and Troy gave a moan. Gabe nearly laughed at the fact that Riley had pushed her ass into his brother.

"We like spoiling you," Gabe growled in her ear, using a washcloth to start working the paint off her. While he worked on her front, Troy did her back. They were a good team, and this was a ritual now. Showering with Riley was becoming one of their favorite things to do.

They moved slowly. Gabe spent a long time making sure every small speck of paint was off her. He marveled at her ink, letting his thumb trace some of the lines of her chest piece. He dipped his other hand lower, now clean and slid it between her legs. He purred at the moan she released when he gently touched her clit. He heard a louder moan and looked at Troy. He had wild, red hair thanks to the paint and water. His brother had probably gone straight for her ass, though, ignoring that he also needed to finish getting cleaned off.

"Troy, clean your hair," Gabe chuckled, sliding a finger deep into her. She gasped, and he guided one of her hands to his shoulder. She took the hint and wrapped her arms around his neck as he fingered her while Troy cleaned himself off. "Tell me what you want," Gabe groaned in her ear. "Tell us, gorgeous."

"I want to ride you," she moaned, and he felt his knees go a little weak. Yeah, he could make that happen.

"You want to be in charge?" Troy whispered, now rinsed of the red. "You want to use us? Lay us on our backs while you take your fill?" Shit, Gabe thought. That sounded even better.

"Yes," she gasped as Gabe pulled his finger out. "Gabe."

"Let's go," he growled, lifting her up. Her legs wrapped around his waist, a practiced move. She did it for all of them, knowing they very nearly felt her feet shouldn't touch the ground.

Gabe didn't bother with drying off, just carried her back to her bed. He sat down so she stayed on his lap and smiled at her.

"Have your way with me," he growled to her.

"I will," she growled back, pushing him down. Gabe felt the wind nearly get knocked out of him as he hit the bed. Troy mumbled something, but Gabe couldn't tell what it was as Riley lowered herself onto him with a sound of pleasure that made his dick twitch inside her.

"Just take it, Riley," Troy whispered as she began to move. Troy was on his knees next to her and Gabe watched them making out as she rode him. "Take what you want from him."

Gabe groaned and thrust upward, making her gasp. He grinned until she pulled completely off him.

"Gorgeous, no, I'm sorry," he moaned, wanting her to get back on.

"Hold on," she chuckled. "I know what I'm doing."

He held his breath as she turned around and slid back on him. Fuck. Now he had the best view of her ass he'd ever seen.

"Bounce on him," Troy whispered, with a devious grin at Gabe. Gabe raised a hand and flipped off his brother. He could barely hold it together as it was. From the position, to the view, he was on edge.

"Be quiet," Riley moaned, pulling Troy in for a kiss. Gabe reached and grabbed her hips, hoping to get her moving before he finished without her. She began to slide up and down him, slow and torturous.

"Oh, fuck, Riley," he groaned. "Please, don't do this to me."

She ignored him, kissing his brother as she wrapped a hand around Troy's cock, stroking it faster than what Gabe was getting. That just wasn't fair. The amount of restraint she had was murdering him. And it was probably what she wanted.

He was enchanted by the sight of her moving on his cock, and he hissed as he felt her tighten those muscles. After a few minutes of that, Gabe braced himself on his elbows and bucked his hips up underneath her again, making her fall into Troy's chest.

"How's that?" Gabe growled softly, watching as her heated eyes looked back at him.

"Do it again," she whispered, biting her bottom lip.

He did as he was told, laying back down and grabbing her hips. He began to meet her slow ride with his own thrusts as Troy wrapped a hand in her hair.

"What do I get?" Troy asked as she made those sexy whimpers they all loved so much.

"I want to suck you," she moaned, and Troy groaned, pushing her down.

Gabe nearly lost it at that. He pulled out of her and moved to get better leverage on her. He also just needed a break. She wasn't ready to cum, and damn it, he wasn't going to finish first.

While Troy thrust slowly into her mouth, Gabe licked her slit, and dove in with a tongue. He slid a finger into her backdoor and began to pump it in and out, listening to her moan on Troy's dick.

Finally, he got her to the edge, and Troy pulled out of her mouth so she could scream.

"Troy, get on your back," she panted. Gabe admired that she still was ordering them around, even as they tried their best to make it too hard for her to think. Gabe backed off while she climbed onto Troy and slid down on him. Then she looked at him.

"You know how much I loved that thing we did in Denver?" she asked with a saucy smile. "I want to do it again."

"Where's the lube?" Gabe asked, rubbing her ass slowly.

"My bedside table, bottom drawer," she whispered, kissing him as she began riding Troy.

"Fuck me," Troy groaned. "Here we go again."

"I love this," Gabe chuckled, grabbing the lube as fast as he could.

"Me too," Riley moaned as Troy pulled her down to kiss him. Gabe got behind her and lubed himself up and then her, sliding two fingers in to make sure she was ready. She gasped into Troy's mouth and Gabe knew it was time.

He slid his fingers out and slowly pushed his dick in, groaning as Riley's scream pierced the air. Troy pulled her lips back to his, holding her until Gabe was all the way in.

After that, there was no mercy. Gabe held her hips as he and Troy pounded into her. Troy kept a hand tangled in her hair, continuing to kiss her to muffle the noises she made. It was rough, and when Troy let her hair go, Gabe grabbed it, pulling her head back.

"Oh, God!" she screamed. "Oh, God! Yes!"

"Is this what our girl wanted?" Gabe growled, keeping the pace relentless. Her answer was just another scream to

God. He and Troy were completely in sync, sliding in and out of her simultaneously.

Then he felt that shiver, that beginning of her orgasm that he wanted so much. He also began to feel her pushing back onto them in time with their thrusts. It was ecstasy, it was passion, it was madness. She was their queen, and Gabe only wanted her to know that as he and Troy drove her onward.

Scratch that. She was their goddess, he told himself as he felt her muscles quiver and tighten on him. Troy's growl was something Gabe could understand all too well as he groaned at the sensation. Her climax was holding them tight, and Gabe's thrusts became shorter and more erratic as he got closer to cumming.

"Oh fuck, Riley," he groaned, shoving deep inside her and holding on until he began to cum. It felt endless. "Oh fuck, gorgeous."

"Christ all-mighty," Troy groaned, panting hard. Gabe saw his brother was drenched in sweat. Gabe was too. So was Riley.

"Oh my God," Riley gasped as Gabe slowly pulled out of her. He helped her off Troy, who couldn't seem to move at all. He laid her down next to Troy and settled on her other side. "That wasn't what I had planned at the beginning of this whole thing."

"I bet it wasn't," Gabe chuckled, kissing her shoulder as he nuzzled into her side. He ran a hand over the smooth skin of her stomach and hips. She was stunning, even sweaty, wet, and disheveled. Like a Goddess. Gabe wondered if she ever had a moment where she wouldn't look perfect to him. He didn't think so. He would remain a devout, reverent lover for as long as she would have him. Looking at Troy, who only had eyes for her in that moment, he realized his brother was also lost in her glory.

"I love you both," she murmured, closing her eyes. Gabe took a soft bite of her ear lobe as Troy answered.

"We love you, too," he whispered, kissing her.

18

RILEY

"I don't think it's safe."

"I don't have much of a choice, right now."

Riley hissed at Brenton, who glared at her. For three days, they had all argued over it. Riley, Troy, and Gabe were against the idea of Brenton and Zachary spending four days in Denver, handling things, being present, and just pushing back against the attempts to screw Kingson Inc. Brenton, Zachary, and Andrew were for the idea, claiming it needed to be done.

"And what if something happens here?" Riley snapped, crossing her arms.

"Then I just trust you, Andrew, and the brothers to handle it," Brenton growled, walking closer to her. She raised her chin in challenge. "Hear that? I trust you. I trust you to keep our home safe while Zachary and I go play stupid games with a bunch of cocksuckers. It is just a few days of lawyers and meetings. That's all. We shove a bunch of lawsuits down their throats to make it more expensive to fuck us than work with us."

Riley bit her lip and backed off.

"Can you please just...not be mad at me?" Brenton growled desperately. "I am trying, Riley. I know what your dad said, and fuck him, but I need to go do this. Andrew is in charge here until I get back, and damn it, we are only a couple of hours away. We will be staying in the condo. You have Thomas and his boys here, along with Sheriff."

"I'm not worried about things here, though," Riley mumbled.

"Then why...why did you ask?" Brenton sputtered.

"Because I told you, I don't think you and Zachary going off is safe," Riley sighed. "Damn it, Brenton."

"Beautiful," Brenton growled softly and walked even closer. Riley leaned on the wall of the hallway as he placed his hands on either side of her. "Zachary and I will do everything in our power not to do something stupid."

"I know," she said, placing a hand on his chest. "Why are people doing this to us?"

"I do not know the exact reason," Brenton murmured, leaning down to kiss her forehead. "I can give you my best guesses, reasons people have tried to hurt the Pride in the past: money, fame, opportunity, revenge. Take your pick. One of them, all of them. We have seen it all."

"Troy and Gabe said you guys were rule-breakers, renegades," Riley whispered.

"We were," Brenton mumbled, moving to kiss her neck and his hands slid off the wall to her hips. "We crushed our enemies so hard that other people did not want to mess with us anymore. We hated this shit, so we figured the more people who were scared of us, the better. They would not start shit if we showed no mercy."

"You guys have never shown mercy in the entire time I've been here," Riley groaned. "So why did they start picking a fight?"

"Because we have," Brenton whispered.

"What?" Riley frowned. What did that mean? The Pride blackmailed people, destroyed lives, killed hunters and kidnappers.

"Cameron," Brenton continued softly. "We should have just killed him. It was weak of us to blackmail him and hope he went away. He was another Alpha, and we played it soft, hoping that we would not need to be so...ruthless."

"Well, he's dead now!" Riley huffed.

"And who knows that?" Brenton reminded her. "You, me, Zachary, Troy, Gabe, Andrew, and your mother. Unless she went out telling everyone, only seven people know Cameron Slater is dead. His son probably suspects or just needs to confirm it."

"Damn." Riley blinked at that. Brenton pulled away and looked down at her.

"Yeah," Brenton huffed. "As all the guys have reminded me, the Pride is softer now. And we have to deal with that."

"Why?" Riley didn't elaborate but she felt like she didn't need to. Why deal with being soft instead of just being the real Pride they were?

"I do not want to go back to being hard," Brenton whispered desperately. "I do not want the death anymore. I do not want to fly all over the world, killing anyone who steps in my path or wants to fuck with me. Riley, we came back to Wild Junction because we were *tired*. We had done our time out there, and this was supposed to be the respite and peace we earned."

Her heart broke a little bit. Not just a little, she realized as it cracked in two. It shattered to pieces to see her strong, gorgeous Alpha look so drained, so weary. He looked so much older than he actually was in that moment.

"Go," she whispered. "If you think doing this will keep

you from going back to that, then I'm okay with it." He would go anyway, but she felt the need to tell him that she was okay. She didn't want either of them sitting around for four days wondering if they were mad at each other or not.

"Thank you," he sighed, pulling her into his chest. The embrace was warm, and she clung to him. It wasn't easy to forget that her men had brutal, hard lives. It was easy to forget that they were young still. They'd done so much, knew so much, that she easily forgot that they were barely any older than her. "Four days. That is it. You stick close to anyone we trust. Thomas and his boys are thinking of coming over for a couple of the days just to show that they support us. They will barbecue for you. Zachary is upset he is missing it."

He left her after that, grabbing his suitcase and walking away. She wrapped her arms around herself and hoped everything would be okay.

19

ANDREW

Andrew finished wrapping the sandwiches for lunch as Thomas strolled in. He grinned at the wolf Alpha that was helping them while Brenton and Zachary were in Denver.

"They come back tomorrow?" Thomas asked without a hello.

"Yeah," Andrew said with a nod. He took a wrapped sandwich and tossed it towards the wolf, who deftly caught it. "Thanks for being here the last couple of days."

"It's no problem." Thomas chuckled, unwrapping it. "You've been feeding us, and I won't lie and say you aren't a better cook than all of us."

"You are a better grill-master than I am," Andrew laughed. "Feel free to come over and work magic like that as often as you want."

"As long as you make that potato salad again," Thomas said with a mouth full of sandwich. "Seriously, that shit was amazing."

Andrew couldn't stop laughing as he remembered the look on Thomas' face when he tried Andrew's potato salad.

He'd begged and pleaded for the recipe all night, but Andrew refused to give it to him.

"You know," Thomas whispered after swallowing. "I've been wondering something."

"Yeah?" Andrew looked back at the wolf, who had jumped up to sit on a countertop. Andrew would have been annoyed, but he knew better than to tell an Alpha to get down. He couldn't even get Zachary to stop.

"How are you the third?" Thomas frowned at him. Andrew gave a heavy sigh.

"I'm more dominant than everyone else," Andrew mumbled.

"I don't think that's the only reason. I'm being nosy, I know, but I like to know who my allies are, and you seem out of place. You cook, you clean, you keep house. You stop arguments before they start. A peacekeeper."

"A Kingmaker," Andrew whispered. He watched Thomas' eyes go wide. "I'm good at stopping arguments, I'm also good at starting them. I understand people. I grew up a child in this household, ignored, required to learn how to get out of trouble. How to read a situation and figure out the best way to handle it. I'm a peacekeeper for the Pride. But I am, in the truest sense, a Kingmaker. The political strategist."

"Well, damn," Thomas muttered, looking down at the half-eaten sandwich. "What changed?"

"Brenton didn't want to be a King," Andrew chuckled. "I went a little crazy. I got so wrapped up in the game that Brenton had to pull me back and remind me why we were even playing it."

"You....You were the mind, while Zachary was the muscle." Thomas insinuated.

"I'm not the most intelligent person, no, but I know

people, and I know shifters. So, it made me good at it. Troy and Gabe are both leagues smarter than me, but my type of intelligence is more helpful in our world than yours. And I am just more dominant than those two," Andrew ended with a smirk. "Now you know."

"Now I know," Thomas said carefully. "You tell Brenton which allies to keep, which bridges to burn."

"I tell him who it's better to kill and who's better to blackmail. I tell him who is a wolf in sheep's clothing, pardon the expression. I tell him who's naïve and who's cunning. I tell him what the servants in their household think since they all trust me. I'm one who rose out of the shithole of being the help to being inner circle, so they tell me things when I meet them. Gossips, the help. Part of the reason we don't have any."

"And I was told you might be the weak link," Thomas snorted. Andrew narrowed his eyes on the wolf, who just shook his head. "By the South Dakota Alpha, the new female. She's trying to lead me into trouble I don't want."

"Get yourself killed so she doesn't see you as a threat anymore," Andrew chuckled, knowing Thomas wasn't so stupid to fall for that bait.

"Yeah," Thomas laughed. "She's proving to be a great Alpha for them, much better than Chris ever was."

"Any word on that?" Andrew asked, continuing the shift in conversation off his checkered past and his old role.

"Nope," Thomas sounded completely uninterested in it. He just didn't care. His scent told an incredibly different story. Betrayed. Hurt. Longing. But *none* of that was Andrew's business.

"Well, I have to head out," Andrew groaned. "Got a fucking meeting with the contractors for the diner."

"I can't wait to eat at this mysterious, destroyed diner,"

Thomas laughed. "Everyone in town continues to tell me how great it was, and how they can't wait for it to come back."

Andrew rolled his eyes. Yeah, the town wasn't making this easy. Every delay he had, another one would find him and ask what was taking so long. He was paying people who weren't working, and that genuinely was starting to piss him off as well. Some even kept taking his money and got other jobs in other towns. He'd started paying them enough, so they weren't working more or feeling stressed. Goddamnit.

He got into his truck and pulled out. It wasn't a far drive to the diner. It never was, but today seemed slower than normal. When he got into the parking lot, he sat in the driver's seat for a moment and just looked at the bare spot where the diner once stood. A casualty to a dangerous game —a game Andrew once played to the edge.

"Fuck," he groaned, putting his head on the steering wheel. Now he needed to go inside the stupidly-cold temporary trailer they had set up to discuss new contractors and find out who he was going to keep, or who was a last, desperate option.

He climbed out and frowned. He was a bit early, but he'd thought many would be there already. He was offering millions in contracts to get the diner back up, and yet, no one wanted to show up a few minutes early to make a good impression? He didn't like that.

"I just want to have my diner back," he snarled to himself. It gave him something to do. It gave him something wonderful and something away from the rest of their lives, away from the politics. But felines had brought his diner into their games, and now he was having a hard time keeping himself from going too deep into it.

He stomped up the steps and pushed into the trailer. He stopped and stared wide-eyed at his guest.

"Andrew Hicks," Jonathan Slater chuckled. "How are you? It's been a long time since I've seen you. We should catch up. Particularly, I want to know why you thought you could scheme and plot and overthrow my father."

Zachary pushed the offer at the other lawyer, a clouded leopard shifter, with a sneer.

"This is what's going to happen to your client if you don't stop playing games with me," he growled. "I'm tired of this. I'm done playing nice. We are suing you into the ground unless you fucking back off."

The clouded leopard, a shithead named Dean, looked over the single piece of paper that Zachary had given him. Then he gave a derisive snort and tore the damn thing in half, making Zachary snarl viciously.

"No dice," Dean chuckled. "Kingson Inc. is just going to have to deal with being on the back foot for a little while. It happens to everyone. You survive, or you don't. We'll meet you in court. Have a nice day, Mr. Woods."

Zachary shot out of his seat with another snarl as Dean stood up patiently.

"You know, you can attack me all you want, but that won't make the problem go away," Dean laughed. "Kill me here. I'll die for my Alpha, but you will still be seen as a weak Pride, brought to your knees by hunters and pure fear."

"I'm going to tear yo-"

"Zachary," Brenton said with a snarl. "Let him go. We will see you in court, Dean. Tell Alpha Travyn that I look forward to bleeding him dry."

"Certainly," Dean said politely, grabbing his suitcase and leaving with a casual stroll.

Zachary turned to his Alpha and bared his teeth.

"What the fuck, Brenton?"

"Killing the lawyer does us no good," Brenton sighed. "And maybe I just do not want to kill anyone."

"Yeah, I've fucking noticed," Zachary hissed. "Where are you? What are you feeling right now that has you so screwed up?"

"Tired," Brenton groaned. "I am tired."

"Tired gets Alphas killed, along with their closest Pride members, their inner circle," Zachary growled, leaning down to Brenton, who didn't acknowledge the challenge at all. "I get it but-"

"Killing him gets us nothing," Brenton growled. "There is just no reason for it. It would mean we have a body, in broad daylight, in our building. We would be seen as completely losing fucking control of ourselves. You know that."

"I know but-"

"There's no buts to that," Brenton snarled, standing up. "Stop fucking arguing with me. If they want to drag this out as far as possible, fine. We have the resources to deal with them. You are looking for a quick and easy solution that doesn't exist."

"Then what do we do?" Zachary sighed, looking away from his Alpha, breaking eye contact.

"We deal with the small shit until Gabe has answers for us on the big shit, like the person who is bribing all these assholes to keep picking at us. Vultures, every single one of them, being paid to pick at us until we are nothing but a brittle skeleton, ready to break into bone dust."

Well, that was a morbid visual. Zachary grunted, trying to banish it from his mind.

"Let's go to my office," Brenton snarled, grabbing his coat. Zachary threw his own on and followed Brenton out of the conference room. They were polite and smiled at all the employees who stopped to say hello to them. Many had been around since Brenton finally took over at seventeen. They had watched the Pride grow up from lanky, terrified teenagers who couldn't trust anyone to strong men who crushed their enemies. Ten years changed a lot.

And in the year since returning to Wild Junction, even more had changed. Or maybe it was the year before, when they played their final game and decided it was time to settle.

"What are we ordering for dinner tonight?" Brenton asked with a sigh as they entered the elevator.

"I was thinking Chinese," Zachary grunted.

"We had Chinese yesterday," Brenton grumbled with a disgusted look. "And I hate the place you always pick. We got it for you."

"We could order from the Italian place, you picky ass," Zachary groaned. "Sometimes I fucking hate you and your snobby ass."

"You will fucking deal with it. I class you, make you presentable to the damn world, you fucking thug," Brenton said mildly. "We need each other, you and I."

"I need you like I need a wart on my fucking balls," Zachary growled.

"That's disgusting," Brenton groaned. They were silent for a moment and Zachary gave Brenton a small smirk. Brenton returned it, and they started howling in laughter. As the door opened on the top floor, they were still losing their minds.

Their friendship was based in petty insults from the very beginning. Brenton had given up on being nice to Zachary, and Zachary hadn't given Brenton the chance to try and build a friendship. One day, Zachary at sixteen, called Brenton a cock-sucking fuckwad. Brenton replied, in that mild tone he'd already mastered, that Zachary was a punk-ass thug that did not know how to tie his own shoes. Zachary tied his shoes. It had them both giggling. It was a start.

"We're fucking weird," Zachary chuckled as Brenton unlocked his office.

"We are but let's continue to pretend we are not," Brenton laughed. "I like making the rest of the Pride uncomfortable."

"You have an image to maintain," Zachary reminded him as he went to grab his seat. Brenton closed but didn't lock the door in case someone needed them. He went to his desk and leaned on it.

"Been sitting too much?" Zachary asked with a smile.

"Yeah." Brenton gave a heavy sigh. "I have."

They weren't in the tallest building in Denver, but their building was a decent height. Zachary enjoyed the view from his spot. He'd convinced Brenton to let him set up next to the big window that was Brenton's wall.

He noticed a glint and narrowed his eyes on where it was coming from. He couldn't identify it and went back to thinking about what to order for dinner. It was probably some trick of the light. He was getting paranoid.

"So, Italian?" Zachary asked, as Brenton just stood where he was.

"Yeah," Brenton sighed. "You know what I really want, again?"

"Huh?"

"Those fucking pot pies Andrew made." Brenton chuckled. "The seafood ones? I loved those things."

"We don't have an Andrew with us right now," Zachary reminded him. It was a damn shame, really, since those pot pies were the fucking best thing Zachary had ever put in his mouth. Well, second best thing, which reminded him of the other person not in Denver with them. "Or Riley, you know...to help pass the time."

"Fuck, I love that woman more than the pot pies." Brenton laughed, but sobered quickly, and Zachary didn't miss it. "Ah, she is mad at me."

"She's mad at both of us," Zachary grunted. "She didn't want us here, doing this."

"I know," Brenton snorted, "but she yelled at me."

"Did you bend her over your desk and spank her for it?" Zachary asked, leaning back.

"No," Brenton mumbled. "It didn't feel appropriate."

"Your problem, not mine. But she had a point," Zachary sighed. "This is all dangerous. Being home, being here. These people could escalate any moment. They were behind the hunters, so what's to say they won't try again?"

"That has been on my mind a lot," Brenton whispered. "A lot."

"We can only hope Gabe finds them before they decide to quit dicking around and try to shoot you. And it will be you, Brenton."

"Let's think on this at dinner," Brenton said quickly. Zachary didn't like Brenton avoiding this. But he also knew that Brenton was always the target. Always needing to stay one step ahead of the shooters, the poisoners, the crooks, and the spies. His Alpha was tired, and so was Zachary. "We have more meetings coming up in about thirty minutes."

"Fucking wonderful."

R iley laughed as Troy squirted oil everywhere when he screwed up a hose. He sputtered and glared at the thing, then turned the glare onto her.

"It's not funny," he growled petulantly.

"It's very funny," she giggled as Finn walked over and sighed.

"You-"

"I asked you to wait on me," he mumbled, hurrying over to Troy and helping.

Riley watched Finn work on her Porsche. It was only supposed to be an oil change, but they had gone crazy and decided to work on it doing something she didn't understand. Gabe walked over and threw an arm over her shoulder.

"How long is Andrew supposed to be gone?" he asked quietly.

"A few hours, and he only left thirty minutes ago. Thomas and his boys left right after," Riley informed him. "Why?"

"Nothing, I just stumbled on some stuff, and I wanted to get his take on it. It can wait."

"Okay," Riley said with a smile. She kissed his cheek and Gabe smiled at her. "Want to tell me what it is?"

"It's nothing major, just another line to some obscure Pride we don't really deal with often." Gabe rubbed his cheek to hers. "Seriously, no big deal. How are you?"

"I'm alright," Riley sighed with a shrug. "Just watching Troy ruin all of Finn's hard work."

"You haven't said much about seeing your dad since he left," Gabe whispered.

She winced. She hadn't, and she'd been avoiding even thinking about it. He was gone again, off doing who knew what, and it was like he'd never shown up to begin with. She'd made her decision, and he had made his. That was it.

"He's gone, and it doesn't matter. He didn't want me for who I am, and I don't want him for who he is," Riley muttered with a frown. "That's how it works right? I'm not totally cold for that, am I? Between him and Mom..."

"No, gorgeous, you aren't cold." Gabe turned her and held her hips. "Zachary's parents didn't want him either. He might be a good person to talk to about this."

"Yeah." Riley nodded, thinking about that. "You're right. I'll talk to him when he gets back with Brenton."

"It's your choice. You could always talk to Abigail about it." Gabe pulled her closer. "She's a great listener. I am too, but I'm not sure I can give you the information you need on this."

"If Zachary isn't helpful, I'll send her a text. How much longer is she staying?" Riley figured the doe would have been gone by now.

"Thomas asked us to keep her here a bit longer," Gabe chuckled. "And I'm still seeing her."

"Brenton, Zachary, and Andrew still haven't," Riley groaned. "Why is that?"

"Because they're stubborn," Gabe reminded her with a grin. "Come on. Brenton will see her when he sees no other option for dealing with his feelings. Zachary will bend and see her when Brenton has. Andrew...Andrew just doesn't really need to? He's pretty secure in who is and how to deal with his emotions."

"Andrew knows how to deal with everyone's emotions," Riley snorted.

"Yeah, he does."

"It's weird sometimes."

"Yeah, it is."

"Do you think Brenton and Zachary need to talk to her?" Riley asked, running her hands over Gabe's chest.

"I do, but it might never happen." Gabe leaned down and kissed her lips gently. "And don't ask me to try and make them."

"I wouldn't," Riley laughed.

Gabe pulled her around and leaned against a wall with her back to his chest. She sighed into him, and they watched Troy and Finn try to fix whatever Troy had broken.

"I should have helped Finn instead of Troy," Gabe chuckled.

Riley only nodded, watching with a deep amusement as Finn tried to get Troy to realize what he'd done. Troy just mumbled incoherently, then left for a shower. Finn gave a groan and looked at her and Gabe.

"Can one of you help me out here?" Finn's voice was like a whisper on the wind. When she'd first met him, he had sounded slick and humorous, but now, Riley felt like there was no life in the fox. He was completely lost, and the Pride could only watch as he wasted away. The only thing keeping him in this world was the fact that the Pride wouldn't let him slip too far away.

Gabe walked over, and they spoke in low voices about whatever Troy had done. Between the Pride, the wolves, and Sheriff, Finn would have more support than he could imagine. Riley just felt he needed some time to grieve, and then a kick in the ass to get him moving again.

Riley didn't let her own troubles with what happened in the compound make her forget what others had gone through. That Thomas had lost so many of his brothers, not just the biological one, Chris, who was off doing who-knows-what, but so many in the inner circle that Thomas was once a part of. James and Antonio went through it all, as well. Sheriff was ripped away from his wife, whom he'd stashed away in hiding. She would have never known his fate. Finn lost his twin. Her Pride was shaken to its core by what was done to her and to them. They had been betrayed by their own kind, and that mess wasn't cleaned up yet.

"You are so far in your own head right now," Gabe whispered, suddenly in front of her.

"How...?" She frowned, looking around him, Finn was gone.

"It's been like twenty minutes. You okay?" Gabe wrapped an arm around her.

"Just thinking about how much has happened to everyone," Riley sighed. "Sometimes, it's easy to think we're just all here and it's always been this way but...it's not. We've known Finn for a month. Only a month, Gabe. Same with Thomas, James, and Antonio. Only a month ago, we were running for our damn lives."

"I know," Gabe mumbled.

"That's not it though. We're not done," Riley groaned. "Brenton and Zachary are off playing games. Andrew is trying to get his own business back up and running. I...I burned a house down and had a vile man sent to prison."

"Yup," Gabe huffed with a nod. "And you're right. We're not done yet. We may never be done, Riley."

"Brenton said something similar. He said he would play the small games because he was tired of..."

"Yeah," Gabe whispered. "We're all tired, Riley. You stand in front of me, ready to go to war and I can't muster the energy. Brenton can't. Zachary is secretly cleaning his guns. Andrew is losing his mind. Troy is getting frustrated over shit."

"I'm going to go paint," Riley said, kissing his cheek.

Ready to go to war? Riley wasn't so sure about that.

22

ANDREW

Andrew spit blood out of his mouth and glared at the lion above him. Jonathan Cameron was not an Alpha. He was just a bully, had always been a bully, and would always be a bully. Punch people around to get what he wanted. Hit them hard enough, and they just stop being a problem.

"You know he's dead," Andrew chuckled, leaning against a wall after Jonathan had hit him. "Right?"

"I figured," Jonathan growled. "Who killed him?"

"Does it matter?" Andrew grunted as Jonathan pulled out a knife. "Why are you here, Jonathan?"

"What? Think Brenton and Zachary are going to show up and finish this? Stop me from killing you in retaliation for ruining me when you ruined my father?" Jonathan pointed at Andrew with the knife.

He should have just run out of the trailer when he saw Jonathan, but Andrew figured he could learn something.

"Other than them being in Denver, why wouldn't they come for you after you kill me?" Andrew asked cautiously. He didn't like the look Jonathan was wearing.

"Because my partner is dealing with them," Jonathan growled, stepping closer, "and once those two are gone and I get done with you, your last few members are going to fall. It's over for the Kingson Pride, Andrew."

There it was, Jonathan had a partner. That was what he needed to know, now he had to get the hell out of the trailer and get to his Pride.

Andrew jumped for the door, and Jonathan slammed into him. Andrew hissed as the knife slashed across his side, and he tried to shove Jonathan back, only to get pushed away himself. It was going to be a fight. Jonathan was now between Andrew and the door.

"Why me?" Andrew scoffed, wincing at the laceration on his ribs. "Why not go after Brenton yourself? Why use a partner for that?"

"The hunters were supposed to kill all of you," Jonathan growled. "I took a huge risk contacting them and sending them after you."

"You supplied them with all of the information?" Andrew growled back but Jonathan shook his head. Andrew needed to keep him talking. Jonathan was a stupid oaf who gloated, and Andrew needed to hear all of it.

"I was given the information," Jonathan laughed, "and a substantial amount of money by my partner to cover any of my costs in dealing with the exchange."

"Then we got free," Andrew chuckled. It also didn't sound much like a partnership. Jonathan was too stupid to realize he'd been used. "A waste of money really."

"It escalated to something bigger than we thought it would," Jonathan sighed, giving an open-armed shrug as the knife dangled in his fingers. Andrew held back. Information. If he could keep Jonathan talking, he could maybe walk out of this alive, and they could stop the entire mess. "And then there was Abel." Jonathan laughed. "That stupid fuck. Killed in his cell two days ago, did you know that?"

No, Andrew didn't know that. They weren't privy to most of the things going on with Abel. There hadn't even been a hearing yet.

"Yeah. Apparently even the worst of shifter criminals don't appreciate when an Alpha tries to buy a shifter from hunters to be a slave," Jonathan chuckled with another shrug. "Well, Abel dying has caused our plans to move a bit faster, but that's fine. I was already looking forward to killing you."

Not Brenton or Zachary, who were both the real threats to Jonathan, Andrew noted. Him. Smaller than Jonathan by probably fifty pounds, and not one of the more dangerous shifting forms. Jonathan could crush him. He filed away the fact that Abel dying was the catalyst for this. That meant something that Andrew would need to seriously consider after he made it out alive. If he could.

"Let's finish this then," Andrew whispered.

Jonathan jumped, and Andrew tried to move, but the confined space and Jonathan's size made it impossible to get out of the reach of the lion. Andrew was slammed into a wall, making the entire trailer shake. The knife sank into his abdomen, and Andrew gave a snarl from the pain. He stomped on Jonathan's foot and brought his knee up, aiming for the lion's balls.

He connected, making Jonathan stagger back for a moment and pull the knife out. Andrew groaned and placed a hand over the wound, looking around desperately for anything he could fight with.

Jonathan roared and came after him again, and Andrew found himself tossed onto a desk, crashing against the furniture with the air knocked out of him. He gasped and pushed himself up to stand as Jonathan kicked his ribs. Andrew grabbed for one of the shit plastic chairs they had and swung it into the lion, making him grunt and drop the damn knife.

Andrew pushed away on the floor as Jonathan recovered. He got himself standing, but Andrew couldn't see where the knife had landed. It at least evened the playing field just a bit.

Jonathan took a swing at him, a massive fist flying towards Andrew's head. He pulled his head back, thankful the punch didn't land. It would have killed him faster than the stab wound. Andrew ducked down and jumped toward Jonathan's abdomen. He hit with a thud, sending them both to the floor. He connected a punch to Jonathan's nose before Jonathan was able to buck him off and force Andrew onto his back.

"I'm fucking tired of you and your fucking pride, you worthless stray," Jonathan growled, spittle flying into Andrew's face as his hands wrapped around Andrew's throat.

Andrew tried everything. He tried punching, clawing, anything but he couldn't get Jonathan's massive hands to stop crushing his airway. He rolled his eyes over, looking for something as black spots danced in front of his eyes.

The knife was nowhere to be seen, but there was a pen. Andrew reached for it, and thanked God when his fingers were around it. He couldn't breathe. He was losing his vision as the black spots also blurred.

He stabbed Jonathan in the arm with the pen, making the lion roar and let go. Andrew inhaled as hard as he could and found that hurt like hell. He desperately pushed Jonathan off him as the lion removed the pen. Andrew barely made it a foot away before Jonathan was able to grab him again.

Andrew saw what he was looking for, though—the knife. He was able to get his finger on it as Jonathan grabbed Andrew's hair. He yanked Andrew's head back and slammed it once into the floor.

Stars danced in Andrew's eyes, but he focused on his hand. He had the knife. He turned as best he could, met Jonathan's sadistically pleased gaze.

Andrew shoved the knife into Jonathan's ear. Jonathan roared and let go of Andrew. Andrew pulled it back out, and, as Jonathan screamed, he pushed the lion back, climbed over him and stabbed straight downward.

The screaming stopped.

Andrew tried to stand and touched his pocket. He needed to call for help.

He couldn't think straight. His head hurt too much.

His phone wasn't in his pocket anymore.

His vision blurred, and he looked down, trying to remember why his stomach hurt.

There was blood everywhere. That wasn't good.

The door opened, and someone cursed.

He needed to make a call. Where the fuck was his phone?

He hit his knees and fell forward, losing sight of everything.

23

BRENTON

"You know what?" Brenton growled after another meeting that went to hell in ten minutes. "Let's get the fuck out of here."

"Thank fuck," Zachary groaned at him.

In twenty minutes, Brenton had lost all patience for everything. He was so done with this. He wanted to go home and curl up with Riley to watch a movie. He wanted to eat Andrew's food and listen to the brothers joke around. He wanted Zachary to lay out on a couch and chill the fuck out.

"Let's get out of here before the next one shows up," Brenton said softly, suddenly missing everything back in Wild Junction too much. His trip with Troy had only taken a day. This four-day trip was suddenly too much, too long. He needed to be home with his entire Pride before he went mad. "Fuck it, we are going home."

"Are you sure?" Zachary asked, grabbing his suitcase. "I mean, yeah let's ditch for the rest of today but we still have shit to do tomorrow."

"I do not care," Brenton growled. "I just fucking do not, Zachary. After the hunters, this shit all seems so goddamn miniscule. Unimportant. You know, when I brought Troy up here, he bitched about it. I can't blame him. Being fucking taken by hunters and firmly believing you will be dead soon really changes things."

"Yeah," Zachary sighed. "I get it man I do, but my job is to keep us safe and that includes all of this shit. We need to do it, Brenton. We have to. We'll skip the rest of today, but we need to be here tomorrow. I hate it, you hate it, but this is the plan we decided on. We have to see it through."

Brenton snarled, and Zachary just stared him down. Goddamnit. Goddamn all of this, Brenton thought, full of rage. His temper was building every moment—every insult they threw at him and the Pride, every annoyance.

"Fine, we'll do tomorrow, but I'm taking the rest of today off," Brenton bit out, and Zachary only nodded to him.

"Let's get out of here," Zachary said with care. "You need to cool your head."

"I would think you'd be just as frustrated," Brenton groaned, wondering why his second wasn't also still pissed off like he was earlier.

"I am," Zachary growled. "But one of us needs to remain somewhat civilized. You know that. It's normally you."

"Yeah," Brenton sighed, letting that sink in. "I hate this shit. We're good at it, we always have been, but I hate it."

"We're not good at this," Zachary snapped, waving a hand around Brenton's office. "We're good at crushing our enemies until they don't have the will to step up and challenge us. This? We're never been so far on the backfoot. We've never bothered with these small games. Brenton, we are no good at this."

Brenton bared his teeth and walked away. Zachary followed on his heels as Brenton looked at the secretary he had. She was human, in her sixties and refused to retire.

"Jeri," Brenton sighed. "We are heading out for the rest of the day. We will be back in tomorrow. Tell the rest of my appointments they can reschedule for any of my free time tomorrow."

"Of course, Mr. Kingson." Jeri gave him a smile and pointed her pen at him. Her gray curls bounced as she gave him a look he could only imagine she also gave her grandchildren when they were bad. There was a twinkle in those brown eyes, and Brenton knew he was about to get a talking to. "We'll get through this. You just keep your chin up and keep trucking along. I'll hold off the hounds baying at the door, but you best come back tomorrow and send them back where they belong."

"Yes, Jeri," Brenton chuckled, leaning down to give the elderly woman a kiss on her cheek. "Thank you, doll."

"Oh, stop that!" Jeri laughed, waving him away. He waited for Zachary to do the same and make Jeri blush. "You boys know how to make an old woman feel beautiful again. Get out of here. Go call Ms. Stern and remind yourselves how lucky you are to have her. She's a good girl, so you boys best do whatever you need to keep her."

Brenton got a solid laugh out of that. Jeri was a doll, and he made sure she knew it. Her husband had passed away twenty years ago, a jaguar shifter that had an unfortunate accident. Zachary enjoyed teasing her, and Jeri was supportive, oddly enough, of their relationship with Riley. Jeri had respect for the young woman who settled them all.

She continued to shoo them away as one of their next visitors showed up. Brenton let the human move out of his way and continued to walk towards the elevator. He heard Zachary growl at the guy and ignored it.

Brenton stepped into the elevator with Zachary and

both chuckled as two others from different floors stepped off to get out of their way.

"I love and hate that they do that," Brenton said with a grin.

"Right? It's always freaked me out a bit, but it's also really cool," Zachary said with a loud laugh. "At least we haven't lost the respect of people in this building."

"Amen," Brenton groaned. "We need some people on our side."

They rode the elevator in silence and ignored the chattering groups of people on the ground floor. Brenton only looked ahead, maintaining the air that he was in control and would remain so. It ate at him that it had never felt more like a lie than in that moment. He wasn't in control. He was slipping. People were noticing. His Pride was noticing.

They were at the door when his phone began to go off. He pulled it out with a frown and saw that it was a private number. He didn't like that someone he didn't know had his private number, something he reserved only for the Pride.

"Alpha Kings-"

"Yeah, look. It's Jessie, Jessie Erikson." She sounded out of breath, and Brenton grabbed Zachary to stop him from walking further. "Look, I've been hanging around-"

"We know," Brenton cut her off with mild authority. "Why?"

"It doesn't matter right now," she panted. "I'm with your boy, Andrew. He's been in a fight. There's a dead guy, the Slater boy."

"Put him on the phone," Brenton snarled. He pushed out of the building and stood in the sun. Zachary hung close to him, nearly on his back to hear the conversation.

"He's unconscious. He's been stabbed," Jessie growled

back. "I called 911 for him already, but I took your number out of his phone to call you. This way, you can call me back. I'll stay here until he's picked up. I've got to get out of here after that."

"Is he alive?" Brenton bit out. "Andrew. Is he alive?"

"Barely," Jessie sighed, desperate. "I got here as he lost consciousness. I'm covering the wound now. He's got a massive bruise forming on his head too. Look. I'm sorry I haven't come around sooner. I've had some problems, myself. I'll...I'll ride with him to the hospital and talk to you. I'll see if they can get him airlifted to Denver."

"They better fucking air-lift him to Denver," Brenton roared. Zachary grabbed the phone from him before Brenton could accidentally crush it. "Fuck!"

"Jessie, call us when he's been picked up, then you fucking ride with him or follow. If you aren't at the hospital, I will fucking find you," Zachary growled and then hung up. Brenton ran a hand through his hair and bent over, taking deep breaths. Fucking Andrew. Dying. This was completely out of control. The Pride was being attacked again, and this time, there was no easy answer like hunters.

"Oh god, Andrew..." Brenton covered his face as he stood up straight again. "Fuck." He couldn't process it for a moment, just standing on the sidewalk. The air was cold, even though the sun was bright. A breeze made the blazer of his suit move, and he just continued to rub his face.

"We need to get to the hospital before him. We need to find out which one he's being sent to," Zachary whispered to him. "We'll figure out the rest once we know he's okay."

"He's too good for this," Brenton choked out. "He always was. He got in this because I was his friend, Zachary."

"He knew the risks," Zachary growled softly. "He's been with you every step of the way. He's learned to be a strong

Pride member and do more than anyone ever expected of him. He's still breathing, now, and I don't think it's going to change. Now we need to go."

Brenton turned to Zachary and slowly nodded. Zachary twisted his head suddenly, looking furious, and Brenton was about to frown at the tiger.

A gunshot rang out. Then a second.

Something slammed into Brenton. It was Zachary, the tiger's arms wrapping around his waist.

Brenton fell to the ground with Zachary on top of him.

"Christ!" Brenton snarled, trying to move as people screamed. He pushed Zachary off him and wondered why his friend didn't fight back. Zachary was dead weight.

"Zachary?" Brenton growled, sitting up and looking at his friend. Zachary was out like a light. "Zachary!" Brenton roared down, shaking his shoulder. He pulled Zachary with him to a car parked nearby, using it for cover, hoping another shot didn't ring out. He rolled Zachary over and nearly lost his stomach.

Even on Zachary's black suit, the blood was obvious. Brenton tore the black jacket open to the white shirt. Then he tore the shirt. He pulled his own jacket off, looking for where the blood was coming from. He needed to put pressure on the wound.

He finally found it. And the second one. Both shots hit him.

"Oh God, Zachary, don't you fucking die on me. Not both of you. I can't fucking lose both of you," Brenton snarled, as people were still screaming and EMTs showed up. So did what felt like hundreds of police officers. "HERE! I have someone injured here!"

Everything was a blur after that. Brenton was forcefully hauled away from Zachary's body. He wasn't sure how, since he didn't think there was a human alive who had the strength. He was continued to be pulled away as Zachary was loaded up on a stretcher and rushed off.

"Sir! Sir!" an officer roared at him. Brenton turned to him slowly. "We need to ask you some questions."

"Ask me at the hospital," Brenton snarled, baring his teeth. Then he ran after the EMTs rolling Zachary away from him. They tried to stop him from jumping in, but Brenton didn't bother giving them an argument. He jumped into the ambulance as they worked on Zachary.

Brenton wasn't sure what he was doing there, but if Zachary was going to die, he wouldn't be alone. Brenton was going to be there for him.

He hoped his enemies had made peace with their gods, because a reckoning was coming. Mercy was no longer an option.

Mercy should never have been an option.

24

RILEY

Riley heard the doorbell first and frowned. Who could possibly be coming to visit? The Pack just left, Andrew was probably just getting his meeting going, and Sheriff was probably working. Abigail? She didn't go anywhere alone; she didn't have a car.

"I'll get it!" Riley called out to whomever may hear her. She was closest and made it to the door in record time. She used the peephole to see two deputies waiting outside the door. Then she saw Sheriff's truck, sirens on, screaming into the driveway. Oh no.

She yanked the door open as the sirens grew close enough to make her ears hurt. Gabe and Troy were suddenly behind her.

"What's going on?" Riley asked quickly as Sheriff jumped out of his truck.

"Andrew's been attacked," Sheriff snarled. He looked at the deputies. "Get out of here."

"Sheriff, we need to question them about the dead body!" one of the deputies complained, looking pissed.

"I'll question them once they know if Andrew is alive or

not," Sheriff growled. "Keep arguing with me, and we're going to have problems."

"Dead body?" Troy whispered, sounding shocked.

"Andrew might be dead?" Riley gasped. Fear raced through her. Her heart felt like it wanted to stop, and she swayed into Troy, who got an arm around her to hold her up.

"What the fuck is going on?" Gabe snarled. "Someone back up and tell us what the hell you're talking about!"

"Andrew was found by Jessie Erickson in the trailer at the diner. He was seriously injured and unconscious. Kids, there was a dead body there. A guy named Jonathan Slater. Looked like a fight happened," Sheriff was telling them calmly, but Riley wasn't feeling calm. Calm was not the word she would use for anything she felt at that moment. "He's being taken by helicopter to Saint Joseph Hospital and-"

Riley didn't hear the rest as she raced for the garage. Troy and Gabe were hot on her heels, and she snatched the keys for her Porsche. She got the doors unlocked as the guys climbed in with her.

"Stop! You three need to-" Sheriff was yelling for them, but Riley bared her teeth as she turned on the engine. The garage door took too long opening in her mind, but once she knew she would fit, she slammed into reverse and heard rubber burn as she spun out of the garage. The deputies were near their own car and had to jump out of her way.

"Gabe?" Troy asked from the backseat.

"I'm calling Brenton. You get Zachary," Gabe snarled. Riley heard the rings from both their phones. She was out of the driveway in seconds and on the highway when Gabe cursed.

"Answering machine," Gabe told them.

"Same," Troy called from the back. "We need to find out what the fuck is going on."

"We need to get to the damn hospital," Riley growled. Then she thought about it. "Sheriff mentioned the guy was Jonathan Slater."

"Cameron's son," Gabe told her with a hiss. "Big beefy mother fucker. It would have been a hell of a fight for Andrew."

"Andrew's lucky he's breathing as it is," Troy, leaning between the seats. "Jonathan's a beast. As big as Zachary and, fuck it all, a hell of a lot meaner."

They were silent for a short time. It was a heavy, pregnant silence full of only one thought. Would they lose someone today? Was this the beginning of the end for them?

"Why would he go after Andrew?" Riley whispered, her eyes on the road. She needed something to concentrate on while she drove. She was going nearly a hundred and fifty miles per hour. She hoped no cops tried to pull her over because she sure as fuck wasn't going to stop for them.

Andrew. Her sweet, country boy, Andrew. Her heart ached, and she blinked back tears. She needed to drive. She couldn't be crying.

"Jonathan would have picked a fight he was sure he could win," Gabe growled softly. "Or it would have been Zachary or Brenton."

"Who are together. He would never have caught one of them for a fight alone, and, if he did, he had a strong chance of losing," Troy continued.

"Yeah. So, he probably had Andrew and watched to catch him alone. He probably knows about our recent troubles and went after him."

"We're missing so much about this," Troy bitched from the back. "There are massive holes in this story."

"We're missing too much," Gabe agreed, looking frustrated. "I didn't grab my laptop."

"We can come back to get it," Riley said, trying to maintain some sense of hope. Andrew was in a helicopter above them somewhere, and he was dying. She had a thought. "Gabe, call Thomas. Tell him what's going on. Ask him if he can pick up the laptop and meet us at the hospital. Troy, call Sheriff," she cursed. The bear was going to be so mad at them. "Ask him to meet us there too. Shit."

"Roger that," Gabe said with some formality. It reminded her that she outranked them. In this moment, with none of their top three, she was in charge of the group. The thought made the situation so much worse. Where were Brenton and Zachary?

"Thomas, hey. It's Gabe and I've got some bad news," Gabe whispered into the phone. It almost felt like saying it louder made it more real. Riley heard Troy get on the line with Sheriff, who bellowed from his end about not waiting for him to continue.

"What do you need?" Thomas asked, and Riley felt a desperate shiver run up her spine at the deadly inflection in his voice.

"My laptop from the house. We got out of there as fast as we could to get to Denver," Gabe sighed. "And with how fast Riley is driving, we might beat the helicopter."

"Done. I'll bring all my guys just in case. You might need hands on deck." Thomas hung up on Gabe. Riley raised her eyebrows at the leopard, who shrugged.

"We don't know if having them or not having them in Denver with us will make a difference yet," Gabe whispered as Troy continued to argue with Sheriff, something Riley was tuning out. "They could help keep us alive, or they could be wasting their time. But I need my laptop, so we can...Riley, I just don't know how deep this is."

"Tell me what you know," she hissed.

"We have the bank account, which was used to bribe our information out of different sources. Information that we found on the hunters. The timeline would suggest that the hunters got the information from whomever collected it. Jonathan was also a benefactor from that account." Gabe took a deep breath before continuing, "And now we may have that piece of the puzzle."

"No one needs to pay Jonathan to kill," Troy growled, hanging up on Sheriff as he roared. "Fucking bear. I love him, I do but damn him, he's a stubborn one."

"You're right. And Jonathan would have struck earlier. Someone is pulling these strings." Gabe nodded. Riley only listened. She just wanted to hear it, listen to it all laid out as she stared at the road.

It was a beautiful day. She couldn't appreciate it. Never had the world seemed so colorless.

"So, what was the money for?" Troy mumbled. "We ruined his dad and in turn, him. He just didn't need the cash."

"Then what's the point of the money?" Riley growled.

"We'll never know from Jonathan," Gabe sighed. "He's dead. As for the rest? The rest is easy...I can tell you who and what the money is being used for. All sabotage against us since we got home. A month of just repeated battering from them. I can link nearly all of it."

"And still no idea who's behind it," Troy whispered. Riley looked into the rearview mirror and watched Troy fall back into his seat. "No idea."

"None," Gabe agreed softly. "Once I get my laptop, I'll

start back in on it. And there were some recent transfers that may lead me to something."

"That obscure Pride you were mentioning," Riley flicked a look to him. "What about it?"

"The Kudo Pride?" Gabe frowned. "Reclusive as hell, mostly based in Japan, but known to let other Prides hire them for shit. Security systems and the like. They are really non-violent, so everyone just lets them be. They don't get involved in politics, so I'm not sure what that's about."

"Interesting," Riley mumbled to herself.

"Yeah, Andrew probably would know more about that," Gabe sighed. "And he's…"

"This is bad," Troy grumbled. "This is all so bad."

"Riley, what's going through that head of yours?" Gabe asked quietly, leaning towards her.

She thought about that question. Andrew may not make it through the day. Brenton and Zachary were MIA, whatever that meant for them. She felt the unbridled rage curl in her stomach past the despair at the thought of losing one of them. She thought about what they knew, what they had gone through up to this point.

"Riley?" Troy pressed.

"I think that if we have to burn Denver to the ground to find out who did this, we will," she hissed. She turned her head slightly to meet Gabe's eyes for a moment, who bowed his head.

"We're behind you, one-hundred percent," he told her respectfully.

"Yes, we are," Troy growled, and she caught a glimpse of his dangerous smile in the rearview mirror.

She'd never seen the brothers look more aggressive than they did right then. She knew, in that moment, that the three of them were at war. Gabe had said they were tired, but she saw no weariness in their eyes or in their postures.

"Here's the plan. We get to the hospital for Andrew. We need to be there for him. Gabe, once your laptop is in hand, start digging and do so quickly. If we need to, I'm not above going after someone who might have information we need." She needed to make sure their bases were covered. "We also need to find Brenton and Zachary. Try calling them again after I'm done. God, if anything happened to those two..."

"I'm sure they are fine and just don't know what's happened," Gabe told her, his voice thick with worry over their family and fury at the ones who picked this fight. It didn't relieve her own worry at all.

"I'm going to ask Thomas about protecting Andrew while he's down. He'll live, he fucking better, but that doesn't mean he'll be up and able to protect himself," Riley continued. "Call Brenton and Zachary."

There was too much wrong. Andrew was critically injured and fighting for his life. Brenton and Zachary weren't answering, still. Riley, Gabe, and Troy were on their own for who knew how long.

They continued in silence, Gabe texting Thomas about where to meet them. Troy was in touch with Sheriff, but the bear was pretty mad they had just run off.

"He wanted us to ride with him," Troy whispered after nearly an hour. "He wanted to keep us secure in case this is a big thing. Also, Jessie said she had gotten Brenton and Zachary on the phone before emergency services and Sheriff arrived. So, they know about Andrew."

"Why does that worry me more?" Riley asked, thinking on it. "That they know, but we can't get ahold of them?"

"Because Brenton and Zachary can fly off the handle

just as well as you can," Gabe mumbled. "You've never seen them truly lose it. If there hadn't been cages-"

"They would have ripped heads from shoulders in the hunter compound," Troy finished. "Remember that day, with your dad? How mad Brenton was, and how ready we all were to fight with him?"

"Yeah," Riley sighed. "A Pride is set by the tone of its Alpha. Me keeping Brenton back was the only thing keeping all of you from a fight."

"Yup," Gabe whispered. "Riley, when we find them, I need you to be ready."

"For what?" Riley frowned as she saw Denver come into view.

"This time, you're not going to be exempt from it. There won't be talking Brenton back down, and Zachary is going to be feeding it. It's a powder keg of testosterone and pissed off lion. And it will rile you up. It's going to make you blood-thirsty."

"I already am blood-thirsty," she growled at him. Gabe shook his head as he continued to explain.

"We're angry, and we're scared. And yes, the three of us want blood. Someone is going to fucking pay for this, but..." Gabe trailed off, and she caught him glancing at Troy.

"She's never experienced it," Troy murmured. "Brenton's been under control for a long time. It's been a couple years since he's snapped."

"What's that mean?" Riley asked, suddenly realizing this was something different. She'd seen Brenton angry and furious, dangerous. She knew Zachary had a temper and could fly off the handle. She'd handled it before, so why was this so different. "Snapped?"

"Brenton likes control," Gabe whispered. "He needs it. Our lives have always been so fucking out of control, that once he got his hands on some, he absolutely needed it. He won't let go, and if someone takes it from him..."

"It's been something he's been fighting since everything started happening with you." Troy picked up where Gabe had left off. "Riley, Brenton's going to be on the warpath when we see him. He's going to be..."

"What we left behind," Gabe mumbled. "Gorgeous, when we find Brenton and Zachary, you're going to see why people were too scared to fuck with us before we came back to Wild Junction."

"Good," Riley snarled. "I wouldn't expect any less from you all. Damn it, if Brenton wants to burn Denver to the ground, then we are going to fucking do it. I want you two to be ready and okay with that."

"Riley, you don't und-"

"Do not tell me I don't understand," Riley growled. Fury reignited in her, that scorching blaze that saw her through Abel. That saw her through the fight for her peace of mind. "And if Brenton's not going to do it, I fucking will. I would do it if one of you was hurt. I would do it for any of you. I was hurt, and I handled him. Now one of you is hurt, and I'm going to handle whoever did it."

"And this is why you outrank us," Troy whispered. "Gabe and me? We're just not as rough as you or Brenton or Zachary. We feel it when one of you gets this way, and we'll follow but we...we're just not that dominant."

She felt it in that moment more than she ever had before. She clenched the steering wheel until her knuckles were white. She needed to call on everything in her, because there was a chance it was just them. It felt good, the idea of being in charge, but it was also terrifying. Before, it had been a game, an idea. A thing they toyed with in the bedroom.

Now it was so very real.

"Keep using those heads, and think about if we've missed anything," Riley whispered, feeling dangerous. She felt out of control, violent. She wanted blood. She wanted enemies on their knees before her, begging for mercy. Mercy she wouldn't grant them.

That scared her a little as well, but it wasn't something she was going to tell them. She needed to appear strong, like Brenton and Zachary would. They needed her to be confident in her decisions.

They entered Denver, and Riley listened to the brothers theory-craft what could have led to this. She growled and hissed at traffic, wondered why there were so many police cars driving around.

Then, Troy's phone went off.

"What, Sheriff?" Troy hissed.

"You're in Denver?" Sheriff huffed. "Get to the hospital as quickly as possible. And keep your windows rolled up."

"Why the windows, Sheriff?" Troy asked softly. Riley felt ill at how Sheriff was speaking. The windows were bullet-proof.

"Turn on your radio or check the news. Zachary and Brenton were shot at while leaving the Kingson offices. Zachary was hit twice. That's all I know," Sheriff growled. "I'm getting there with the wolves. We'll be there as fast as possible, but you three have never been in a more dangerous position. People are trying to fucking end all of you. The timing suggests it was right after Andrew was found or during his ride to the hospital. Call me if anything gets in your way. I'm on the line with Denver's police to make sure you are covered. State troopers are about to flood the city, and the SSTF is furious."

Troy and Sheriff ended the call. Gabe turned on the

radio as Riley felt her heart pound dangerously fast. It felt like it would leap out of her chest.

They couldn't get ahold of Brenton and Zachary. Now they knew why.

"-Woods. Sources say that it was a possible hit job, but no one has any real information. Brenton Kingson is holed up in the hospital that Zachary Woods was taken to, and all attempts to speak with him have failed. It's believed that he was the target or they both were."

"Denver's playboys have finally made the wrong people upset?" A female voice. "And where is the rest of their little group of trouble makers?"

"Turn that shit off," Riley snarled. She didn't want to hear a bunch of humans wonder why someone tried to kill Brenton or Zachary. She wanted to know if Zachary was alive.

"This isn't the game," Gabe roared. "This isn't how we fucking do things, you mother fuckers."

"What?" Riley snapped, looking over to him as she was forced to stop at another red light.

"We never do things in the daylight like this. Accidents. Deaths in your bed or your home. You don't fucking try to assassinate another shifter in broad fucking daylight. We live too close to human society for that. We can't just off each other where people can see, the SSTF would take us all in. The SSTF's number one job is to stop exposure. This is going to bring them back in." Troy growled. "Brenton's probably a wreck. He learned about Andrew then gets fucking shot at? Zachary was hit?"

"He probably lost his phone in the madhouse," Gabe mumbled. "And Zachary's phone is probably at the hospital with his other stuff."

"We need to get to the hospital," Riley growled, watching

the light turn green. She slammed on the pedal and felt it kick them all back in their seats. She weaved through the slower traffic, cutting people off.

"Riley, please don't kill us on the way there!" Gabe growled.

She ignored him. If there was one thing Riley did better than them, it was speed. She ran a red, right before the cross traffic could ever start moving. The hospital came into sight, and she didn't bother finding a parking spot. She drove them straight up to the front door and cut the engine, jumping out before Gabe and Troy could say anything.

She ran into the building and marveled at the quiet of it. To everyone else, this was a regular day. To her, it was a nightmare come to life. She would never forget the soft peaceful music they played over the speakers and how at odds it was with her own emotions.

Troy and Gabe were right behind her as she reached the desk with a receptionist.

"I'm looking for several people," she said quickly. "Andrew Hicks, Zachary Woods, and Brenton Kingson."

"And you are?" The woman frowned at her. "Because lots of people are looking for Brenton Kingson. I won't even ask how you know about the other one not on the news."

"Their girlfriend," Riley growled. Riley read the woman's name badge. Heather. "Heather, I don't have time to argue with you."

"Oh really?" the woman scoffed. "Girlfriend? Like I've never heard that one before."

Riley bared her teeth. The Pride's relationship wasn't well known enough for people to buy it, yet. It's why the news people said that Zachary and Brenton were both still playboys. It annoyed the hell out of Riley.

"Look, bitch," Gabe growled. She finally noticed the

brothers behind Riley, and Riley hissed. "I'm Gabe Walker, and if you know what's good for you, you will tell us where they are! If you don't, I will sue this hospital into the fucking ground, buy it, then fire you!"

Riley raised her eyebrows and slowly turned towards Gabe. She knew the brothers were rich, but she'd never seen them flex it. The Walker fortune was nearly at the level of Brenton's, but they just let it sit and did their own thing.

"Ah, yes," the woman stammered. "You must be Riley Stern then. I was told to keep an eye out for you all. Come with me."

"Thought so," Troy growled softly as the woman stood up and began to lead them towards an elevator. "Where are they?"

"Mr. Kingson was given a private room to wait in. Zachary Woods and Andrew Hicks are both in surgery. I was told to make sure you got to Mr. Kingson as quickly as possible."

Riley took a long moment to think about that. Both were in surgery, and they probably would be for hours.

"Why this hospital?" Riley asked Gabe quietly as the woman got into the elevator with them. "It's the same one I was brought to after..."

"This is the only one where...our people work," Gabe whispered to her. "And that means we can hide bloodwork, write off anomalies, and things like that. Nearly every major city on the planet has one hospital we can feel safe going to. Hospitals are also a safe ground, in a sense. The employees just do their job and don't get involved. They help people, no matter the politics."

"That's good," she mumbled as the elevator dinged on the right floor.

"When Mr. Woods and Mr. Hicks are out of surgery, they

will both be placed in this room, for security reasons and at Mr. Kingson's insistence," Heather continued, seeming more flustered than even before. "He's in a very bad mood." She knocked once on the door and the growl that was returned had Riley a bit scared.

"We have it from here," Riley said quickly, hoping her voice wasn't shaking like her knees were. She opened the door and saw him.

She'd never feared Brenton because he was Brenton. She dealt with the fear induced by her troubles knowing it was never his fault.

Seeing him now made her genuinely scared.

His gold eyes nearly glowed with a feral rage she couldn't match. His entire posture screamed that he was on the edge of violence, muscles tense and ready to strike out. His lips were pulled back in a soundless snarl. She wondered if he was about to shift, since his canines seemed bigger than normal. Everything about him seemed just not-quite-human anymore.

"Brenton?" she called softly. He growled back.

Now she understood. Zachary's fast temper was normally right under the surface. Her tiger was capable of great violence, and he was quick to anger, but also quick to step back. Zachary balanced this beast. He was the temper Brenton wasn't allowed to unleash.

Brenton was controlled, a force to be reckoned with. Calm and in charge. When Troy said 'snapped', he'd meant it. The temper that bubbled underneath Brenton's mild tone and business-like approach to all things wasn't even close to human. If something stepped on the toes of this...man in front of her, he wouldn't hesitate to break its neck without a thought.

"Brenton?" she called again, stepping closer. "It's me."

"He knows," Gabe whispered. "He knows it's us. He just needs a moment to reel himself back in."

"I've never seen..." She didn't know how to finish that.

"This is what makes us different from human. Right now, the lion is in charge," Troy mumbled. "We are, at our most basic level, the animal inside of us, not the human skin we wear. Riley, you know this. It was your cheetah's rage that drove you to ruin Abel. This is us. Brenton, being the Alpha he is...he's more. And he's holding back."

"Stop talking about me," Brenton snarled, turning away from them. "If she doesn't understand it yet, then nothing will teach her."

Riley snarled at his words. She did not come for this. Not this asshole from the night of the bar.

"Don't fucking speak about me like that, you goddamn prick," she snapped, stomping over to his side of the room. "You don't get to lash out because you're upset. I won't fucking allow it."

He growled and turned back to her, closing the distance between them. She saw that it wasn't just rage in his eyes though.

"What I am fucking terrifies you!" he roared. "And this entire thing will never work if that keeps up."

"Then stop trying to scare me," she whispered, acknowledging the hurt in his eyes. "Then don't turn this on me. Yeah, Brenton, you are a scary mother fucker right now. I'm not the only person in the room that's scared of you though. Troy and Gabe are, and you weren't a jackass to them. Every human who's probably run into you since this started is scared." She swallowed a lump in her throat. "You are."

"I'm not scared," Brenton hissed.

"You're scared you might lose Zachary, or Andrew, or both," she continued, ignoring his outburst.

"Stop," he growled. She ignored that too.

"I know because I am, too. I'm terrified of losing them. I need them like I need air. Brenton, love, don't push everyone away. Don't try to make this harder on us. Be angry at the right people, don't be angry at me."

"Riley, stop," he commanded, and she felt her mouth glue shut. Fucking asshole. Then he leaned in and kissed her softly. His canines were still somehow too long, and one hooked her lip piercing. He tugged it, cursed softly. He unhooked himself and stepped back. "I'm sorry. I'm not right in the headspace right now."

"Well, I don't think you ever have been," Riley mumbled with an eye-roll. "But today, I can forgive it. Two of our family members might not make it through the day."

"I think it was one shot for each of us," Brenton sighed. "I think Zachary moved in time to take his and mine, the fucking idiot."

"We were told about Andrew by Sheriff," Gabe finally spoke up, coming closer. "Thomas and the pack are also on their way with the bear. They are bringing my laptop. Brenton, we're still flying blind."

"You three know about Slater?" Brenton asked, and Riley was happy to see his eyes were becoming more human by the minute. He was falling back into the tightly controlled Brenton she knew. But now, she had seen the true beast under the skin, and she was never going to un-see it.

"We do," Troy sighed. "We've been thinking about it all for the entire drive here, but we just don't understand."

Riley let Gabe and Troy get Brenton caught up, but in the end, they all knew the same things. Her mind wandered just a little. She remembered the sight of Brenton and thought about it. This was the man she fell in love with. This was the beast that claimed her, sent her to her knees and enjoyed the sight. For a moment, she let the idea of that take her away from the rest.

It made her a little hot. She felt the idea of him behaving that way in the bedroom make her warm and a bit excited. Just for a moment.

"Riley," Brenton coughed. "I'm not sure where your head has gone, but now is definitely not the time."

Oops.

"I definitely want to know what she's thinking," Troy mumbled. "Might help us all deal with this until they get out of surgery."

Riley opened her mouth but couldn't figure out what to say. This hadn't been what she intended.

"Sheriff and the wolves are on their way," Gabe sighed. "We wouldn't have much time."

"I've never been in the bedroom with you two, before," Brenton growled softly. "I'm not too sure I could handle it, anyway."

"Yeah, there's a reason for that," Troy said with a nonchalant shrug. "You and Zachary can dominate all you want outside the bedroom. I don't particularly want you ordering me around in bed. Her? Definitely, but not you."

Riley frowned at the weird conversation they were having. What brought this on? This made no sense.

"We could try," Gabe offered, spreading his hands. "I'm down."

"Shit," Troy mumbled. "We could try. She would probably like it."

"You think?" Brenton murmured, looking back at her. She didn't like the glint in his eyes.

"How did we get here?" Riley asked, feeling a bit freaked out. "We need to be finding out who did this."

"You started it," Brenton purred dangerously.

"I...I was thinking about how you might be in the bedroom, out of control like that," she mumbled quickly. "A thought for another time, trying to think of something else..."

"Ah," Brenton huffed. "We'll shelve our ideas as well."

"You know..." Gabe began, a sly grin coming over his face. Troy looked like he had the same thought.

"Oh, man," Troy chuckled. "Are we thinking the same thing?"

"We've never all been with her." Gabe grinned. Troy grinned back.

"We all know why that's never happened, either," Riley hissed. "The fighting for dominance and other nonsense would be a mess."

"I could step back if I needed to..." Brenton said quietly. "So could Zachary...Andrew would just enjoy the entire scene of it...It could work."

Mad men. Riley was in love with mad men.

"Shelve it," she growled as Brenton leaned to kiss her again.

"Of course, we do need to focus on the task at hand."

"Nothing much to focus on," Gabe reminded them. "We could run over everything we already know, but it gets us nowhere. I'm not even sure I can find the information we need."

"Then what do we do?" Riley asked, frustrated. "What?"

"We wait," Troy sighed. "We wait to see if our family makes it out of this hole."

They did. Riley curled up into Brenton on a couch while the brothers had the hospital's staff bring in a table and some comfortable chairs. 'Comfortable' chairs. She couldn't believe it, but they convinced her they were fine.

An hour passed. Then two. She began to feel uncomfortable with it. The playful mood the guys had fallen into was long-dead, only a temporary bright spot to the dark day they had found themselves in. She stretched while Brenton went to find them drinks and food. No one came with word about Andrew or Zachary. Brenton brought back vending machine trash, but they all ate it without complaint.

They waited.

"Right this way," Heather's voice cut through the thick, overpowering silence. Riley looked at the door, and all four of them were ready to fight as the door opened and Sheriff stood in the doorway.

"Well, hell," Sheriff growled, "I'm impressed there aren't bodies in the room. Would have thought you would kill anyone trying to come in."

"We've had a moment to calm down," Brenton growled back, softly.

Riley saw Thomas, James, and Antonio behind the bear, all slowly making their way in. Brenton was still tense, even as Gabe and Troy calmed down. Gabe began working in silence on his laptop while Troy talked to James and Antonio about protective measures. Her ideas, since Brenton had agreed with them.

"Brenton," Thomas greeted him carefully and Riley realized why Brenton was tense. He was waiting for the other Alpha to bend the knee even in his Pride's moment of weakness, two members down. "I'm here to help. We agreed to be partners in this."

"Thomas. We did," Brenton mildly replied. "But I need to know if I will go home with an ally or a new enemy just waiting for the right moment to strike."

"I'll never be that enemy, Brenton. Not because I like you, though I do. I like her." Thomas pointed at Riley. "And if your Pride falls, so does the little cheetah I've come to consider a friend. She doesn't deserve to fall, and she loves all of you, therefore you don't deserve to fall."

"I knew I liked you," Brenton huffed, holding out a hand. They shook as Riley stood in bewilderment. What the hell? What?

"Wait," Riley cut in, waving a hand around.

"Don't, kitten," Sheriff groaned. "Just don't ask. Let them posture and play. Alphas have to come up with excuses to be allies, and you're the one they chose. They aren't allowed to just be friends. It's ridiculous, but it's how things are done."

"I can't be the only reason," Riley scoffed as Thomas and Brenton began speaking, wandering away from her.

"You aren't," Sheriff chuckled. "You're the only one they're willing to admit in public."

She huffed and narrowed her eyes on the two Alphas. Weird. She knew there were more reasons. She'd heard Zachary discuss them, she'd heard Thomas discuss them. Why would they not bring them up here?

"Don't think too hard," Sheriff groaned, poking her in the forehead. She hissed and glared up at him. "You have better things to worry about than how Alphas play their silly little games."

"You're right," she mumbled, a bit perturbed. More important things. "We haven't heard anything about the guys yet..."

"You probably won't until they are certain they have something to tell you," Sheriff sighed. "Kitten, there's a lot happening. How are you?"

"Angry," she snapped. "Mad as hell."

"Well, nothing is on fire," Sheriff coughed, covering his mouth, "so I don't think that's the only thing."

"I'm worried," she sighed, collapsing back on the couch, "and I have nothing to do right now."

"Let them all work it out," Sheriff groaned, sitting next to her. "You and I can just keep our eyes and ears out for anything about the guys. Want to do that?"

"Yeah," she mumbled, "we can do that."

25

RILEY

Riley fell asleep at one point and woke up to the door opening. The room had fallen silent after discussions had ended hours before. She looked up at the clock on the wall and felt her heart stutter.

Eight hours. Eight long hours.

"Brenton Kingson?" a female voice called in softly. Riley sat up straight and frowned. She didn't recognize the voice very well. A distant memory. Riley saw a flash of ice-blonde hair.

"I thought I told you to meet me here," Brenton growled softly, next to Riley again on the couch. Sheriff was on her other side.

"I had some things to take care of," Jessie sighed, walking in. Riley was astounded to see her again. Jessie Erikson had helped kidnap Riley months before, along with Riley's ex, Trevor. Her world had changed so much since the last time she saw the lioness. Jessie still had the ripped and rocking body that Riley remembered though. "One very major thing," Jessie coughed softly, "but I have been in the hospital the entire time. I promise."

"Well, damn," Thomas groaned. "Now we have a pregnant female in the mix. What in God's name is going on?" He looked over to Riley and Brenton, and Riley felt Brenton shrug with her.

"When I was trying to get to Andrew, knowing something was going down, I realized I couldn't shift," Jessie sighed, rolling her eyes up to the ceiling. "Sure enough, I'm about ten weeks along."

"You can't shift?" Riley asked, confused.

"You don't know any female shifters, do you?" Jessie laid her eyes on Riley. "Once a pregnancy progresses far enough, we can't shift. The science behind it is sketchy, at best, but it's our lot in life. Don't let them knock you up, it's a pain."

"And who knocked you up?" Brenton asked carefully. "And damn, you must have been pregnant when they caught your scent on our property."

"It would have been too early for it really to be noticeable in my scent, but yeah, I've realized," Jessie growled softly. "When I got here, a male grabbed me and asked if I was fucking crazy. I told him I just found out myself, so he ran the lab work and I've been dealing with that. So please, tell me how much more fucked up will this day get?"

"You know about the shooting?" Gabe asked from his spot.

"Yeah. All over the news, still. Whoever is after y'all doesn't give a damn about the rules anymore. They just want you dead." Jessie crossed her arms, and Riley tried to catch her eye. Jessie wouldn't look at her. That irked Riley to no end.

"So, what have you been doing around here?" Brenton asked with care. He stood up slowly but didn't go closer to the lioness, who stayed within a foot of the door.

"I heard about the hunters," Jessie sighed. "And I heard the chatter and bitching from the felines near my area. I settled in Georgia, teaching at a gym. I haven't spent any of your money...well I bought a house."

"And, you came here?" Brenton asked softly. He seemed just as confused as Riley.

"I wanted to offer help. You need numbers, people. A strong front. I owe you all that, all right? I know this all started because my...my old Pride decided to help Cameron. I'm not stupid. So, I felt like I should come back and help."

"Honorable," Troy mumbled from his spot.

"I'm lost and confused," Thomas grunted. "Can someone catch me up on why a pregnant lioness thinks this is partly her fault?"

"She helped kidnap me," Riley offered him. "Someone was trying to bait my mother into revealing herself, a guy named Cameron Slater. They succeeded in kidnapping me. The guys found out how to save me with her help, since she turned on the kidnappers when they got too crazy for her and killed her Alpha. It's a pretty fucked up story, really. Cameron's son, Jonathan, is the person who attacked Andrew today."

"Felines," Sheriff growled. "Thomas, that's really all there is to it. They are fucking felines, and we'll get aneurysms trying to figure it out. Just...don't look too far into it."

"You know, Sheriff, I think you might be right," Thomas mumbled.

"I know I am," Sheriff huffed.

"Alright," Brenton growled. "Jessie, you want to help?"

"Yes," Jessie told him, squaring her shoulders.

"Welcome to the Pride," he growled.

"What?" both Riley and Jessie yelped.

"If you think I am letting a pregnant female wander around in this mess without taking some action about it, you have both lost your minds," Brenton snarled. "Sit down, relax and just...do not fucking get hurt, please. Also, tell Gabe who the father is. We will track him down for you. He can join too."

"Now, wait a fucking minute," Jessie hissed. "I'm not joining your damn Pride. I'll follow orders, you'll pay me, but my Alpha is dead, and I'm not serving a second one."

"Why not?" Brenton growled.

"Because you'll never give me the position I deserve," she snarled back.

Riley raised her eyebrows and looked between them before touching Brenton's shoulder.

"She and Abigail can live together?" Riley offered softly. "Or maybe Finn?"

"You are right, I will not make you my second. Hell, I would not even put you in my inner circle. Can you blame me?" Brenton growled, ignoring Riley.

"No, but that also means I'm not joining your Pride. I'm not a Kingson shifter. I will never be a Kingson, and you'll never convince me otherwise. You fuckers are a breed of your own," Jessie hissed defiantly.

"Fine," Brenton growled. Riley gave up on stopping this. "After all of this, you can disappear again."

"Thanks," Jessie snapped. "Not like I'm as useful as I planned to be anyways."

"She has a point," Riley mumbled. She saw Jessie hold a hand protectively over her stomach. She didn't smell any fear from the lioness, but it made Riley sigh. "Who's the father?"

"I don't know," Jessie mumbled softly. "I've only slept

with humans recently and...well let's say my bedroom has a revolving door at the moment."

"Tell me about it," Riley huffed, looking pointedly around the three of her men in the room, who all just grunted softly. "You must have a lot on your mind. Sit down, relax. We're in limbo on Andrew and Zachary."

"Have you all tried the SSTF, yet?" Jessie asked as James jumped up and freed a chair for her. It was a little sweet, really.

"Why would we?" Troy mumbled. "Those pricks won't get involved."

"Um, yeah they would now," Jessie laughed with derision. "Brenton Kingson and Zachary Woods were shot at by snipers in broad daylight. I guarantee you, they are real fucking involved now."

"But will they help us?" Riley asked. "And would it really help us?"

"Or just leave us appearing weaker than before?" Gabe added as Jessie shrugged.

"You would need to convince the hell out of them, that's for sure. They would just slap the person on the wrist, since it's an annoyance to them to need to clean this up, but I promise you they've figured it out. Or they will sooner rather than later." Jessie sighed. "One of the guys from my old Pride was a prior member. He'd been kicked out after ten years for getting involved in the politics. It would be a risk for whoever you go-"

"Call my dad," Riley told Gabe quickly. "Now."

"No," Brenton snarled. "We are not asking your dad for help."

"Wait," Jessie snorted. "Your *father* is in the SSTF?"

"Yeah," Riley sighed. "He is."

"And your mother is Isabella Gordon?" Jessie continued, looking shocked. "Is that what I'm hearing?"

"Yup," Thomas mumbled from behind her. "That is what you are hearing."

"Good Lord," Jessie laughed. "That's something else."

"Drop it," Brenton growled. "It is not important, and it does not change anything. Riley, we are not asking for his help."

"Damn right, we are," Riley hissed. "He's an in we can use to find out who did this! Who's still doing this!"

"No," Brenton said with a finality that made Riley narrow her eyes. "That's final. Gabe, Troy, if you make that call, I will hurt you."

"Oh wonderful," Gabe mumbled, looking at Troy. Riley hissed at Brenton, pissed.

"Brenton," Riley growled. "We can do this. We can convince him to help us!"

"And if we cannot?" Brenton asked softly. "Can you live with the knowledge your father would let you and the rest of us die?"

She stuttered after that. Brenton was serious. The room got a heavy silence as everyone processed why Brenton didn't want to contact Keith Stern.

He could say no. He could turn the Pride down and let them get torn apart. And that was a final betrayal to Riley that Brenton wasn't willing to risk.

"Okay," she whispered. She wasn't willing to risk it either. Her heart couldn't even take the idea of him denying them. She sat back on the couch with Sheriff. "You're right."

"I am sorry," Brenton said quietly.

"You have nothing to be sorry for," she replied, suddenly weighed down. "Not you."

"Well, damn," Jessie whispered.

"I want you back in Wild Junction. Go to the mansion, I'll have someone meet you there." Brenton sighed at her. "You might as well have the best security money can offer while you're here in Colorado."

"Sure thing." Jessie gave a fake salute. She stood back up and sighed. "Oh, one other thing...did you hear that Abel Cartona was murdered in his cell the other day?"

"No," Brenton growled softly. Riley's head shot up. He was dead? She wasn't sure whether she should cheer or be mad that her plan for him to suffer in prison was ruined.

"Yeah, couple days ago, I think. Someone shanked his dumb ass, thought you ought to know." Jessie shrugged. "Anything I should know about the mansion?"

"There's a security room attached to the garage," Gabe told her, standing up. "Let me get your number, and I'll tell you how to turn it all on when you get there."

"Thanks."

"Jessie?" Brenton called as she was finishing exchanging numbers with Gabe. Riley looked between them. Jessie looked up from her phone with a frown. "Thank you."

"For?"

"Saving Andrew," Brenton whispered. "I am sorry you are getting dragged into this."

"I chose to be in this," Jessie huffed. "I didn't realize the... other thing until today, so, it's not like I was purposefully taking a risk to something other than myself." She waved over her abdomen when she said it. "I'll stick at the mansion in case you all need me to do anything. I might be a rogue, now, but consider this my official declaration of being an ally to the Kingson Pride. And...no need to thank me for Andrew. He fought hard. He's a good male."

"Rogue?" Riley asked quietly, looking to Brenton.

"A shifter, always a feline or wolf, who completely rejects

the Pride or Pack-based lifestyle," Brenton whispered. "Tons of them, and they are normally harassed and thrown out of areas by the ruling Pride or Pack, since they can be seen as a threat."

"Learning something new every day," Riley mumbled.

"I'm going to go," Jessie told them quietly.

"Go on," Brenton sighed. Riley felt drained and realized that Jessie never even spoke to her.

"I'll be right back," Riley whispered to him and walked after Jessie. Once in the hallway, she grabbed the lioness' arm and swung her around.

"Yes?" Jessie asked quietly, looking perturbed at Riley holding her arm.

"I never got the chance to say thank you," Riley said quickly.

"Your Alpha just did," Jessie groaned with a frown.

"For helping me in the cabin," Riley whispered. She watched Jessie pale, and she took a step back from Riley.

"Don't ever thank me for that," Jessie hissed. "Ever."

"Why not?" Riley hissed back. "You might have been a part of it, but you also saved my life."

"I know. And I was hunted for months, myself, by my old Pride as they searched for everyone. I need that entire incident to die and stay dead, Riley," Jessie growled softly. They were both trying to keep the staff from hearing them. A nurse passed and they both watched her walk away before turning back to each other. "Months. They had no idea what happened in the cabin that day. They knew I had been there, and we had all been there. No bodies were there, and no cabin was there when they finally investigated. If they had found me, I would be very dead."

"Why?" Riley asked gently.

"Because, while I saved you and helped your Pride, I

technically betrayed my own. Sure, Trevor killed our Alpha, but he was still..." Jessie closed up and looked away from Riley. "I would prefer if we never bring it up again."

"Are they still looking for you?"

"Yes," Jessie bit out. "They will always be looking for everyone. All those bodies aren't something a Pride can just forget. Sure, they have a new Alpha, and they continued on with business, but they won't rest until they have answers."

"Stay in Wild Junction," Riley offered, carefully. Jessie was obviously easy to spook, to chase off. "It's not just about you anymore."

"What do you..." Jessie looked confused, and Riley watched realization dawn on her. "I can't run from them if they catch up to me and I have a kid."

"No," Riley whispered. "You can't."

"Fuck." Jessie looked even paler than before. "I want to keep it."

"Then keep it...and live in Wild Junction," Riley said plainly. "I know, we have a lot of problems, our little town, but...we have Sheriff, and Thomas with his Pack, and Finn, a fox we met in the compound...Abigail is a doe who's staying in town for a little while..."

"Look at y'all, just building a regular old shifter community," Jessie snorted but she looked thoughtful. Riley had some hope.

"Think about it while you stay on the estate," Riley sighed with a shrug. "And your kiddo can grow up with a ton of other shifters."

"I don't know what its form will be, being a half-breed. Definitely feline, but it would be nice to have another tiger or leopard and shit around, just in case it's not a lion," Jessie mumbled, still thoughtful. She looked back to Riley with a nod. "I'll think about it."

"Good." Riley nodded. "Have a ride back?"

"Yeah, I have my own car," Jessie said with a weak smile. "I'll give your boy, Gabe, a call when I get there."

"Be safe," Riley murmured as Jessie began to walk away.

"You, too."

Riley didn't go back to the room immediately. She leaned on the wall and wondered how they all ended up here. Felines...Plots thick for everyone around them, dragging entire communities down with schemes and dangerous plots. It was all madness.

It didn't have to be. That's what Riley had a real problem with. Other shifters were just fine. Packs fought over land and resources, that made sense. What did felines fight over? Money? Reputation? Respect? Just for fun?

None of it made sense to her. She could understand the animals in them. She could understand Brenton's feral rage, the Pride dynamics, the new concept of rogues, but not why felines felt the need to try and murder children. Or fight over wealth when it wasn't particularly hard for them to get more of it. Petty things like screwing each other's wives became deadly plots where people, innocent people, died.

"What is this fucking life?" she mumbled to herself. Jessie was running from people she once trusted because she decided to save Riley, who had been innocent, herself. What the hell was that?

She didn't know how long she had stood there, propped against the wall, when Troy walked out to her.

"You okay?" Troy inquired softly, leaning his shoulder onto her wall. He looked down with concern, and she sighed.

"Why are felines like this?" she asked, crossing her arms. She kept her voice low and her eyes on the lookout for passing humans. "Why this? Why can't we be more like the wolves or, even better, the bears?"

"That's complicated," Troy whispered with a frown. She glanced at him and saw he looked thoughtful and also...a little worried. "There's a few reasons, I think."

"What are they?"

"We're cunning," Troy groaned. "You know it. You are cunning, even if it's not your go-to thing. You know how to plan and be patient to get what you want. You know what buttons to push to get the response you're looking for. We, as a species, are cunning. We are patient predators, us felines."

"Okay." Riley bit her bottom lip with a nod. "And?"

"I need you to imagine something for me, for this next part," Troy told her cautiously. "Imagine a court. Not a courtroom but...a medieval court. A King or Queen, and the social climbers that dance around them."

"Not a hard visual," Riley snorted. "Where are you going with this?"

"The Kingson family name wasn't always their name." Troy leaned down closer to her and whispered in her ear. "Felines are good at political intrigue. We dance the shifting politics of court. The only thing that's changed is our titles."

"Andrew said that the Kingson family took the king in their name too seriously," Riley mumbled. "Why?"

"Because they used to be kings," Troy continued to whisper. "Pretty girl, we felines are like this because we used to do it in ballrooms instead of boardrooms. Felines, we've always been smart enough to amass wealth and power." He took a deep breath then, and Riley waited, her eyes slowly going wide. "Modern times meant modern changes. We just changed the arena, but since humanity has been able to count wealth, felines have fought over it. We've bickered and played games. And the Kingson family is the last direct line to what once was. You think this is bad? Six-hundred years ago, we would have been taken by a hired mercenary band, and no one would have blinked an eye. You would have never met us because we would have all been dead as children."

"But, why?" Riley hissed.

"Because they can," Troy growled softly. "Because they have the intelligence, and they know players. Because petty squabbles like sleeping with each other's wives ruined families back then. Because illegitimate children weren't just a skeleton in the closet, they ruined a lineage. A mistress could kill the wife because the man held the power to make one of them the most powerful woman on the earth. Riley. I hate it. Gabe hates it. We all fucking hate it. We weren't raised to play the game—we were forced to survive them younger than most others, but this is what we are."

"I'll never participate," Riley snarled.

"Pretty girl...you already have," Troy said with a broken crack to his voice. "You jumped off that ledge. For whatever reason, and yours was a fucking good one, you jumped. You're in this now. People see you as a player, like they do any of us."

Riley opened and closed her mouth. She turned slowly to look at Troy again, and she knew she probably looked shocked.

"I. Am. Not. My. Mother," she bit out slowly.

"I never said you were," Troy growled. "Damn it, you need to learn the distinction. We're all players in a sick game that we need to survive, and it sucks. But, it's not like you picked the fight. You aren't petty like them. You aren't her. I think you worry about becoming her because it might feel so easy to slip that far, but you are too good for that. Are you a touch violent and a whole lot pissed off? Yeah. But you aren't cold or unfeeling."

"There are two types of players," Brenton's voice broke into the conversation. "Those who get the thrill of the game, who play it to the hilt for the sheer rush...and those who play to win the game, no matter the cost. Your mother is one of the first. She does not care. It is a wild game to her, to see how far she can push our straining system until it breaks. You are the second. Most people in the second group play for one reason, and that is survival or love, or some other emotional thing. The difference is the heart. You have one, your mother does not."

"What he said," Troy sighed. "The Pride, we all play for the same thing. To win and live another day. We hold ourselves to some rules: we've never hurt children, and we've never left orphans behind."

"So..." Riley gave a long sigh. "This is just what we are."

"Did it feel good to get Abel?" Brenton asked carefully.

"Yes," Riley said, her voice strong. It damn-well had.

"Then you have your answer," Brenton whispered. "Yes, this is just what we are. But it does not mean it is *only* what we are."

"Well, obviously," Riley snorted. "Why did you come out?"

"I am getting pissed off with no news on either of the guys. I am about to go harass the nurses station." With that, he walked away. Riley pushed Troy gently.

"Go stop him," she hissed. "Before he gets us all thrown out."

"We won't get thrown out," Troy chuckled. "Pretty girl, you missed something important that I just told you."

"What's that?" Riley scrunched her nose at him.

"*King*son," Troy laughed. "And no one says no to the King, pretty girl."

She stuttered. She thought that particular point had been an exaggeration, not a statement of fact.

"You'll need to ask Brenton for the specifics on his family history, but yes...when we felines played in ballrooms, it was his family who stood over everyone and ruled. At least in Europe and most of North America, anyway. I wouldn't say it was a global thing. Though, once globalization started to happen, the more business-orientated Kingsons spread their influence across the globe." Troy chuckled.

"Madness," Riley mumbled. "All of this is madness."

"I know," Troy said, pulling her close to kiss her forehead. "I know."

"And all of you were basically groomed to be his Pride," Riley pointed out, wondering if it were really that simple.

"Yes and no..." Troy made a face as he thought about it. "It was definitely our parents' intentions, and Geoffrey's, but...it didn't go the way they planned. If they had done it their way, if they hadn't been vulnerable, people like Gabe and I would have been used against Brenton at every turn, so our father could gain more wealth. We wouldn't be friends and family. Andrew wouldn't be in the group at all. Zachary...his situation was more complicated because his parents didn't want him at all. His own strength made him an asset, even as a child, to our predecessors."

"Oh, the webs we weave," Riley whispered.

"This is a game that was started decades before any of us were even born." Troy nodded. "Now we just need to survive it."

"When does it end? How does it end?" Riley asked softly.

"It doesn't," Troy told her sadly. "It just doesn't."

Riley swallowed a lump in her throat. That didn't bode well for them.

"Let's get back inside before Brenton gets what he wants," Troy groaned, opening the door for her. She stepped inside just as they heard Brenton growl. Troy gently pushed her all the way in the room and closed the door behind them. "Let's just pretend we didn't hear that..."

"Is everything alright out there?" Sheriff asked, standing up.

"Yeah!" Riley stammered. "Complet-"

"It has been ten hours, you fuckers, I want to know what the fuck is happening!" Brenton roared, making things shake a little.

"Dear God," Thomas sighed, but Riley saw he had a small smile. He thought Brenton was amusing, and she smacked him in the stomach. "What was that for?"

"Don't find this funny," she snapped. "It's not."

"I'm sorry. He reminds me of myself, and I'm glad to see y'all have an Alpha willing to tear down a hospital for you." Thomas groaned, rubbing his stomach. "Please don't do that again. I am an Alpha, remember?"

"Not mine," she taunted and stuck her tongue out at him. Troy threw a hand over her mouth while Gabe growled softly.

"That belongs to us," Troy whispered in her ear softly. Sheriff began to cough. "Not the wolves." He pulled her all the way back to the couch in that position, his arm wrapped around her from behind to cover her mouth. "Brenton will have my balls if he thinks I'm letting you go around with your tongue out."

She licked his hand, because she could, and he pulled it away. Then he wiped it on her cheek.

"Finally!" Brenton snarled outside the door. He barged

back in, looking like he was about to eat someone. "They will have word for us in fifteen minutes."

"Thank god," Riley sighed. "Did they give you any information in the meantime?"

"Both surgeries had a couple complications, but nothing major, other than their initial injuries," Brenton sighed, calming down again. She'd never seen him get riled up and need to come back down so much. "They were waiting for both of the guys to be out of the danger zone and become more stable. Andrew lost a lot of blood because of the trip it took to get here. Zachary had a lung collapse. We will know more when they come in."

Riley's heart clenched. A lung...major blood loss...two of her guys had come so close to dying that it made tears well in her eyes, and the playfulness she had with Troy disappeared...again. Another tiny bright spot on the darkest day of her life.

"Do they know how many of us there are?" Gabe asked, looking around at the motley crew of them. Riley wondered the same thing, and they had been there long enough for the shift to change.

"They are sending in two shifter doctors. They will figure it out before they even open the door." Riley was happy to hear the mild, casual tone come back to Brenton. She didn't know if he was actually calming down or just bottling it up, but he was at least not terrifying the staff.

"So..." Troy sighed. "We wait."

"We keep waiting...Gabe, have you gotten anything?"

"No, Brenton," Gabe conceded softly. "Nothing. I'm sorry."

"It is fine," Brenton growled softly. "It is fine, my man." He patted Gabe's shoulder as he walked by. "Anything else interesting happen?"

"I told Riley about your family," Troy mumbled. Riley watched Brenton slow his walk and begin to tread carefully.

"Why would you do that?" Brenton asked, crossing his arms.

"She asked why felines play games like this. The answer to that question is-"

"Complicated," Brenton finished with a groan, and he looked up to the ceiling as he ran a hand through his hair. "Yeah...So, about five generations ago, my family let the monarchy die and invested everything from it into a more modern power. Monarchies were dying all over the world, slowly but surely. They got out before people could take them out. Then they realized they could remain on top with the new system and way of doing things. They didn't need to constantly rule from a figurative and literal throne, but they could rule in spirit from a mountain of wealth and allies."

"Felines," James sighed. "Always got to be doing something."

"Yup," Thomas huffed. Brenton turned to him slowly. "Now, you are missing some details for her."

"Like?" Brenton asked, a frown causing wrinkles in his forehead, wrinkles Riley had never noticed before. Were they new because of everything going on?

"There's still a small group who thinks you should be completely wiped out. Or the other small group that wants a real feline ruler again." Thomas shrugged. "Either of those could be the problem."

"I ignore them. They are so few, on either side, that they do not have the resources to make a play for it." Brenton sighed. "But you are right. Those two tiny little factions do exist."

"I don't like any of this," Riley mumbled, looking at Troy, who shrugged in the same way Thomas had. A 'this is our world' kind of shrug, and there wasn't anything she or anyone could really do about it.

A knock at the door finally drew their attention, and Riley held her breath. The doctors were here.

"Alpha Kingson?" One called in and Riley's nostrils flared at the scent. It was the doctor who treated her ages ago.

"Come in," Brenton called, and the entire group watched them walk in, tentative and unsure.

"I wasn't expecting so many people here." Doctor Serrano tried for enthusiasm, but it fell flat. Brenton made a derisive noise, and that made the doctor sigh. She hadn't seen the jaguar in a very long time, and their last encounter had been him asking if her Pride hurt her. How things had changed.

"What's the news, Serrano? Tanaka?" Brenton looked between them. Tanaka was looking at Sheriff, nodding slowly.

"Your leg seems perfectly fine now," Tanaka told Sheriff, who nodded.

"Thanks, Doc," Sheriff grunted. "Now tell us how the boys are."

"Ah, Mr. Hicks was my patient. He needed a couple of transfusions. Luckily, we have several mountain lions who fit the bill and offered their help. His most severe injury, however, is the head wound. It appears he was hit with something with great force. He will definitely have a concussion but, he lucked out with no hemorrhaging in his brain. He might have some memory problems, but we need him to wake up, first, to know for sure." Tanaka was completely calm and professional. Riley almost wanted to claw his eyes out. He showed absolutely no emotion. "He's stable, though, and doesn't need any assistance breathing, so we can bring him in here while he recovers. We're just waiting for anesthesia to run its course and keeping him for a few more hours of constant supervision in case we misjudged the head injury. Right now, we believe it should only be some hairline fracturing around his forehead, nose, and left orbital socket."

"Good," Brenton sighed. "Thank God."

"So...he should be okay?" Riley asked, biting her bottom lip. "Andrew will make it through this?"

"The odds are in his favor on this, pending anything unexpected," Tanaka told her, finally cracking a serene smile. She sniffed and realized this patient man was a... bear? A sun bear, she finally pinpointed. The image of his secondary form was firm in her mind after a moment.

"And Zachary?" Troy directed at Serrano.

"Collapsed lung, a spinal injury which shouldn't lead to any paralysis, and a number of internal injuries we had to clean up. One of the bullets passed through, but the other bounced around and caused mayhem. We've stopped all the bleeding for now, but there's still a possibility he will have problems. I recommend absolute care with him in terms of his back. A simple strain on it could further damage the fractured vertebrae and lead to serious issues." Serrano didn't have the same calm as Tanaka. He was uncomfortable in the crowded room, looking around at all of them. "Are we in danger for helping you, Brenton?"

"I don't know, but this is a hospital. So, unless you're deciding to drag it into the fight by choosing sides...I don't think you should worry," Brenton growled softly.

"Of course," Doctor Serrano coughed. "I can also have Mr. Woods down here in a few hours, after seeing how he comes out of surgery and making sure there isn't some bleeding we might have missed. Thank you all for being patient. We're doing our best."

Riley snorted. None of them were truly all that patient, but it wasn't like they could barge into the surgery ward and do it themselves either.

"Ms. Stern, it's a pleasure to see you again." Doctor Serrano took notice of her and she nodded, throwing a small wave. "I trust you've been in good health?"

"As good as can be," she mumbled. "I'm talking to a therapist, now."

"I can imagine," Doctor Serrano muttered, seeming none too surprised by that. "I hope it's going well."

"Definitely," Riley whispered, looking at the floor. She wasn't really seeing Abigail as a therapist, but the friendship with the therapist...well, therapy still seemed to happen.

"After they are moved in here, how long before we can expect them to be awake?" Brenton asked quickly before either doctor could dismiss themselves.

"Zachary, anytime in the next...four to ten hours? Maybe earlier. Whenever he decides to wake up, really. He's just asleep at this point." Doctor Serrano spread his hands with a small shrug.

"Andrew might not wake up," Tanaka whispered, "because of the head injury but we're hopeful he'll be up in the next twenty-four hours."

"Andrew might not wake up?" Gabe mumbled, looking from the doctor to her and finally to Brenton. Riley saw how pale her Alpha was. She remembered that he and Andrew had known each other since they were practically babies.

"Keep us posted," Brenton choked out, looking dazed by Tanaka's admission to Andrew's health. "Keep...please, keep us posted."

"We will, Alpha Kingson," Doctor Tanaka said softly.

And with that, the doctors left, and Riley watched her Alpha fall to his knees and cover his face. She stood and walked slowly to him and touched his shoulder gently. He responded by pulling her close and holding her, his face on her stomach.

"Brenton," she whispered, her own words too thick with pain. "Brenton, we'll make it. He'll make it."

He didn't say anything, just held her. They stayed that way for a long time, until Troy came over and was able to convince him to let her go. Brenton dropped himself onto the couch, and so did every Pride member in the room. It was a tight fit, but Riley was thankful for the bodies.

As the day ticked over into the next, they were still unsure if they would be whole once it was all said and done.

26

RILEY

She didn't move. She ate whatever was given to her. She drank when she was asked.

And she waited.

Jessie called, and Gabe helped her set up the mansion's security.

"Here they come," James whispered from the door. "They are bringing both at once."

"Thank God," Brenton sighed.

Riley swallowed and tensed as the door opened, and she saw Zachary first. Tubes and wires were everywhere. He was paler than she could have imagined. He looked battered, and Riley couldn't imagine he was having a peaceful rest.

She stood up slowly as they positioned his bed and hooked everything back up in his new location.

"Oh my God," Troy mumbled, and Riley turned back to the door as Andrew was brought in.

He was a mess. There was bruising over his entire forehead, and the area around his left eye was swollen to the point she wondered if he could open it. The same bruising went over his nose and across one of his cheeks. It was such a mess that she nearly didn't want to recognize him. The man in that bed couldn't be her Andrew.

"If they wake up, please call us immediately," a nurse told Brenton quietly. She was a wolf shifter, as well. "I'll be giving you a schedule of their regimens, when and who will be delivering their medications. We want you to feel safe here while they heal."

"Thank you," Brenton told her, but Riley could tell he wasn't really paying attention. He sounded distracted.

She stumbled over to the space between the beds and looked between the two pieces of her heart. Two battered, broken, pieces.

"Can I have a chair?" she asked softly and waited. Thomas brought her one without bothering to say anything. She positioned it so her back would be to the wall, and she sat down, curling her knees up to her chest.

Back to waiting.

"Are you okay?" Thomas asked her as she started to zone out, ready for another long battle against her own tears.

"No," Riley whispered. There was no point in lying about it. "Look at them, Thomas. Look at them. After everything, after what we did in Texas, we are still here... with them, hoping they live through the day."

"The doctor said Zachary should be fine, if he takes it easy," Thomas reminded her, kneeling in front of her. "And if you or your guys need anything, you tell me. Ya hear that?"

"You're a good guy, Thomas," she sighed. "You know that?"

"I like to think I have good friends, and they deserve the best from me," Thomas said gently, with a small smile. "Me and the guys don't know how we got so lucky to meet you all in that nightmare. We'll do whatever is needed."

"Keep an eye on my boys?" she asked, searching his face.

"Which ones?" Thomas whispered.

"The ones who can walk and go get themselves hurt, too," she groaned. "I...I need to stay here with these two. I can't miss them waking up."

"I'll do my best," Thomas sighed.

"We are not going to do anything stupid," Brenton said from his spot across from Riley. He sat at Zachary's side, in the back corner of the room where he could see everything. "We do not even know what we are going to do next."

"That is a problem," Thomas grunted. "The boys and I would fight for you, but we need a target. We need the who."

"If they went through all of this," Troy spoke up from Andrew's side. "They will try again. We're two Pride members down..."

"If we weren't on our knees before this," Gabe whispered. "We are now..."

Brenton's growl shocked them.

"I go to my knees for no one," he snarled. Riley looked back over to him slowly. There was a fury in his eyes that she could relate to, and yet it was deeper than she could muster.

She was tired. She understood it now, what Brenton, and Gabe, what they all had told her. It was exhausting, holding on to the fight, the rage, to see the next day. The constant battering from outside forces coupled with the need to continue moving forward to survive.

"I bet that isn't true," Thomas growled back. "And you can't fix this if you don't admit it's all gone to hell."

"Thomas," Troy snapped quickly. "Do not push him."

"He's right," Riley sighed, and they all turned to her. She met Brenton's eyes. "We're on our knees, Brenton. We could soldier on through Cameron, and hunters, and politics...but we can't soldier on through this. We're on our knees. The ground we had has been yanked out from underneath us."

"Riley," Brenton growled softly.

"No, Brenton," she hissed. She pointed at Zachary between them. "Look at him. Then look at Andrew. Then you tell me how we haven't been brought down to rock-fucking-bottom. Because, let me tell you, I am. I thought I had reached the lowest point of my life in that fucking compound...I had no idea how much worse it could get, and I'm not even the one hurt."

She couldn't hold back the tears any longer. She placed her head on her knees and cried. No one said anything. No one judged it.

Her heart was shattered at the lifeless-looking bodies that surrounded her. Andrew may never come back. Zachary may never be the same.

Thomas backed away from her slowly. One didn't touch another Alpha's lover when the lover was emotionally vulnerable like this. It was Troy who ran his hand through her hair, comforting her. She could smell his own tears now that he was close.

"We need a plan," Gabe whispered to someone. "We need to figure out how to survive this. We can't hide in a hospital until these two have hopefully healed then figure it out. The likeliness that we're all dead before either of them wake up is only growing."

"Every shifter on the planet is now watching," Thomas mentioned as he retook his seat. "Every single one. Even though you kids are young, you have a name and a reputation. You also have the history of the Kingson Pride behind you. Everything you do, until this is resolved or you fall, will be watched."

"You are right," Brenton sighed. "It's six in the morning?

I'll head to the condo, clean up, address the press and get back to business."

"You could get hurt," Riley growled softly. "I don't want you out there."

"I do not have another option, Riley," Brenton growled softly.

"Stay here," she whispered.

"He can't" Sheriff groaned from his spot. "He just can't. It's one thing to hide in the hospital while waiting on word for Zachary and Andrew, but he can't hide now. The longer he hides, the weaker you all appear to be."

"But you don't have to go out alone," Antonio spoke up softly. "Take the brothers."

"And leave Riley here by herself?" Brenton snarled. "Are you mad?"

"She's not by herself," Thomas snapped. "You think we would all just leave her here in the hospital while you go out and do what you need to do? Don't be daft, Brenton. It doesn't look good on you."

Riley felt that verbal tongue lashing from across the room.

"This is why I'm not friends with other Alphas," Brenton hissed. Riley bit her bottom lip. Was Brenton's stubbornness going to chase off their only allies? Thomas was a friend, not just to her, but also to Zachary.

"I've got age and experience on you," Thomas growled. "And military training to protect her. I'm not stepping on your toes by being the ally that I promised to be. Or a friend to her. Quit your shit."

"Men," Riley mumbled, looking to Troy.

"Men," he muttered back in a deadpan tone meant to amuse her. It nearly made her smile.

"Cute," Brenton growled at them. She met his gaze and watched his eyes soften. "Okay."

"Good. I wasn't intending on leaving unless you killed me first," Riley huffed. "I'm going to be here when they wake up."

"I know," Brenton sighed, running a hand through his hair. "They wouldn't want it any other way. Troy, Gabe...let's get back out there."

"I hate all of this," Gabe grunted. "Let's go look like nothing's wrong."

"Impossible," James threw out. "But definitely try."

"Thanks for the vote of confidence," Troy groaned, kissing Riley after he sent a glare at James. James only shrugged.

"We can hold things down here, but what goes on outside this room is more important. You aren't just down two Pride members, you're missing your Alpha's two closest. This is bad shit." James sighed. "We're all going to die. The other felines will never forgive us for being Kingson allies as the Kingson Pride fell."

"Probably," Thomas snorted. "Let's die on our feet though."

"So much confidence," Gabe bit out, shoving his laptop away. "I'm so happy to have the wolves around. Troy, let's get the fuck out of this stuffy ass room before I try to murder them."

"Good idea." With that, Riley watched the leopard brothers exit, both mumbling angrily about how the wolves were pushing buttons. She looked over to Brenton, whose narrowed eyes on Thomas concerned her.

"Funny," Brenton snarled. "Keep her safe, Thomas. Sheriff, I'm counting on you too."

"Will do, Brenton," Thomas chuckled.

"We got it from here," Sheriff confirmed, throwing a hard look at Thomas.

Brenton walked over to her, swooped down for a goodbye kiss and left without another word.

"I don't need all of you being assholes," Riley hissed at the wolves. "What the hell?"

"They would have dragged their feet if we made it easy for them to be here," James sighed.

"And you want them going out there pissed off and ready for war, not down and defeated," Thomas added. "You just worry about these two. Let those three do what they do best."

"What's that?" Riley growled.

"Play the game," Thomas whispered.

She didn't converse with any of them after that. The wolves made a schedule to be guards outside the door. Sheriff spoke to his wife about remaining in Denver. He also called his deputies about Jonathan Slater's body. Andrew had legal problems as well. No one knew what happened in the trailer except him and Jonathan. Jonathan was dead.

She looked over Andrew and gently touched his unbruised cheek. A tear rolled down her face at the sight of him. She didn't want to imagine what Jessie had found. What he might have looked like on his way to the hospital.

"Be okay," she whispered to him. "You both have to be okay for me. The Pride needs you, love."

Her words were ignored by the other shifters in the room. She could only hope Andrew heard them. She wanted the rage back, she wanted the anger. She wanted to be furious and fight, but Andrew's battered face was a stark reminder of failure. Zachary's still body was a constant reminder of their problems.

She was tired of it all. She just wanted things to be

normal again. She wanted concerts and picnics and new piercings. She wanted new tattoos and races cheering on Gabe. She wanted coffee in bed with whomever else was there. It could be one of them or just her and Star.

"Shit, Star," Riley groaned. "That poor cat." She turned to everyone else. "Do any of you have Jessie's number from Gabe? I want to make sure my cat doesn't starve."

"It's good," Thomas told her with a smile, "that you remember the world keeps spinning through all this. Gabe told her about Star. You must have missed it. Your cat is fine and happy. She apparently likes Jessie more than the guys."

"My cat has her priorities right," Riley chuckled, laying her head down on Andrew's bed. She would give him a load of attention before turning to Zachary. "She knows that all my guys seem to be bad news."

"Boys are bad news, period," Sheriff grunted.

"Mmm." Riley smiled to herself. "But they lead to such good times."

"Things I never wanted to hear," Sheriff growled. She gave a weak laugh, while the wolves snickered at Sheriff's uncomfortable muttering over never needing to hear about Riley's personal business.

"I love them so much, it hurts," she whispered after a few moments. The laughing died down, and one of the wolves left the room.

"I know, Kitten," Sheriff said gently. He rubbed her back, and she sat up and looked at Zachary's bed. She turned her chair, so she could finally give him some attention.

Looking at him, there, she realized he could have just been asleep. The bullet wounds weren't visible. He seemed to just be in a deep sleep. She took his hand and squeezed gently.

"I need this to stop," she mumbled, too full of emotion. "I need this to end up okay."

"We'll figure it out," Sheriff lied to her. Never had Sheriff lied so blatantly. It was all over his scent, all over his posture, and filled the words.

She didn't call him out on it because she wanted to believe the lie. She needed to believe the lie.

27

GABE

G abe showered quickly, ignoring his brother who shaved just as fast. They all had grown some nasty stubble over the last twenty-four hours.

"I think I know what we need to do," Gabe mumbled as he turned the water off. "But...it will be a fight."

"What are you thinking?" Troy asked, rinsing off his razor. He rubbed a towel over his face while he looked over to Gabe.

"We need to try and swing some help from Keith," he sighed. Troy cursed.

"Brenton will never go for it. I can't blame him. I don't particularly want to see how much that ass doesn't love his daughter," Troy growled. Gabe knew he was frustrated and could empathize. He was, too, and it was beginning to eat at him. He scratched aimlessly at his arm before forcing himself to stop.

"Brenton has to be the one to do it," Gabe whispered. "He's the only one who has a snowball's chance in hell of convincing Keith to help us."

"Yeah, I know..." Troy sighed. Gabe looked into the mirror and met his brother's silver, mercury eyes. Troy was never colorful, but he seemed downright washed-out in that moment. Exhaustion, pain, sadness, and regret all warred in those eyes. "We would need to have a solid argument for it."

"All of us dying," Gabe grunted. "All of us dying, including Riley is the argument."

"Well, shit."

"Yup."

GABE WATCHED Brenton sit down at his desk and waited patiently for the right time.

They had been in meetings all morning. Condolences from every single piece of shit they saw. People looking at Gabe and Troy, realizing that Brenton had to call upon the two lowest-ranking members of his Pride just to have backup. They were a small Pride, but it had never been like this. Gabe and Troy were last resorts, always, and for good reason. Zachary had the legal expertise and the brute strength. Andrew was a kind face that knew how to read people.

Troy and Gabe did paperwork. They had proven in their earlier years that being much more was a pointless endeavor. Their problems had been their focus, and they didn't normally do the public side of the fighting. They could handle the behind-the-scenes shit, but most of the Pride's enemies never saw them.

"You have something on your mind, both of you. Say it now while we have a break," Brenton sighed.

"I was just thinking about how Troy and I never do this

kind of stuff," Gabe mumbled. Troy coughed and glared at him. Shit. This was Gabe's idea and he knew Troy wasn't going to bite the bullet for him. "And something else."

"What is it?" Brenton asked, frowning at him.

"I'm stuck. I don't have the tools or resources to find out who's behind the account. I think we need to ask...or beg, for help," Gabe groaned. "Brenton, I've been tracking Keith's every move since he left. Obviously. He's still here in Denver, working through the SSTF's Denver office, on the fall of our Pride. We need to take the risk."

"I will not ask that man for anything," Brenton growled.

"Stop being a stubborn ass, Brenton!" Troy roared, shooting out of his chair. "We've done all we can! Zachary and Andrew are down. Andrew might not come back...We don't have options anymore. We need to start using every resource we have, and Keith is a possible resource. His fucking daughter is drowning in this, just like we are."

"If he says no, Riley never has to know. She never has to know we even tried," Gabe whispered, grabbing his brother's arm. "Brenton, we're out of options. This is all we have."

"And who would go beg?" Brenton asked, looking furious and nearly defeated. "Who?"

"You," Gabe said, feeling the ache of knowing it would kill his Alpha to do it. "It has to be you. If one of us went, Keith could very well laugh us out of the room. But you're our Alpha. Your going is a sign, a show, to him that this is it for us."

"I hate both of you sometimes," Brenton growled softly. "You know that?"

"Yeah," Troy grunted. "But Zachary would say the same thing. Andrew. They would both agree. It's time to take the risk. Damn, Brenton...we've been through so much. But this is bigger than anything we've ever handled."

"Zachary and Andrew are currently incapacitated," Brenton hissed.

"If it were me and Troy, they would lose their minds, too!"

"So would I!" Brenton roared, standing up so fast that papers flew off his desk. "Any of you!"

"Then go talk to Keith," Gabe sighed. "Because it could be us next time. Or Riley...or you. Brenton...we're falling apart. This might already be too broken to fix, but damn it, we can't ignore our last option."

Brenton growled softly. Gabe just waited. He'd backed Brenton into a corner on this. He'd never seen Brenton make so many mistakes before, but they had been trying to play this like normal felines instead of like the Pride they were.

"Riley told us in the car that she would do anything for the information we needed," Troy whispered. "Anything. You might have struck the idea down while she's hurt and reeling from Andrew and Zachary, but I bet once one of them wakes up, you're going to hear this again. She's going to put her foot down. Zachary will. Andrew would."

"So, you two are trying to get me to do this now," Brenton sighed, turning away from them. "How did we end up here?"

"We're not playing our game," Gabe told him, walking closer. He sat on Brenton's desk and looked out the same window. "We're playing their game. We need information to shift this back in our favor. We need to play our game, our rules, our schedule. We need to know who they are. Hell, we need to find the person or persons who shot at you and hit Zachary."

"You are right," Brenton mumbled. "We have not been playing our game."

"Will you go?" Troy asked, taking the other side of Brenton.

"I'll go."

28

BRENTON

Brenton silently stood in the hotel lobby, keeping an eye out for any agents he could recognize. Gabe had told him that Keith and his team all had rooms here for the duration. Keith was room 405. Brenton spent a second debating between taking the stairs or risking the elevator.

"Fuck," he muttered distastefully. Brenton was about to beg a man he hated to help save his Pride, a Pride that included his daughter. He reached the elevator and waited. He hoped no one would call the press about his presence there. He'd already released a statement saying he was working with the authorities about the situation. He wasn't, but he knew better than to say he was going to find who did it and murder them.

The authorities wouldn't help anyways. Brenton clenched his hands. The SSTF would have told the Denver police department to stand down. A police chief somewhere was learning about shifters and being sworn to a lifetime of silence in exchange for not pressing this or making it more public.

Games. Rules. Players.

In the end, Brenton was trying not to strangle every single one of them. He wanted to toss the figurative game to the floor and eviscerate the opponent who refused to step out and show themselves.

"What floor?" A man asked Brenton as he stepped on the elevator with a small crowd.

"Fourth, thank you," Brenton said, trying hard to maintain the calm he was known for. The mildness. He worked hard to keep it, since the lion under his skin was normally too intimidating. Brenton had mastered it when his father beat him for being more dominant than him. By the age of ten, Brenton could talk like a businessman that ran companies with a deceptively gentle nature. It was something he kept up over the years, as he noticed humans didn't tolerate him very well when he wasn't in control of the lion.

Brenton almost missed his floor, he was so lost in his thoughts, but being on Keith's floor made him remember with sudden clarity how he had gotten there.

Brenton was stumbling. He was unsure of himself for reasons he didn't understand. Hunters. Riley. His feelings. Keith. The SSTF. Zachary. He couldn't find the root of his uneasiness.

He'd never loved a woman like her. The Pride had always been his brothers, but now the stakes seemed higher, and he was failing.

He walked slowly to Keith's door and pounded on it. He knew Keith was in his room. Gabe had confirmed it before Brenton entered the building. Security cameras had caught him going to the ice machine and returning.

The click of the lock being released made Brenton tense. The door opened slowly.

"Liam, I thought I told you-" Keith's eyes went wide at the sight of Brenton.

"We need to talk," Brenton said politely. Keith nodded slowly, opening the door completely and allowing Brenton to walk in.

Brenton looked around. He'd never been in a normal hotel room. The tiny, cramped one-room standard. There was a small kitchenette, a coffee maker, a bottle of Jack Daniels on the counter. A recently poured drink. Brenton took a long sniff, paying attention to what he caught.

Keith had been drinking, that much was obvious, now that Brenton was looking for it. He shouldn't have missed it when the door opened, but he was very good at ignoring scents. Every shifter got good at it as they grew up, or they would be constantly distracted by things.

"Why are you here, Brenton?" Keith asked, locking his door.

"To ask for your help," Brenton said quietly, letting that sink in for Keith before continuing. "The Pride is on its last leg. We do not know who is doing this. We do not know who shot Zachary. We do not know where Slater fits in on all of this. You are cleaning up the public side of this, and I am asking you for your help."

"You want to know what we know?" Keith carefully inquired.

"Yes." Brenton felt his heart clench. His Pride was crushed at the idea of it. He'd never needed this. He'd never wanted to beg for help. "Keith, I have two guys in the hospital. One might be crippled if we are not careful, the other might never wake up at all."

"Which one might not get up from it?" Keith asked, grabbing his drink.

"Andrew," Brenton whispered.

"He's the good one of you lot," Keith grunted. "Damn shame."

"Everyone loves to underestimate him," Brenton sighed. "Slater did."

"Why would I risk my career for this?" Keith scoffed. "Andrew is a good kid. But you? Brenton, you are your father's son. Everyone in the SSTF knows it."

Brenton snarled at that.

"See?" Keith pointed at him with his glass. "Violence first."

"We have been trying a nonviolent approach, and it is failing. People are getting hurt," Brenton growled.

"A bunch of renegades who never followed the rules," Keith said with disgust. "You had to think it would catch up with you eventually. The bodies, the disrespect to other felines. Nearly a decade of it, you had to know that eventually one of the more powerful enemies you have would strike hard."

"Your daughter," Brenton snapped.

"Excuse me?" Keith stumbled, glaring at him.

"Your daughter is going to get hurt," Brenton growled. "And she doesn't fucking deserve that, no matter what you think about her actions. She is fierce and gorgeous and her heart is too fucking big to be destroyed. And here you stand, judging me and the guys I grew up with like you fucking know something."

"She can walk away," Keith mumbled. "She's not in too deep..."

"Liar," Brenton snarled. "We both know that is not true."

"You never should have dragged her into your world," Keith groaned.

"She never would have been, if you had stuck around for her," Brenton hissed, a meanness settling in him. It was time for a slap of reality to the entire affair. "She would have gone to college and become a great painter. She might have gotten the Fever and shifted, but she would have had a father who fucking loved her-"

"I do love my daughter," Keith roared, throwing the glass. "I just..."

"Have some real fucked up priorities," Brenton snarled. "You went from wanting to avenge your dead wife to wanting to repair your make-believe honor over being tricked by her. And then you let the SSTF fuck your daughter sideways and leave her with nothing."

"Don't..."

"Don't what? Tell you that the people you work for are just as corrupt as the rest of us?" Brenton roared. Riley had told them what Keith had said. It had all made so much sense. Brenton knew there was more than one feline at the top of the SSTF. It was something they would do. They didn't out Riley for being Isabella's daughter. Instead, they decided to make her life so hard that she could never rise up. With a stubborn mule of a father like Keith and Isabella's pure cunning evil, Riley, in theory, was a threat to the stability to the feline world. Shit, the shifter world.

The Pride's little cheetah was a force to be reckoned with. And she'd been brought to her knees by two men in hospital beds, a father who didn't know how to love, and so much more.

"They screwed your daughter. They screwed your being in her life in the process. They could have set her up with a shifter family who understood her, who could have introduced her slowly to the world and kept her out of danger. Instead they threw her into foster care," Brenton growled. "You blame me, her mother, all of this, for creating the girl who only ever wanted you to love her, but you refuse to take part of the blame or even level it at the SSTF. They fucked you. They fucked her."

"Why does this matter?" Keith sighed. He looked at the shattered glass on the floor and grabbed a small bag. Brenton watched him begin to clean up.

"I'm trying to get you to understand that your career with the SSTF is meaningless," Brenton snarled, "because it was built on the idea of using you against Isabella, and it was strengthened by the pain your daughter had to go through, so you could run off on your little quest. And now you hide behind it like you are somehow better than us."

"Where is she?" Keith asked, slowly picking up pieces of glass.

"At the hospital, a complete wreck."

"Does she know you're here?"

"No."

That made Keith look back up and narrow his eyes.

"Why not?"

"Because I did not want her to know if you turned me down. She does not deserve to hear 'I love you' from you, then know that you are okay with letting us die." It was a harsh, bitter truth that struck Keith. The human's hands began to shake. "Why are you drinking at ten in the morning, Keith?"

"Because I've been thinking about something Sheriff told me," Keith sighed. Brenton could smell tears. "He told me I already failed the most important mission of my life... and he's right. I've been here, watching you all fall, and trying not to remind myself that my daughter is a part of this. That she can...she will die with all of you. Because she's too much like me...She'll fight to the bitter end for what she wants."

"You always compared her to Isabella," Brenton said

carefully. Keith was hammered, and it was beginning to show. Brenton wasn't sure if he should use it against the poor, sad man or walk away before he accidentally broke him completely.

"Because I never wanted to admit that her temper comes from me," Keith groaned. "Lily was calm, always so calm. She didn't have that fire. She was a balm, easy going. Peaceful. Riley gets her temper from me. She's...she's so much my daughter that it hurts so goddamn much."

"And you do not know how to fix it," Brenton whispered sadly. "Fuck, we are more alike than we knew, Keith."

"What?" Keith's words were becoming slurred. Brenton went to help him clean up the glass and threw it away. He helped Keith off the floor and to sit on the edge of the bed.

"Keith," Brenton sighed. "We can fix this. Not apart, but together we can fix this. I can stop people from hurting her and you...Damn, I can help you fix things with Riley."

"We need each other," Keith mumbled. "Fuck. I hate you."

"I hate you too," Brenton groaned. "Can you get me what I need?"

"Yeah," Keith hiccupped as he said it. Brenton nearly pitied the man. He was destroyed by a woman he loved, then accidentally destroyed the other one. He'd been pulled into their world without ever realizing it. How could anyone have expected this man to pick up the pieces of his heart and just move on after losing his wife? He was intelligent, trained to figure it out and complete the mission.

"Did you drink after..." Brenton wasn't sure how to phrase it.

"Yeah...Riley was too young to know, but I drank a lot after losing Lily. Suddenly I was a single father, no future ahead of me. My life's work down the drain...Yeah, I drank a lot until I found the SSTF."

"You should talk to Troy and Gabe, one day," Brenton told him softly. "They both deal with addiction problems."

"I've heard...Those boys are too young to have gone through all that," Keith grunted.

"We all are," Brenton murmured sadly.

"Fuck...you're only twenty-nine..." Keith groaned, rubbing his forehead. "It's easy to forget."

"Do you want me to stay?" Brenton asked gently.

"No...I'll get the information to the hospital...But, Brenton, this is closer than you realize. That I can safely say here."

"Are we being listened to?" Brenton tensed and nearly cursed to himself as Keith shook his head.

"No, but it's almost eleven. I'm about to have a meeting with my team I can't miss."

"Can you make it to that this drunk?" Brenton frowned at the older human.

"Yeah, half of them will be, too," Keith chuckled. "We're a bunch of fucked up fools, my team. We actually had to do your protection detail because we're in trouble already for some other shit."

"Good Lord, and you all are supposed to uphold the law..." Brenton groaned, running his hand through his hair.

"Get out of here before one of them comes to tell me everyone is ready. And Brenton?" Keith grabbed his arm.

"Yeah?" Brenton didn't know what to think.

"Thank you for loving her," Keith mumbled. "No matter who her mother was and what that woman did to your family."

"I will never judge someone on the actions of their

parents," Brenton whispered. "And she is an honor to love. Help me keep her around."

"Of course. If it gives me any chance to know her again, I'll do it," Keith continued to mumble. "Go on, young man."

Brenton got out of the room faster than he thought possible. Tears were in his eyes. Keith was a broken man who had lost everything, from a combination of his own actions and a world he didn't fully understand. Felines were getting out of control in their games, if the SSTF was sly enough use Keith like this and ruin not only Riley but also him as revenge against Isabella.

Brenton didn't like thinking about that. The SSTF was not his concern. Keith, maybe, but not the organization he worked for.

He slipped onto the empty elevator and sighed.

Back to waiting.

Back to the games.

Back to wondering who the players were until Keith came through for them.

29

RILEY

R iley sat in that room for hours. She played cards with James, Antonio, and Sheriff for much of it, while Thomas held guard at the door just in case.

"Have you slept yet?" James asked her as he dealt another hand.

"No," she mumbled. She was exhausted. It was now hitting twenty-four hours after she had learned Andrew was attacked.

"I got a nap in earlier, you should go do the same," James continued. "I say this because you tried to say you had a pair of nines but one of them was a six. You should get a nap in."

"No," she mumbled again. She would sleep when at least one of her guys was awake. She would sleep when Brenton or one of the brothers got word to them on a breakthrough on this. She would sleep when they had a real plan.

"Alright," James sighed, looking away from her to Sheriff, who gave a shrug.

"She's not going to go to sleep until she passes out on the

table," Sheriff told James. "I'll make sure to put her on the couch when that happens."

"Screw you," she muttered, glaring at the bear.

"Don't get feisty with me," Sheriff growled softly. "I'm here to help you and the boys. I'm not here for your attitude, Kitten. I'm here to make sure you all make it through, and I'll be damned if Brenton gets back or Zachary wakes up and they get pissy about you not sleeping."

"One more round, then," Riley yawned, barely covering her mouth.

"Fine," James threw in some chips. "Let's get this going."

They had barely started when Thomas opened the door, looking confused at them.

"Riley," he called to her. "There's someone here to see you or anyone from the Pride."

"I'll handle it," she sighed, dropping her cards on the table. She got up slowly and ignored the sway and stumble as she did. She really did need to sleep. When she got to the door, she could smell him. She straightened her back and prepared herself for a moment. "I've got it, Thomas."

"I'll stay close," he mumbled to her as she passed him.

Riley looked over her dad warily. He looked like a mess. He'd been clean-shaven the last time she saw him, but now he sported a beard that looked a little unkept. He reeked of alcohol, and his clothing was casual and wrinkled.

"Riley," he greeted her carefully. "I was hoping for Brenton or..."

"Any of the guys?" she offered, walking a little closer. "Why?"

"I brought something." He spoke like a child who was caught with his hand in the cookie jar. His words were a bit slurred. "I might have gotten here earlier than they thought I would..."

"Why are you here?" she pressed as he patted his pockets.

"I can't keep watching this," he told her, slurred and soft. "I'm sorry, I can't find..."

She waited, tapping her foot on the plain tile floor. She was tired, confused, and losing patience with the drunk man in front of her.

"Why are you drunk?" she asked, finally grabbing his jacket and pulling him out of sight from the curious nurses.

"Ah, daughter, I'm sorry," Keith groaned. "I never wanted to see how much of my daughter you were...There's no way you aren't mine...You only look like her, but you couldn't be more different as a person."

"Dad?" She frowned at him and looked over to Thomas, who shrugged, looking worried and confused himself.

"Brenton gave me a verbal beat down earlier," Keith mumbled. "And Sheriff did while I was in your home...I'm so stubborn, and I'm sorry. Oh, fuck there it is," Keith finished, pulling a small USB stick out of his pocket. "Tell Brenton, I did my part. Riley...you never deserved any of this. Not me, not what I let the SSTF do to you...Not the kidnappings, not the hate, or my judgement. I hope you remember I do love you."

She took the USB slowly, wondering who the man in front of her was. She also hoped he hadn't driven. She would file away what he said about Brenton for when she had her Alpha in front of her.

"Do you want to come in and sit down?" she asked softly.

"No, I can't look at those boys in there," Keith grunted. "We let it happen. The SSTF. We knew it was about to go down, and we were told to stand down and just do clean up. But...Riley, I don't want you to die. I don't want you to be alone anymore, either. I hate them, those boys, but they are so much better to you than I ever have been."

Riley swallowed a lump in her throat. She couldn't say anything as he sighed and leaned on the wall.

"I drank a lot when you were little, after Lily died," he mumbled. "I ignored you when I could get away with it, when you wouldn't notice. I barely knew you...barely knew who this daughter of mine was, even as a babe. I didn't think. And then, I started to completely ruin your life after I joined the SSTF...then I left you."

Riley bit back her own tears. What was this? Her father had only put on a strong, stubborn front. Who was this vulnerable man with her? Why was his apology, years too late, making her want to cry?

"I don't think you'll ever forgive me," Keith said as he gasped for air. "I convinced myself you were Isabella's daughter and had nothing of me in you. It made it easy to push you away and forget the broken man left with a six-year-old girl after your mother..."

"Dad..." Riley tried for words. She wanted to hate him. She felt it building in a small portion of her heart.

The rest of her foolish heart was just happy to hear that her father actually did love her and was willing to admit he screwed it all up.

"I should go," he mumbled. "They are going to fire me for this."

"Would that be a bad thing?" Riley asked gently.

"I don't know anymore," Keith groaned. "I guess I'll find out."

"Dad, did you drive here?" She touched his arm and he shook his head.

"I had one of my guys call me an Uber, that stupid taxi app thing," Keith mumbled.

"I'll have someone here call you one," she whispered. "Or I'll have Sheriff drive you back to...where are you staying?"

"DoubleTree, in the middle of downtown, close to the office," Keith answered her.

"Hold on," she told him and looked over to Thomas, who was wide-eyed and shocked. "Watch him?"

"Yeah..." Thomas mumbled.

"I know you told me there was history here, but I think he's got other things on his-"

"You're a smart man, Thomas," Keith chuckled. "Avoiding the SSTF like you did."

"Yup," Thomas groaned, grabbing Keith as he swayed. Thomas looked at Riley and bared his teeth. "Believe it or not, tons of their force are drunks. There are some costs to living the life they do."

"I can believe it," Riley muttered, going back into the room. She looked at Sheriff and sighed, wiping her face off. She was exhausted and emotional and none of this was okay with her. "I need a favor, and if you do it, I'll lay down for a nap."

"Anything, Kitten." Sheriff smiled, standing up.

"Drive my father back to his hotel," she started, then held up the USB stick. "And take this to Brenton in his office."

"Brenton just called your phone, he's on his way with the brothers," Antonio told her with a raised brow. "What's that?"

"I don't know. My dad just said, 'tell Brenton I did my part'," Riley sighed. "Can you drive him back, Sheriff? He's drunk."

"Well, damn," Sheriff groaned. "Yeah, should have figured this was going to happen, with an agent like him. I'll handle him, then give his team a damn beat down for letting him wander around by himself in this situation."

"Maybe you should leave the rest of the SSTF out of this," Riley suggested, remembering what her dad had said about being fired.

"Maybe," Sheriff grunted, and Riley didn't like how angry the bear sounded. She watched him walk out and just stayed in the room as she heard Thomas and Sheriff tell Keith it was time for him to go get some sleep.

"Is this seriously a thing?" Riley mumbled, looking at James and Antonio.

"Thomas had a bout of alcohol problems while he was in the Marines," Antonio told her, frowning. "When lives are constantly on the line and you see the shit they do..."

"Yeah," Riley huffed. "I get it, I just..."

"He's your dad, and it must be hard knowing that the asshole that is Keith Stern is also a man fighting his own demons," James sighed. "I take it you won't be napping until you get that thing to Brenton."

All these guys, and they cared too damn much.

"I accidentally lied to Sheriff," Riley mumbled. "I have no intention of sleeping, now."

"Of course," Antonio snorted. "Well, sit down. We'll keep playing until something else happens. Nothing we can do with that thing until Gabe gets here with his laptop."

"Exactly," Riley yawned. "While we have nothing going on...I've been meaning to ask something."

"What's up?" Antonio gave her the cards Sheriff had been playing.

"Why does Abigail avoid you all like the plague?" Riley had noticed it, what felt like centuries ago.

"No idea, but you're her friend, right?" James looked at her hopefully, and Riley became a little uncomfortable.

"Yeah?" Riley threw some chips into the center without checking her cards.

"Tell her we want to hang out," James mumbled.

"Okay," Riley coughed. "Are you guys...?"

"She's pretty," Antonio muttered under his breath. "And Thomas wants her to join the Pack and keep her nearby, since we seem to have use of her nearly constantly."

"I don't think it's just Thomas," Riley chuckled softly, realizing what was happening. Riley gave it a year before she wasn't the only woman in Wild Junction who had too many men to handle.

"We want her in the Pack before Kingson decides she might be good in your Pride," James told Riley quickly.

"Oh, you don't need to worry about that," Riley huffed. "Pride is family. Brenton only tried to force Jessie in because he feels weirdly responsible for her. Because of how much she's helped us."

"It's also the pregnancy," Brenton huffed as he walked in. Riley stood up too quickly and stumbled from her lack of sleep. He caught her and held her to his chest. "You okay?"

"I'm fine," Riley yawned again. "Just feeling the lack of sleep now."

"Of course," Brenton murmured down at her. "So, yeah... Jessie being pregnant makes everything in me a little on edge. A female shifter shouldn't be rogue, not when she's pregnant."

"Is that a thing?" Riley asked, going on her tiptoes to pull him down for a kiss. He growled against her lips as she kissed him.

"Yes," he whispered. "Shifters' pregnancies, not being able to shift...they can be hard on females."

"I'll have to remember that," she whispered back as his arms wrapped around her waist.

"Do we get hugs and kisses?" Troy spoke up, stepping around her and Brenton with Gabe right behind.

She smiled over at him and Brenton let her go without complaint. It was a testament to their relationship that none of them ever tried to push the others out. There was some squabbling over who got time, but it was never a serious issue.

"Come here," Troy chuckled, pulling her close. She rubbed her cheek to his until he purred and kissed her. "We all missed you and those two."

"I missed you guys, too," she murmured, kissing him again.

"Now me," Gabe grunted, pulling her from Troy.

"I have something for you," she sighed, wrapping an arm around his waist. She held the USB to him and he took it slowly as she kissed his cheek. "My father dropped it off only about ten minutes ago."

"Damn," Brenton coughed. "Well..."

"Yes, Brenton," Riley swung her eyes back to him. "You should explain."

"I told him to," Gabe whispered in her ear. "We needed to, and I thought it was better if you didn't know in case he wouldn't help."

"He was drunk," Riley told them. "Very drunk."

"He was drunk when I spoke to him a few hours ago," Brenton grunted.

"He wanted me to tell you that he did his part," Riley said with a bit of bite. "What's your part?"

"I would ask you to give him a chance," Brenton said with a softness that touched her. "He's a broken man when he's not in public."

"He seemed like a broken man, here. I didn't know what to do with it or how to deal with it." Riley pulled Gabe in for

---

his kiss after that, and he smiled at her. He quickly set up at the table, James clearing the card game.

"Have any of you slept?" Antonio asked quickly.

"We rotated on taking naps between meetings," Troy groaned. "Sucked, but those twenty-minute power naps will come in handy."

"Riley." Gabe touched her shoulder gently. "Why don't you take a quick nap while we go through what Keith gave us?"

"But..." Riley frowned, watching Gabe plug in the USB.

"Please?" he asked quietly. "We'll wake you up the moment we know anything new."

She sighed and nodded to him, looking over at the couch. He kissed her cheek and whispered how much he loved her before she made her way to the only place to sleep in the room.

She lay down and watched the brothers sit close together at the laptop, Brenton leaning over them with his hands on the backs of their chairs. James and Antonio sat on the other side of the table. She fell asleep as Sheriff got back, but she didn't know how long that took.

30

TROY

"What do we have, Gabe?" Troy asked an hour after they all knew Riley was actually asleep instead of just staring off into nothing.

"I'm working on it," Gabe mumbled, typing furiously. "A lot of this I've already figured out. But they started to break down where the money came from. Offshore accounts, several of them."

"So..." Brenton sighed. "We still do not know who the money is coming from."

"No," Gabe groaned. "But now I have a better lead on it. Some of these transactions can get buried really easily. I might be good, but we're talking hacking into banks that I don't have a physical connection to. I'm going to need more time but...this is good. He gave me some good stuff. Better leads. Shell companies, pass-through companies. I just need a few hours to follow the breadcrumbs."

Troy raised an eyebrow at his brother. Well, wasn't that some shit. They could end the day knowing what to do with themselves.

"Keep on it, and thank you," Brenton said quietly.

"No need for thanks," Gabe chuckled. "Call Keith and thank him. I promise he didn't give us everything, but...he probably gave us what he could without raising every red flag."

"That is all I needed from him," Brenton said shortly. "Thank God."

"You boys and your technology," Sheriff groaned. "Tell me in twenty-four hours we can all go home."

"Cranky without Mrs. Bear?" Troy offered him a small smile. Sheriff just narrowed his eyes at Troy. Troy shifted uncomfortably. "I need us all to chill out for just a moment. Fuck, I need a drink."

"Stop that," a groan came from across the room. Troy's head swung toward the beds, and he cried out in joy at the sight of ice-blue eyes and a pissed off look visible on Zachary's face. He shot up from his chair, and Gabe knocked his own over as he did the same.

"Zachary," Brenton breathed out. One moment they were huddled around the laptop, the next, Troy was nearly on the bed trying to hug Zachary, who protested violently.

"Get off me. Fuck, I hurt, asshole," Zachary snarled as Troy laughed. Tears were in his eyes, and he grinned at Zachary who had a small smile himself.

"You nearly..." Gabe trailed off as he stood behind Troy. "Fuck, it's good to see you awake."

"How long have I been out?" Zachary groaned, looking between them. Troy glanced at Brenton, a man who looked like he'd found God again.

"A bit over twenty-four hours," Gabe answered, leaning forward and putting his forehead to Zachary's. Troy swallowed his emotions as Zachary raised a hand slowly and held Gabe's head to his. Once Gabe moved over again,

Troy did the same. Zachary was a glue they often forgot about.

"Brenton," Zachary groaned as Troy backed away again. "My brother."

"Zachary," Brenton choked out and Troy wondered if Brenton had ever been so shaken, so shocked, or so thankful.

Brenton stepped closer, sat on the edge of the bed and leaned forward. Troy watched as they embraced slowly, Brenton's head going onto Zachary's chest. Zachary gently laid his hands on Brenton's back.

"How are you?" Brenton asked quietly. Zachary chuckled weakly, and Troy nearly wanted to strangle the tiger. He was about to try and be funny.

"I was shot, Brenton!" Zachary tried to laugh. "How the fuck do you think I am?"

"Ass," Brenton groaned.

"How are you?" Zachary grunted, pushing Brenton back. "How are all of you?"

"We're trying our hardest to hold it together," Brenton sighed. "Look to your right."

Troy and Gabe cleared the way for Zachary to get eyes on Andrew.

"Oh, shit," Zachary whispered. "Is he going to be okay?"

"The knife wound and minor and moderate bruising will be fine. The head injury though..." Troy tried to make it sound better than it was, but there was no avoiding that Andrew looked like he'd been pummeled into the ground.

"Turns out, being shot in the back twice is better for you than whatever happened to Andrew," Gabe mumbled. "They don't know if he's going to wake up. He could very well be comatose."

"Don't freak out," Brenton whispered, holding Zachary

to the bed as the tiger tried to get up. "There was no hemorrhaging in his brain, and the CT scans came back fine. A lot of broken bones in his face, but no obvious damage to his brain."

"Let me up," Zachary snarled. "Let me up to see him."

"Zachary," Troy hissed, helping Brenton hold Zachary down. "You can't. You have a small spinal injury that could be exacerbated by physical activity. You can paralyze yourself, and that would do none of us any good. As a shifter, healthy and in your prime, you are healing quickly, but you were shot in the back twice. Probably by a high-powered sniper rifle. You can't just jump out of bed like nothing happened."

Troy rarely used anything he had learned about medicine for any good. He knew a lot of things, he studied more in his free time. He paid attention to doctors and, if he had the time, he'd be out there learning more about what Andrew and Zachary needed.

Now was the perfect time to put his foot down.

"Why does it hurt so much?" Zachary groaned, easing back into his pillows.

"You were shot," Brenton sighed.

"Fuck," Zachary hissed, then he added more softly, "Where's our girl?"

"I'll get her up. She's going to be mad we haven't yet," Troy chuckled, patting Zachary's leg.

"I'll get some coffee," Gabe groaned. "She's only gotten about an hour of sleep in the last day..."

"Then let her sleep," Zachary muttered, looking around Brenton to Troy near the couch. "She's beautiful when she sleeps."

Troy looked down at her and smiled. He kneeled slowly, ignoring Zachary's request to let her sleep. She was going to stab one of them if they didn't wake her up for this. He gently shook her shoulder, trying to ease her up instead of startling her.

"You all are being real quiet," Zachary grunted. Troy heard some shuffling and remembered the other people in the room. He looked over his shoulder to see Sheriff shuffling closer to Zachary.

"We didn't want to interrupt," James mumbled. "It's good to see you awake, man."

"Thanks James. Antonio, nice to see you both here. I'm just going to assume Thomas is nearby." Zachary shifted uncomfortably in his bed, and Troy could smell the anguish from pain. Zachary could have a tough face all day, but they all knew he hurt. James quickly mentioned that Thomas was on watch outside the door before Zachary leveled his pained stare on Sheriff. "Sheriff, got something to say?"

"I thought I had lost you, boy," Sheriff growled. "Don't get shot again."

Troy couldn't stop the laugh as he watched Sheriff, for the first time, lean down and hug Zachary. Sheriff had never really admitted he even liked them all that much, much less that he cared for them.

"I have coffee," Gabe mumbled from behind Troy. Troy nodded quickly and went back to stirring Riley from her short slumber.

"Pretty girl," Troy whispered. "Pretty girl, Zachary is awake."

That did it. Her eyes flew open, and he saw her nostrils flare as she took in the scent of Zachary and his pain. Troy fell back on his ass as she sat up.

"Zachary," she cried out, hauling herself up and diving to the bed. Troy felt tears come to his eyes as he watched her blonde waves flying around when she climbed onto the bed and held Zachary. "Zachary." Her voice was choked with tears, and Troy swallowed a lump. He was always amazed with how big her heart was, how deeply she felt.

"Riley," Zachary whispered, holding her.

"I love you," she sobbed. "I thought you were going to die, and…"

"It's okay, Riley," he continued to whisper. "I love you and the guys too much to go down like that."

Troy knew there wasn't much to say to that. Zachary was awake again, and that was a ray of hope for them. Keith had brought them information—another beam of light on the dark time the Pride had fallen into.

Now, they just needed to hold on to the light while they struggled to get out of the hole they were in.

31

ZACHARY

Everything hurt. Even his damn toes felt like they had been crushed and broken. That annoyed Zachary.

What pissed him off was the fact that someone had shot him and tried to kill Brenton in broad daylight.

Zachary held Riley while the Pride got back to work. Brenton caught him up quietly as Riley fell back to sleep, curled into Zachary's side. She barely fit on the bed. Hell, he barely fit, but it was okay. He wanted her there. He needed her there.

"What's the game plan?" Zachary asked quietly.

"Find out who is doing this and then crush them." Brenton made a frustrated noise. "But..."

"We're losing," Zachary grunted. "Let's admit it. We're losing."

"Between you, her, and those two." Brenton nodded towards the brothers. "I am pretty fucking tired of being told we are down."

"Brenton, someone tried to assassinate us. I'm not sure how I'm alive," Zachary snorted. "We're losing."

"I know," Brenton sighed. "Fuck, I know. Gabe could know who is doing this any minute, though, and then we can make our plans."

"There's only four of you who can do anything," Zachary reminded him. "And, I'll be real, only three I'm willing to put in harm's way."

"You couldn't stop her if you tried," Brenton chuckled. "If she wants to fight, we need to let her and make sure she is prepared for it...but I have an idea on that."

"I'll trust your judgement," Zachary growled softly. "But if she gets hurt..."

"Kill me, please. I will welcome it. I'm pretty tired of any of you getting hurt, to be honest."

"It was me or you, Brenton. It had to be me," Zachary whispered.

"No, it didn't," Brenton mumbled sadly. "Zachary, I told you that it never had to be you."

"And, at the time, I believed you," Zachary sighed. "I know better now."

"I have never asked you to die for me," Brenton snarled softly. Zachary saw a flash of something dangerous in those gold eyes and realized what he'd missed in the last day.

Brenton was hanging on by a thread. Their Alpha was about to snap, lose all his control and hurt someone.

"No, and I know you never will, but I'll do it anyway," Zachary reminded him carefully. "I'll do it because it's the best thing I could ever give you for everything you've done for me."

"I did not do anything that important..." Brenton looked away from him, and Zachary reached out to touch Brenton's arm.

"You taught me how to live, how to trust. You gave me a foundation of real family that later helped me realize I

287

could love. Brenton, if dying in your place is something I can do for you, I will. Every time. And not only you." Zachary took a deep breath as Brenton gave him a pained look. "Between your pride and good heart, Andrew's guidance, and the brothers teaching me how to smile...and her...Brenton, I would gladly die for any of you. Don't ever think I regret that."

"I hate you, you fucking prick," Brenton mumbled.

"I love you," Zachary whispered. Brenton's head lowered onto Zachary's shoulder.

"I'm falling apart," Brenton murmured so quietly that Zachary nearly didn't hear him over the incessant beeping of the machines around them. "It's never been this hard. Having her, having a taste of a normal life and freedom, has made this all so much harder."

"I know," Zachary comforted him. "Brenton...I think maybe you should...You should fall apart, let go."

"Excuse me?" Brenton looked back up sharply. Zachary met his brother's gaze.

"I think it's time for you to let the lion out of its cage. I would do it for you, as I have for years. I would be the hardness, but I'm bedridden." Zachary poked Brenton's chest. "You hide it, the beast, the thing that makes you so dangerous. It's been...years since you went there. I know what it does to you, but I think it's time for you to let him out one more time. He knows how to play the game and win it."

"I..."

"You've lost faith in yourself," Zachary hissed. "It's been written all over your face and your posture for weeks. We failed to handle Cameron appropriately and almost lost Riley. You made a mistake in how to handle things after we escaped the hunters in Texas and got home. You need to get back on track and remember what made us great. We've made mistakes before, but we never let it get to us. We picked up the pieces, and we hit back harder."

"Yeah..." Brenton sighed, looking down at his hands. Zachary watched him run one of those hands through his hair as he stood up.

"Go watch those two," Zachary grunted at him, hoping he could set his Alpha to a task to keep him occupied.

"Do not tell me what to do," Brenton snorted.

Zachary threw his idea out the window. Fine. Brenton would need someone else to push him over the edge if he wouldn't listen to Zachary.

He pulled Riley in a little closer, ignoring the pain in his back and the rest of his body. He had holes in him, and he knew better than to try and ignore them. He grabbed the little button that would knock him out. He needed to heal. He needed to trust those smart leopards to do what they did best.

He needed a fucking nap.

He hit the button, and it didn't take long for the morphine to kick in and take him down into dreams of their past. Of his past.

SOMEONE SHOOK HIM AWAKE, and he snarled, trying to grab the hand that was touching him. No one was allowed to fucking touch him, not after what he'd gone through. He caught it and hated that the hand was strong enough he couldn't break it.

He'd been caught in a shitty dream about cages. Instead

of the hunters, it was his parents, calling him an uncontrollable monster. A wild thing that they could never tame or teach. A thing they would need to hide or give away. Unworthy of them. Unintelligent, dangerous, and crazy.

He'd only been eight.

They had never tried to teach him how to read or write. They had made their judgment based on his form and had given up on him from there.

Tigers had problems, and Zachary dealt with them every day. Some days were worse than others. No matter what, another tiger shifter, normally dark skinned, what humans might call "exotic", would always judge his pale cast and his ink-black hair. His ice blue eyes. His parents had just been the first.

The last time he'd been truly bedridden was when his father had caned him. Zachary had been eight and had snarled at him. Zachary was looked down on because he was a white tiger, he always had been. He had also been looked down upon, like Brenton, for being too dominant as a child.

He squeezed the hand harder, making someone whimper.

"Zachary," Troy whispered, obviously in pain, "don't hurt us. We need to move Riley." Zachary released the hand quickly.

"Then move her," he growled, coming out of the nightmare. He was still pissed off, though. He didn't know why being a white tiger irked him in that moment. He couldn't remember for a moment why his back hurt so fucking bad.

"We can't," Brenton growled back. "You have got her completely curled up into you. Let her go. A nurse is here to check your injuries."

Zachary cracked his eyes open and hissed at the light in the room. Why couldn't they keep it dark? As he took in the hospital room, he remembered where he was and what had happened. His anger slowly receded as he took in the scent of Riley curled up with him, and Brenton who was leaning close to him. He could see Troy rubbing his hand with a grimace.

"How long have I been out?" he asked, realizing he did have Riley completely trapped. She was still sleeping peacefully, but his arms were locked around her, and his legs were tangled into hers. He slowly worked himself out of the mess, one of his IVs nearly getting tugged out in the process. "Fuck, that hurts."

"Thank you," Troy mumbled, picking up Riley slowly. Zachary watched him put their girl on the couch and tuck a blanket over her.

"Only two or three hours," Brenton sighed. "After this, I want you back asleep though. I will get them to drug you if I must. We are still working on it."

"Fine," Zachary snarled. "Sorry for maybe getting a little violent there."

"You were not sleeping easy," Brenton told him. "We knew what we were getting into. A nightmare?"

"Something from when I lived with my parents," Zachary grunted. "I'm fine."

"Alright," Brenton sighed.

Zachary let the nurse roll him to his side and change his bandages. A second nurse did the exit wound on his abdomen. They mumbled about how well he was doing and that there were no signs of infection or bleeding at the sutures. He didn't pay attention, knowing Troy was going to memorize all of it and bother him about it later.

"Would you like a mild sedative to help continue

resting?" the male human nurse asked, holding a small syringe.

"Lay it on me," Zachary mumbled.

He was, once again, out in minutes.

32

RILEY

S he woke up a little when she was moved off Zachary's bed. She watched him get checked, and then she fell back asleep, thankful that he wasn't giving everyone too hard of a time. If there was ever a moment they would all accept cranky, grumpy Zachary, this was it. Yet, he stayed well-behaved, and she smiled at Brenton, stretching slowly.

"You should also sleep more," Brenton whispered to her.

"No," Riley groaned, rubbing her forehead. "No, I need to be up as much as possible. That was a good nap, though."

"Okay," Brenton sighed, taking a seat at the table on Gabe's left. Troy was on Gabe's right and they continued to work, puzzling out who was coming after them.

She sat up slowly as Gabe slammed his laptop shut. She narrowed her eyes on him and noticed he was pale, his eyes wide with fear. And rage. Something swirled into emerald green eyes that made her worry.

"Gabe," Troy bitched, smacking Gabe's chest. "What the hell?"

"I saw that, Gabe," Brenton snarled. "Open the laptop."

Riley frowned and walked closer.

"Brenton..." Gabe swallowed the lump in his throat. "Fuck."

"Open. The. Laptop," Brenton growled. Riley could barely understand the words that came out of his mouth.

Gabe slowly opened the laptop back up and pushed it toward Brenton. Brenton pulled out his phone, dialed a number and waited. Riley, as she made her way around the table to see the screen, saw Troy pale and heard him curse wildly.

"No fucking way. Not again. Not this. Not..." Troy pushed out of his chair and began to pace.

"Anything we need to know?" Thomas asked with a yawn. Riley didn't like the anger and frustration she could smell coming from her guys.

"I'm going to destroy her," Brenton hissed, his jaw set. Thomas sat up straight. James coughed. Sheriff looked startled.

"Tell me what's going on?" Riley said carefully.

"Lana Cartona is what's going on," Gabe whispered. "Or rather, Lana Kingson, if she uses her maiden name."

Riley stumbled to a stop, looking around the room for someone to tell her who this other Kingson was. It was Troy who noticed her confusion and sighed.

"Abel's mother," he said with a bite. "The bitch who tried to have Jameson poison us all as kids. The bitch who hired women to fuck us and kill us in our own beds."

"Brenton, this is the first time we've caught her in the act," Gabe growled. "It's fucking time to teach her how we play the game."

"He said his parents were on his side to try and get him in charge of Kingson Inc." Brenton snarled. "He fucking said it."

"But we thought he wasn't connected to the hunters," Riley groaned. "He wasn't connected to the hunters, damn it! He had no idea who sold us out. He found out about them through a contact in the state force."

"Fuck," Troy groaned. "She's right."

"His mother was trying to set him up with an easy victory," Gabe scoffed. "Sounds like Lana."

"He was murdered in his cell a few days ago..." Thomas whispered from his spot.

"That is why the game escalated without warning," Brenton growled. "Her fucking precious boy was dead and she..."

"She's out for blood," Thomas finished for him.

"I am going to call the lawyers and get everything-" Brenton started, looking mean and ready.

"Then let's give it to her," Riley whispered. Her cheetah hissed and spit. Violence should never be the answer. "Let's stop playing her games. Let's stop playing all the games."

"What do you mean, pretty girl?" Troy asked carefully.

She met Brenton's eyes, those gold, hard stones. He knew what she meant. He might not want to hear what Riley was about to say, but she was going to anyways.

"She might be your aunt, Brenton...but I hate this. I'm tired of hearing about the political games and the underhanded dealings of this...community. Abel...Cameron and Jonathan. Andrew and Zachary were both supposed to die because of this bitch. All of you were supposed to die years ago." Riley took a deep breath. "I'm not letting you all keep playing *games*. I am tired."

"So am I," Brenton whispered.

"So...let's stop playing the games," Riley said, straightening her spine. "And let's start fighting like the animals that we are. If she wants blood, let's fucking give it to her."

"Now, Kitten," Sheriff stuttered.

"No, Sheriff," Riley snarled, feeling the rage build up inside her. "This needs to be over. Every shifter on the planet is watching? Then let's show them what the Kingson Pride does when we're done playing by their fucking rules. Let's stop playing the cards we're dealt," Riley snapped, taking the card deck off the table and throwing it across the room. "And let's start teaching the other players what it fucking means to fight for their damn lives."

She was furious. The Pride should have killed this bitch years ago. This horrible woman who went after children. This awful woman who was willing to let them be killed and skinned.

Riley would never embrace the fucked-up politics of the feline world.

But she would embrace the cat inside of her. Always. She embraced the vengeful, cunning rage and fire to get back at Abel. She embraced the hunt. Her cheetah hissed and snarled, pacing somewhere deep in Riley's soul.

"I have an idea," Brenton growled with a smile. "Gabe, find out who tried to kill Zachary and me. The actual shooters."

"Are you sure?" Gabe asked, looking back at his laptop.

"Yes," Brenton growled softly. He stood and walked over to her. Riley growled softly as her lion ran a hand through her hair and pulled her in for a kiss.

"You are the second person today to remind me that we are all just animals," he growled into her mouth.

"And these games are so very human," she whispered.

"They are, aren't they? We felines have become so enamored with our wealth, power, and intelligence that we have all forgotten what it means to be wild. Truly wild. Truly free."

The conversation felt like they were discussing something dangerous. Riley felt a thrill in her bones. The politics had dragged the Pride down...it was time to throw the politics away.

"I did it," Riley smiled, feeling dangerous. "I showed the world what it cost someone to fuck with me and fuck with all of you."

"I should have taken that to heart sooner," Brenton growled. "But we're going a bit harder this time."

"What's the plan?" she asked, holding on to him.

"We're going to kill them," Brenton growled softly. "I would have with Abel. I should have with Cameron. That was the start of this. I should have put that man in his grave for taking something that belonged with the Pride. It was a sign of weakness."

"Then let's show them we aren't weak," Riley purred, pulling him down for another kiss.

She felt blood-thirsty. She felt violent. Brenton apparently did as well, because he bit her lip as he pulled back from the kiss. His growl and the fire in his eyes thrilled her.

She looked over to the brothers, who were both grinning. Troy winked at her, and she winked back, making him chuckle.

"Are you okay with this?" Brenton asked her softly. "I'm going to do some things that you may not like."

"Will it help us be safe? Will it end this? Will it scare people off from fucking with us anymore?" she asked, looking back up at him.

"Yes," Brenton growled.

"Then, yes. I'm fucking stoked," she hissed. "Let's do this."

"I'm actually terrified," Thomas whispered.

"Me too," Sheriff grunted. "I need to leave. I can't be party to this anymore..."

"I know," Brenton said mildly towards the bear. "Go, before we say anymore that would put you at odds with your job. We've put you through enough, old bear."

"Thank you," Sheriff sighed. "Kitten, you be careful."

"Always," she chuckled, hugging Sheriff tightly. "You have a safe drive home. Tell Patty hello and we're okay for me?"

"Of course," Sheriff chuckled. She watched him grab his jacket and leave after that. Thomas and James waited patiently to see if the Pride was going to call on them for more.

"You will stay here and protect these two," Brenton said softly, gently without his normal commanding undertone. "Please?"

"Of course," Thomas said politely with a nod. "I wouldn't leave them undefended for anything."

"We appreciate that," Riley told him, walking to hug Thomas close.

"I was wondering when the fierce cheetah I met was going to come back," Thomas chuckled. "We wolves, we never played like the felines. You're in my territory, going out like this. You'll need to strike hard and fast. No mercy, no survivors. If you want to show everyone you're done playing games, you need to mean it."

"There's a chance it just won't work, too," James sighed. "But I think you'll do fine. Just make sure you all survive the night."

It took Gabe an hour to track down the assassins once he had Lana's name. Riley was proud of him. After everything their little Pride had gone through, Gabe was coming out the other side stronger than ever, now able to admit his failures while also continuing to work hard. Troy was a constant support, and she knew, when this was over, she might not ever need to worry about how they were doing with their issues. So damn strong, those two, even if they hadn't realized it for a long time.

"I love you," she whispered in his ear as he wrote the names down.

"They are still in Denver, since they can't get the second half of their payment until the job is complete," Gabe growled, looking over his shoulder at her. He kissed her slowly. "I love you, too, by the way."

"I know," she chuckled. She stole a glance at Thomas and Brenton looking over floor plans of Lana's winter home. Lana was hiding all the way out in New York. Brenton and Riley were going to get on a plane, fly out and make a quick visit to her and her husband, Abel's father.

Tomorrow, the Cartona Pride would no longer exist. The entire family would be wiped out, just like the Slaters.

Riley couldn't fucking wait.

"I got the jet waiting on standby for you two," Troy called out from the other side of the room. "You'll have about an hour drive when you land."

"Do we tell anyone that we're doing this?" Riley asked.

"No," Gabe told her quickly. "We strike, and we walk away. The SSTF won't come after us for it, they've made it abundantly clear they don't care who wins or loses this.

They don't want to arrest her for nearly exposing us...hell, they might be happy we are taking her out of play."

"I can't believe you guys never went after her before," Riley sighed.

"My decision," Brenton said mildly, looking up at her. "I never wanted to go after her because I never wanted to be the last Kingson. I never wanted to do it."

"Well..." Troy chuckled, and Riley wondered what the joke was. "Since it's all your family that's ever really caused us problems...maybe if you have no family, we might actually have some peace."

"Yeah," Gabe snorted. "A bunch of shit-disturbers, your family."

"It is the Alphas," Brenton groaned. "If your families had as many Alphas as mine, they would have been pains as well."

"Are you okay knowing that you're about to have...no family left?" Riley asked him softly.

"I have family," Brenton answered her. "I might be the last Kingson tomorrow, but I will still have family."

"Amen," Troy chuckled. "Fucking amen, my brother."

It made Riley's heart swell. Family. That's how all of this had started. They had offered her a real family again.

"It's not just your family," Riley chuckled, walking towards Brenton. "Mine has been a pain too."

"We are not hunting down your mother," Brenton said quickly, pointing at her. "She is absolutely not our problem."

"You're right. I'm going to let my dad run around the world and try to figure that one out. She hasn't been causing any real problems since that thing with Cameron, either," Riley told him, holding back a grin as she leaned into him.

"I love that you all can grin and joke a bit while planning the deaths of at least four people," Thomas laughed, shaking his head. "Reminds me of when I was a Marine, and we were sent out on a mission."

"I would say I value human life and shouldn't laugh while planning this...but I don't really value the life of a woman who has tried to kill my guys for over two decades. I don't value the lives of hunters who refuse to value my life. I'll do whatever it takes and sleep easy, if it means my guys and I finally get to have a safe life. A peaceful one." Riley snarled towards the end, that anger and ferocity coming back to the surface for a moment.

"Good, because this is survival of the fittest and it's time for you to reclaim your spot at the top of the food chain." Thomas looked to Brenton after that. "I hope, that if you all ever have children, no one ever picks on them or hurts them."

"Oh?" Brenton frowned at him and Riley tilted her head to the side.

"Riley would remove heads from shoulders over it. I'm a little worried you might smother any future children as it is," Thomas laughed, throwing his head back.

"That is a very good point," Brenton chuckled, grinning. Then he slid his gaze to Riley. "Children, huh? You think so, Thomas?"

"No," Riley growled softly. "No. You give me at least five years of no one trying to kill us, or any of our friends, and I'll consider it. Also, won't I be in my prime for like...forty years or more?"

"Yeah," Troy laughed. "Plenty of time, Brenton. Let's not rush it. Shit, man."

"I am not rushing anything!" Brenton laughed. "Thomas brought it up. Let's get back on topic, please. Gabe, you were saying the assassins are still in town. Tell me more."

"I should have looked harder into the Kudo Pride. They

were used as a go-between for hiring them. Those shits finally chose a side, or maybe they have always done this and never gotten caught. Troy and I can handle the assassins. Hopefully. They are a couple of Asian Golden cats. We should be able to over-power them if we take them by surprise. They got paid ten million up-front, with another ten million when they're done." Gabe was reading from notes he'd taken.

"What was their exact assignment?" Riley asked, watching as Gabe sighed.

"Brenton. And Zachary, if possible. Andrew was Jonathan's problem. The rest of us? Who knows. Lana may have thought we would just go into hiding. Take cover, lick our wounds."

"Or let you all get comfortable and slowly destroy you," Brenton growled. "Lana is a master politician, another reason I never wanted us to fight with her. She used to follow the rules to a tee."

"But for as long as she's alive, she'll be looking for a weakness," Thomas finished. "Is she an Alpha?"

"Yes," Brenton sighed. "My father married her off to Cartona to keep her antics out of his way. She was more dominant than him. Hell, she is more dominant than her husband. I would bet my fortune that she technically runs that Pride."

"Why does she want us, then?" Riley asked. "Why does she want you dead?"

"My guess?" Brenton frowned. "It is not money, that is for certain. Abel may have been vindictive over it, but he was always too weak to even get his father to declare him as his heir. He was a jealous prick. Lana, though, has never cared about the money."

"She wants the power," Riley whispered, remembering

what the brothers and Andrew said about the Kingson name. "She wants to be the Kingson Alpha..."

"She wants to rule," Brenton whispered back. "She wants to be the Queen. And she can do it. She is smart enough to make it happen. She must have seen us go easy on Cameron-"

"I don't care." Riley shrugged, cutting off Brenton's explanation of his aunt's motives. "I don't care about the reputation of the Kingson name or any of the other stuff. What I do care about is keeping everyone here safe and alive. I don't give a damn about her motivations or what's at stake for her. All I need to know is what's at stake for us, which is our family. My family. Your family." She put a hand on his chest, and he nodded at her.

"Then let's get this done." Brenton's face was stone, but his eyes weren't. They showed Riley so much. His anger, his pain, his love, not only for her, but also for the entire Pride.

"You two be safe," Troy told them. "Stay safe."

"You too," Riley said.

"Come home to us," Gabe whispered, coming to hug her, then Brenton after he stood up. "Troy and I will head out after nightfall."

"Good," Brenton said, holding Gabe's shoulders. "I'll call you when we land. And when it's done."

"Good." Gabe smiled.

33

RILEY

They landed in New York without incident. They slept most of the plane ride, gathering the energy they needed for the long night ahead of them. Riley felt better for it, and Brenton seemed ready for what was to come next.

"I have done this before," Brenton sighed. "This entire thing. Flying out to kill someone."

"What?" Riley frowned at him as they loaded into a car that had been prepared for them while they were flying.

"About a year before I met you," Brenton began quietly, looking off into the distance as he started the car. He got them moving off the tarmac for the dark journey to Lana's home. "The entire Pride loaded up and we went after someone who...Andrew had that girlfriend, remember? His only serious relationship."

"Yeah, I try not to ask about her," Riley sighed. "But I know the story. Human girl while Andrew went to culinary school. It ended because she wanted to get married, and that was never going to work for Andrew and the Pride. She realized she would never get what she needed and left."

"Yup," Brenton mumbled. "She did not know about shifters or anything having to do with our world. Well, those last couple of years before coming back to Wild Junction were hard on us. They all were hard, to be honest, but those...We were constantly getting shit from people. And one day, Andrew got a picture in the mail. Andrew, our good guy who could talk anyone into anything. Who knows people. Who genuinely cares and loves and wants happiness around him."

"Brenton?" Riley wondered where he was going with this.

"My Kingmaker," Brenton whispered. "He did that for me. He never liked it, but it was a talent that could be used for good or evil. It got to the point where Andrew couldn't turn it off, he was losing himself a little. Then he got a letter in the mail from Kathleen. She met another guy, and they were getting married. Another shifter. We went to the wedding."

Riley crossed her arms and continued to listen as Brenton turned them onto a lonely highway.

"The shifter told her all about our world...and then left her at the altar just to break her heart. And to laugh in our faces that he could, and we hadn't protected her."

"What happened?" Riley asked quietly.

"She killed herself," Brenton finished.

Riley gasped, covering her mouth.

"She was broken. And Andrew couldn't handle it," Brenton sighed. "So, we loaded up, hunted him down. Hunted his friends down for helping him hide. Hunted his Alpha down for not controlling his Pride and letting some small fry fuck with us. Killed his entire inner circle, because they tried to protect the Alpha."

"How many?" Riley wasn't sure she wanted the answer.

"Twelve," Brenton growled. "By the end of it, we killed twelve people. Then Andrew went a little mad and began plotting for me to take over the entire feline world to stop it from ever happening again. I bought him the diner, instead. We redecorated the mansion, and we moved back to Wild Junction. People were terrified of us, Riley, and we didn't even have normal dealings with that Pride."

"Oh my God," Riley mumbled.

"Can you blame us?" Brenton sighed.

Riley thought about it and shook her head slowly.

"No. Will they fear us after this?"

"Lana and the rest of my family members have found that I can be lenient to them. The world knows this. I would rather destroy their business and their reputations than kill them, like Cameron. I asked Andrew and Zachary what could be done besides killing him. I didn't want to kill my uncle. I didn't want you to think we were capable of it. A thousand things. Andrew offered blackmail. Cameron's reputation was always important to him, so ruin it."

"Will they fear us?" Riley asked again.

"They will be petrified," Brenton whispered.

"Good." They fell silent, and Riley quickly texted Gabe.

RILEY: How are things at home?

GABE: Andrew still out. Zachary awake and bitching. We head out in thirty for our targets.

"THAT IS GOOD," Brenton murmured. "I'm more comfortable

with Zachary being awake and injured than just the wolves being there."

"Me too," Riley whispered. "Is that it?" She nodded toward a house coming into view, and Brenton nodded.

"That's it," he sighed. "Riley...I'm going to kill her."

Riley looked over to him with a frown.

"You mean..."

"I mean, you will let me take charge of this, and I will kill her." Brenton's tone was stern, and his face had become a cold mask.

"Why?" she asked him softly.

"Because I have to," was his only response as they passed through the gates to the property.

"What's the plan?"

"We are going to play nice house guests. Have a coffee. I will eventually ask to speak to her alone. I will kill her...and you will kill her husband." Brenton sighed. "You are going to kill her husband, Marco, because he supported Abel, and I have a feeling he's going to find you enchanting. Young, healthy, fiery."

"We didn't bring any guns," Riley reminded him. "How am I going to kill a grown lion?"

"The same way you killed the last one," Brenton chuckled. It was dark, dangerous. He pulled something from his jacket pocket. They had changed into new clothing and showered on the jet, so they looked fresh and ready to have a small gathering with family. "You are going to stab him. Aim for the eye. This is big enough to end it." He handed her the switchblade, and she took it slowly.

"We're about to murder two people in cold blood," she mumbled to herself.

"We're about to kill the competition. You asked for this," Brenton reminded her.

307

"Well..." Riley smiled. "She started it."

"Damn right, she did," Brenton snarled, and Riley saw that his canines, once again, seemed a little too long. She could feel his anger and his rage feeding her. "And we're going to fucking finish it. For Andrew. For Zachary. For us. The Pride. Our family."

Alphas set the tone of their Prides. Brenton's was one of death. This was going to be a night of horror for their enemies and benediction for the Pride. With the world watching as they fell to their knees, Brenton and Riley were going to give them the middle finger and fight back.

Riley could nearly feel Brenton's lion prowling inside him, ready to strike at the ones who'd fucked with them one too many times.

Brenton parked in front of the mansion and stepped out. Riley waited. This was for show. Brenton got her door for her as a butler ran out. He took her hand and helped her out. She kissed his cheek as Brenton growled at the butler.

"Go tell my aunt and uncle that I would like to see them. I want to offer my condolences over Abel."

As the butler ran inside, Riley raised an eyebrow and looked at her Alpha.

"That's cold, love," she murmured, "since we're the reason he's dead."

"He is the reason he is dead," Brenton snarled. "They know that, even if we helped him to an early grave. They will accept us. Watch."

Sure enough, the butler came back out and ushered them in. Riley was anxious for what was next.

34

GABE

"**A**re you two ready to go?" Thomas asked them quietly.

"Yeah," Gabe growled with a grin. He was feeling ramped up. Ready. It had been a long time since he'd felt good about violence. It hadn't been while rescuing Riley or running from the hunters...no, the last time he'd been happy with violence, ready for it, was when he and the Pride went out and slaughtered a Pride for what they did to Andrew's ex. That had felt good. So did this. Better than any high Gabe had ever experienced.

Which was why Brenton had chosen that moment to pull them out of the violent world of shifters and drop them back for a peaceful life in Wild Junction. The Pride had always been too vicious for the world. They had pushed it away, hidden it since going home.

It was time to remember who they were and what they could do. What they had done before.

"Be safe, you two," Zachary called out with a groan to accent why they were stepping over this line one last time. Hopefully it was the last.

"We'll get them back for this," Troy promised Zachary, who nodded.

"I know," Zachary whispered, his ice blue eyes piercing them. "Then, since Riley isn't here, come back and give me a cuddle."

"That's fucking weird. Never say it again," Gabe mumbled. Zachary's laughter told Gabe that the tiger was fucking with them, but he looked at Troy and saw something twinkle in his brother's eyes. "Don't go there, Troy. Not tonight."

He knew Troy was going to make some obscene comment about being game for a cuddle with Zachary. Troy couldn't resist. He watched Troy practically eat the comment he was about to make and swallow it.

"Fine," Troy sighed. "I'll stay focused on the task at hand."

"Let's head out," Gabe chuckled, patting his brother on the back. "Zachary, we'll call Thomas when we're done."

"And if you never call, I'll know why," Zachary growled. "Come back. I don't tell you two this enough, but you're my damn family, and I don't want to lose you."

Gabe smiled at him as he walked over to the tiger.

"You don't need to say it often," Gabe muttered, hugging Zachary. "We know."

"I should be out there with you," Zachary sighed. "I can't handle being stuck here."

"Z...we got this. You kept Brenton from being hurt. You helped push him to remember who and what we are. So did Troy and I. So did Riley. We have it from here. Rest easy. If Andrew wakes up, you can be here for him. Play cards with Thomas and bitch about how much you hurt."

"Go, before I try and get up to leave with you," Zachary snarled, and Gabe patted Zachary on the top of his head before jumping away. Zachary had tried to grab him, but it was time to get going.

"Be good," Troy called as Gabe followed him out of the room. They waved to James, standing at the door and got more solemn with every step.

"You ready for this?" Gabe asked softly as they made it to their Range Rover.

"Are we ever really ready for this?" Troy asked quietly. "We're about to get up close and personal with two assassins hiding out in a rough part of town."

"Yeah," Gabe sighed, turning the vehicle on. "I feel good, though. Like Brenton took the leash off."

"He did," Troy said with a grin, "and I do, too. Plus...fuck these guys. You don't come into our city and fucking shoot us."

Gabe pulled out of the hospital parking lot and started through the dark night that had settled over Denver. He knew Riley and Brenton were just beginning their own dangerous play to end this.

They rode in silence. The roads were clear, so Gabe took liberties when he could. He ran a couple red lights and drove a bit too fast.

His leopard prowled, stalked, happy to be on the hunt. It was a need and a high. A proof of strength and power. Troy and Gabe were stalkers, and tonight they were feeding the animals inside them and going on a hunt.

"We can't fuck this up," Gabe whispered. "There's no room for failure."

"I know," Troy growled softly, checking his sidearm in the passenger's seat. "There never is when it comes to this."

Tomorrow, the Kingson Pride would be on top or nonexistent.

Gabe parked them nearly a mile from their objective. He cut the engine and looked at his brother.

"Do you think Riley and Brenton are okay?" he asked softly.

"By now, they are probably playing Lana and Marco into a false sense of security. I trust them," Troy sighed. "Is Lana our only worry? Will we really be done after her?"

"I think so," Gabe mumbled. "Her allies will scatter to the wind. The Cartona Pride will fall apart without anyone holding it together, and everyone will know Brenton is tired of the games. The next time someone screws with us, we go on the hunt. Troy, I think this is something we should have done a long time ago."

"I agree," Troy said, opening his door and jumping out. Gabe followed him, and they both went to the back of the Range Rover. In the trunk, there was a compartment normally used for tools. After the hunters took them, Zachary had gone crazy and changed its purpose. Gabe pulled it open and found what he knew would be there.

A variety of guns, from a single assault rifle to a shotgun, and a handful of handguns, from a revolver to a Glock, were stashed inside. Gabe ignored the guns, though. He picked up a couple blades. This was going to be a close quarters fight, if they would be sneaking into their tiny rented apartment.

"Carry a sidearm just in case one makes a break for it," Troy whispered, and Gabe nodded slowly. He grabbed a holster, strapped it on and slid a revolver in that Troy had already checked. "There won't be any reloading."

"Yup." Gabe knew that. He wasn't intending on using it. He looked over Troy's set up. Troy would be using a shotgun, with a hunting knife in case one of them got too close. The real difference between Troy and Gabe...How they preferred to kill people.

"Let's do this," Troy snarled with a grin, pumping the shotgun. Gabe grinned back but didn't say anything as they locked up the Range Rover and snuck off into the darkness. They cut through alleys, ignoring the pimps, the drug dealers, and the prostitutes. In return, they were ignored.

Gabe and Troy got to the apartment building quickly enough, and Gabe pointed to the fire escape.

"I'll climb up first," he whispered. "Follow me up when I clear it." Gabe was a silent climber. Troy was decent, but Gabe knew that if these guys were looking out for anyone, they would notice Troy.

"Roger that," Troy whispered back, giving Gabe a quick thumbs-up.

Gabe looked at the three-foot vertical jump he would need to make to grab the ladder. This was the riskiest part of the climb. He crouched, bracing himself on the balls of his feet. He didn't jump for the ladder though. Too risky, Gabe judged. He hit the brick wall and found places to hold before he slid back to the ground. He wished momentarily that he could shift and get away with it. His leopard form would find this climb easy.

He scaled the brick slowly and didn't touch the steel fire escape until he knew he could get both feet on it without a sound. He looked down at Troy and knew he would need to kick the ladder down to help his brother up. Troy had an amazing sense of balance, but snow leopards couldn't climb like African leopards.

Gabe motioned to Troy to give him a moment and continued his climb up to the third floor. He kept his steps silent and his body low. The only sound he could hear was the wind and the soft background noise of a television playing the news.

He found the window he wanted and grinned, listening.

The news was playing more stuff about Brenton and Zachary, the shooting in Denver. No one was talking, and Gabe heard a snore that told him one of them was asleep. Gabe looked back down at Troy and pulled his cellphone out.

GABE: Go to their front door. Leave the shotgun, we'll come back for it. I'm going to let you in.

HE WATCHED Troy read the text and nod. Troy deposited the shotgun behind a bag of trash. Gross but effective.

Gabe looked back in the window and slid it open. Gabe would scoff at it being unlocked, but he realized there just wasn't a lock on it. They went cheap, finding this fucking rat's nest to hide in.

Gabe walked quietly to the front door, through the tiny living room, trying not to wake up the one sleeping on the couch. He flipped the lock on the front door and pulled out his knife.

Right on time.

An arm came around Gabe's throat and yanked him back. A stabbing pain radiated from his side and Gabe snarled, grabbing the arm and flinging the other shifter over his shoulder. He hadn't noticed him coming close, since the entire dingy apartment reeked of the two assassins. The shifter slammed into the front door just as Troy was trying to push it open.

"Gabe, what the fuck?" Troy growled, breaking it down to get it open as the assassin charged Gabe.

The second one was also awake now, coming after Gabe from behind. Gabe cursed and dove into the kitchen before either could stab him again. Troy came in guns blazing, taking two shots. Gabe saw him hit the first assassin, but it wasn't fatal. Gabe pulled the knife out of his side as the second one dove on top of him.

With a snarl, Gabe shoved the second one off him and rolled so that he was on top. He was still holding the knife and tried to stab the asshole. He met resistance as the assassin struggled to stop Gabe from shoving the blade into his chest. Gabe felt the guy buck underneath him and was nearly thrown off, getting shaken enough that his attack was stopped. The assassin disarmed him and threw a punch, connecting to Gabe's jaw.

That did knock Gabe off him. Gabe hit the tile floor and growled in pain. He heard other scuffling somewhere else in the apartment and briefly wondered if Troy was okay.

Gabe stood up quickly and looked for his own knife, since the assassin held the other one.

"You think you can come after us? Kill *us*?" the assassin growled. Gabe grinned, grabbing a coffee pot.

"I think I can," Gabe snarled. The assassin jumped at him, and Gabe shattered the glass coffee pot against the side of his head. The shifter screamed in agony, and Gabe grabbed the knife before it hit the floor and shoved it into the shifter's gut. He yanked it back out and slit the assassin's throat.

As blood began to pool on the floor in the kitchen, Gabe hissed in pain, wondering where his brother was.

"Troy?" He called out. "Brother?"

"Here," Troy groaned. Gabe walked into the single

bedroom and found Troy holding his shoulder, panting over the second shifter. "How are you?"

"Stabbed," Gabe hissed, touching his side, feeling the warm, wet blood beginning to soak his side. "Let me get what I need then we can use the fire escape to get out of here before any of the local cops show up."

"Pictures?" Troy asked. "Also, Zachary is going to be so mad we got hurt."

"He'll deal," Gabe sighed, pulling his phone back out. He was amazed that it wasn't cracked. He took a picture of the dead shifter in the bedroom then walked back out to the kitchen to get one of the other guy.

"Let's go," Troy whispered, watching Gabe. Gabe nodded slowly, looking over to his brother. Troy was grinning, and Gabe couldn't resist smiling back. "Who are those for?"

"Sending one set to Keith so he can come cover this up, because that's his fucking job." Gabe chuckled in pain as he walked to the window. Already they could hear the distant screech of sirens. He climbed out before continuing, Troy right behind him. "The other set is to the Kudo Pride."

"Good idea," Troy groaned as they hustled down the fire escape. Troy kicked the ladder down with a clang and they both slid down the sides. Gabe was getting dizzy from blood loss, but they couldn't be here when the human cops arrived. They would get arrested, and they did just murder two people. No matter what the SSTF or Brenton did, nothing would save them from a very long jail sentence if local law enforcement caught them.

"We got to move," Gabe grumbled as Troy grabbed his shotgun. "Fuck, my knife."

"I got everything of ours before we bounced," Troy told him quickly.

"Finger prints?" Gabe groaned. "Fuck, let's just get moving. The SSTF can fucking take over."

As they ran, Gabe sent the texts. One to Keith, telling him there was a shifter mess that needed to be cleaned up quickly. Gabe and Troy's fingerprints weren't on record in any city, anymore, so he wasn't sure he could get arrested at this point, but he would feel better if the SSTF just did their job. They didn't want to get involved in politics? Fine, they could clean up the messes then.

As Troy helped him in the Range Rover, Gabe lay in the back.

"Just the stab for me," Gabe mumbled. "You?"

"Dislocated shoulder," Troy hissed. "Put pressure on that with this."

Gabe felt something fall over his face and realized that he had a jacket on top of him. He pressed it over the wound and grumbled at how bad it hurt. As Troy got them moving, Gabe sent the second text to the number he'd found for the Alpha of the Kudo Pride. A quick reminder that the Kudo Pride shouldn't choose sides like this again...or Kingson Pride was going to take a long vacation in Japan to meet with them. It wouldn't be pleasant for the Kudo Pride.

"Let's just get back to the hospital and get fucking Serrano to look at us," Troy sighed. "And send Brenton a text. We're done on our end, and he'll want to know, no matter what's going on."

"Yup," Gabe whispered.

GABE: We're done. All on you and gorgeous, now.

35

RILEY

R iley and Brenton were led into a gorgeous drawing room with comfortable couches and beautiful paintings on the wall. Brenton kept her directly at his side, his arm casually around her to keep her there. She didn't fight it, accepting the warmth he offered. She had found one issue with New York and this house. It was colder than Colorado.

"If you can wait here, Alpha Cartona and Lady Cartona will be with you in a moment," the butler told them with deceptive calm. Riley could smell how nervous the male was, but he didn't let it stop him from doing his job. "I can bring you refreshments in the meantime."

"No thank you," Brenton replied crisply. "We're fine."

"Of course, Alpha Kingson," the butler mumbled before leaving them. Riley looked up to her Alpha, one of the loves of her life, and saw that he was different. This was not a man she was used to. She never saw him set his face in such a cold, dispassionate way.

"Brenton?" she whispered softly.

"Don't speak," Brenton whispered back. "They will have

this room bugged to hear what their guests discuss before a meeting."

Riley didn't say anything to that, letting Brenton lead her to a couch and sit them down. What was there to say? Riley and Brenton were here to kill his aunt and her husband, the Alpha of a rival Pride. They were done playing the games from across the country and were taking the fight to their enemy's doorstep.

No, there really wasn't much to say about it.

It was silent for a long time, and Riley felt Brenton twirl a finger in her hair, something he would do while they lay in bed together. It made her ache for a moment, missing those quiet moments. It was barely thirty-six hours after Andrew was attacked and Zachary was shot, but...everything felt like an eternity ago. Not even two days...

"Brenton!" A sultry female voice entered the room as the door opened. "My nephew, to what do we owe the pleasure of your visit?"

Riley looked over and stood up as Brenton did. The woman the voice belonged to looked like a female version of him. Brown hair, perfectly straight, cascaded over her shoulders. She had the same pure, molten gold eyes, and Riley saw they shared the shape of their eyebrows.

And she was young. Well, she looked young. By appearance, Lana Cartona looked like she was only forty, which meant she was probably closer to eighty. Years on Riley and Brenton. Years of these games, these dangerous plays for power, and Riley saw the calculating spark in her eyes.

"Auntie," Brenton purred, a coo that made a shiver run up Riley's spine. Riley only heard that tone from Brenton when they were in bed together. "I just heard about Abel and wanted to see how you and Marco were doing."

Riley looked around Lana and saw where Abel got his looks. Marco smiled bitterly at her. Marco knew this wasn't a social call, and he certainly knew who Riley was. Riley and Marco watched Brenton and Lana kiss each other's cheeks and begin chattering about something to do with wine and stock prices.

"Wine is soaring, you should invest," Lana laughed. "This new generation of humans are in love with it the way the Gen X'ers weren't."

"I like my scotch, personally," Brenton chuckled. "And I invest in things I like."

"You and your father," Lana giggled. "He loved his scotch as well, do you remember that? You were so young when he died."

Riley stiffened as Brenton led her back to the couch. Riley threw a glance up to Brenton's face. Whatever he was feeling wasn't on his face or in his scent. He was completely closed off to the world.

Riley knew that Brenton remembered though. His father beat him when he drank too much. Brenton was careful with his own drinking because of it. Riley knew that much. Riley also knew that Jameson killed Brenton's father for Lana. A glass of scotch and a long drive to clear his head. Written off as a drunk driving accident. Geoffrey had been poisoned.

Jameson had also tried to kill Brenton and the guys for Lana.

"Love," Marco coughed out. "Let's get a fire going to warm this room up."

"A fire sounds like a good idea," Lana sighed happily. "Jones! Come in and build a fire."

Riley watched the butler silently enter, and they waited in silence while he got to work. It didn't take long, but the seconds ticked by for what seemed like an eternity. It was a heavy silence. Lana continued to smile gently at Brenton and Riley. Riley resisted the urge to shift uncomfortably.

"Fires are so nice in the winter," Lana whispered as Jones left. "Aren't they, Ms. Stern?"

"They are," Riley replied, ignoring the near-glare Marco was giving her. "You can call me Riley."

"You may call me Lady Cartona," Lana answered with a cutting smile. "Looking at you two is a blast from the past. You look like her, your mother."

"I've heard," Riley mumbled.

"And Brenton? He's the spitting image of his father. The Kingson stamp of looks, they are inescapable." Lana was still smiling, and Riley was resisting the urge to slap the smile off her face. "So, you've come to talk about Abel?"

"And offer our condolences," Brenton told her mildly. "Plus, it's been so long since we've seen each other, Auntie."

Riley hated that word. Auntie. She hated that Brenton admitted any relationship to this woman.

"Hopefully, my boy will rest in peace," Marco growled softly. "Thank you for your condolences."

They all settled into their seats as Jones brought drinks Riley and Brenton hadn't asked for. Not even their hosts drank from them or ate the tiny sandwiches and pastries laid out between them.

"I'm sure he will," Brenton sighed. "He played the game. It happens."

"Oh, I know," Marco snarled. "I'm going to offer you an apology. I'm not sure what got into his head, trying to go against you." Such a lie, Riley realized. All that statement had been a lie. Abel's parents had supported his attempt to take over Kingson Inc. after Brenton was dead or thrown out.

"It was foolish, I agree. I would have given him a seat on one of my boards, if he had asked for it. Brought him back in. That's what family does for each other." Another lie, Riley could smell. But, again, not a single shifter in the room called it out.

"Of course, it is," Lana whispered.

From there, Brenton, Lana, and Marco talked aimlessly about memories of Abel when he was younger. Riley stayed quiet, listening angrily about the man who molested her in a hellish room. She could taste leather and rust. She could feel the cold, wet blindfold over her eyes. The breath on her ear.

Then Brenton's phone went off.

"Excuse me," Brenton sighed politely. "I just can't get away from it all anymore."

"The life of a successful businessman and Alpha," Lana laughed. "Geoffrey had similar problems. He normally gave his phone to Walker, so he could ignore it for an evening."

Walker, Troy and Gabe's father by last name.

"That, I did not know," Brenton chuckled, unlocking his phone and reading whatever was there. "I don't think I could trust the Walker boys with my phone for any length of time."

That wasn't a lie. Gabe would break into it, and Troy would put a bunch of nude men all over it as the background and delete all of Brenton's apps—just so they could laugh when Brenton lost his mind. Riley knew this because it had happened to Zachary, once. She never left her phone unattended when those two were feeling like some trouble was needed.

"Ah," Brenton sighed. "Well isn't that something..." Riley saw Brenton relax just a little bit. She wondered if it was one of the guys.

"Good news?" Marco asked, frowning at Brenton.

"Yes." Brenton smiled at his uncle. Riley watched Brenton put the phone away. "Lana, I wanted to know if you had any older photos of our family. I've been meaning to show Riley some pictures of me as a child, and I realized I had none."

Riley was confused. That wasn't a lie.

"Oh, of course," Lana laughed. "Come, we'll go find some. I know I have them around somewhere."

"Be good," Brenton whispered in Riley's ear, kissing her neck before getting up from the couch. She smiled at him and held his hand for a moment.

"I'm not going anywhere," she teased. He nodded to her and left with Lana. The moment the door closed, Riley narrowed her eyes on Marco. "Your son was a monster."

"Your Pride is falling apart." Marco growled happily. "Brenton and Lana are going to talk about what he can give her to stop this. There isn't anything, but she'll wring him and the rest of you dry before it's over."

"Doesn't change the fact that your son is dead," Riley hissed. "And I'm here, free."

"You got the SSTF involved in our politics," Marco snarled. "When you should have been told that it's not allowed."

"Forgive me," Riley chuckled darkly. "I know murder is forgivable but what he did to me was not. I wasn't the first one to break your stupid fucking rules."

"The hunters," Marco growled softly. "Just because no one admits it doesn't mean it never happens. And you? You would make a fantastic slave. Doesn't matter now."

"Why not?" Riley asked, her hands in her pockets. Even the fire couldn't warm up this room.

"I'll make you a deal, darling," Marco chuckled meanly.

"You stay here. Let Brenton go back to Denver and his tiny little Pride by himself. You'll have everything you want in exchange for being my mistress. You're pretty, and if you claimed all of those guys, you must be good at something."

"Aren't you married?" Riley said with disgust. Her right hand gently held the switchblade. "Won't she not appreciate that?"

"She and I haven't been in a bed together since the night we conceived Abel," Marco snorted. "I got my heir out of her. Now I need a new one, and I'm not willing to risk her, again. Plus, she's getting to the age where she'll be useless for it. I would rather have her as a political ally than a lover."

"You astound me," Riley whispered. "Why would I ever take that deal when I get to go home to someone like Brenton? Every member of the Pride is more appealing than you."

"I figured I would offer," Marco sighed. He stood up and wandered away from her, to a small bar in the corner. She watched him take out a bottle and pour a drink. "Lana always gets what she wants, by the way. If she wants the Kingson Pride to finally fall, it will."

"Why now?" Riley asked, standing up.

"Hell if I know. I just told her that since Abel died, she better do it quickly, or I would get involved." Marco smiled over to Riley. "She likes the long game, Lana. She made a dangerous play with the hunters because the Slater boy was willing to be the go-between, but since that failed and escalated much further than she intended...she went back to what she knows best."

"So-"

"No, I think that's all I'll be telling you," Marco chuckled. "You and I have other business. My only child is dead because of you."

"A lot of people seem to be dead because of me," Riley mumbled, pulling the switchblade out of her pocket as Marco walked back toward her.

"Back to my offer," Marco purred, sitting next to her. "You're young, healthy, and obviously have some of your mother in you. I can see why my son made such a stupid decision to get involved with the hunters to have you and to get to kill Brenton himself."

She didn't let him keep talking. She flipped the blade open and turned to stab him. He grabbed her wrist.

"I'm not stupid, little girl," he snarled, standing up and taking her with him. "I know Brenton wouldn't leave you alone with me, if he didn't have a reason. I was giving you a chance not to die. And when I'm done with you, I'm going to have my guards execute your Alpha if he doesn't fall in line and give Lana the deal she wants."

"We're not here to play politics or make deals," Riley hissed. "We're here to kill you both."

Marco paled a little, shocked by that revelation. She tried to pull away, but he pulled her hard closer to him and she felt the bones in her wrist grind together. She cried out at the pain, bringing a knee up to slam Marco in the balls. The pain caused him to release her, and she stumbled back several steps, wondering if he'd broken her wrist. He recovered quickly and charged at her. She jumped out of the way and went for his back. He turned around before she connected. His back was to the fireplace in the middle of the room.

Riley jammed the knife into his left eye with a victorious snarl before he could stop her. She saw the life leave his other eye.

She yanked the knife out and tried to get away from the blood that sprayed out. She felt some hit her cheek and watched Marco's body fall back into the fire place. His clothing lit up, and Riley went to the bar for some water, to stop the smell of burning flesh from completely overwhelming her.

It was like over-cooked bacon, and that disgusted her. She found a pitcher of water, and hoped it was enough. She doused the flames as well as she could and collapsed back onto the couch.

Riley waited patiently for Brenton after that, wondering if any of the staff was going to come in.

It only took a moment for her to smell Brenton and Lana outside the door.

36

BRENTON

Brenton followed Lana out of the drawing room. He knew Riley would be fine. She was faster than Marco, and she had a weapon. He trusted her, like she had constantly asked him to. It was time he extended that trust in her ability to do her part.

"In here," Lana murmured with an arrogance that made Brenton's temper flare. He'd been holding it back all night, letting her verbal stabs land, letting her feel powerful.

He stepped into the room she had indicated and found himself in their ballroom. The clack of Lana's heels as she walked across the room to turn on some music pissed him off. Every single one echoed in the room and made his head hurt.

He wasn't only pissed off, though. He wanted to do this because it was his duty. It was his decision to leave Lana alone for years instead of crushing her earlier. Marco was Lana's figure-head, and when Brenton had cut her out of Kingson Inc, Marco had become Lana's bank account.

"She's pretty," Lana chuckled. "Marco is going to fuck her."

"I'm sure he will ask," Brenton said with disgust. "She will not go for it."

"Are you sure?" Lana giggled, walking back towards him. "Dance with me, Brenton. You've always been an exceptional dancer. We can talk and listen to the music. Jones is finding the pictures and bringing them to us. He left the moment you asked."

"I have not done formal dancing in a long time," Brenton sighed. He took Lana's hand and waist gently and began the waltz, letting her follow him.

"It's like riding a bicycle," Lana laughed. "So, why won't your little Isabella get with my husband? Your Pride is a mess right now and ours isn't."

"Riley is just not the type," Brenton told her with a small growl. "Why did you restart this, Lana?"

"Slater," Lana said with a smile as they spun around the room. "Not the boy, though he was a useful tool."

"My uncle Cameron," Brenton groaned. "I knew it."

"Not just him..." Lana laughed as Brenton spun her with his hand. "You have a female now."

"And?" Brenton frowned at that.

"Women were always the down-fall for the Kingson men. You fall in love. Geoffrey did. With the wrong one. He liked your mother, but he loved Isabella. It was her betrayal that led to the start of his fall. He lost Cameron as an ally, as well as many others in the feline world. And now, here you are, with a little Gordon all to yourself."

"Stern," Brenton snarled, pulling Lana close to him. "I have a Stern."

"Why is that important?" Lana frowned at him. "Either way, you have a female, you showed a moment of weakness with Cameron, and I knew you would be easy to handle. Too easy. I wasn't expecting the hunters to fail so spectacularly, but after that? Brenton, how does it feel to lose?"

"I have not lost, yet," Brenton growled. "I'm still alive. Your assassins aren't."

"Excuse me?" Lana jerked her head back and away from him.

"My boys just texted me. They handled that particular problem," Brenton snarled viciously. "Tell me, how does Riley lead to my downfall? Why do you care about her?"

"I'm your aunt," Lana whispered. "The only other true born Kingson left, besides you. I can't let you have an heir, Brenton. It would ruin everything for me. It would be so much more work to deal with you and another heir. I worked so hard to take Geoffrey out, only for you to somehow keep surviving. I'm not letting the cycle continue."

"There's nothing I can give you, is there?" Brenton finally asked. He'd hoped. He kept it so far down that Riley and the guys didn't know he'd hoped. He didn't want to do this. He didn't want to truly be the last Kingson. He didn't want to kill her.

"No," Lana told him peacefully. "But you can buy some peace."

Brenton shook his head as they continued to dance. He spun her out and back into his chest one time before stopping the dance.

He didn't want to do this.

But his love would never be safe with Lana walking around.

His brothers would never be safe.

Any children he had. Their lives would be hounded by her and any children she had, trying to reclaim what she had lost her chance at.

No one he ever cared about was ever safe.

And Brenton was so tired, even as his lion begged to end the woman completely at his mercy. His pain and his rage warred inside him. His human side was fighting its hardest not to completely fall to his lion. He wasn't going to kill a woman in a fit of rage.

Lana was completely at ease. She knew he'd never wanted to kill her.

"I am stopping the cycle," Brenton whispered, holding back tears. He slowly wrapped a hand around her throat.

"You were always much too sentimental to follow through on this, Brenton," Lana laughed, trying to walk away. He only registered her shock that he didn't release her for a second.

He broke her neck quickly.

He didn't let the body drop. He held it carefully, her back to his chest.

Lana had always been a much better Kingson than he had been.

A tear rolled down his cheek as he realized he was alone.

There was no one left on the earth who understood what it meant to be a Kingson. The pressure of generations of leaders on their shoulders.

He was alone.

He lifted her body easily, ignoring how awful if felt to carry the dead weight. He stepped out of the ballroom and saw Jones in the hall. The butler went a deathly white and took a couple steps back.

"You will find them in the drawing room. They fought with each other and, finally, their toxic marriage ended itself," Brenton whispered.

"Of course, Alpha Kingson..." Jones whispered.

Brenton knew Jones would listen, so he turned away from the butler and walked slowly back to the drawing room. He caught the lightest scent of burning flesh and resisted the urge to vomit. He opened the door with one hand and saw Riley leaning back on a couch. Marco's body was smoldering.

Brenton said nothing as he gently laid Lana on the opposite couch. He said nothing as Riley stood.

They walked out together, and neither said anything until Brenton started the car and drove them away.

"Is it over?" Riley asked softly.

"There is not a shifter on this earth who will feel safe from us now," Brenton replied, holding back a wave of pain.

"Good," Riley sighed.

"How do you feel?" He looked over her face.

"Fine," Riley mumbled. "Truthfully, I feel fine. I did what I needed to do to keep the Pride safe. How do you feel?"

He didn't know how to answer that, so he didn't. He got them back to the jet, knowing it was ready to leave at a moment's notice.

He didn't answer her as it took off. He didn't answer her nearly an hour into their flight. Instead, he stumbled back to the bedroom and let go.

He cried, holding his head as he sat on the bed. He cried for a lost childhood. He cried for a missing family. He cried for a mother he never knew, a father who only cared about his potential as an Alpha. He cried over his brothers, children who never had their own dreams because they were chosen for him. He cried for Riley, a beautiful, fierce soul who did whatever it took to protect those she loved. He just cried.

Then he stopped crying and looked up to the ceiling. He was out of energy. He hoped desperately that this was all over. His heart felt like a stone in his chest, weighed down from it all.

"Brenton?" Riley called, opening the door to the bedroom on the plane.

"You can come in, beautiful," Brenton sighed, lying back. He heard her walk to him.

"Are you okay?" she asked softly, looking down at him.

"No..." he mumbled, staring at her. He loved those amber eyes and those golden waves.

"It was hard for you," Riley whispered, "because she was family."

"Yeah," Brenton groaned. "Not just family..."

"You're the last Kingson."

He wondered when his beautiful woman became so adept at knowing what was wrong. He loved her for it, though.

"Yes." he whispered back up to her. She climbed onto the bed and threw a leg over him to straddle his waist.

"You'll always have me," she sighed. "And Zachary. Troy and Gabe...and Andrew."

He closed his eyes at that thought. They weren't out of this yet. Andrew...

"I know," he groaned. "I know...it's just hard."

She kissed his face, and he wrapped his arms around her waist and rolled them over.

"How does your lion feel?" Riley asked him as he kissed her neck. He stopped and looked into her eyes.

"He's never been more pleased with himself...except once," Brenton growled softly.

"And that other time?"

"The first time I made love to you," Brenton whispered, kissing her gently. "And every other time."

"When we land, I want you to hold on to that," Riley chuckled. "He's okay. Your soul is okay, and you will be, too. Though, admittedly, our souls are wild animals."

"Yes, they are," Brenton laughed. He sobered for a moment. "I stepped back from being what I am for too long. I took the Pride home and shoved my lion away, shoved away what I was capable of in an effort to try and walk away from everything. We all did. Leashed them and tried to do things differently. Riley, thank you for reminding me what I am. Reminding me and the guys what we are. It was a hard thing to do...but it was the right thing to do. You did it with Abel, and I knew it scared the piss out of shifters everywhere. Instead of stepping up to the plate and continuing it, I backed down. Played their games instead of fighting like the lion I am."

"We aren't playing their games anymore," Riley said with heat, and Brenton nodded.

"No, we aren't. If they want to mess with the Kingson Pride, they better expect a fight," Brenton growled. "And I'm glad we found you. I'm glad we found a woman who understands what we are and holds us to be that. I'm not sure how we got so lucky with you."

He really didn't. She was everything the Pride once was and more. She had heart and fire. She was willing to go the extra mile to protect everything she held dear, instead of just surviving in their harsh world. She had grown so much, from the feisty thing, happy to get revenge on Cameron to a woman capable of taking initiative and claiming what was hers.

"I'm glad I found you all because you gave me a place to discover who I am," Riley sighed, and he heard a happy note to it. "Let's take a nap, though. I'm exhausted, and this is a long plane ride."

"Good idea," Brenton chuckled.

Later, he noticed his heart felt lighter, holding her to his chest. He twirled a finger in her hair.

He would do it again. He would kill her again, if it meant his loved ones were safe. If leaving Lana alive meant never holding Riley again, he would kill his aunt. Testing a bike for Gabe and Troy. Cooking damn muffins with Andrew or eating his food. Arguing with Zachary.

He wanted all of it, and she had wanted to take it away from him. From them, the family he was so lucky to have.

He would kill her a thousand times over.

He would kill anyone for them.

And he was done feeling sorry about it.

37

RILEY

W hen they landed, the news was already out. Marco Cartona and his wife, Lana Kingson-Cartona, were found dead in their homes.

The story? Marco murdered his wife as she stabbed him. No one believed it.

Riley thought it was far-fetched herself, but Brenton only shrugged.

"No one needs to believe it, except humans. And the police will not examine the bodies. They will be quietly buried in the Cartona family plot alongside Abel. The people who worked for them will be given jobs all over the world with other prides. And everyone will continue on with their business."

"Yeah," Riley snorted. "I figured."

"You want to know what is next?" Brenton asked, looking over her face. She smiled at him.

"What?"

"We are going to check on the boys." Brenton chuckled softly. "Oh...and I need to turn my phone back on and listen to it blow up."

She watched him do just that. The moment the phone was back, she glanced at the screen.

Fifty text messages. All from Zachary.

"The brothers took a couple minor injuries," Brenton whispered to her.

"Yeah, they sent me a text telling me." Riley chuckled.

"Zachary is probably telling me to get to the hospital to kick their asses for getting hurt, but that's actually not what I need to do next," Brenton sighed. "I need to make a call, from the mansion."

"Do you want any of us there for that?" she asked softly as they walked to their Range Rover.

"No. It's nothing, really. A lot of people will be telling me how sorry they are. The truth is...there is no one else around who is brave enough to try what Lana did. Because no one was safe the way Lana was. And, in the end, not even she was safe."

"It feels so easy," Riley sighed. "All tied up in a bow. Lana played a game and if...if my dad didn't help us, we would have lost."

"I know," Brenton whispered. "But we have something else to worry about."

"Andrew," Riley groaned. "We'll get him back, right?"

She didn't like how Brenton didn't answer her, but there was no reason for them to lie to each other now.

"Let's get to the hospital," Brenton said, opening the passenger door for her. She climbed in and rode quietly, checking Brenton's messages for him.

"Nothing really that important," Riley chuckled softly. "Jessie sent you a text calling us 'stupid, crazy motherfuckers' but that's about it."

"We just assassinated two people, Riley," Brenton chuckled. "We are kind of stupid, crazy motherfuckers."

Well, he had a point, Riley thought.

They made it to the hospital and walked into the room. None of the wolves were on watch anymore. They found Zachary in his bed, whining about how Gabe and Troy got hurt. Riley pulled her jacket down further to cover the bruise on her wrist from Marco. Troy and Gabe somehow wedged themselves precariously on either side of him, and Riley held back a laugh.

"How long have they been like that?" Riley asked Thomas, watching Brenton go over and slap each brother on the stomach.

"About four hours." Thomas laughed. "They told Zachary if he didn't quit bitching, they were going to give him the cuddle he asked for. He didn't stop bitching."

"Weirdos," Riley snorted.

"How do you feel?" Thomas asked her this time.

"Good," Riley shrugged. "For the first time in a long time, I feel like it's all over."

"This is how wolves deal with things, we just fight and kill each other," Thomas chuckled. "It does have a nice sense of finality to it, doesn't it?"

"Yeah," Riley murmured, watching Troy fall off the bed, onto his back. Brenton howled with laughter, and Zachary laughed until he winced. Gabe was smart enough to get off the bed before he also fell.

At that moment, Doctor Tanaka walked in and smiled at all of them. Riley was surprised by the snarl Gabe and Troy both released. It made the doctor pale.

"You two have something to say?" Brenton asked them, ignoring the doctor for a moment.

"Tanaka used to be a member of the Kudo Pride," Gabe hissed. "I didn't think you would come back in here, today. I figured when we figured out who the assassins were, you would disappear."

"I'm a doctor, Mr. Walker," Tanaka growled, and Riley raised her eyebrows. She didn't think the doctor had it in him. "I left the Kudo Pride fifty years ago and never looked back. Please don't accuse of me of that nonsense ever again."

"Sorry," Gabe mumbled. "I'm a little...worked up."

"That is completely understandable," Doctor Tanaka acknowledged with a nod, calm again. "I was just getting in and figured we could try something, now that it has been a couple of days."

"What is that?" Brenton asked softly.

"Smelling salts," Tanaka chuckled. "He has normal brain activity, and we haven't yet hit the point where I'm comfortable saying he'll be comatose. He could just be resting deeply as he heals."

"Why didn't we try this sooner?" Brenton growled.

"I wanted to make sure you had a stable Pride for him to heal in," Tanaka whispered, looking sad and a bit guilty.

Riley sucked in a breath. She looked over at Brenton, who looked murderous.

"Doctor Tanaka, please, proceed," Riley told the shifter quickly. "Please."

"I care for my patients, not just physically, but genuinely," Tanaka continued, "and I didn't want to wake him up, only for all of you to fail and be unable to protect him as he heals. But...well news has already reached this hospital. It seems Alpha Kingson has finally crossed the final line of his humanity and killed his most powerful enemy. I feel good trying this now."

"For a neutral party, you really follow politics," Brenton snarled. "Wake him up."

Tanaka said nothing after that, only went to the bed and

cracked open something. Riley edged closer, and felt Troy wrap his arms around her from behind.

She held her breath as Tanaka placed something under Andrew's nose.

And she cried out as Andrew winced and shook his head, only to groan.

"Careful, Mr. Hicks. You were seriously injured and still have several injures to your head and abdomen."

"Fuck," Andrew groaned. Riley watched his good eye open and saw tears fill it. Her vision went blurry and she staggered forward. "Guys, it's Slater and Abel is dead and-"

"We know," Riley cried out, putting a hand on his good cheek. "Love, we know. It's over."

"It's over?" Andrew groaned, looking over her face and then, turning his head gingerly towards Brenton to her left.

"Lana," Brenton sighed. "I killed her."

"I'm sorry," Andrew whispered hoarsely.

"Nothing to be sorry for," Brenton chuckled. "Not you."

"Brenton?" Andrew grabbed Riley's hand and held it to his good cheek, his eye closed again.

"Yeah, buddy?"

"I want my diner back," Andrew moaned, "and only the diner. No more of this. I'm so done with all of this."

Riley laughed softly as Brenton told Andrew he could have whatever he wanted. Riley watched Troy and Gabe slide up to Andrew's other side, whispering their own thanks that he was back.

"When can we go home?" Zachary growled from his bed, and Andrew frowned.

"Zachary, why aren't you over here?" Andrew seemed so confused.

"Because I was shot right after you got stabbed," Zachary snarled. "Shit, I'm not mad at you. I'm just-"

"Cranky," Riley finished. "Zachary is cranky."

"Of course," Andrew laughed and began to cough. Then he winced and groaned. She could only imagine how much his face hurt from the broken bones.

"Let's go home," Brenton whispered. And Riley agreed. In every part of her, she agreed.

38

ANDREW

The Pride spent a week catching Andrew up on everything that had happened in the forty-eight hours he'd been out of commission. They also coddled him, tucked him into bed, and treated him like he needed to be handled like glass.

Today he was going to cook, though. And nothing they did could stop him.

He felt smothered. He'd never been the one who needed to be taken care of. He was the one who took care of all of them. He had learned to cook, divided up chores, and was responsible for the house so they could feel safe—so they could live quietly.

He didn't want to admit he might need the help.

For the entire week, it had eaten at him.

The problem he refused to admit to them. Because if they knew, he wouldn't be allowed to do anything, anymore. He could lose his place in the Pride and in the family.

He opened a recipe book he ordered offline and sighed at the recipe he wanted to try. 2 eggs per serving. Milk.

Flour. Vanilla extract. He ran through all the ingredients, like normal, before going to the fridge to pull them out.

He pulled out everything and rechecked the recipe as Troy and Gabe wandered into the kitchen and passed him. He was happy that they didn't stop and ask him if he needed help. They then ruined that.

"Hey, Andrew" Troy walked back in. "Need any help?"

"No," Andrew groaned. "You aren't coming anywhere near my kitchen. And we aren't eating another dinner consisting of takeout."

"Okay," Gabe chuckled. "We're still setting Jessie up with her own place, so we'll be back later."

"How's she doing?" Andrew asked quickly. He was curious. A pregnant female was now going to settle down in Wild Junction, a strange occurrence. And she'd saved his life. He owed her.

"Good. Apparently the baby is healthy. We've tried tracking down the possible fathers but so far, nothing. She's resigned herself to a life of single motherhood at this point, but Brenton and Riley have already promised her that we would help in any way," Troy told him with a smile. "She had wanted to be more helpful with everything but..."

"She was helpful enough," Andrew mumbled.

"She was," Gabe agreed, "and now she's buddy-buddy with Riley and Abigail. It's terrifying."

"And Phoebe, that human Riley used to hang out with. She's apparently really cool," Troy groaned. "We now have a gaggle of women running around Wild Junction. Those four tore up Rocker's the other night."

Andrew chuckled with a nod. He'd heard Riley get home, singing at the top her lungs as Brenton carried her inside. He'd been laying around in the den when Brenton dropped her on a couch. She then proceeded to fuck him while Andrew just watched in semi-shock, and mostly amusement.

They were all living their lives again, slowly but surely. They were fixing things they'd neglected, relationships that had fallen to the wayside, building a real life for themselves, knowing that their worst enemies were gone.

Except him. He was carrying a secret. He was broken, and he didn't know if he could tell anyone.

"Go on, you two, and help her," Andrew told them.

Andrew waited for the leopards to leave before refocusing on the recipe. He mixed, added dashes of salt, stirred.

It was a meat pie that he'd never tried before. It was a pretty pedestrian item, but he figured if the Pride liked it, he could add it to the diner's menu and see how the town enjoyed it.

He slid the two pies he'd prepared into the preheated oven and set the timer. Forty-five minutes. He slowly sat down at the bar and waited.

"Andrew?" Riley's voice made him turn, and he smiled at her. The swelling around his face had decreased enough that he could use both eyes and he was insanely happy for that, just so he could see her face.

"Hey, darling," Andrew purred as she walked over to him.

"Cooking? You must have decided that Brenton's coddling was too much?" she asked with a smile. Andrew groaned.

"Yes. And Troy's...and Gabe's. And yours, actually." Andrew chuckled. She laughed softly and kissed his cheek.

"Well, we're all just following Brenton's lead," Riley whispered with a small pout.

"Liar," Andrew growled softly. "Troy and Gabe, yes. You?

You are just enjoying being able to tell me what to do." He watched a smile spread over her face.

"Yes, I am. Does this mean I'm higher in the ranks than you?" she teased in a small growl.

"No," Andrew purred, wrapping a hand around the back of her neck. "No, it doesn't."

"Prove it," she whispered, and Andrew pulled her close slowly into a kiss. It was a soft kiss, it had to be, since his face was all fucked up. He and Zachary were also banned from...strenuous activity until they were healed. Andrew hated it.

"You know I can't," he snarled. "Don't tease me."

"Did you hear what happened to Brenton this morning?" she asked. Andrew frowned. He'd been told something...but he couldn't remember what it was.

"Uh," he searched for the words. "Remind me, I must not have been paying attention when he told me..."

He knew he'd spoken to Brenton about something...

"Some guys pledged their eternal support to the Kingson Pride, astounded by our 'resilience and personal strength in times of great peril.'" Riley laughed. "They weren't a part of Lana's scheme."

Andrew honestly didn't know what she was talking about. And that made him not okay. He continued to listen to her talk about this meeting Andrew was sure he'd heard about before. He'd been with Brenton just earlier in the day...

He zoned out, thinking about it.

"Andrew, your timer is going off," Riley chuckled. "Earth to Andrew?"

"What timer?" Andrew frowned.

"Oh, love," Riley whispered. "You put something in the oven."

"Fuck," Andrew growled, rushing over to the oven as it went off. "I don't know...what's going on with me."

"Andrew, how often is this happening?" Riley asked softly as he pulled the meat pies out.

"I normally remember things when someone else mentions them," Andrew whispered. "But some things are going missing completely."

"How much is going missing completely?" Riley inquired with a warning in her tone. She wasn't going to accept him pulling rank or trying to hedge the conversation.

"Twice in the last week," he sighed. "I remember meeting with Brenton after his meeting this morning, but I don't remember what was said. And the other thing... something about the Kudo Pride."

"They offered us their support as apologies for being used as a go-between for the assassins," Riley told him as he set the pies out to cool.

"That," he mumbled. Tears pricked his eyes. He had a great memory. He could memorize recipes and now he was constantly checking them, just in case. And now things were slipping.

"Andrew," Riley sounded so sad, and Andrew felt his breath catch in his throat. "Tanaka said you might deal with this. And it could be permanent. You should have told us."

"I was always the one who took care of everyone," Andrew whispered. "Always."

"Let us take care of you," Riley pleaded. "Let us do this for you. You didn't deserve this. You just wanted to be something for Brenton and the Pride, and it got you hurt. Let us take care of you for a little while."

"It's hard," Andrew whispered. He didn't want to lose his role in the Pride...

"Are you done in here?" she asked him softly. He nodded and let her take his hand. "Come on, let's go."

"Riley, I'm not allowed to do any strenuous activity," Andrew growled softly.

"Then I'll make this easy for you," Riley chuckled. "But I think you need to relax and lay in bed. After that, we're going to call Doctor Tanaka and tell him what's going on."

"You better make this good enough that I forget that second part," Andrew purred at her, following her up to her room.

"I'll do my best," Riley chuckled, "but you need some loving."

He did. Goddamn it, he really did.

She got her door for them and locked it behind her. He pulled her to his body and slowly, and so gently, kissed her. He let her rain kisses across his bruised and battered face as he tugged her shirt up.

"Slow," Riley whispered, pulling back from him. He let her undress him instead. He felt tears in his eyes as she kissed every inch of him. He backed up and sat on the bed at her direction, a light push. Completely nude, he watched her kneel down in front of him and lick the underside of his shaft.

"Oh, fuck," he groaned, closing his eyes for a moment. "Darling..."

"Hush," Riley chuckled. He opened his eyes to see her take the tip of his cock in her mouth. He watched as she went further, making him moan.

He didn't want it to end, but his balls tightened when she was able to take all of him. He hissed and wrapped a hand in her hair and pulled her back gently.

"Please," he groaned. "Don't end me like this. You'll completely undo me if you keep that up."

She laughed and got to her feet, letting his hand fall from her hair. He took her waist in both hands and pulled her close to stand between his thighs.

He tugged her shirt up and purred when she didn't stop him. He kissed her breasts as he revealed them, loving the soft, creamy skin. He threw her shirt away and unclipped her bra, letting in fall to the floor between them. He didn't care about the black lace or the dainty bows. He only cared about being with her and remembering it.

He took one of her nipples into his mouth and listened to her gasp. He ran his tongue over it and felt goosebumps raise on her skin. He purred, gently palming her other breast, making her back arch so they were pushed out to him even more. His free hand roamed down and undid her jeans, and she pushed them down, along with whatever little thong she had on.

"Naughty," he growled, getting a glimpse of it around her ankles.

"You like it," she purred.

"I do," he chuckled.

"Lay back on the bed for me, Andrew," she whispered, and he scooted back so his back was against the still-cracked headboard. They really needed to replace it, but Andrew heard a small rumor from Zachary about a plan to get her a completely new and bigger bed.

"Come here," he growled. She crawled across the bed to him, and he held his breath as she straddled him. He slid a hand between her legs and used his other hand to pull her face to his. He rolled a thumb over her clit and covered her cry with a kiss. He slid two fingers into her, happy to know she was already completely wet for him. He already knew she was turned on, he could smell it, but something about feeling that wetness was a pleasure.

She broke the kiss and moaned into his shoulder. He growled as she bit down, and he pumped his fingers faster. He wanted more. He wanted to roll her over and worship that ass he loved so much, but that wasn't in the cards for at least a month.

Then she accidentally hit the stitches on his side and he groaned, letting his head fall back to the headboard. A worse idea. That made his skull rattle and he could feel every single facial fracture he had.

"Fuck," Andrew cursed. The pain made him stop the important work he wanted to be focused on.

"Oh, Andrew," Riley looked horrified. "I'm sorry! This was a bad idea."

"Don't move," he growled, throwing in every ounce of dominance he had into the command as she tried to get off his lap. "I'll be fine. Let me have this, Riley."

He watched her eyes go wide, and she settled back where he wanted her. He didn't normally throw rank around, not in bed. Here, he wanted them to be equals, but he wasn't going to be left with blue balls because she felt bad.

"This happened to me," Andrew continued to growl, "and it sucks, but I'll survive. And Riley, don't take away my pride by treating me like an invalid. I fought for the Pride, and I won, like I always have. Like I always will."

"Andrew," she breathed out, gently touching his bruised cheek. "I know but...I never thought it would be you."

"I'm not built for it...any of it," Andrew swallowed. "I've always been what Brenton needed from me. Housekeeper, cook, political mind when they couldn't manage on their own...I promised myself as a child that my Alpha deserved my best. But...my friend, Brenton, deserved everything.

Anything. And I'll give him that, no matter what. And, darling? I'll give you that."

"Why?" Riley whispered, looking teary.

"Because Jameson once told me that I would be thrown away." Andrew held back tears too. "And I haven't been. But...it's possible now. I'm broken."

"No," Riley cried out to him, holding his cheeks gingerly. "No, Andrew, we would never throw you away. You belong with us, even if you want to only run the diner and be comfortable. Even if you need a little help. You're mine. I would never let anyone push you aside. Brenton would never do that to you either. Zachary, Troy, and Gabe will always be at your side. You belong to us."

Andrew cried softly, those old things Jameson said to him coming to the surface. Who did he believe, Riley or the man that raised him? A man he killed to protect his brothers.

Riley kissed him, and he gasped as she slid down on him. He hadn't expected that.

"Darling," he growled softly as she gently wiped his face.

"Mine," she whispered. "I love you. More than you can ever know."

He let her ride him, groaning at every stroke. He held her close, letting her whisper sweet nothings to him as she took him. She reminded him that she loved him, reminded him that they all did, in their own ways.

He let his hands roam, remembering her, every single inch. The new scars from their war to survive. The tattoos he loved to see on her precious creamy skin. The dusty rose of her nipples.

She picked up her speed as he let a hand drift lower again and rub her clit softly. A gentle touch to send her over the edge and take him with her.

He listened to her cry out at his touch and felt her climax begin. She rode him through it, the rippling of her inner walls driving him mad.

He took her chin with his free hand and pulled her face to his. He kissed her as he followed her, shooting deep into her.

They were both left panting and wet-faced. They had both cried. Andrew wiped the tear tracks off her cheeks.

"I love you," he whispered, full of emotion.

"I love you too," she whispered back. "Forever and ever. Through it all."

"I should talk to Brenton about this, shouldn't I?" he asked, holding her to his chest. She didn't fully relax, probably afraid of hitting his stitches again.

"You should. I can make the call to Tanaka and let him know. I'll get an appointment scheduled."

He swallowed more tears before they could start. He was broken. He didn't know if he could be fixed.

But he had her. She would help him through this. He could trust that.

Now, he needed to tell his friend and Alpha.

THE MEAT PIES WERE A SUCCESS. Riley had helped him prepare the rest of dinner, which they kept simple. Green beans, mashed potatoes. Simple.

After dinner, Andrew found Brenton just standing in the backyard, looking out over the woods.

"Anything wrong?" Andrew called out, kicking off his shoes to enjoy the grass beneath his feet.

"I am lonely," Brenton whispered. "And I am not sure why."

Andrew sighed, walking closer. It looked like Brenton had something he needed help with as well.

"When did it start?" Andrew asked, moving to stand next to Brenton. They had been here before, as youths. They stood like this while waiting for Zachary, Troy, and Gabe to come back after hiding Jameson's body away. Andrew had been a wreck...so had Brenton.

Here they were again. Both wrecks.

"The moment I killed Lana," Brenton said, devoid of emotion. "I would do it again. In a heartbeat. She was never really my family...but she also was the only one who understood."

"She also tried to kill us...a number of times," Andrew reminded him. He'd always told Brenton to handle her, and Brenton had always stepped back. He would kill any of their enemies...except her. Brenton always had a soft spot for the few family members he had left. His uncle Cameron. His aunt, Lana. The last connections he had to his parents and the bloodlines that had made him.

It was that tiny soft spot that had started this mess.

"She understood what it meant to be a Kingson and the pressure the rest of the world dropped on you," Andrew agreed, continuing when Brenton didn't. "She was also a cunning, dangerous woman who wouldn't miss you. She wouldn't feel lonely. She would go have a bunch of kids, finally, and take the figurative throne. Don't miss her."

"I don't want it." Brenton mumbled. "To be the last. Damn, Andrew...this is my family. This. If I could make you all Kingsons with me, I fucking would. You all deserve it, being here with me and for me all these years. Loving the same woman as me. I would give you my name for that. And then I wouldn't be alone..."

Andrew choked on that, his eyes filling with tears.

"I need to tell you something, Brenton," Andrew whispered. He couldn't keep it to himself and Riley any longer.

"Let's hear it," Brenton sighed, looking sadly at Andrew.

"I'm having...some short-term memory problems...Riley and I scheduled an appointment with Tanaka and a specialist for next week." Andrew said it as fast as he could. "I don't remember the exact day..."

That hurt. Andrew couldn't remember. He had it on his phone, but he didn't want to check it.

He felt big arms wrap around him and stood a little paralyzed, for a moment. Brenton was hugging him. This wasn't a rare thing, he just hadn't been expecting it.

"Why didn't you tell me sooner?" Brenton asked, a small growl in the question as he nearly crushed Andrew.

"I was scared," Andrew muttered, "that it would be too much of a problem for you to want me around anymore."

"You were my first friend, Andrew," Brenton groaned, pulling back. He held Andrew's shoulders, and Andrew felt unnerved by Brenton's gaze. "I am sorry, but I own your dumb ass. You are not going anywhere. You humble me. You remind me that normal people are out there and that they are capable of incredible things. And I love you like a brother."

"I won't be as good as I once was," Andrew pressed the topic and Brenton chuckled.

"Andrew, I was never letting you get involved again, anyway. You have done enough and more. You *never* had to prove yourself to me. Funny enough, when we were kids, I just wanted to prove myself to you. The older one that knew what real hard work was. Fuck, man."

Andrew pulled Brenton back into the hug and, silently,

they stood in the grass until a soft laugh could be heard. Andrew snuck a glance and saw Riley smiling at them. The face she wore was very much an 'I told you so,' which made him laugh too.

"We are going to help you," Brenton chuckled. "Every step of the way. If this is permanent, then fine. We can deal with that. Andrew, it is over. There is no one left for us to fight. With Lana gone, no one is going to stand up and try again. I have spent the last week telling every feline shifter on the earth that we are out. There is no reason to mess with us." Brenton put his forehead to Andrew's so gently, Andrew wondered if they were even touching or if they were just that close. "You can be whatever you want to be. House husband, diner owner, chef...Andrew...you do not have to be anything for me anymore, except you. And here. You need to be here. For her, for me. For Troy and Gabe, who still somehow need a father-figure, or at least an older brother who is around. For Zachary, who needs someone to soften him a bit."

"Plus, who's going to watch me get completely fucked sideways?" Riley teased and both males turned to her. Andrew bared his teeth in a grin as Brenton growled low, readying himself to go after her.

She stuck her tongue out, and Brenton snarled. Andrew laughed as Brenton ran after her. She was quick as hell, but Brenton had longer legs. Andrew walked slowly, knowing he would find them in her room when he got there. Brenton would keep the door unlocked for him.

He felt lighter. Things were still dark for him. He just had to trust his family to help him through this. And hope that he never forgot a single minute of his time with them.

He could be whatever he wanted and not what he was

needed to be. He could step back from the politics. He could fight with them, for them...and he could live a quiet happy life when fighting wasn't necessary.

He also had an idea. He would need Riley's help though. And Zachary's. Troy and Gabe would just need to agree to it.

39
_____

ZACHARY

January

Zachary groaned as Doctor Serrano checked his back one more time.

"The wounds have healed up, though they've scarred. Unavoidable. How are you feeling otherwise?" Serrano was pleased with Zachary's recovery, but Zachary wasn't.

"My back always fucking hurts," he growled. "Always."

"The muscles need to rebuild their strength," Serrano sighed. "And the fracture on your vertebrae is still healing."

"How much longer? It's already been a month." Zachary was used to smaller injuries that healed so much faster thanks to whatever made shifters faster healers. They were well into a new year, a cold January. Zachary was ready to be healed.

"I would give it another month and an x-ray just to be sure," Serrano told him, keeping it light, as if there was no permanent damage. "Something is on your mind."

"Yeah," Zachary growled. "I just want to heal right."

"You are healing perfectly well. You just need to be patient."

Zachary snorted.

"I'm going to go," he mumbled, standing up from the examination table.

"Are you taking your medications?" Serrano asked quietly.

"No," Zachary snarled. "I flushed them."

"Why?" Serrano frowned at him and Zachary rolled his eyes.

"Because I have a recovering drug addict for a brother, and I don't want him to feel the itch. Andrew's are kept under lock and key, at Gabe's request."

"I'll write you another prescription," Serrano groaned. "You need the muscle relaxers to keep your back from spasming."

"I really don't," Zachary hissed, and, for the first time, Serrano hissed back.

"You do, you stubborn ass of a patient. I understand that Gabe has problems, but he knows how they can be avoided. You just don't want to take them, but you need to. I'll call Brenton in here if you need a dressing down from your Alpha over it, try me. Or better yet, Riley. She seems to get all of you to do exactly what she wants."

"I outrank her," Zachary mumbled, feeling petulant. He didn't need to get thrown back into the doghouse. He'd just gotten out of it. "Please don't call her. I'll start taking the meds and lock them up with Andrew's. There's no reason to call her."

Zachary was already still in some trouble because he pulled a muscle trying to workout when he wasn't supposed to. Riley and Brenton...and Andrew had all given him a verbal beating over it. Then Riley left his bed until he was feeling better and as punishment for being careless.

Yeah, she had them figured out. He had been on his knees last night for her, apologizing for being insufferable over his injury.

"I thought so," Serrano chuckled, handing him a slip. Zachary took it and shoved it in his pocket. "The pharmacy here in the hospital will get them ready for you by the time Andrew is out of his appointment. How's he doing?"

"Better," Zachary sighed, rubbing his lower back. "He's adjusting, and so are we. He thinks it's a bigger thing than it is. I'm just happy he's alive. I don't care if he can remember what he made us for breakfast or not."

"He's not worried about breakfast," Serrano told Zachary gently. Zachary narrowed his eyes. "He's worried about not remembering moments with all of you. And you need to understand that."

Zachary snarled. He did understand it. He just didn't know what to say about it. He didn't want Andrew to feel like he was useless or losing them. He just didn't know how to fix it. And then there was Brenton, who floated between being so content and pleased with their life...and miserable because every feline shifter on the planet was watching him, waiting for the last Kingson to make a move, to do something.

The only ones Zachary could count on to be right in the head were the brothers and Riley. The brothers, of all fucking people. He loved them to death, but there had been a time when those two were the *last* people he could rely on. Now, they were shining examples of having problems and continuing on.

Pricks.

He was mildly jealous of them.

They had somehow grown into real fucking adults over the last year in Wild Junction.

Zachary knew that was Riley's doing. She loved them, she pushed them to talk about their issues and overcome them. She reminded them that there was so much more than the bottom of the bottle, booze or pills.

Zachary left the exam room and saw her waiting patiently for him.

"Hey, baby," he purred, pulling her into his chest.

"Hey, Zachary," she chuckled. "How's my big, cranky tiger?"

"Cranky," he growled with a smile. "He would like to get pet."

"I'll pet you when we're home," she laughed, kissing his cheek. He didn't like that his back hurt when he leaned down for her, but that was something he was going to ignore. Absolutely nothing was going to stop him from getting kissed by her.

"You can pet me in the car," he growled playfully. "You like playing around in the backseat, I know."

He watched just a small tinge of pink enter her cheeks. He remembered driving home while Brenton gave her an orgasm. She was remembering too.

"We could have Brenton drive this time," he whispered in her ear, "and Andrew can watch me blow your fucking mind." He loved the way her breath caught, which distracted him from the small slap to his stomach. He gave a soft grunt, rubbing the spot.

"You can't talk like that in the hospital. Plus, you have to drive. Brenton is going home tomorrow with Troy. We're taking Andrew home, where Gabe is waiting. Remember?"

He had. A pity, really. He would have to wait until they

got home and tucked Andrew into bed...probably hers. Zachary would even let Andrew have a go.

They walked silently, exchanging dirty looks, on their way to Andrew's room. Brenton and Troy were both in the room, as well. Zachary felt like it was too small with all of them in there, but he wanted to hear how Andrew was.

"What did I miss?" Zachary whispered to Brenton.

"His face is healing fine," Brenton sighed. "The memory problems will probably be permanent."

"We can handle that," Zachary reminded him.

"We can," Brenton agreed with a strong nod.

"I can hear you two," Andrew growled softly. Zachary was happy to see that Andrew hadn't lost all of his hard edge that he hid so well. That streak of dominance and passion underneath the calm, loving nature.

"You won't remember it in an hour," Troy teased, making Andrew snort.

"You can't make me laugh about this. It's not funny." Andrew chuckled softly. "Seriously."

"Too soon?" Troy asked, looking around the room.

"Too soon," Riley told him with an eye roll.

Zachary watched Tanaka read over papers and examine x-rays and cat scans of Andrew's head.

"We'll keep monitoring but, everything is healing nicely. Mr. Hicks, I wish I could do something more, but this is where we enter the great unknown. The brain is a tricky thing. We didn't notice any damage and still don't, but these things are complicated."

"You say this every time," Andrew sighed. "I know, Doctor Tanaka. It's okay. If it's a problem forever, then I have support to help me. I'll start taking notes and dealing with it."

"Yes, you do have support," Tanaka said with a wistful,

happy note. Zachary saw the doctor look over the Pride. Everyone was in attendance, except Gabe, who got caught up in a meeting with one of the Walkers' clients. "You have a good family to help you through this."

"I do," Andrew confirmed, sliding off the bed. "Are we done?"

"We are, you're free to go," Tanaka chuckled. "Call me if anything changes, please."

"We will, Doctor Tanaka," Brenton said, shaking the shifter's hand. "We will."

Zachary led them all out into the hallway and casually threw an arm over Andrew's shoulder.

"Ready to head home?" he asked.

"Yeah. I am, please," Andrew groaned, nodding. Zachary took a long look at Andrew's face. The bruising was mostly gone, except for the worst parts on his cheekbones. His nose was now slightly crooked, but it wasn't awful. It added something even more rugged to the long-haired outdoorsman that Andrew embodied.

He would be fine, Zachary told himself. They all would be.

"Brenton, Troy, you both be good and safe," Riley mumbled, kissing each of them. Zachary and Andrew watched and waited.

"We will," Brenton sighed. "We will. This is all just clean up. Everyone wants me to know that they were just swayed by Lana...and they want to make sure I never make a play to be bigger than I am now. They are willing to leave us alone if I do not try to be what the Kingson family once was."

"Yes, yes," Riley mumbled, waving her hand. "Go deal with them. Tell them that we're more of a family than a Pride now. It's the truth."

"It is," Brenton chuckled. Troy grinned and clapped

their Alpha on the back, and Zachary watched them leave. Then he pulled on Riley and tugged her to walk between him and Andrew.

"I have an idea," Andrew said quietly as they walked to the Range Rover they brought to Denver. "And it's going to sound crazy."

"What's it about?" Riley asked, curious.

"Our family," Andrew told them with a smile, "and finally being a real one."

Zachary's eyes went wide as Andrew explained.

It was a fucking crazy idea.

Zachary loved it.

"I don't need Brenton's signature to do it," he laughed. "I have power of attorney."

"Yeah," Riley whispered. "And this fixes one other problem."

"What's that?" Andrew chuckled.

"I was never going to marry any of you because whose name would I have taken?" Riley smirked with a shrug.

"Well, damn," Zachary groaned, turning on the Range Rover. "Thanks for finally admitting that, baby. I appreciate it."

"It's the truth," Riley laughed. "Think Troy and Gabe will go for it?"

"They will," Andrew whispered. "I've already talked to them about it, knowing they have their own things they'll need to deal with if we go through with it."

"So, when do we want this done?" Zachary asked from the driver's seat. Riley sat next to him while Andrew lay down in the backseat. "It could take me months to get it all set up."

"What about my opening? It's going to be in April, right

after my birthday. And...well, you all know what I paint. Us. Our family, our friends. It's the perfect time."

"Yes," Andrew laughed. "I like that. Write it down, so I remember it in an hour and don't ask again. Please."

"I can do that," Riley chuckled.

Zachary considered the plan, Andrew's scheme. It would solve a lot and it would make one Alpha so happy.

It might also scare a lot of people, but Zachary didn't really give a shit.

Zachary only ever had this family. One he was willing to throw his life away for.

He would be honored to throw the Woods name away and be a real family.

40

RILEY

February

F ebruary came faster than Riley had thought it would. December was a blur of danger, death, and the beginning of healing. January was hoping for recovery.

But she had something to do, something she had promised for February. She couldn't put it off any longer, and he had called her first.

Riley walked into the little sandwich place on the town square. She'd avoided it since her last talk with Haley. She never came back to it.

Today, she was meeting her dad, though, and it was a nice place to sit for a talk.

"Riley," his voice reached her, soft and sad. She also heard just the tiny bit of hope in it.

She looked over at him and swallowed. There he was, her father. Keith Stern. Brown hair with a hint of gray in it, strong build, older face, wrinkles she still wasn't used to.

He'd helped them. Now, she needed to give him a chance.

She wanted to, even if Brenton hadn't promised that he would give a gentle push for her to try.

"Dad," Riley whispered, walking over to him as he stood up from his seat.

"I quit my job," he told her hurriedly. She stopped in her tracks and let that register. "I thought a lot about it. And I heard your Pride finally told everyone that you were out of the game. And I heard what you all did with the information I gave you..."

"Woah, Dad. Stop. Stop for a minute." She held up a hand and walked over to him. "You quit the SSTF?"

"I did," Keith huffed.

"Why? They meant everything to you. The mission, catching...criminals." Riley couldn't just come out and say 'Mom,' but they both knew who she was referring to.

"Because they weren't everything to me," Keith whispered, "and it took me too long to see that what should have been my everything was something I pushed away, thinking I couldn't handle it. And how they treated you? I should have known back then. I should have stepped up and backed out of the mission to go back to you. I failed you. In so many ways. So, I quit before they could fire me for cleaning up everything that happened in December. And for helping it all happen."

Riley was at a loss for words. She tried to make the mental jumps to figure out what changed. He must have noticed because he just helped her walk out, and then they were wandering the small town square.

"I'm not comfortable with what happened in December, but I would like to be a part of your life again, if you'll have me." he mumbled, looking a bit guilty. Scratch that, he looked very guilty.

Riley had something they needed to clear up, though.

"If it happens again, will you run for the hills?" she asked him softly. "If the Pride goes out and does it again. Can you live with knowing your daughter is completely okay with killing someone who threatens who she loves? Can you accept that?"

"I..."

"We're wild animals, Dad, wild souls who will do what we need to do to protect each other. I'm okay with that being in me. I'm okay with knowing that I'm capable of violence and ruthlessness in the effort to protect them. I'm okay with knowing they are capable of those things to protect me. I need you to be okay with it, too. Or at least accept it."

This was too important. Riley held her breath. She would walk away from him if he couldn't. There was no going back for her. There was no rewinding the clock to the content, semi-lost woman she had been. There was nothing she wouldn't do to protect what was hers. Her men were her territory, and she would fight to the bitter end, no matter what.

She couldn't do less than that anymore.

"I can accept it," Keith mumbled after a long silence. "Because I should have done it...years ago for you...for our family. And because I didn't, we lost our family, each other."

"We did," Riley agreed.

"I was a coward, and while I'm uncomfortable with knowing what you can do, what your boys can do...I respect it. You all are strong. And I want to be a part of it. I won't get in your hair...I have no ground to stand on, I won't butt in where I'm not wanted, but I want to be around. I want to meet this daughter I lost because of my own idiocy."

"And Mom?" she whispered.

"Her enemies will track her down, eventually. She's gone to ground. Though...have you seen her?"

"Once," Riley admitted to him. "I told her I was staying with the guys. I didn't want a psychotic mother over them."

"When?" Keith frowned at her.

"I'll show you the tape later, but last April. It's a story," Riley snorted.

"So...I'm not looking at being a grandfather, am I?" Keith shifted uncomfortably. Riley raised her eyebrows and gave him a wide-eyed stare.

"No. No. No, no, no." Riley shook her head, terrified at the idea. "At least five years of no craziness before any ideas of that."

"That's good," Keith coughed. "I'd like to get to know all of them before I even consider thinking of any of them as sons-in-law."

"Well..." Riley sighed. Already she was feeling better about this. He seemed willing, and she knew she was. After everything, it was time to fix things. He was giving away something that meant so much to him and meeting her on her ground. She would give him a chance. "There's something you should know."

And she told him the plan Andrew came up with, and how she was doing it.

He only groaned.

"I guess I'll just have to get used to them. There's no chance you're ever leaving them?"

"Not a chance," Riley laughed. "Not a chance in hell."

41

ANDREW

March

A ndrew grinned in the late March sun as the mayor of Wild Junction cut the ribbon on the rebuilt Starry Night Diner. There was a party going on in the parking lot, and he found himself bombarded by people from every direction. Many asked how he was feeling, others just wanted to check in and see if they still had jobs.

In the end, he didn't fire anyone. He just didn't want a fight over it. He wanted his diner back, he wanted the town happy again. He wanted something that was his. Purely his.

"I'm so happy for you," Riley laughed, kissing his cheek. "I'm so glad it's back, and it's stunning."

"I'm glad, too," Andrew chuckled, pulling her close. He gave her a hard kiss, and people cheered. Brenton clapped him on the back and pulled him into a hug the moment Andrew was done with Riley.

"This is what I want for you," Brenton whispered, holding him. "Just this."

KRISTEN BANET

"Thank you," Andrew mumbled, holding Brenton.

Andrew was still third in the Pride, and he always would be. But they'd had no trouble since December, and it seemed like they were about to get the rest and peace they always wanted. They had finally earned it.

Every day was a challenge for Andrew, though. He took notes, he reread recipes, he forgot seeing someone when he saw them again an hour later.

He had hated it to begin with, but now, looking back, he was just thankful to have the days. He could take the small challenges, if it meant seeing amber eyes waiting for him to help him cook breakfast. Troy kept his gas tank filled since Andrew seemed to forget if he had gotten gas nearly every time. Gabe left him notes on his dashboard about pretty much anything. Zachary threatened to kill anyone who even bumped Andrew's head. That one annoyed Andrew a little, but he understood Zachary's issue. A second head injury could screw Andrew more than he already was.

And Brenton. He didn't treat Andrew any differently, except one thing. He told Andrew how much he meant to him more often. Brenton just did that for the entire Pride.

Andrew knew he was still shackled with being the last of his family. The Pride was working on fixing that, though.

"So, do I get to try that famous pie and shit I keep hearing about?" Thomas called out, jogging over to them, holding a beer. Andrew laughed as Zachary hugged the wolf. Brenton only shook Thomas' hand.

"Yeah, there's some on that table over there. It's four dollars a slice but you can tell them you're with us," Andrew chuckled. "I'm sure Troy will give you a piece."

"I fucking hope so," Thomas groaned, eyeing the table where Troy and Gabe were selling the food that Andrew and the kitchen staff had hustled to get ready for the day. "Those two ate all of my ribs last week without blinking an eye."

"Yeah, they do that," Riley said, giving Thomas a hug. "Come on, I'll convince them to feed you. Where are the others?"

"Off hounding Abigail to stay, I'm sure," Thomas grumbled. "Tell me, Cheetah, think we can convince her to stay?"

"I think she will." Andrew missed the rest of that conversation. Abigail was thinking it was time to go back to her practice, but she was dragging her feet.

Zachary was taking bets on how long before she left. Andrew had a grand on her staying in Wild Junction. He had another five hundred on her joining the Pack like Thomas was begging her to do. Zachary wasn't buying it, but Andrew was certain of his bet. He had a feeling he was going to make a lot of money off the other guys in the Pride. The only person who thought he was right was Brenton, who was smart enough not to get in the pool.

"Andrew," Sheriff's growl hit him, and Andrew winced. Brenton growled softly with Zachary.

"Did I do something?" Andrew asked cautiously, looking over at Sheriff and his wife, Patty. Andrew and Patty were becoming cool. She was a doll in the kitchen, and she had offered a couple of her own recipes for the diner's new menu.

"No," Sheriff huffed. "Why didn't you tell us you were going to name that blueberry cobbler after Patty? She cried, I sniffed. It was awful. Come here and give her a hug."

Andrew laughed and walked over to hug Patty, who held him gently.

"You are such a good boy," Patty chuckled. "Don't let this old bear give you a hard time, he cried, I sniffed."

"Thrown under the bus by my own wife," Sheriff groaned.

"Riley does it to us," Brenton mumbled. "I feel your pain."

"You deserve it," Sheriff growled.

"So do you," Zachary coughed.

"Come on, let's go see Ruth and let her cry on you for a little while," Patty said politely, pulling Andrew away from Brenton, Sheriff, and Zachary who were starting a small argument about who deserved what.

By the end of the day, he was exhausted but happy. He sat on the back of his truck and watched Troy and Gabe steal leftovers and put them in their Range Rover. Riley was whispering with her dad; a man Andrew was developing a small amount of respect for. He came to dinner, talked with the guys, and genuinely seemed to try and get to know them —not their reputations, but the men they actually were.

They were wild, and brash. Ruthless men who would do anything for their own safety and each other. But they loved. Andrew didn't know how they were all so capable of loving so much.

But Riley showed them that they could, that they always had. And that had led them to this. Finally having the life they had dreamed of and more.

"There could always be more trouble," he sighed to himself.

"Yeah, there could," Brenton said mildly, taking a seat next to him. Zachary sat on his other side with a grunt.

"Can it happen after my gallery opening?" Riley asked loudly from where she stood with Keith.

There was still that. Andrew couldn't wait. He stole a glance at Zachary, who grinned.

The gallery opening was lining up to be quite the event. Between their idea with Riley and something *Brenton* was working on in secret for them...

The gallery opening was going to change them forever. In all the best ways.

42

RILEY

April

R iley smiled at the paintings on the walls around her. She'd made every single one. Every painstaking hour, every moment she was in her room, dedicated to capturing the things that made her happy. She looked out over the people watching, family and friends, visitors from other prides, socialites and shifters from Denver.

"Welcome to the opening of my gallery, Wild at Heart!" she announced, her eyes teary. She was met with cheers, her guys hollering and screaming like a bunch of hooligans how much they loved her.

She had chosen the name for a purpose. Every single subject of every painting was a shifter. Some she had met in passing over the last few months, some she loved with every breath she took. And they always would be the subject of her work. Something about the human intelligence behind those animal eyes entranced her on the canvas. She couldn't resist painting them, couldn't resist trying to capture the humans inside the animals, or the animals inside the humans.

To any human who didn't know, she did portraits of wildlife and humans, a strange mix. But next to a painting of Brenton in his study was a lion yawning in the field on their property. A painting of Andrew hung next to a painting of a cougar laying in the sun on a rocky ledge. The same for Troy, playing in the snow or sitting on his motorcycle. Gabe, covered in grease or a shadow in the night. Zachary, shirtless, every tattoo painted with accuracy, and a large white tiger jumping into the stream.

And on it went.

She stepped down from the chair she was standing on, the only way for her to be close to tall enough for the announcement. She laughed as her men kissed her cheeks and swung her around.

"I'm so proud of you," Keith whispered when she hugged him.

"Thank you," she mumbled back, squeezing him.

"You should have had this sooner," he sighed.

"It's in the past," she reminded him. "We have a future, Dad. Let's keep our eyes on it." As he nodded, she went to drift around the party.

"Kitten, this is wonderful," Sheriff grunted, pointing at a painting of him and Patty. Riley smiled and hooked her arm with his.

"You can have it," she whispered to him. "I painted it for you both."

"Really?" He frowned at her and she nodded slowly.

"I've put a lot of these paintings up for sale, the animal ones, but the portraits are for the people who stood for them. So, your bear may be sold off tonight, but not this one. This one is going to go home with you. If you want it."

"I would love it," Sheriff mumbled. "Thank you."

"Of course," Riley chuckled. She touched Sheriff's cheek. "You gave me so much more than I ever thought I could want—a protector, a cheerleader. A father."

"You have one of those, again," Sheriff grunted, throwing a look over at Keith, who was talking to Andrew about something.

"I can have two," Riley reminded him, flicking his nose softly. "Big old bear. Don't be daft, as Thomas says."

"Fine, fine," Sheriff laughed, waving her hand away. "Any weddings he and I will fight over in the future?"

"No," Riley told him plainly. "I don't think a big dress and flowers are in my future. I don't think it's necessary. I love who I love, and I have them. No one is going anywhere and...well, we have this plan, you see."

Sheriff was howling while she walked away. She was grinning and looked around. Who else needed her for a moment?

The wolves were arguing with one of her employees, a young shifter she'd hired who was trying to get into the art world. A rogue. She drifted over to them and listened in.

"Look, we just want to buy the painting of the doe, alright?" Thomas growled. "It's not like I don't have the money."

"We aren't selling tonight, I'm sorry sir."

Riley gasped and edged a little closer. The drama floating around the wolf Pack and Abigail was juicy and Riley wanted to learn every piece of it. Zachary knew something, but he wasn't offering it up. Abigail was flustered whenever Riley asked.

It wasn't Riley's problem though, she was just happy to be a bystander to the unfolding issues. Abigail was still dragging her feet, and the wolves were still trying, for reasons unknown, to get her in the pack.

Well, Riley huffed, not completely unknown. It was obvious the wolves quite liked Abigail.

"Let them buy it," Riley finally intervened as Thomas got growly. "He has the money, he runs a successful little bar in Wild Junction."

"I do," Thomas confirmed. "I closed on Rocker's back in February. And it's only been doing better since I took over."

"Are you sure, ma'am?" Rachel asked quietly, unsure. "You know if we let one get sold..."

"It's fine," Riley laughed. "Remember to calculate your commission on any sales. And if they have a red tag on the title, they are not for sale."

"Of course!" Rachel nodded, smiling. She was a coyote shifter, and she was always happy. Riley wondered how she even found such a peppy, bright young woman to work for her. Not very young. Riley was only about five years older than her, putting Rachel around twenty.

She wandered away, listening to Thomas, James, and Antonio begin planning where they were going to put the three-by-four-foot painting in their little farm house on the outskirts of Wild Junction.

Then she hit a smell that made her sigh. She wasn't shocked by it. She'd expected it. She found Finn staring sadly at a painting she'd done just for him.

"Are you okay?" she asked softly, walking up to his side. He nodded silently. "It's for you. To help you remember, since I know you don't have many pictures of him."

"Thank you," Finn whispered.

Riley and Finn looked at the painting for a long time. She had asked Finn to run with the Pride one night, and she'd been stunned by the beautiful red fox he'd become.

Later inquiries led her to learn that Finn and his twin, Huck, had been identical, in human form and shifted form. So, she had painted them together. Two red foxes playing in deep woods, a game of hide and seek. Light dappled throughout.

"You got it so right," Finn finally choked out. "Thank you."

"I'll have someone take it to the apartment for you," she told him kindly, touching his arm. Someone she'd met on happenstance, now a part of this strange community she had. She just hoped someone taught Finn how to live again.

The conversations continued all night, Riley telling people how to get their paintings delivered to their homes and offices. People congratulated her, but she found she only had eyes for a certain group.

After the party died down, the thing she'd been anticipating was ready. She locked the doors after the last guest left and turned to her Pride. Brenton wrapped an arm around her and kissed her softly.

"Tonight was lovely," he whispered to her. Grunts and nods from the other guys said they agreed with Brenton's sentiment.

"Thank you. Brenton," Riley started, "we've been keeping a secret from you."

"I have noticed," Brenton growled softly. "For months now. Any of you want to tell me what is going on?"

"We may have done something crazy," Troy laughed. "Like *really* crazy."

"It was my idea," Andrew mumbled. "From something you said and...we know the politics and the pressure on your shoulders from other Alphas has been rough."

"They just want to keep making sure we will never cause any trouble, at least purposefully," Brenton sighed. "It is what comes with my name, I know that."

"But you don't have to do it alone," Zachary growled softly. "Because we're family."

"I already know that?" Brenton frowned at Zachary, and Riley snorted. She watched him turn the frown on her.

"Yeah, but you carry your name like a burden, and we don't like it. We don't want you to feel alone, even surrounded by all of us." She pulled her wallet out of the purse she'd had to carry all night. She then pulled out her new driver's license.

She waited for all the guys to do the same.

"What did you all do?" Brenton growled, narrowing his eyes. She handed him the ID and watched him read it. Watched his eyes go wide.

"We're family," Riley whispered as Brenton took all their driver's licenses.

"You're all mad," Brenton mumbled.

"We're all Kingsons," Gabe laughed. "Because damn it, Brenton, we're family."

Riley watched a tear roll down Brenton's cheek. It was impractical and stupid. But they had done it anyway. For him to understand what this meant to them.

On her driver's license, she was now Riley Kingson. Then there was Zachary Kingson, Andrew Kingson, Troy Kingson, and Gabe Kingson.

Wildly stupid, and it was the only thing they thought would be enough to show him that he wasn't alone. That he really did have a real family, not just in heart or in name, but in both. It helped her know this was her family. Her place was with them.

Zachary and Andrew caught him before he fell. He clung to them and held on for a moment. Then he grabbed the brothers and held them.

Riley screamed when he got to her and swung her around.

"This is going to piss people off," Brenton laughed. "Oh, why would you all do this?"

"Because it was the right thing to do," Andrew chuckled. "You said you would give us your name. I decided that we should take it, shoulder the burden with you. And Brenton, it makes us family, just like Riley said. And she brought up a good point."

"What's that?" Brenton frowned, holding her close.

"I'll never have to choose which one of you to marry," she whispered, "because you all belong to me, and I belong to all of you. We belong together."

"Well," Brenton coughed, looking over at the guys, who snickered. "Thanks for this, guys. For being so good at secrets."

"Yeah man, it was a pretty hard line to ride." Zachary chuckled. "Now give her the damn thing."

Riley sputtered as Brenton pulled a small box from his pocket. It wasn't small enough to be one ring though, so Riley didn't know where this was going. He opened it slowly and revealed six rings, simple and gold, like his eyes. Four of them had a tiny stone in them, one had all four stones, and the final one was pure gold.

"We know marriage isn't your thing," he whispered. "But I think we can have something to make this official anyways. No weddings, just us. Forever."

She felt a tear roll down her cheek as she nodded. Brenton slid the ring with all the stones on her finger and the plain gold onto his own. Zachary's had a small sapphire. Troy's had a diamond. Gabe's had an emerald. Andrew's had a ruby.

"Brenton's gold gives us a solid base," Gabe told her. "And you keep all of us."

Riley pulled him in for a hug, and Gabe held her for a moment. She cried and nodded, unable to find the words.

"Are you okay?" Andrew asked as she released Gabe. She kept nodding.

"I love you all. Forever. Always," she whispered. "No matter what."

She couldn't wait to see where their lives would lead them. Maybe there was more trouble on the horizon. Mostly, she figured there were only happy adventures for them to come. New discoveries about each other, about their love, and their future.

But she knew she would always have them. This family that stormed into her life.

And that was all she could have ever wanted.

ABOUT THE AUTHOR

KristenBanetAuthor.com

Kristen Banet has a Diet Coke problem and smokes too much. She curses like a sailor (though, she used to be one, so she uses that as an excuse) and finds that many people don't know how to handle that. She loves to read, and before finally sitting to try her hand at writing, she had your normal kind of work history. From tattoo parlors, to the U.S. Navy, and freelance illustration, she's stumbled through her adult years and somehow, is still kicking.

She loves to read books that make people cry. She likes to write books that make people cry (and she wants to hear about it). She's a firm believer that nothing and no one in this world is perfect, and she enjoys exploring those imperfections—trying to make the characters seem real on the page and not just in her head.

She *might* be crazy, though. Her characters think so, but this can't be confirmed.

You can join her in being a little bit crazy in The Banet Pride, her facebook reader's group.

facebook.com/kristenbanetauthor

twitter.com/KristenBanet

instagram.com/Kbanetauthor

ALSO BY KRISTEN BANET

The Redemption Saga

A Life of Shadows

A Heart of Shame

A Nature of Conflict

An Echo of Darkness

A Night of Redemption

Age of the Andinna

The Gladiator's Downfall

Wild Junction

The Kingson Pride Series

Wild Pride

Wild Fire

Wild Souls

Wild Love

The Wolves of Wild Junction

Prey to the Heart

Heart of the Pack

27092961R00217

Made in the USA
San Bernardino, CA
25 February 2019